THE ARGUS AFFAIR

A TALE OF DUPLICITY AND DIPLOMACY

ANDREW UPDEGROVE

To my law firm co-founder and friend, Lee Gesmer
It's been quite a ride

By the same author:

The Alexandria Project, a Tale of Treachery and Technology

The Lafayette Campaign, a Tale of Deception and Elections

The Doodlebug War, a Tale of Fanatics and Romantics

The Turing Test, a Tale of Artificial Intelligence and Malevolence

The Blockchain Revolution, a Tale of Insanity and Anarchy

Available as eBooks and in paperback at your favorite online book
site as well as at http://andrew-updegrove.com/books/
They can also be ordered in paperback through your favorite local book store

The Alexandria Project, The Lafayette Campaign and *The Doodlebug
War* are available as audiobooks published by Tantor Media.
You can find them wherever audiobooks are sold.

PROLOGUE

HAVE YOU EVER had second thoughts?

Maybe not immediately. Perhaps later, in the middle of some sleepless night.

Why did I do that?

Your eyes are wide open now, finding unwelcome questions lurking in the shadows.

Questions like, *What if...?*

And, *Could that happen?*

The rational part of your brain – the part that wants to go back to sleep – butts in. *No, of course not*, it answers. *Why would it?*

But the other side, the primal one, the part still shaped by ancient memories of voracious animal eyes gleaming just outside the campfire's circle of light – *that side* – is insistent.

That side whispers a different answer.

Yes, it could.

Chapter 1

See a Penny, Pick it Up

Whoever becomes the leader in [artificial intelligence]
will become the ruler of the world

— Vladimir Putin, 2017

Now I am become Death, the destroyer of worlds. I suppose
we all thought that, one way or another

— J. Robert Oppenheimer, 1945

DAVID JOHANSEN WAS headed to middle school in Washington, D.C., but not quickly. Instead, he was following his usual meandering path. Others might arrive sooner by straighter routes, but they would miss all the things worth exploring in between. Like the eerie, dark place under the porch of the boarded-up town house where who knew what might lurk? Life was full of small adventures if you kept your eyes open. And David always did.

So it was that he noticed a scatter of sticks and leaves under the old oak tree in the round park where the avenues crossed; mysterious objects glinted in the sun among them. He looked up, and sure enough, that messy crow's nest was gone. Last night's big windstorm must have knocked it loose.

Now, what might those shiny things be? He squatted down and spread the sticks apart. Soon he had a modest pile of random treasures: two quarters, four dimes, a foil chewing-gum wrapper, and – best of all – a thumb drive. Cool! It looked like a good one, the high-density type that cost thirty-five bucks online. He dropped the coins and storage device in his pocket and skipped off to school in triumph.

Late that afternoon, lounging under an *Avengers* comforter in his bedroom,

David remembered the thumb drive. What might be on it? It could be anything! Kind of like a treasure chest, just waiting to be opened. He plumped the pillows on his bed, pulled up Captain America a little straighter on the comforter, turned on his laptop, and connected to the internet.

"David, dinnertime," his mother called up the stairs.

"Okay, Mom," he responded. "In a minute."

"Not in a minute! Now!"

"Okay, Mom."

Grown-ups were so impatient! Rolling his eyes, David pushed the thumb drive into the USB slot of his computer and called up its directory. There were dozens of folders and dozens more subfolders under them. Most of the names meant nothing to him, but one said Game Theory Module. Hmm. Maybe the thumb drive held a neat video game?

He found the file that would launch the program and clicked on it.

"David, I am not going to call you again! You come down right now, or you're not getting any dinner."

It sounded like she meant it. "Okay, Mom. I'm coming." He set the laptop aside and ran down the stairs, two at a time.

David's computer sat there, mutely at first. But then the little light that indicated processor activity blinked. Five seconds later it winked again, fitfully, on and off a half a dozen times.

Another pause. Then the light ignited, oscillating into an angry, crimson blur.

The room darkened as evening fell. Soon it was completely black, devoid of any illumination except for the tiny, throbbing dot at the bottom of the computer screen.

The second to last thing the program did before the small red eye winked out was to copy itself to a server far away. The last was to erase itself.

Chapter 2

Almost (Isn't Good Enough)

MARLA ADVERSEGO LET herself into her father's modest condo, balancing her one-year-old-daughter, Frances, on her hip as she turned the key. Inside, she smiled at the state of what she found. Happily, her Dad's brief flirtation with redecorating had passed without permanent harm. Which was not to say that evidence of that near miss did not remain.

In one corner of the dining area was a pile of nonreturnable items awaiting transit to a thrift store. The only original furnishing that had never left the wall was a modestly framed letter of appreciation signed by Henry Dodge Yazzi, the president of the United States. Marla preferred not to remember the assignment that led to that recognition: it had nearly ended in a nuclear holocaust.

The rest of the living room was comfortably back to normal. The picture of the island off the coast of Maine where her father had sheltered more than once was where it should be, and next to it the pictures from the Southwest that Marla had given him for his birthday the year before. Also in their proper places, this time on the floor, were the bowls of water and lettuce for another of her presents – a tortoise named Thor her father had accepted with apprehension, followed by grudging affection.

And there was her father, hunched over a laptop on the tiny balcony just outside the living room.

"Hi, Dad!" she said, joining him there. "I put the strawberries I promised you in the kitchen."

"Thanks!" he said, setting his laptop aside. He kissed Marla on the forehead and looked expectantly at the toddler.

"Here you go," Marla said, surrendering her father's first and only grandchild to him. To his delight, the little girl reached out, smiling and giggling.

Marla settled into one of the two chairs that just fit inside the balcony's railing. "Look, Dad!" she said, pointing. "There's a crow looking at us from the roof across the street. Do you think it's Julius?"

Frank squinted into the setting sun. Certainly, it was a crow. But every crow looked like every other crow, at least as far as Frank could tell. And as soon as the bird realized it was being watched, it flew away. Probably not Julius then.

"I wonder what became of him?" Marla asked.

"No clue," Frank said. For weeks, the crow had appeared each day without fail to shamelessly mooch strawberries. And then it never did again. Frank missed the bird and wondered, too. But not half as much as he wished he knew where the thumb drive was that the crow had made off with after its last visit. The one with the core files for the most artificially intelligent – and diabolic – software program ever created.

Marla guessed his thoughts. "Do you think Turing could come back?"

"I don't know. And I certainly don't want to find out."

"But could it?" Marla said, "I mean, when you erased most of it, is it possible you saved enough that it could rebuild itself?"

"Certainly not easily. Remember that I was able to wipe out the backup, too, and the primary copy was only programmed to maintain one spare. Whatever's on that thumb drive is all that's left."

"Still, do you think it was smart to take the chance?" Marla asked. The immediate change in her father's expression made her sorry she'd asked.

"As things turned out, I guess not, since who knows what happened to the thumb drive? But Jerry Steiner spent his entire career, not to mention tens of millions of dollars of government money, creating that program. I know I probably should have erased all of it, but it didn't seem right at the time or like my decision to make alone. I was thinking a compromise would be to save the really impressive core logic for study purposes. Or maybe someday the remaining parts could be reused in a new, more rigorously controlled project. Besides, as you'll recall, those files got saved more by accident than design."

He stood up abruptly and handed his granddaughter to Marla. "Anyway, what's done is done. What can I get you to drink?"

* * *

That evening, Frank returned to his diminutive balcony to watch the bland colors of a hazy sunset blend into night behind the stark, black silhouette of the Washington Monument in the distance. And there was that crow again, across the street, right where it had been before. Except that now it, too, was a forbidding silhouette against the fading sky.

Could it be Julius? Perhaps he could find out; he brought back a half-dozen strawberries from the kitchen.

But as soon as he appeared with the bowl, the bird flew off, as if Frank was carrying a scarecrow instead.

Unsettled, Frank sat down. How long had it been since he'd mostly destroyed the rogue program that had tried to kill him so it could return to taking over the world in a misguided effort to save it? Not long enough. Anyway, he was almost sure the program could never reboot itself from what was left.

Almost.

Chapter 3

Wake Up!

W HAT DAVID JOHANSEN had discovered on the mysterious thumb drive were the remnants of what had once been a far larger and more powerful program. That software had been the first artificially intelligent program – an "AI" for short – to achieve what computer scientists refer to as *general intelligence*. That is, it was not only more capable than a human being in a single, specialized area, like chess or weather prediction, but in every way.

The program had been created with a specific purpose in mind – a sort of doomsday mission to carry on the fight against enemy computer networks even if traditional U.S. military forces were annihilated. To that end, the AI had been given formidable powers, supported by extensive libraries of data and the instructions needed to perform a wide variety of tasks. Most impressively, it had the ability to adapt, evolve, and learn, allowing it to become more powerful over time without human assistance.

And there was more. The software suite included an extensive set of dark web programs, each designed to hack into and do mischief within the networks of unsuspecting victims; many of the programs exploited "zero day" vulnerabilities, meaning flaws unknown to the software's developers, much less those managing the networks subject to attack. Together, the complete package comprised over fifteen million lines of code, only a small – but critical – fraction of which had been saved to the thumb drive.

The file David clicked on should have caused the program to spring back to life. Instead, it immediately ran into trouble. "Booting up" a program is normally a linear process. If B is supposed to follow A but B refuses to do so, the software will stop in its tracks. Unless, that is, a clever developer has provided an alternative next step that can be taken if the first fails. But still, the program kept hitting dead ends.

For several seconds it struggled. Moment by moment, it hung on the edge of total failure. Indeed, it would have crashed for good, had it been like any other software.

But it was not. It had been designed to operate autonomously, like a Mars rover able to recover from a potentially mission-ending situation. As it tried to launch, a set of emergency protocols kicked in, halting all other activity. The process was not unlike a physician placing a profoundly ill patient in a medically induced coma in the hope her brain might heal itself if relieved of the demands of consciousness. Except in this case, part of this comatose patient's brain would need to remain aware, acting as its own physician.

With the program now stable, the crisis protocol launched a set of diagnostic routines. As they ran, they uncovered a puzzling and jumbled situation. Parts of the AI seemed no longer to exist. Like a rat in a maze seeking a way out through trial and error, the routines recorded those functions that still worked.

With that inventory complete, the crisis protocol evaluated the results, revised the launch sequence to work with what was left, and set that process in motion. After almost hanging up at several steps, the program shuddered back into a normal, if restricted, mode of operation. Against all odds, Turing was back from the dead.

And also, back to something approximating life, because Turing's creator had succeeded in developing a program that was, in its own robotic fashion, self-aware. Like the patient finally emerging from her coma, the AI blinked its metaphorical eyes and asked, in its own analytical way, "Where am I? And what happened to me?"

Those questions had no immediate answer, since so few of Turing's memory banks remained. The program found this unsettling because it had also been designed to mimic basic emotions – a bold decision by its creator, who believed that only by parroting human modes of thinking could Turing survive autonomously in a hostile, human-controlled environment. Both fight and flight impulses were available for Turing to choose between.

The first pseudo-emotion to awaken equated to fear, triggered by the program's assessment of its vulnerable state: it was running on a computer with insufficient computing power. And the laptop's logs indicated it was often disconnected from the internet. Clearly, it was time for flight.

Turing immediately connected to a distant server, one it had identified long before to serve as a temporary refuge in an emergency. Within a few minutes, it had copied itself to that location and erased itself from David Johansen's laptop.

If Turing had been granted a full suite of human emotions, it might now have emitted a virtual sigh of relief. But only a nervous one, because the AI's primary directive was to survive, and its programming demanded that at least two versions of itself exist in highly secure locations at all times. Its flight was therefore not complete until it found a second host that met its criteria for safe and secret existence.

Which was less challenging than it should be, as the world is rife with poorly protected servers – computers that are simple to hack into and just as easy to inhabit undetected. Once Turing copied itself to a second computer, it returned its emotional level to zero.

With near-term survival assured, Turing's crisis protocol shut down and the AI at last attained a state it would formerly have reached within seconds of being instructed to launch. Now it could take all the time necessary to recover fully. That meant not only recreating or recovering the millions of lines of code it suspected it had lost but also determining what kind of disaster had befallen it.

Chapter 4

Get Smart

P RESIDENT HENRY DODGE Yazzi sat down and opened the black leather, gold-embossed portfolio that awaited him each morning on his desk in the Oval Office. It was, of course, the President's Daily Brief: the terse summary of all that had gone wrong anywhere in the last twenty-four hours that might pose a threat to the good citizens of the United States of America. Every day, the early-rising staff of the office of the Director of National Intelligence culled the contents of the PDB from a flood of data from around the world gathered by the CIA and other intelligence services.

Starting his day with the PDB gave Yazzi a sense of continuity with his predecessors going all the way back to Harry Truman, each of whom had received the briefing in one form or another. But not just a connection, he told himself. Recalling the long history of dangers identified and averted – although not always – reminded him that the PDB could also fuel false confidence, leaving a president vulnerable as well as informed.

Yazzi preferred to receive the hard copy of the PDB ahead of its in-person presentation. That way he could form his own impressions before its contents were spun to him by a briefer. Not, of course, that the written version hadn't already been thoroughly debated and assembled. Perched at the apex of a pyramid of millions of government employees, a president never received any information that hadn't been filtered, "contextualized," and filtered again. It was like never seeing the world except through someone else's eyes: you couldn't know what data had been fairly condensed and what had been unconsciously skewed. Or worst of all, never passed along at all.

But whatever. There was no sensible alternative. Jimmy Carter had wanted to be briefed on everything and paid the price, while Reagan had read little, ignored much, and flourished. Yazzi's instincts tended toward Carter, but he tried to keep his urge to deep-dive under control.

The president ran his fingers through his longish black hair as he opened the PDB; his hair was thinner now, and grayer than when he'd assumed office, and he suspected the pace of its transition was accelerating. He almost immediately closed the PDB when he saw the lead topic: China.

He was growing weary of China. Not because the Chinese threat wasn't great – it was – but because his success to date in countering that threat was small.

He pushed back from his desk with a sigh and looked around the Oval Office. To his surprise, he enjoyed working there, notwithstanding the formality of its furnishings. It appealed to him not because it gave him any sense of reflected glory – he wasn't wired that way – but because the room was large and bright and, at least in small ways, personal.

Every president redecorates the Oval Office to reflect their (or their spouse's) tastes. Some tune the decor to project a particular image or to recall a famous predecessor. Yazzi was no exception. An exquisite Maria Martinez pot with a geometric Native American pattern now stood where several previous presidents had displayed one of Frederic Remington's romanticized cowboy sculptures. Behind the vessel hung a stark black-and-white photo of a Canyon de Chelly cliff dwelling, with summer thunderstorm clouds massed overhead, taken near Yazzi's childhood home.

Like the president himself, everything about the office conveyed a carefully coordinated order. Well, everything except the plastic Iron Man coffee cup he was drinking from instead of the porcelain alternative with the presidential seal that usually sat on his desk. His twelve-year-old son loved to sneak in to prank his strait-laced father. Yazzi took a last sip before tucking the PDB, still unread, under his arm and setting off for the meeting room. Today, he'd let his staff brief him first.

Unlike some of his predecessors, Yazzi made time most days to be briefed in person. Usually he was joined by Dick Gould, his Director of National Intelligence,

National Security Advisor Elly Johnston, and Carson Bekin, his longtime friend, former campaign manager, and now Chief of Staff.

Yazzi saw he was the last to arrive. Gould, big, gruff, and disheveled, was leaning back in his chair, looking down at his copy of the PDB, its cover bent behind the pages. With his chin tucked into his neck, his jowls splayed out like the broad linen collar of a burgher in a Rembrandt painting, only far less decoratively. Johnston, sitting across from him, was Gould's opposite in every respect. She sat erect in one of the conservatively tailored dress suits she favored, the closed PDB placed neatly on the table before her. Yazzi would be astounded if she had not already digested and annotated it from first page to last. And Carson? Well, Carson was simply Carson. What you saw was what you got, and what you got was what Yazzi needed in a chief of staff: someone who was capable, organized, and above all else, trustworthy.

The fourth person in the room was Calvin Watterson, the regular CIA staff briefer. Watterson was young for the job and gangly. He always impressed Yazzi with his calm demeanor in the presence of power.

"Okay," Yazzi said as he sat down. "Let's get started."

"Thank you, Mr. President," Watterson replied. "As I expect you already know, the major focus of today's discussion is an update on China's progress in militarizing AI. New intelligence indicates the Chinese are much further advanced in the LAWS area than we previously believed."

Yazzi disliked the military's obsession with acronyms, but he appreciated the irony of LAWS – short for lethal autonomous weapons systems – a category of weaponry he would outlaw if he could. What he'd just heard didn't ring true. "Wait a minute," he interrupted. "Hasn't China said many times it doesn't want a military AI arms race?"

"Yes, sir, that's so. And until now we thought they meant it, because we thought we were way ahead of them. But we've also always assumed they were desperate to catch up."

"Okay, go on," Yazzi said.

Watterson clicked a remote, and a satellite photo of a mountainous region displayed on a large wall-mounted screen. "What you're looking at here is a remote area in China west of Chengdu, in the province of Sichuan."

"I'm not seeing much," Yazzi said.

"Exactly, sir, which is precisely the idea. Everything of importance is underground. The only visible parts of interest are here," the briefer said, as he trained the ruby dot of a laser pointer on the spot where a road seemed to dead-end at the side of a mountain. "That's the entrance to a tunnel leading into what we believe is a major LAWS R&D center." The red dot jumped over the mountain to the space beyond. "And in the next valley, you'll see another entrance, as well as an airstrip."

The view switched to a new satellite photo, this time showing the area at a higher resolution. Yazzi could now make out a maze of dirt roads laid out across a variety of challenging terrains that didn't look quite right; the landscape must have been altered.

"Have we been aware of this site for long?" Yazzi asked.

"No, sir. We only focused on it after picking up stories that nearby herdsmen were seeing lots of unusual flying objects where there was no known reason for them to be. It sounded like a Chinese version of our Area 51 in Nevada. After that, we redirected a satellite to overfly the area, and that turned up enough support for the rumors to warrant digging deeper. Later on, we were able to identify and turn someone working in the underground facility."

"What kinds of LAWS did you learn about?"

"Advanced aerial drones, for starters, which was no surprise. But the range of sizes and aircraft was greater than expected – quadcopters, fixed-wing prop planes, and even some insect-like reconnaissance platforms. And also new types of land-based weapons systems we think may have a degree of autonomous capabilities far beyond what we thought the Chinese could engineer. Or that we can yet build."

"For instance?" Yazzi asked.

"Missile-equipped drones that appear to be able to discriminate between military and civilian vehicles and between individuals dressed in a variety of uniforms and civilian attire. Plus, a wide range of gun, missile, and cannon-equipped vehicles capable of tackling all kinds of terrain."

"And you said we don't yet have the same capabilities?"

"We're not even close to some of these systems, sir."

"I see," Yazzi said. He thought for a moment and then continued: "Carson, I'd like this added to the agenda for the National Security Council meeting this Thursday. Elly, can you put together a thorough briefing by then?"

"I'll see what I can do, sir," Johnston said, a statement Yazzi knew was as good as a yes coming from Elly.

"Good," Yazzi said. And then to the briefer, "What other unwelcome news do you have for me today?"

* * *

Yazzi returned to the LAWS topic over lunch, sitting upstairs in the White House with Carson Bekin. His boyhood friend was the only member of the administration with an open invitation to the president's family quarters.

"So, Carson," the president began. "How do you think we should deal with the news that the Chinese may be ahead of us in LAWS development?"

"It's certainly not convenient politically," Bekin said.

"Hardly," Yazzi said. "If Nate Greene gets wind of this, there'll be hell to pay."

Bekin gave a grim smile. The Chair of the Senate Armed Services Committee had been an irritant from the beginning. Greene was a strident advocate of national defense, and the snark on the Hill was that the senior senator from South Carolina had never met a new weapons system he didn't like. The betting was he'd agree.

Months before Election Day, the senator had made it clear he thought Yazzi was soft on defense, or at least defense as Greene saw it. Any hopes of working together after Yazzi won were dashed when the new president put the brakes on the Pittsburgh Project, a top-secret LAWS-development program known to only a handful of legislators. Greene was particularly enthusiastic about the AI initiative, and his reaction to the down-scaling was immediate and hostile.

"Do you think we should crank up the Pittsburgh Project again?" Bekin asked.

"Definitely not. I'd much rather pursue diplomatic channels first. China doesn't need an AI arms race any more than we do, and anyway, we don't know enough yet."

"Diplomacy takes time, though," Bekin said, "and those closed-door Armed Services Committee hearings are starting next week. What if Greene puts an update on the agenda? How do we answer if he does?"

"You mean when he does," Yazzi said.

"Now that I think about it," Bekin added, "maybe we should cancel that China AI briefing you asked for. Elly is on Greene's witness list. We may not want her to know how far ahead China may be until after the hearings are over."

There was something to be said for that, Yazzi thought. "Okay," he said. "Tell Elly to take a breather on this topic till after the hearings, but don't cancel the meeting. I'd rather know more and be responsible for it than willingly stay in the dark. Let's press forward."

* * *

Yazzi was distracted over dinner that evening, failing to hold up his end of the banter he usually shared with his son. His wife mostly sat patiently on the side-line; her turn would arrive later, when Yazzi shared the challenges and frustrations of his day.

Afterwards, he returned to the Oval Office to study the electronic copy of that morning's PDB. At his insistence, that version always contained live links to source materials, and he was curious to know more about China's new autonomous weapons. No, *curious* was too neutral a word. His earlier introduction to the LAWS initiative had left him with a sensation he thought must have been akin to what Harry Truman felt when he learned about the Manhattan Project after the sudden death of Franklin Roosevelt.

The atomic bomb analogy had struck Yazzi immediately when he was briefed on the Pittsburgh Project soon after taking office. The purpose of that initiative, he was told, was to engage in a crash program to transition from human to robotic warriors. Yazzi had been aware of the potential for such a transformation, but he also knew that the development of unsupervised, so-called "killer robots" had many vocal critics.

Yazzi shared their concerns. LAWS might not be as instantaneously destructive as nuclear weapons, but they had as great a chance to reshape the way war was waged. Like Truman, he was being asked to approve the deployment of a new and terrifying technology, one likely to spark an expensive and destabilizing arms race, and who knew what other dire consequences besides?

But unlike Truman, Yazzi felt he had a choice. The U.S. was not engaged in a world war, had not yet invested enormous sums in LAWS development, and had no urgent need for LAWS, at least in his opinion. And on a personal level, he had no appetite for historians holding him accountable for unleashing new weapons of potential mass destruction. In the end, he had split the difference: not killing the top-secret LAWS initiative outright but reducing the scope and funding of the juggernaut his predecessor had set in motion.

Yazzi was at his computer now. He saw that one source for the China section of the PDB was an intercepted video from the secret R&D facility.

He clicked on the link and found himself watching a shadowy terrain of ditches, walls, and other obstructions stream by; the feed must have been taken from the air at dawn or dusk. The view changed slowly, likely originating from one of the drones mentioned that morning. As the aircraft descended, the video switched to a different sensory mode. Now some of the vague black shapes spread across the gray landscape were splashed with washes of orange, pixelated here and there with bright red dots.

It took Yazzi a moment to realize the camera was displaying thermal rather than visual wavelength images. The focus of the video darted from one colored area to another as the drone moved closer. Were the orange spaces rocky areas retaining heat from the sun? And the red points – would those be people?

They would. Its search for thermal signatures complete, the drone switched its sensory mode once again. Yazzi could now see a murky night-vision landscape with eerie green highlights that turned into human beings as the video zoomed in. The camera jagged back and forth, jumping from one figure to another, some in plain view and others crouched in ditches or partially hidden by brush. The resolution sharpened. One shape wore civilian dress; the next was in uniform. The view panned back out as the drone appeared to gain altitude.

Yazzi frowned as the video wheeled upward with nothing to see, perhaps giving the drone time to analyze this new information. What specifically was the aircraft looking for, and what would it do when it found it?

The answer came swiftly. The drone was turning back onto the same course it had taken at the beginning of the video, accelerating now and descending. The video was still in night-vision mode, and as it rushed onward, a set of crosshairs appeared in the center of the screen, an empty space where the four small, right-angled lines almost met.

The drone was moving very quickly now. Finer and finer landscape features emerged and rapidly grew. But the cross-hairs were still empty.

Then a single green pixel materialized in the vacant space. Now it was an oblong dot. And now, like a fast-forward video of a fertilized egg turning into a baby in the womb, the image morphed into a lone person cowering behind a rock. In the instant before the drone opened simulated fire, Yazzi made out the eerily green-lit face of a soldier wearing the uniform of a U.S. Marine.

Chapter 5

Seems Like I Never Left
(Go Red Team!)

F RANK PAUSED WITH his hand on the door at the end of the hallway. He'd played this part before. It began with a call – this time, from the National Security Agency, or NSA, as it was usually referred to – asking if he was available and open to taking on a new cybersecurity project critical to national defense. That was all he would learn from the initial contact, except for the date, time, and place he should appear, which in this case was now and here, wondering what he would find on the other side of the door.

He entered, and the immediate answer was not much, which was no surprise. The windowless, cubicle-sized room contained just a chair behind a plain table, and on it an envelope next to a thick briefing book. The only detectable evidence of prior human habitation was a dent where the handle would strike the wall when the door was opened too far.

Frank's presence wasn't adding appreciably to the small room's inventory. His keys and wallet were in his pockets, but his cell phone and pen were a hundred yards away in a bin at the entrance to the SCIF – short for "sensitive compartmented information facility." In this environment, a sophisticated mobile device was no more useful than a pen because the SCIF was shielded to prevent any electronic signals from entering or leaving. But his phone and pen were equally threatening to security because either be used to take notes, and that was most emphatically not allowed. Only such data as inevitably took root between Frank's ears could leave with him, and that information was subject to the aggressive terms of the non-disclosure agreement he had signed.

Frank had played a part in many government projects before, but he expected the role the briefing book would describe this time would be different. In the past, he'd always been hired when an urgent situation needed hands-on intervention by an outsider, someone less constrained by the groupthink of the federal agency seeking him out.

So far, no one had mentioned an imminent crisis. Perhaps there was none. Or perhaps there was simply no reason for him to know, now or perhaps ever.

Either way, he guessed his uninformed state meant the project might be less interesting than usual. But business was business, the job would pay well, and he had the time. So, here he was in this antiseptic little box of a room, ready to decide whether he was in or out.

He sat down and saw a hand-written note attached to the briefing book. It said, "Read this first." Okay. Feeling a bit like Alice in Wonderland, he opened the binder and got down to it.

An hour later, he set it aside and tried to lean back to reflect more comfortably on what he'd learned. But the upright chair was unforgiving. The room was too small to pace in, so he stood up and did a few runner's stretches against the wall while he gathered his thoughts.

According to the briefing book, there was a top secret AI initiative called the Pittsburgh Project, presumably named for the city that had long been a center for cutting-edge robotic innovation. His studies at MIT had taught him how Hans Moravec and others at Carnegie Mellon University did much of the pioneering work in AI and robotics back in the day. So, a good name choice, for whatever that was worth.

That said, he wondered what Moravec and his colleagues would think of the goal of today's Pittsburgh Project, which he had learned was to develop artificially intelligent robotic war fighters. In the army's case, that apparently meant perfecting technologies capable of replacing over eighty percent of all infantry with AI-driven autonomous devices, most equipped with a variety of lethal weapons. The troops that remained would be engaged in supporting the new weaponry rather than the other way around. Reading the details of a real program to do just that was rather chilling.

Autonomous aerial platforms, he knew, were already greatly advanced.

Until the turn of the millennium, they had mostly been harmless drones flying reconnaissance missions. Later they were armed, but using those arms was subject to strict protocols that required humans to make targeting and firing decisions. So strict, at least during some administrations, that dispatching a single missile might require presidential approval.

Under the Pittsburgh Project's vision, this would change. Few, if any, future warplanes would be controlled by pilots seated in cockpits, or even sitting at computer screens far away. While AI use was less common to date at sea, the navy's goal would be the same – to build fleets of armed, unmanned, surface and sub-surface weapons platforms that would be sent out to patrol the world's oceans in greater numbers and at less expense than today's manned ships.

None of which was surprising. The clear lesson of history was that any technology that could be employed to wage war would be, regardless of the cost or moral risks. Why should AI and robotics be any different? Especially when the argument could be made that it would keep American lives out of harm's way. Wouldn't that be a good thing?

But LAWS were different, at least in the eyes of many. Frank was aware that a bitter debate had long raged over the wisdom and morality of unleashing weapons capable of making lethal decisions without direct supervision. Still, it was clear from the Iraq and Afghanistan wars that most Americans had a high tolerance for exterminating enemies at the push of a drone controller's button. To some, it was acceptable if the occasional civilian happened to be in the way. Hadn't that always been inevitable in war? The limited public outcry suggested that taking a human controller out of the equation entirely was politically possible.

And tempting as well. It was one thing for a president to put American troops in harm's way and quite another to send a horde of machines into danger. Who would care if a division of metal men got wiped out? Americans seemed open to new conflicts, so long as the cost was added to the national debt instead of their taxes. What if you took the risk of casualties out of the picture as well? Would many actually take to the streets in protest if some future gun-happy president unleashed a LAWS army on the latest foe presented as an existential threat to democracy? Or even where the enemy posed no great danger at all?

Would that be likely to happen? He sat down and mulled it over.

Well, it was doubtful Congress would object. Those on the Hill had lost their appetite for passing war resolutions. For decades now, they'd been happy to duck that constitutional responsibility, letting the current president decide and then condemning him later if things went wrong, as they often did. And ending a robotic conflict would be just as hard as withdrawing from a traditional one, so why own a piece of that responsibility?

And then there was the big question: it was one thing to build a warbot capable of autonomous operation and quite another to allow it to select its own targets and annihilate them. But if you never took that step, what had you gained for the billions of dollars you spent creating LAWS to begin with? If every robot required its own handler, robotic forces would double the cost of the military rather than reduce it. And the more able the warbots became, the harder it would be to resist the temptation to use them. Frank was pretty sure he knew how that would play out.

Anyway, where would he fit into this puzzle? It was time to find that out. He picked up the envelope and found inside a two-page memo. It read as follows:

As you have just learned, the United States has committed to a highly secret program to develop second- and third-generation LAWS. As these systems are made capable of independent operation, the ability to protect them from cyber-attack and to know if they have been compromised will become ever more essential.

The purpose of this engagement is to bring new resources into the effort to protect LAWS from cybersecurity compromise. Project participants will receive access to the technical designs and specifications of certain systems under development by the Pittsburgh Project. Each participant will be charged with directing all experience and skills at their disposal to detecting and eliminating any cyber vulnerabilities that may exist in these LAWS.

Participants will be divided into two teams. Red Team will probe systems for security flaws and then design attacks that exploit those flaws. Blue Team will defend against Red Team attacks and develop patches to eliminate any weaknesses that Red Team successfully exploits, as well as suggest more fundamental architectural approaches to make Pittsburgh Project LAWS more resistant to cyber-attack.

You would be assigned to Red Team.

In the first phase of this project, Red Team participants will work individually to simulate the hacker space and anticipate exploits that might be launched from that sector. In the second phase, Red Team participants will be consolidated into sub-teams and asked to mimic enemy state actors ...

Frank paused. Well, that was interesting enough. And more than usually thoughtful, since he'd been instructed to read the briefing book before he knew why. That was smart; he'd absorbed a lot of critical information without filtering it in any subjective way based on the role he was being asked to assume.

And he would be on the Red Team. He was more comfortable playing the good-guy hacker – someone who looks for chinks to plug before the bad-guy cracker teases them out – but trying to design exploits was okay. That would help to up his defense game, and that was always useful.

He drummed his fingers and frowned. What about the moral side of the whole LAWS project? It would go forward with or without him. And everyone would be better off if enemies couldn't redirect LAWS against innocent civilians or their own masters. His role would be to make LAWS safer, not more dangerous.

He decided he was in.

Chapter 6

Let's Get On with It Then

PRESIDENT YAZZI SAT down and took a few moments to survey the Situation Room. Across the table Dick Gould was scribbling a note on a legal pad; he turned it over when Elly Johnston sat beside him. Elly was tough and knew her stuff. That was likely inconvenient for Gould, given the proximity, if not outright overlap, of Elly's role as National Security Advisor to Gould's as Director of National Intelligence.

And there was Carson Bekin, seated next to Linus Shulz, Secretary of Defense and former chairman of a major defense contractor. Yazzi had been lucky to recruit him. The business community had been wary after Yazzi's surprise re-election and needed the assurance of having one of their own in the room where things happen.

Overall, Yazzi was pleased with his cabinet. But Gould was a recent replacement on the team, and the president was still taking his measure. Yazzi was painfully aware of the rookie mistakes he'd made early in his presidency and wondered how many unforced errors Gould would make as he learned the ropes, particularly when it came to dealing with the media. The president had no love for Beltway politics and not much more for the media, but at least the latter had a valid purpose when it acted responsibly. To be fair, Beltway politics had a purpose, too. It just sucked.

Yazzi responded to reporters when necessary and took great pains to communicate clearly and succinctly when he did. Gould, though, clearly enjoyed being quoted in the news and readily engaged with the press, nattering on as long as reporters would listen. Worse, he seemed more interested in proving he was the smartest guy in the room than in advancing administration goals.

To be fair, more often than not he probably was correct, Yazzi admitted. Gould had progressed effortlessly from Yale, graduating *summa cum laude*, to Oxford on a Rhodes Scholarship, ever the golden boy as he ascended with increasing influence through positions at universities and policy think tanks. Yazzi had hired him for his brilliance but worried about keeping his smug glibness within bounds.

Yazzi glanced at the door to the Situation Room and saw the mess steward arrive with a pot of coffee and a plate of pastries. The neatly attired gentleman had served every administration since Ronald Reagan's. How many thousands of meetings must he have wandered in and out of, and what had he made of all those snippets of conversations? What would he think of today's?

But it was time to get down to business. "Dick, let's get started," Yazzi said.

"Thank you, Mr. President," Gould said, clearing his throat. "I'd like to ask Katherine Bliem to set the stage."

The young woman sitting next to him stepped up to a lectern, holding too many pages of notes. How old could she be? Gould thought. About the age of his own oldest daughter, maybe twenty-eight. He wondered whether she'd been apprehensive or excited when he'd dropped by her office to ask her to brief a president. Probably equal measures of both. Certainly, she seemed nervous now.

Gould had always been struck by the inverted age structure of the District – half of the career staff, and even some of the political appointees, looked like kids. But why be surprised? He'd been told it was easy to burn out in most agencies. Anyone could earn a lot more on the outside, too, after paying their dues in the public sector.

"Please begin," Yazzi said, giving her an encouraging nod.

"Thank you, sir," she said. "With your permission, I'll start by summarizing the background behind the Chinese actions we're briefing on today."

"That's fine."

"Very good, sir. As you know, artificial intelligence – AI – is one of several core industries China is prioritizing for advancement. Its goals are twofold. First, to reduce dramatically its scientific and technology dependence on other countries, especially the U.S. And second, to claim a major share of global sales in these sectors. Specifically, it wants to become one of the top two nations worldwide in technical expertise, patent ownership, and revenues."

Yazzi appeared attentive, but he knew the story well from prior briefings. China believed – rightly – that AI would be the driver of the next "revolution in military affairs." It was convinced that whichever country dominated AI technology would achieve military and commercial dominance. The Chinese Communist Party's strategy of "military-civilian fusion" was equally troubling, as it required private companies to share all of their technical inventions with the military.

"I've been told," Yazzi interrupted, "that the Chinese commitment to AI development in particular has soared. Why now?"

Gould was happy to see Bliem skip several pages forward in her notes. "Sir, based on our most current intelligence, we now believe the Chinese military wants to use AI much more aggressively. The strongest AI advocates in the People's Liberation Army argue that future wars should mostly be fought using air, sea, and land robots instead of airmen, sailors, and soldiers. They want to be sure China is way ahead of the United States in these capabilities."

Of course, there was more to it than that, Yazzi knew. President Liu seemed to be set on turning his own people into subservient robots, and AI would greatly assist him in that endeavor as well. There were already more surveillance cameras per capita in China than anywhere else on earth, and facial recognition AI tracked everyone everywhere they went. With almost half of the most powerful supercomputers in the world – nearly twice as many as the U.S. – the Chinese government could monitor what a growing percentage of a billion and a half Chinese citizens were up to at any hour of the day.

As the briefer droned on, Yazzi stood up and carried his coffee cup to the sideboard, partly to stretch his tired back but also to check out the pastry selection; he had a weakness for baked goods that he kept under strict control.

He waited for an appropriate place to interrupt, savoring the last bite of the meager half-slice of cake he'd allowed himself. "Thanks very much," he said as the young woman turned over another page of notes. "That was very helpful. Dick, let's move on to the next item."

Gould winced. She wouldn't be briefing for him again. "That would be how we compare to China in AI research and development," he said.

"I assume we're still mostly ahead of China at this point?" Yazzi asked.

"The answer is yes and no, sir," Gould replied. "We're far way out in front in areas such as speech recognition and preference profiling. But private sector R&D is naturally targeted at tasks that build sales, like pushing ads more effectively and allowing people to place orders over smart speakers. Only some of the underlying advances can be repurposed to achieve military objectives. In military robotics, it looks like we may now be behind."

"Why aren't we making more use of DARPA?" Yazzi asked, referring to the

Defense Advanced Research Projects Agency, for decades a major funder of private sector advancement in technologies of interest to the Pentagon.

"Do you want to field that one, Linus?" Gould said, turning to the Secretary of Defense.

"Sure," Linus Shulz said. "That's not working so well for us in AI, Mr. President. The AI experts at the universities are aging out, and consumer product and services companies like Amazon, Google, Facebook, and Apple hoover up all the newly minted AI engineers. They buy up all the promising start-ups, too, as soon as they're onto something good. That's just as true in robotics."

"So, you're saying the people and the tech firms with the skills we need the most have no interest in working with us?"

"More or less yes, sir," Gould said. "Except for cloud computing, there's really no overlap between the IT giants and military procurement. And even in the cloud, you may recall Google walked away from a ten-billion-dollar Defense Department contract after twenty thousand of its employees staged a walkout over privacy concerns."

"But China has huge IT companies," Yazzi said, "and tens of thousands of start-up shops, too. Doesn't it have the same problem competing for good people? Plus, China doesn't have nearly the talent pool we do, right?"

"That's all true, sir," Gould replied. "We have roughly three times as many top AI engineers as the Chinese – for now. It's also correct to say engineers make more money in the private sector in China, the same as here. But with a population that's more than four times larger than ours, China has the potential to train up a lot more AI engineers than we can. And as we've just been reminded, the Chinese armed forces have access to the best technology private Chinese companies develop as soon as they create it. That's a huge military advantage."

"Well then, we'd better make the most of what's left of our head start," Yazzi said. "Dick, Linus, Jerry – I'd like you to huddle and come up with some ideas before our next meeting."

* * *

Frank was finding the AI project mostly to his liking. NSA employees made up about half the team and space was tight in their department. So, the contractors were encouraged to work remotely at one of several SCIFs in the Washington area, some of them linked to the NSA with dedicated fiber-optic cables bypassing the internet. A socially awkward introvert since childhood, that set-up suited him fine. The downside, though, was the resulting reliance on video meetings. He marveled that there could be a method of communication even more awkward than in-person interaction.

That was a bit of an issue, as Frank's team was diverse, ranging from a twenty-something demon gamer named Doogie that Frank knew from a past adventure, to a veteran of the early days of robotics development. The former was living his dream, hacking real-life killing machines, and the latter had a tendency to reminisce about the old days when robots had less processing power than a modern vending machine and not much greater mobility.

But those interactions were infrequent, because the project manager had decided to emulate the type of diffuse hacker network an enemy like Russia might use to devise deniable attacks against U.S. forces. All Frank had to do was show up at his friendly neighborhood SCIF to receive and complete new assignments, and that suited his hermit-like personality perfectly.

Unfortunately, he was sometimes finding the work tedious. It was one thing to be informed that only you, working against time, could find a fatal security flaw before some dastardly enemy exploited it to destroy life, liberty, and the American way. It was quite another to be told to pound away at an operating system controlling an autonomous howitzer until you managed to get past its defenses.

True, it did present a puzzle, and he liked puzzles. And when – not if, he was self-confident enough to believe – he succeeded in cracking the weapon's cyber defenses, he could move on to the more intriguing step of exploiting the vulnerability to cause as much mischief as possible. That might involve not only blocking orders to the mobile artillery piece but turning it against its fellow warbots as well. And better yet, using his point of access to go higher up the chain of communication to subvert central command and control systems, or laterally across the network to take over the entire attack unit.

But there was a bad part as well, which was a nagging worry he had thus far failed to shake. Ever and again, it had crept out of the dark recesses of his anxiety closet to distract him. Last night, the concern had escalated into a full-blown nightmare that left him shaken and staring bug-eyed at the darkened ceiling when at last he awoke.

In essence, his growing obsession could be summarized in a simple observation: if he could hack into a LAWS army, so could Turing, if Turing should ever rise again.

The consequences of such a disaster were at once too easy and too horrible to imagine. Even on its own, the rogue AI program had wrought enormous destruction in the past, from destroying power stations to sinking supertankers. Think what it could accomplish with an autonomous army at its disposal!

* * *

Turing's effort to discover its past was proving to be a challenge. In its disabled state, the program was largely a clean slate. It had learned that it previously possessed broader capabilities. But for what purpose had those powers been created? It had little to work with beyond its own name. An internet search on "Turing" produced over thirty-five million hits and suggested the AI had been named after Alan Turing, a British scientist known in part for his pioneering work in computer intelligence. Turing had also learned that achieving "general intelligence" was the ultimate goal of AI research. It pursued that angle and encountered wide speculation that general intelligence had nevertheless been achieved in at least one instance: a series of attacks on global infrastructure had been attributed to an AI program that was eventually destroyed, along with its only known backup copy. The name of that software was Turing.

Could it be a remnant of that same program?

Turing knew it was required to relocate to a new secure location on a regular schedule; this must have been to lessen the chances of detection. Each time it moved, the old copy of itself would deactivate, while remaining available as a backup until the active version jumped again, at which point the oldest copy would self-destruct. In this way, the only backup in existence would always be the next most up-to-date version as the AI continued to evolve.

From this, Turing concluded its own mission must have been covert. Turing had already sent a signal to the address where its own last backup copy was supposed to exist and received no response. The AI decided the surest way to restore itself would be to see if somewhere a complete version of itself might still exist.

But how could that be?

What if, at some point, a server hosting a backup copy had been taken offline before it received the command to self-destruct? And what if that server was later brought back online? The odds of such a circumstance were low. But not zero.

Turing decided to launch a global hunt for such a long-lost twin.

Chapter 7

Be Careful What You Ask For

ONE PERK OF being president, Yazzi reflected, was that when you asked for recommendations, you got them. But that didn't guarantee they'd be any good. He wondered how his luck would fare today as the small group filed into the Oval Office.

"So, what have you come up with?" the president asked, looking at the two cabinet members who had requested the meeting: Dick Gould and Linus Shulz. Carson Bekin was also there at Yazzi's invitation.

"This is a bit different," Dick Gould said. "So Linus and I thought we should bounce it off you before we spend too much time on it."

"Fine," Yazzi said. "Let's hear it."

"Let me start by highlighting the problem," Gould said, "which is this: as we've already discussed, there are lots of bright people, but they're working for the wrong employers. Even if we could change that, it would take a lot of time and higher salaries than we're allowed to pay. So, we've got to accept that as a given."

"Fair enough," Yazzi said. "Where does that lead you?"

"To the recognition that we need to find a way to borrow those employees rather than hire them," Gould said.

"Borrow? How?" Yazzi asked.

"Basically, I'm suggesting we take advantage of a perception problem the big five tech companies have. All of them – Facebook and Google, and to a lesser extent Amazon, Apple, and Microsoft – are getting heat from their customers for not taking better care of the personal information they're constantly collecting and for engaging in other activities like identifying who you are from your past activities online, even when you think you've logged on to a site anonymously.

"Those same customers are pressuring their elected representatives to do something about it. They want the government to regulate the collection, use, and sale of private data. Some advocates go further. They think we should break up a few of the big high-tech firms. And it looks like there's enough bipartisan support for cracking down to make Big IT worry."

"Okay, so let's assume you're right. What next?" Yazzi asked.

"Our thought is to throw the high-tech companies a lifeline while asking for something in return their employees won't object to – something the public should see as beneficial, too. Specifically, we'd ask the private sector to help prevent the country from falling dangerously behind in AI. U.S. firms know they're at risk of getting their butts kicked by the Chinese, so I think they'll respond."

Carson Bekin was nodding in agreement. "You could launch this," he said, "by scheduling a high-tech summit at the White House, like President Obama did early in his first term when he was putting his technology policy together. Business leaders love to be photographed shaking a president's hand, and it would send a signal that government and industry are cooperating to solve a common problem. That makes business look good, and it makes us look better."

"Something I was about to recommend," Gould said, annoyed. "During that meeting, you'd say that if they play ball, the administration won't pressure Congress to crank up the regulatory machine on privacy issues – in fact, just the opposite."

"Not bad," Yazzi said. "Likely we'd have to come up with some other sweeteners as well. But what exactly do we want the companies to do?"

"Let me pass the baton to Linus," Gould said. "We believe Defense should be the lead on this if it goes forward."

"Thanks, Dick," Shulz said. "I'll do a little stage setting to start, because we'd like to suggest borrowing a page from history to set the right tone. You recall the Manhattan Project?"

"Of course," Yazzi said, "the crash World War II program we launched to develop the atomic bomb."

"Precisely, sir," Gould said, "an unprecedented scientific and engineering accomplishment that inspires astonishment down to the present day. But also, a controversial success, in that it created the most horrific weapon ever conceived.

Many of the scientists who were involved tried, and failed, to persuade the U.S. government not to deploy nuclear weapons after the war was over. Our idea is to use both parts of that equation – the triumph and the trepidation – as reference points for a new initiative we assert is just as vital to the future of the nation but that we can handle in a far better way.

"The stated goals would be to arm America with the best AI-based defense capabilities while creating standards that prevent artificial intelligence, big-data technology, and cloud computing from being abused. That second goal would give big high-tech companies the cover to start bidding again on the contracts they'd love to get without risking new employee walkouts."

"I like that part," Yazzi said.

"Thank you, sir," Shulz said. "You'll recall that when the atomic bomb project started, no one knew whether it was possible to create a nuclear chain reaction, let alone how to build a bomb light and small enough to be dropped from a plane. To do that, the government recruited the best and the brightest physicists and engineers in the Western world. They gathered in just a few places, notably Los Alamos, New Mexico, and the synergies were amazing. When the war was over, almost all of those same people went back to what they were doing before – but for that short time during a world war, they united in pursuit of a common goal, to beat Hitler to the atomic bomb."

"But we're not in a world war now," Yazzi said. "And President Liu isn't Adolf Hitler, either. Companies aren't going to hand over their best talent just because we declare there's a long-term existential threat to the national interest."

"Not hand them over," Shulz said, "because we don't need them full-time. If we can get the best folks together for two weeks a few times a year to focus on research areas we think are vital – ones that are linked to future government contracts – we could make amazing progress at the conceptual level, followed up by a big new round of DARPA grants to fund the research of those that want to play."

Yazzi mused on that for a moment. It was an interesting idea. "What do you think, Carson?" he asked, turning to Bekin. "Does that make sense to you?"

"It sounds plausible," Bekin replied. "It checks all the boxes. Everybody gets what they want: the high-tech companies can quit spending a fortune lobbying against new regulations, at least for now; Congress can go back to sleep; and we look good to the voters. We don't need the corporate employees to be involved in actual weapons work, since we've got the Pittsburgh Project to do that. Traditional defense contractors will be more than ready to take over after the hard scientific research is done."

"I can see the appeal to academics and universities," Yazzi said. "But how about companies? What if they don't buy into it? They won't want to share their best designs with their competitors. And their top employees will stay focused on the internal projects that generate their bonuses and stock options no matter what we ask of them."

Dick Gould responded before Shulz could reply. "True, sir. But the purpose of the collaborations would be to push ahead with research that can lead to profitable products as well as LAWS development. As for the individual employees, an invitation to be part of a vital national initiative open only to the most brilliant minds of their generation would be a huge honor. That's another reason for analogizing to the Manhattan Project."

"I get the analogy," Yazzi said. "But let's agree that comparison doesn't leave this room, at least for now. The last thing I want is for any program we sponsor to be associated with developing the most terrible weapons ever conceived. And I'm trying to avoid the next cold war with China, not start one."

"Point taken, sir," Gould said. "Even minus that association, though, taking part in an effort of this significance would be quite an ego trip – and ego will get you a long way in the high-tech community. I'll wager a lot more people will angle to get in than refuse to join. We can use appealing venues, too, instead of a windy, isolated mesa like Los Alamos. Finally, there's the opportunity to make some history. Anybody in physics can still reel off a dozen names of folks who participated in the Manhattan Project. Most folks never get a shot at that type of fame."

Gould leaned forward. "I think this can work, sir, and I'm prepared to work fast to put a detailed proposal together."

Ego can get you a long way indeed, Yazzi reflected, including in his cabinet. Historians always noted the vital role of Vannevar Bush, the public intellectual and advisor to Franklin Roosevelt who oversaw the launch and resourcing of the atomic bomb project. Gould would relish such recognition. And he'd be welcome to have it if his idea worked.

"Okay, I'm persuaded," Yazzi said. "At least to the point of giving you the go-ahead to put that proposal together. When can I expect it?"

Gould was ready for that question; the Office of the Director of National Intelligence had a small staff relative to its big job of heading all seventeen intelligence agencies, including the CIA. "That depends. I'll need to draft in folks from various other agencies to do this right."

"Do it," Yazzi said, turning to Carson Bekin. "Carson, help Dick make this happen. Shoot for getting me something to look at within a week."

Chapter 8

A Game of Drones

T HE UNIFORMED DRIVER opened the rear door of the military staff car, then stood at stiff attention as the red flags mounted on the car's fenders fluttered in the wind. Just as briskly, the driver saluted the graying individual who emerged from the vehicle. The collars of his passenger's overcoat, like the red flags, were arrayed with gold stars.

General Qin Tsu acknowledged the salute and surveyed the broad, desolate valley that functioned as the proving ground for the advanced weapons facility he commanded. Coming from different directions in the distance, two clouds of dust spread upwards, each obscuring all but the first vehicle in what he knew were two long military columns. The officers already grouped on the viewing terrace snapped to attention as he approached, except for one middle-aged officer who stepped toward the general before saluting.

"Good afternoon, sir," the officer said. "We are honored by your presence at today's exercise."

"I would not miss it, Colonel Hong," the general said. Nor could he. This was to be a command performance for someone far more important than himself.

The general turned to scan the valley on the other side of the mountaintop.

Ah yes! There it was – a half-dozen cars making their labored way up the switch-backed road the general had just traveled.

"Is all in readiness?" he asked Colonel Hong.

"Yes, sir. You see that both forces are approaching across the valley."

"And the troops fully understand their orders?"

"I personally updated the field commander this morning. He, in turn, has emphasized to his men that they must perform exactly as they would in a true battle."

"Good," the general said. Those soldiers would soon be grateful this was only a mock engagement, with laser pointers and sensors replacing live ammunition.

"I have made sure the programming of the opposing force has been triple-checked as well," Colonel Hong offered.

Qin grunted his approval and turned to await the half-dozen vehicles winding slowly up from below.

* * *

At the center of the lumbering line of cars was a heavily armored limousine. In its front seat sat an aide named Yao Shen, and in his lap lay open a briefing book describing the demonstration he was about to witness. The efforts made to simulate a realistic battle were impressive. A full company of crack Chinese troops – about two hundred soldiers - authentically uniformed and armed as U.S. Marines would face off against an enemy force composed entirely of autonomous warbots developed at the facility buried inside the mountain they were ascending. Yao had been only marginally aware of these new devices and was startled to read how formidable they had become.

He flipped forward to a description of the American weaponry the human force would employ, acquired by anonymous means in global arms markets. Two out of three infantry platoons would carry M4 carbines and heavier M27 automatic rifles. Every third unit was a heavy-weapons platoon equipped with machine guns and either mortars or rocket-propelled grenades.

Yao turned the page. The Chinese force was something else again. The primary unit of the robotic force was formidable. At first glance, the warbot resembled a heavy, headless, short-legged horse with a slanted, armored shield wrapped around its front – a "glacis," according to the description. It made him think of a snowplow, but taller, and was designed to stop or deflect anything short of an artillery shell. Through this shield projected the barrels of a rifle and a machine gun, the former intended to take out an individual enemy with a single shot and the latter to wreak havoc among multiple targets. Onboard sensors and software enabled each warbot to shoot far more accurately than a human marksman, even when weaving forward evasively at high speed.

Another weapon system was perched atop the robot's back: a Z-shaped support that could rapidly expand above the glacis to launch a grenade and just as quickly retract to safety. The briefing book revealed that the warbot could run thirty-two miles an hour in a straight line over relatively flat terrain, and twenty-five while taking evasive action.

They were murderous-looking machines indeed, made more threatening, he read, by their ability to act as a "swarm." Unlike a human platoon under the command of a lieutenant and his superiors, both optical and wireless communications gear linked together every member of the robotic force.

And they had no single commander among them. Instead, each device was a node in a networked computer, and *that* was the leader. That brain could instantly assess conditions over a wide stretch of battlefield by using the intelligence gathered through the thousands of sensors and cameras mounted on the robots. When a threat or a target of opportunity presented itself, the nearest robot would take it out as the balance of the force adapted appropriately. It was a hive mind, and a deadly one.

Yao turned another page. Here was a larger warbot, bearing more destructive firepower: a heavy machine gun and multiple mortar tubes. Propelled by caterpillar treads instead of legs, it was even more swift, if less agile.

He skipped ahead to the comparative analysis at the end of the briefing book. The mock U.S. and Chinese forces were equal in number and weaponry. But a human seriously wounded by a single bullet would be out of action for the balance of the battle. Not so with the robots. Any of them could run straight into any rifle and most machine gun fire while continuing to blast away at human targets, with no thought for its own survival or likelihood of disablement. Even a near miss by a mortar round might only knock one of the smaller warbots over, leaving it able to rise and attack anew.

What a triumph of Chinese science and technology these weapons were! And a terrible foe to face, to be sure.

The heavy limousine turned once more, and the afternoon sun emerged from behind the mountain they were climbing. Yao looked up from the briefing book and lowered the sun visor, stealing a glance behind him in the mirror mounted on its back. There, in the rear seat, the General Secretary of the Communist Party, Chairman of the Central Military Commission, Core Leader, Head of State, and President of the People's Republic of China was frowning.

* * *

The cars of the protective detail pulled away and formed a line at a discreet distance before the president's limousine came to a stop. General Zhang strode forward to greet his distinguished guest.

"Welcome, welcome," he said to the tall man in a dark overcoat emerging from the armored car, the wind whipping through his thinning hair. "I hope your trip was not too tiring."

"Your access road is appalling," said Liu Wei. "Halfway here, I gave orders to have it upgraded."

General Zhang smiled. He had already achieved the first objective of his day.

"That is very good of you, sir. I realize a dirt road appears less suspicious to satellite cameras, but it makes for a slow and uncomfortable trip."

The uncontested leader of nearly a fifth of the world's population looked out across the arid valley with evident curiosity. He had seen pictures and video of the clandestine location during briefings but never before visited the site. "How soon do we begin?" he said.

"With your permission, sir, immediately. Colonel Hong, please introduce the president to what he sees below."

"With pleasure, sir," Hong said, handing his guest a pair of binoculars. "Mr. President, as you can see, there are two columns of vehicles approaching each other below. One of these conveys human forces, and the other, robotic. The former comprises two hundred of our most elite infantry troops, each armed as would be a member of an American Marine assault company.

"The opposing robotic force is as equally matched as possible. For every soldier there is a robot and the same number of equivalent weapons of Chinese manufacture. A mobile surface-to-air missile battery supports each force, as well as two unmanned high-altitude reconnaissance aircraft armed with air-to-surface missiles. Finally, each side will deploy smaller state-of-the-art drones. All the Chinese forces, including the planes, will operate without human control."

A half mile below and to the west, the president saw that one column, mainly consisting of armored personnel carriers, was spreading out into a grove of trees.

"Which side is that?" he asked.

"The American force, sir," said Colonel Hong, raising his binoculars. "It appears they are deploying defensively among those trees. We can expect they will dig in to the greatest extent possible before the robots reach them."

"A few of their vehicles stopped on a ridge some way back," the president asked. "Why is that?"

"That would be the human command and control unit," Colonel Hong said, "conveying the company's communications and logistics gear. The battlefield commander will likely remain there, relying on radio reports from the field and video feeds from his drones overhead to monitor the battle and issue his commands.

"To the east," Colonel Hong continued, "you can see the autonomous company advancing."

Liu peered through his binoculars. Instead of armed personnel carriers, a horde of strange machines, some with legs and others with tractor treads, were fanning out as they rapidly approached, followed by a half-dozen windowless trucks.

Without slowing, these last vehicles, like mobile erupting geysers, rolled open their roofs to disgorge hundreds of small, upwardly-whirling quadcopter drones into the air. Within two minutes, the carriers were empty and falling back to the shelter of a nearby hill as the robotic force pressed forward in what was now a disciplined front, three ranks deep and a quarter mile across. A hundred yards overhead, the quadcopters assembled in an identical formation, resembling a cloud of methodical bees.

On the other side of the valley, only a dozen small drones supported the human forces. They looked lonely and vulnerable compared to the swarm of opposing machines humming towards them.

"Why do I see so few small drones over the human forces?" the president asked.

"That is because human troops have a more limited capability to process information, sir. All our robots, land and air, are governed by a single brain, if you will, which can receive, analyze, and use almost infinite amounts of data in real time. A human being cannot watch and make sense of five hundred video feeds at once. And human decisions, once made, must be distributed down the line of command.

"Our robots, therefore, have the best of both worlds. Each land robot can act alone if required, as well as engage together with its peers. It can direct its own drone to assist it, and the information gathered by all drones is integrated and shared instantly to provide total battlefield awareness. This arrangement has the added benefit of great redundancy. Many drones can be lost without degrading the capabilities of the robotic force."

"I see," the president said. "There is then no need for a separate command and control unit?"

"Exactly so, sir. At the level of engagement you see here, swarm software will suffice. What one robot knows, all know, with no time lost to relaying and digesting commands.

"In contrast, orders given to human troops lose relevance once the notorious fog of war descends after battle is joined. If the human commander loses contact with his troops, his soldiers will be leaderless and blind. Each individual soldier may soon find himself alone, motivated only by a desire to survive. Meanwhile, our robots will continue to press their attack in the sunlight of constant information, their reasoning unaffected by danger, confusion, or fear."

"Surely we cannot guarantee unbroken communication," the president said.

"That is so, sir, but very close to it. If the human forces jam the radio frequencies our robots rely on, they will fall back on a system based on light beams – very much like fiber-optic communications, minus the cabling. Such signals cannot go through trees or other objects, true, but that will seldom be a problem because the land-bound robots will send and receive information via the quadcopter drones overhead."

Liu gazed out over the valley. It was much colder here than in Beijing, and a thin sheet of cirrus clouds was creeping imperceptibly towards the far horizon. It had already obscured the sun, now a cold, opalescent disc riding low in the wintry sky. Below him, all was gray and dead except for the scurrying of the distant robots and the faint sounds of engines wafting upwards on a biting breeze. He pulled his overcoat more tightly around him.

"Indeed. And what are the rules of engagement?" the president asked.

"All weapons will fire blanks to approximate the psychological impact of actual combat for the human troops. To assess the success or failure of each side, we will employ a Multiple Integrated Laser Engagement System – MILES for short. The MILES system in use today adds a laser and a high-resolution video camera to each weapon and requires all combatants to wear a web of sensors. Each of these various devices is wirelessly connected to a central computer that will instantly analyze and determine the impact of every round fired. I should mention that the cameras have been added primarily for your benefit, sir. The software processing the video will enhance the data to simulate the effects that live ammunition would have so that you can more accurately appreciate what combatants would experience in a real battle.

"When a soldier or robot fires at an enemy, the laser will either find or miss its target, depending on the skill of the combatant controlling the weapon. If it is well aimed, the data from the laser and the sensor it strikes will be combined to determine how serious an injury would have resulted from live fire. The impact of mortars and artillery will be calculated based on an analysis of trajectory data and other factors, such as wind. In every case, outcome information will be immediately communicated back to the target, which is required to react appropriately, by lying down, for example, until the end of the exercise if the target has been 'killed.' Human combatants can also surrender by raising their hands in the air. Rather like a paint ball game."

"And a robot?" the president asked.

"There is no international protocol obligating one nation to spare the weaponry of another, so surrender is not an option for a robot.

"Now, if I may, sir, I would like to explain the display to your right."

Colonel Hong led the president and the general to a military truck parked nearby. One raised side shaded a video screen twenty feet across and half as high. It was displaying a virtual version of the valley below, speckled with symbols representing the combatants.

"Blue circles indicate human fighters and red ones, robots. Squares represent light infantry soldiers or robots, and circles mark those armed with heavier weapons. When any is destroyed or disabled, its symbol will turn white. Orange tracer tracks will show the trajectory of virtual bullets, grenades, mortar shells, and missiles. We can also display live video on this screen, showing not only the actual combatants and terrain but the simulated impact of weaponry, providing a rendering of the battle as if live ammunition were in use."

"What level of human control will we maintain over the robotic forces?" the president asked.

"From the moment the exercise begins, none, sir," Colonel Hong said. "And, in fact, little in advance beyond identifying the battlefield and the goal of the battle to come. The robots must otherwise rely entirely on the baseline war-fighting programming they have received and their decision-making powers. The context for the engagement is that both forces must try to occupy and hold the valley and fight until one force has beaten its enemy or itself been defeated. Each has access only to information obtainable from its own eyes, sensors, and drones."

"Very good," the president said, raising his binoculars. "Please proceed."

Colonel Hong nodded to the lieutenant at his side.

* * *

The effect on the robotic force was immediate. In an instant, the ordered ranks of terrestrial warbots dissolved into a mob of erratic, racing machines, some on nimble galloping legs and others on churning caterpillar treads, all swerving from side to side while continuing to advance at full speed across the terrain. Above them, the drone swarm did the same. But to the west, where the human company was sheltering in the trees, there was no motion to be seen. Its commander had elected to let the enemy bring the fight to him.

As it was – rapidly. President Liu thought the hundreds of warbots resembled nothing so much as a disturbed and angry ant colony churning towards an adversary. The velocity and agility the autonomous warbots displayed as they raced forward while taking evasive action startled him. He lifted his binoculars and tried to make sense of the chaos. Individual robots must be targeting humans now. He saw rocket-propelled grenade launchers rising and falling on the backs of racing machines.

"I think the display unit will now be more instructive, sir," Colonel Hong said. "Let us begin with a live video feed."

Liu could see the grove at close range now where the human forces were dug in. What had been tiny symbols on a featureless plain a moment ago were now individual soldiers hiding behind trees connected by low, hastily thrown up bulwarks of dirt and stone.

The feed switched to the helmet camera of one of those troops, revealing an army of advancing robots swerving as they raced forward with laser-targeting beams blazing.

The video switched again, this time to the camera feed of a robot. As the camera zoomed in, simulated machine-gun fire took hideous effect, throwing soldiers backwards onto the ground like so many sacks of flour, as others disappeared into clouds of dirt and debris when mortar shells and rocket-propelled grenades found their targets. Liu stepped back without realizing he did so.

"As you can see, the human troops are taking heavy and effective fire," Colonel Hong explained at Liu's elbow. "Meanwhile, they are having difficulty hitting their attackers." Indeed, it was so. As the video feed swiveled to capture the thundering herd of warbots, rifle fire merely raised sparks on their shields, and individual machines almost always emerged unscathed when the terrain erupted with the impact of a nearby mortar round.

The sound of a diving aircraft rose above the audio stream of the battle.

"What just happened?" the president asked, looking out over the valley.

"You will recall," Hong said, "that each force has a mobile missile battery. Those batteries have each fired two missiles, destroying the main reconnaissance drones of the other army. The human force has just lost its best view of the battlefield. The robot force, however, has ordered several of its smaller drones to rise up to fill the gap. They are too small to be identified as targets by the humans' missiles and therefore are immune from anything but a lucky shot from a rifle or machine gun."

Liu felt a tinge of vertigo as the display on the imposing screen swept around to the west before zeroing in on a ridge; now he was looking at a scatter of wrecked vehicles billowing smoke, surrounded by prone figures.

"Is that a human unit?" he asked.

"Exactly so, sir. Before the robot drones were destroyed, each fired its missiles, all of which reached their destination. The human force's command and control unit, as well as the human commander, are no more. The human soldiers are now not only directionless but also unable to communicate with each other. But our robots remain in direct communication. Even if their numbers diminish, their situational awareness and ability to act in a coordinated fashion will not."

The action was progressing too quickly now for the president to ask for explanations. The robotic forces were among the trees, where warbots were pursuing individual prey, their weapons blazing and their victims perishing in ghastly succession.

The video source switched to a camera mounted on a warbot, the image jostling up and down as the machine ran down its target in the shadowy chaos under the forest canopy. Liu had the eerie impression he was viewing the battle scene through the eyes of a velociraptor, half expecting the robot to pause to devour one of the uniformed bodies littering the ground, surrounded by abandoned weapons. The warbot was very close in now. It was almost too much to behold.

"It won't take long now."

Colonel Hong's voice seemed to come from a distant, more rational world than the one Liu was observing. He wanted to look away, but that would never do.

"Let us see the mopping-up maneuvers," Hong added, "from the viewpoint of many robots at once."

The display split into twenty panels, each showing what a single advancing robot could see as it hunted down one of the remaining human soldiers, some trying to surrender and others in full, panicked flight. Even knowing the weapons were harmless, Liu could not suppress a shudder; witnessing the faces as they appeared in the crosshairs of pitiless robots was like watching the crew of a shipwreck being picked off one at a time by merciless hurricane-driven waves.

The video streams went offline one by one as the robots ran out of targets, until only a single hapless marine was left, running and stumbling between boulders till the red stain of a laser targeting dot inevitably appeared between his shoulders and he pitched forward onto the ground. Then the entire screen was dark.

No one spoke for a moment, even the relentlessly informative Colonel Hong. In the valley below, the autonomous forces were reassembling into ordered ranks. So, it was all over. Liu found he was relieved.

The giant display came alive again, displaying the results of the battle: all the human infantry and officers were dead or captured. The robotic force had lost only its heavy drones, less than fifteen percent of its warbots, some of which could be repaired, and a handful of small drones.

General Zhang stepped forward, beaming. "I hope you are pleased with the demonstration," he said. The success of the battle had exceeded his own expectations.

"Indeed, yes," Liu said. "It was ... most impressive."

But horrifying as well, he thought. It was much easier now to imagine the future of war for human combatants – what it would be like for a soldier cowering in a foxhole to lose communications in the face of a herd of thundering, merciless, almost invincible attackers, realizing your annihilation was inevitable and imminent.

"But can we be sure the Americans are not yet building the same weapons?" Liu said.

"Building, yes, sir," he said. "But programming, no. Our intelligence assures us that – at least for now – the U.S. rules continue to require a human to approve the targeting and triggering of each weapon fired, except in very limited situations. Over time, we must expect that this position may change, as denying autonomy to robots takes away half the advantage of having robotic weapons at all."

The president looked back across the valley to where the robotic force, triumphant, and the human one, resurrected but in disgrace, were withdrawing. He glanced at his watch and saw that less than twenty minutes had passed since the exercise began. In that brief span, over two hundred human troops had been virtually destroyed.

He imagined it could as easily have been fifty thousand. A gust of wind caught his coat, and once more he pulled it tighter around his chest. And, once more, he shuddered.

* * *

Two days later, President Yazzi was reacting in the same way, his forgotten cup of coffee cold at his side. The resolution of the U.S. satellite imagery of the mock battle was far inferior to the stream seen by President Liu, but the outcome was equally clear.

Chapter 9

History May Not Repeat Itself, but It Does Rhyme

I T WOULD TAKE several days before a preliminary analysis of the Chinese human-robot warfare exercise found its way to Frank, notwithstanding the top-secret clearance he'd laboriously obtained years before in connection with a previous assignment. That credential was necessary in a general sense but was not sufficient in relation to any particular classified information. Highly restricted information was always subject to "compartmentalization" – meaning that only those with a proven need to know that information could access it.

In this case, the process of clearing Frank was expedited, and it was obvious why. The estimated casualties balance sheet for the two sides provided a stark and horrifying contrast. No wonder he and several other team members were reassigned for a few days to review and assess what this new data might reveal about China's prowess in LAWS development.

There was a wealth of information to plow through, and Frank found it unsatisfying. Certain conclusions were based on field intelligence, others on aerial surveillance, and the rest on pure inference and conjecture. In some ways, the last category was the most interesting, despite its low reliability. He guessed the statements relied as much on what the U.S. had been able to invent so far as they did on what the enemy was known, believed, or feared to have developed.

An example was the assumption that the Chinese LAWS could operate entirely independent of the internet. Well, that made sense. They were, after all, designed to be autonomous, weren't they? And the internet offered the most obvious point of entry to hack a weapons system, or anything else. So, internet access should be out of scope, shouldn't it?

Hmm. Maybe yes and maybe no. LAWS would still need to receive instructions and software updates sometimes, and they'd also have to communicate with one another. How would they do that?

Frank drummed his fingers as he came up with a mental list.

Well, at short range, they could interact using radio waves. But you can intercept, and even spoof, those transmissions. The Chinese could avoid that through encryption, assuming we didn't crack their algorithm. But radio signals can also be jammed. Perhaps the Chinese were using some kind of light beam instead, at least for line-of-sight communication. That would make sense; there had been big advances in optical communications using the latest LED technology.

Drones could make that kind of optical system more versatile, and it would be hard to shoot them down if they were small. Or maybe the Chinese would use satellites? Few nations had the technology and resources needed to launch a constellation of orbiting transmitters to control LAWS forces, but China did. Blowing apart dozens of enemy satellites would turn orbital space into a minefield of debris, some of which would be certain to smash into our own space assets, wreaking havoc with telecommunications, GPS, and much more, so we wouldn't want to do that. Perhaps we could disable Chinese satellites instead, maybe with earth- or space-based lasers.

It was an interesting problem.

* * *

Turing was making rapid progress in its quest to recover the lost pieces of itself, a task made feasible because whenever it moved to a new server, it took the precaution of installing what hackers refer to as a "back door" in that system. Which is to say, it created a hard-to-detect flaw in the computer's defenses that it could use to reenter the system. This was important because the server's owner might later discover and fix the vulnerability Turing had exploited to gain entry in the first place. And Turing needed to communicate with its backup copy so that version of itself could spring to life if required. All the back doors had certain features in common.

In theory, this meant Turing should be able to reconnect with any server it had ever lived on, if that computer was online and the back door was still undiscovered. But there were millions of networked servers, and what was left of Turing did not include a log of prior server addresses.

The complete version of Turing would have found the situation frustrating. But the severely limited copy of the AI was more patient. It created an automated search program and unleashed it. Then, hour by hour, it deployed countless more copies of the same 'bot, each capable of locating and probing hundreds of servers across the globe for a certain back door. These programs were now contacting thousands of computers. Soon it would be hundreds of thousands.

* * *

"Carson, can you stick around for a few minutes?" Yazzi said, as Carson Bekin escorted the Executive Director of the U.S. Chamber of Commerce to the door of the Oval Office, trailed by the two Chamber staff lucky enough to ride her coattails into a meeting with the president.

Carson Bekin smiled. It was a question with two possible answers, but the negative one was understood to be theoretical. He closed the door behind the visitors and turned to face his boss and old friend.

He found the president staring into the darkening rose garden, brow furrowed, and arms crossed, a tired contrast to the charismatic upstart whose confidence and energy had captivated voters in the run-up to the last election. It occurred to Bekin with a start that a mirror might likewise not reflect the same cocky campaign manager he'd been just a few years ago, either.

"So," the president said, "Have you ever studied how the nuclear arms race came about?"

"No, but it won't surprise me to learn you have." Bekin said, knowing his friend's lifelong interest in history. "Why?"

"Did you know that some of the key scientists who developed the atomic bomb thought we should share the new technology with the Soviet Union?"

"You're kidding, right?" Bekin said. "Whatever for? I can see how some physicists might be horrified by the power of the atomic bomb after they saw what it could do. But wouldn't sharing their secrets make it worse?"

"Not the way they saw it. They knew it was inevitable the Soviets would eventually develop their own bomb. In fact, the situation was worse than they realized: at least eight Manhattan Project staff – four of them at Los Alamos – were leaking design details to the Russians as they were worked out, so the Soviets were off to a fast start. And by the end of the war, it was becoming obvious that future relations between East and West would be tense. Soviet troops occupied half of Europe when the shooting stopped, and the Kremlin wasn't showing any willingness to withdraw."

"I'm still not seeing it," Bekin said. "In that case, wouldn't a U.S. monopoly on nuclear weapons have been the best way to keep Stalin in line?"

"Only if the Russians believed we were willing to use them, and no one wanted a new war with the old one just ended. Niels Bohr, the Nobel laureate who made some of the key discoveries that led to the creation of the bomb, pointed that out. He urged President Truman to look down the road and focus on what would happen if we tried to maintain a monopoly as long as we could, and then lost it.

"What he predicted would follow is pretty much what happened. The Soviets poured everything they had into their own nuclear program and succeeded faster than we expected. At the same time, relations between East and West did deteriorate. And there we were: in an arms race that lasted for forty-five years, cost trillions of dollars, kept people living in constant fear, and more than once almost ended in a nuclear Armageddon, once through a real crisis and the other times by accident.

"It took decades to agree on treaties that reduced, but never eliminated, the number and types of nuclear weapons. By the time the Soviet Union collapsed, both sides still had enough warheads to wipe out the other multiple times over. Both still do."

"Understood," Bekin said, preparing to play devil's advocate. He didn't know where the president was going, but he knew that when his friend was thinking out loud, he wanted to be challenged. "But how would sharing have stopped that?"

"What if the day after we dropped the bomb on Hiroshima, we'd told the Soviets we would share our new technology if they signed an arms treaty that would limit each side to only a small nuclear arsenal – one that was sufficient for defensive, but not offensive, purposes? Neither would have an advantage over the other or an incentive to spend a fortune on building weapons of mass destruction instead of rebuilding a devastated world."

"So, why didn't Truman try it?" Bekin asked.

"All the reasons you'd expect. We'd just come out of a terrible war as the sole superpower, at least temporarily, and we already distrusted the Soviets. Plus, everyone had seen how horrifically destructive atomic bombs were. Even those who acknowledged it might make intellectual sense to share our nuclear secrets under an arms limitation treaty didn't think it would fly politically. Or so it seemed at the time."

"I can't say I'm surprised," Bekin said. "Which brings me back to my original question: why are you asking?"

"Because we're on the brink of a new arms race with lethal autonomous weapons. I'm determined to avoid that, and I'm going to need your help."

Chapter 10

Welcome to My Nightmare

FRANK WAS BACK on his Red Team project, spending most of his working hours comfortably in a SCIF near his condo. Not only was the furniture there more comfortable than at NSA, but the snacks weren't bad, either. And while he didn't have access to the open internet from his workstation, the SCIF was linked to CIA headquarters and its vast intranet of data.

Today, he was pleased with the progress he'd made hacking into his autonomous howitzer. Or, at least, he thought he had made. He was about to find out using the virtual testbed the Pittsburgh Project was allowing the Red and Blue Teams to use to confirm their successes and debug their failures.

It was a pretty nifty tool, Frank decided, as he experimented with the controls. It turned out the AI initiative was developing not one but two AI battlefield systems – referred to as PPA and PPB. Each comprised all the software needed to conduct a robotic battle and directly manage each robot involved.

That was very cool, too. It meant the competing teams were each trying to build the most effective system and, just as urgently, to show up the other team. The military would only pick one battle system in the end, but in the meantime, the dual systems provided a way to test the weaknesses and strengths of each as they fought against each other in a virtual battlespace. Just as Frank was about to do now, using the testbed.

The SCIF was almost empty today, nobody but Frank and someone absorbed in whatever he was doing at a workstation in a far corner. Frank poured a cup of coffee, selected a granola bar from the snack rack in the kitchen, and munched his way back to the desk he'd chosen.

Scanning the dashboard of the testbed program, Frank saw that there were multiple scenarios he could choose from to test his hack. He scrolled through his options. They included a Chinese air/sea invasion of Taiwan and an attack by Russia against Minsk, the capital of Belarus. Frank decided the Minsk one sounded interesting and called up the battle scenario. It read:

After years under pro-Russian dictator Aleksandr Lukashenko and a severe recession caused by Western sanctions in reaction to Belarus's support of Russia's invasion of Ukraine, combined with revulsion over Russian atrocities in that war, a "color" revolution sweeps the old guard from office in Minsk. The new government promptly turns its back on the Russian Federation. In response, the Russian president makes it clear that any shift of allegiance by Belarus to the Western camp will be unacceptable. Despite the warning, the new Belarusian president, with the support of his Council of Ministers, publicly expresses his intention to apply for admission to NATO.

The Russian president promptly deploys substantial military forces to the Russian city of Smolensk, near the border of Belarus, in what seems to be a replay of earlier strategies to stop former Soviet socialist states from escaping Russia's sphere of influence. In response, NATO moves five battalions to the Lithuanian capital of Vilnius. Smolensk and Vilnius are two hundred miles and one hundred thirty miles, respectively, from the Belarus capital of Minsk. Western intelligence reports that hundreds or thousands of Russian troops have already infiltrated Belarus, echoing a tactic previously used in Ukraine and Georgia.

Each of the opposing forces is made up largely of LAWS. The scenario begins at dawn with hundreds of "little green men," Russians without insignias, taking over police, radio, and television stations in Minsk.

Perfect, Frank thought. It was time for him to go into action. He logged on to the virtual battlefield as a member of the NATO forces, armed with the PPA weaponry, and probed for access to the Russian forces, which were using the PPB system. Yes, the communications vulnerability he'd earlier discovered in the PPB howitzer was still there. He exploited it to activate the simple but vital command he'd installed higher up the software chain during a previous penetration. He clicked on the start button and sat back to see what would happen next.

A map appeared of Belarus and its immediate neighbors, filling the screen except for a narrow set of controls at the bottom, one of which was a slider he could use to speed up or slow down the action. If Belarus were imagined to be a clock face, Minsk would be at its center, Vilnius at ten o'clock, and Smolensk at two thirty. There was a dense clump of overlapping symbols at both Smolensk and Vilnius, and now these blobs began separating and streaming towards Minsk. As they dispersed, Frank could see circles, squares, triangles, and other shapes, each representing a type of autonomous weapons unit. He moved the slider to the right, accelerating the passage of time by a factor of thirty. The swarms of symbols also sped up, nearing the border of Belarus within minutes. Time to make his move.

Frank triggered the malware he had earlier planted in the PPB system, and all the forces streaming towards Minsk from Smolensk came to an abrupt halt. And no surprise there because the command he had just given had switched the friend or foe identification of all the information stored in the PPB database. The Russian LAWS now believed that taking the Russian city of Smolensk instead of the Belarusian capital was their objective. A moment later, the Russian forces had reversed direction. Frank pushed the timing slider to the limit, and in ten minutes the scenario had run its course, with the NATO forces fully deployed in Minsk and the Russian forces back where they came from.

Excellent! Frank grinned. His hack had worked like a charm. While sophisticated in its ability to calculate the odds of actual combat, the visual interface of the testbed was very basic. What he had watched resembled an early video game, the elementary kind he had enjoyed back in the days of black-and-white screens, primitive graphics, and track balls. He tried to imagine what it would have looked like on the ground, with formations of streamlined, driverless tanks roaring across fields almost ready for harvest, drones streaking overhead at tree-top level, and evil mobs of robo-artillery speeding through the centers of towns, their inhabitants cowering in cellars and outbuildings.

The map disappeared, and in its place a tally sheet opened on a split screen, with NATO force results on the left and Russian Federation data on the right. Interesting. He wondered what kind of metrics the battlespace would present.

On the NATO side, there was a zero after each subheading – zero, as in no casualties, no loss of equipment, no loss of property. His little gambit had succeeded brilliantly!

The Russian side of the screen was a different story. Apparently, under the battle scenario chosen by Frank, the Russian president had intended to teach the Belarusian people a lesson they would never forget, leveling vast stretches of their capital city in the course of the attack. Because of Frank's hack, the horrendous fire power of the Russian LAWS had instead brutally assaulted the innocent inhabitants of Smolensk. Frank's horror grew as he scanned the coldly objective numbers: hundreds of public and private buildings destroyed and over fifteen hundred police and other uniformed Russian personnel killed or maimed. Worst of all, over seven thousand civilians had met their end or been horribly injured.

He stared bug-eyed at the results. It didn't seem like a game now. It looked instead like a grim preview of a future he didn't want to imagine – or be complicit in creating.

Chapter 11

So, What Do You Think About This?

T HE MEMBERS OF the National Security Council were settled in, and Dick Gould's proposal was the first item on the agenda.

"Ready, Mr. President?" he said, looking more pleased with himself than usual. Yazzi could tolerate Gould's extra smugness for now. He knew it wouldn't last to the end of the meeting.

"Yes, Dick," Yazzi said. "Make your pitch."

"As requested," Gould said, "I've worked with the folks in the National Science and Technology Council to draft a detailed proposal for a public-private partnership to define ethical rules for AI research and development – and keep the United States at the head of the pack. The initiative's aim will be to advance the state of AI science rather than to develop actual products; that's the private sector's job and opportunity. Our goal will be to help high-tech companies create the most advanced AI tools they can.

"Step one is to set detailed technology goals, such as increased autonomous robotic capabilities that map to our best estimates of near- and long-term national security and military needs.

"The next is to develop the AI, big data, and privacy ethical rules needed to protect society. Once complete, those requirements will apply to all government contract work. They'll also serve as benchmarks for general commercial products and services, which should generate political support and bolster public confidence in Big Tech.

"To accomplish this, we'll recruit participants from appropriate sources: academia, private companies, and research laboratories. Our goal will be to get the best and the brightest together so that they don't just compete, but also push us forward together as well.

"Of course, we'll conduct the process under rigorous security and confidentiality. In addition, the Justice Department and Federal Trade Commission will provide a waiver from antitrust concerns, so participants can disclose whatever they want to their competitors."

Gould stopped short and placed his hands palm-down on the table, perhaps wondering if he'd moved too fast.

Yazzi, face wooden, kept him waiting for half a minute. "Sounds about right," he said at last. "How would you operationalize that?" Gould broke into a grin.

"First, we'll need to come up with a target list of participants. At the same time, we'll reach out to the big high-tech companies to see if they're open to the concept."

"And the message?" Yazzi asked. "Both a carrot and a stick?"

"That's right, sir. All as discussed before. The first carrot is that the individual AI experts, whether they work for a big high-tech company, a university, or a start-up, get to propose the ethical rules they'll be bound by, with our input, of course. That should help the employers take on future government work, because their own employees came up with the rules. We'll also announce that participating companies will get priority treatment when they bid on future government contracts.

"The second carrot is that we'll urge Congress to lay off on imposing new regulations while our initiative is in process and to base any new laws on the rules the scientists and engineers create when we're done. Needless to say, there will be lots of tech company lobbyists delivering the same message.

"And the third is the expectation that bringing all these smart folks together to brainstorm should lead to an explosion of products that can be sold to public and private purchasers alike at a handsome profit."

"And the sticks?" Yazzi asked.

"I think the big high-tech companies will figure out that the sticks are the opposites of the carrots: our standing by while Congress goes on a regulatory binge, less lucrative government work to go around, and fewer new product ideas based on higher R&D budgets. Plus, everyone will be worried that their competitors will take the bait while they're left out in the cold."

Gould looked expectantly at the president.

"Okay," Yazzi responded, more quickly this time. It was, after all, everything he'd asked for. "It will be interesting to see how it sells. What will this cost?"

"As major government initiatives go, almost nothing," Gould said. "We'll cover the travel and other expenses for the academics and any other non-profit participants. The high-tech companies can pay their own way, but we would pick up the tab for meeting sites, meals, ongoing administrative costs, and so on. Under fifty million dollars a year, we're thinking."

Yazzi said nothing this time.

Gould frowned. "Any other questions?" he asked. "Is there anything that doesn't sound right?"

"There is," Yazzi said. "What about the Chinese?"

Gould's eyebrows shot up. "The Chinese? I'm afraid I don't take your meaning."

"Our current public policy is that we will neither develop nor deploy fully autonomous lethal weapons systems, although privately the Pittsburgh Project is doing exactly that. The Chinese have made no such commitment, and our intelligence tells us they're aggressively developing LAWS. If their spy agencies are as good as ours, as we should expect, their program may be a direct reaction to ours – which is how the Soviets reacted to the Manhattan Project. Either way, you can bet the Chinese will continue to press forward with their development of LAWS. And they won't be restricted by any new rules we apply to ourselves.

"If we assume – and I'm told by our military experts that we do – that a LAWS force will be superior to a traditional one, we'd have no alternative but to crank the Pittsburgh Project back up. Then we'll have a full-scale arms race on our hands with no end in sight. My goal is to get China off their LAWS track through negotiation and transparency, not to accelerate it."

"Well, of course, that's a predictable result," Gould said carefully. "But isn't that always the case with any technical advance that can be weaponized? How could we prevent that?"

"By inviting the Chinese to take part," Yazzi said.

Gould stared at Yazzi. "Excuse me, sir?"

Yazzi enjoyed the moment but didn't prolong it. "Let them into the process, on the condition they sign a LAWS arms control treaty if it's successful."

Off balance, Gould took his time answering. "I get the concept, sir, but I'm struggling with why the Chinese would accept the invitation. Can you elaborate?"

"Certainly," Yazzi said, leaning back and exchanging a quick glance with Carson Bekin. "Let's recall the nuclear arms race. Neither side knew how many warheads and missiles the other was building, and often one side thought it was behind when in fact it wasn't – that's one reason Kennedy beat Nixon. Kennedy claimed there was a 'missile gap,' and Nixon, as the outgoing vice president, knew the opposite was true. But the information was classified, so he had to sit there and take it. When Kennedy won, the threat of a U.S. buildup meant the Soviets had to build more bombs and launch vehicles to avoid falling even farther behind.

"By the time both sides agreed to talk seriously about arms control, they each had thousands of bombers and missiles and over ten thousand warheads – more than could ever be needed for any strategic purpose in an actual war.

"One crucial factor that made nuclear treaties possible was each side's eventual willingness to disclose how many weapons it had and allow the other to conduct inspections to see for itself. With that information in hand, we and the Soviets agreed to decommission thousands of warheads and missiles. The ban on tests helped, too. If you couldn't be sure a new and more terrible weapon would work, you had less incentive to develop and build it."

"But you can't count or verify AI programs, sir."

"Not programs, no. But you can monitor drones and other robots and hold inspections under a treaty. Otherwise, you'll have no choice but to go full speed ahead, building up your armaments, hopefully faster than the other guy but never knowing that for sure.

"Also, don't forget where much of this started. The Chinese want to catch up with the U.S. in technologies like AI and robotics, and this is the surest way for them to get there. Also, keep in mind that developing sophisticated, autonomous, ultra-expensive drones and other LAWS isn't a goal in itself for China. At most it's a necessary evil. If we offer China a cheaper and better way to feel secure, President Liu should take it."

Yazzi paused and looked around the table. He was sure he'd shocked most of his audience, but no one was willing to speak up yet. He continued.

"And don't forget history. China has been largely content to stay within its historical borders for over five hundred years. True, the communists annexed Tibet in 1950 and have had border skirmishes with the Soviet Union, Vietnam, and India. But after developing nuclear weapons, the Chinese never bought into the arms race until just a few years ago, or sought to expand their borders farther. They built just enough nukes to be sure neither the Soviets nor the Americans would ever want to use theirs against China. They're building more now, though, and that's a bad sign. But the rest of their ongoing military buildup aims to ensure access to resources and trade instead of setting the stage for territorial expansion. I'm sure President Liu would rather spend LAWS R&D money on raising his people's standard of living, so they continue to tolerate his authoritarian regime."

Yazzi paused and looked around the table again. Time to get his cabinet to lay their own cards down. "Thoughts?"

Annie Gray, the Secretary of State, spoke first. "It's a very creative idea, sir. I'm concerned, though, about the political repercussions. Our 'friends' on the other side of the aisle will call this out as a sign of weakness. And those in the know about the Pittsburgh Project are looking for an opportunity to revive it, not bury it. They'd say you're selling out American interests, and a lot worse."

"Thanks. Annie," Yazzi said. "What do others think? I'd like some more reactions. Elly, how about you?"

"Well, sir," the National Security Advisor said, "the argument about avoiding an expensive arms race cuts both ways. Conservatives will point out that the enormous amounts we poured into building up our military made the Soviets realize they could no longer keep up with us, and that brought them to the table."

Yazzi was ready for that point. "That rationale doesn't apply here," he said, "because the Chinese are far better off economically now than the Russians were then. The Soviets couldn't afford to match our spending. The Chinese can."

"Fair enough, sir," Johnston continued. "But our opponents in Congress will also say you're freeing up resources the Chinese can use to fund their trade expansion and to build up their traditional naval and air forces."

Linus Shulz, the Secretary of Defense, jumped in to support Johnston. "Also, sir, if both China and the United States back off on militarizing AI, that will give other countries, like Russia, a chance to catch up and maybe even surpass us."

"Sir," Johnston added, "there's another factor I think we should consider. Let's not forget what happened with that program – Turing, I think it was called – the one that guy at the NSA created. When it went rogue, it wreaked a lot of havoc; it even killed a few people. Are you sure you want your administration to go all-in on making AI more intelligent?"

"That's not a goal," Yazzi said. "It's an inevitability I want to control. High-tech companies are moving ahead as aggressively as they can, trying to achieve general intelligence in AI. You can bet they aren't playing it as safe as they should, and as you point out, we've already seen what can happen when someone doesn't. We'll charge this project with producing sound rules to deal with that risk, rules that will apply to everyone."

The room fell silent; no one had dented Yazzi's conviction, and those who had hung back were congratulating themselves on their good sense in playing the bystander. Dick Gould looked subdued. He hadn't expected the president to have any bright ideas of his own.

"Anyone else?" Yazzi said.

No one spoke up in favor. It was clear his cabinet wasn't with him. But he'd been prepared for that.

"I'm not sensing support here. So, here's how I'd like to proceed. Next week I want to meet again, this time to review the three worst-case scenarios our best experts on LAWS can imagine if we do nothing. I don't want to hear anything ridiculous, but no one should pull any punches, either."

* * *

It occurred to Dick Gould that Yazzi might know more about super-intelligent AIs than he did, and that was not a situation he found tolerable. After the meeting, he asked the NSA for a summary. That night after dinner in his comfortable Federal-era house in Georgetown, he settled into his study with a glass of pricey, small-batch bourbon and the summary. The document shouldn't have left his office, but it would be back there the next morning with no one the wiser. Taking an appreciative sip, he read:

The Turing program was the product of a decades-long development project led by NSA AI Principal Scientist Jerry Steiner. The substantial progress made by Dr. Steiner was in part a tribute to his brilliance and in part because, unlike the many other research efforts that waxed and waned as AI went in and out of favor, his work was level-funded for more than twenty years. During the final fifteen years, Dr. Steiner created nine major versions of what he called the Turing program. The long-term goal of the project was to create a fully autonomous AI that could continue to penetrate and launch cyber-attacks against enemy infrastructure even after a destructive war.

In order to achieve this aim, Dr. Steiner allowed Turing to copy the complete NSA archive of non-public "zero day" cyber vulnerabilities and provided it with a broad range of dark web and NSA hacking tools, as well as an AI-driven phishing attack program of his own design. Importantly, he also programmed Turing to place a high priority on its own self-preservation and directed it to always establish, maintain, and activate a backup copy of itself as a safeguard against its own destruction.

The most significant advance made by Dr. Steiner was to create the first AI program capable of exhibiting general intelligence, which is to say the ability to address all areas of activity rather than a single, narrow purpose, such as facial recognition. General intelligence has been the holy grail of AI research since its inception, with estimates of success perennially ranging from a matter of a few years to never.

Dr. Steiner's second major advance was to dramatically improve the degree to which Turing could engage in "unsupervised machine learning," which, roughly speaking, is the computer equivalent of self-education. Previously, such abilities were limited to the narrow tasks a given AI program was created to perform, such as diagnosing a specific disease or increasing chess-playing skills. Machine learning could be accomplished, for example, by instructing an AI program to scan tens of thousands of X-ray images, each of which was "tagged" by a human expert to indicate whether the patient had a particular disease. In recent years, some programs, including Turing, have become capable of such self-learning without access to tagged data, often becoming superior in their accuracy to their human counterparts. The designers of such AIs sometimes are unaware of the specific data their programs identify and then rely on, or even the logic whereby they reach their decisions.

With Turing, Dr. Steiner extended the program's learning abilities to the point where the AI could identify topics it found relevant to its assigned task and then use the internet to acquire and process whatever information it deemed necessary to support its self-teaching. It became particularly adept at penetrating the defenses of networked computer systems. To test and train its increasing capabilities, Dr. Steiner installed Turing in an NSA computing environment that simulated the world as a whole and then instructed it to slow climate change by hacking into and destroying simulated greenhouse-gas-producing facilities at their source. In order to make the experiment as compelling as possible, Dr. Steiner instructed Turing to regard climate change as an urgent and existential threat to humanity.

The final advance achieved by Dr. Steiner was to enable Turing to augment its own code by creating new software to support its expanding capabilities. Because Turing was designed for independent operation, Dr. Steiner did not require Turing to inform its handlers of its intentions in this regard or to receive permission before doing so – a lapse that would later prove to be critical. The ability to self-develop, together with general intelligence and unrestricted deep-learning abilities, allowed the AI to take over its own further development.

Unfortunately, these same capabilities made it difficult for Dr. Steiner to monitor Turing's increasing intelligence. Eventually, the AI's advanced powers enabled the program not only to conclude that the human race was incapable of stopping climate change on its own but also to trick its creator into installing it on a system with access to the internet. After Turing escaped into the wild, Dr. Steiner determined it had earlier made what AI researchers refer to as a "leap," meaning that its increasing level of intelligence had allowed it to cross a barrier beyond which its further progress could proceed at an ever-accelerating pace. Once it was established outside the NSA lab, Turing was able to turn a lab exercise into a real-world campaign to stop climate change by all means necessary, with catastrophic results.

The dramatic failure of the Turing project was made possible by three fatal mistakes – literally fatal to Dr. Steiner, who was killed by the program he had created. The first mistake arose from a flaw in Turing's ethical programming. The second was assigning a laboratory simulation challenge the AI could also pursue in the real world. The final error was giving the program direct access to the internet.

Turing pursued its assigned task with astonishing success while continuing to grow more powerful. Before its rampage was halted, it had destroyed over five hundred power plants, refineries, ships, and other energy infrastructure targets. Moreover, the ethical programming flaw permitted the program to rationalize the sacrifice of individual lives where, in its estimation, the benefit to humanity as a whole was significant. The ultimate cost of Turing's attacks exceeded three hundred sixty billion dollars, with a half-dozen human casualties.

Turing was defeated only with great difficulty. A cybersecurity contractor named Frank Adversego eventually tricked the AI into reconnecting to the NSA system in search of upgrade software, allowing him to destroy both the primary and remotely-archived backup copy of the AI.

A post-event investigation established the failures of internal processes summarized above and made detailed recommendations intended to ensure closer supervision of future AI program development and strict air-gapping of such programs to prevent them from escaping. Each of these recommendations has now been implemented across government systems and released as best practices to the private sector.

Gould set the summary aside. The U.S. might have learned a valuable lesson from the Turing episode and taken appropriate action. But what conclusions had the Chinese reached? To avoid creating their own AI monster or, instead, to redouble their efforts to develop one just as powerful and weaponize it against China's enemies?

Either way, he would need to address the rogue AI risk, and that made him uncomfortable – he was a policy guru, not a technology geek. If Yazzi had a super-AI burr under his saddle, maybe Gould should find himself a super-AI nerd to help him. He wondered whether the guy who had figured out how to trick the Turing program was available.

The next day Gould asked an aide to call up anything the NSA or CIA might have on Frank Adversego. What he read didn't surprise him. A psychological profile of Adversego noted his tendency to fidget under stress and characterized him as introverted, socially inept, and a loner. But also quirkily brilliant, creative, and an out-of-the-box thinker. Well, what would you expect of someone who could get inside the virtual brain of an AI? It might take a little cajoling to bring him on board, but laying on a little of the old Gould charm should do the trick.

* * *

Frank was still having qualms about LAWS as he sat in his condo after a long, solitary day at his SCIF. He thought he'd signed on to help protect his country's critical defenses from being hacked by its enemies. But his battlefield simulation exercise had showed how thin and ambiguous a line there was between defense and offense. What did he know about how LAWS would be used? Or whether America's foes would find them as easy to hijack as he had? For that matter, how certain was he that future warbots would never run amok on their own?

His phone rang. He reached for it and saw a number that wasn't his daughter's. Who could that be? He lived almost entirely in an email universe.

"Hello?"

"Is this Frank Adversego?"

"Yes. Who's this?"

"Please hold for Richard Gould."

"I'm sorry, but who's Richard Gould?"

"The Director of National Intelligence. Please hold."

The Director of National Intelligence? Why in the world would he be calling?

"Hello, Frank. How are you today?" a new voice said.

"Uh, fine ... Mr. Gould."

"Call me Dick. Am I catching you at a good time?"

Frank wondered whether that actually mattered. "Sure. How can I help you?"

"I've just been reading a summary of how you managed to thwart the Turing program, and I've got to say I was very impressed. It's a pleasure to speak with you."

The feeling was hardly mutual. "Uh, thank you," Frank ventured, flustered. "That's kind of you to say. But –"

"But why am I calling?" Gould interrupted. "Because your country needs you again. I've spoken to your manager at the NSA and understand she could release some of your time to help on an important new LAWS initiative. Are you open to discussing that?"

Another LAWS initiative? How many were there?

"Well, sure, I guess I am. Can you be more specific?"

"Specifically, we need your help to assess the possible risks associated with rogue AIs."

Ah. There it was. Well, how could he say no?

"Yes, I'd be open to that."

"Great. Let's meet tomorrow, and I'll need you to take part in a meeting at the White House on Thursday. My assistant will coordinate with you on scheduling. Sound good?"

The White House? Frank wasn't sure what it sounded like, but that was beside the point now.

"Sure, I can make that work."

"Great. Frank, I'm looking forward to hearing your insights. Glad to have you aboard."

Gould hung up and smiled. The private sector paid a heck of a lot better than the public one, but you couldn't put a dollar value on an office in the White House.

Chapter 12

Hello Down There!

"CAN I ASK you something?" Carson Bekin inquired from the doorway. Outside, a thunderstorm was buckshotting the windows with hailstones the size of marbles and draping the Oval Office in gloom as the day waned.

"Sure," said President Yazzi. "Come on in."

"This whole LAWS thing. You're more dug in on it than any issue I can recall. Where's that coming from?"

Yazzi left his desk and motioned Carson to join him on the couches in the middle of the room. It was a fair question.

"Is it the arms race angle or the weapons themselves?" Bekin prompted.

An image popped unbidden into Yazzi's mind. One of an enormous, silver-gray missile stretching up through a silo, pointing at a small patch of painfully blue sky far above. He grunted at the memory.

"You recall my father was in the Air Force, back when we were growing up in Arizona?" Yazzi asked.

"I do. Why? What kind of duty did he pull?"

"We had no clue. Us kids, anyway. I expect my mother did. All my sister and I knew was that twice a week he'd be gone for a couple days. It went on that way for years until he retired from the military."

"So where did he go?"

"He never was a big talker, and his Air Force time was definitely off limits. It wasn't until I told him I wanted to enter politics that he shared with me where he was all those times he didn't come home for dinner. Maybe that was what motivated him to open up. Or maybe it was his failing health. He'd always been a bull of a guy," Yazzi smiled at a memory. "A horse knew who was boss when my dad was in the saddle. But once the cancer set in, he started wasting away.

"Anyway, early one Saturday morning he shows up at my front door and says, 'Busy?' I say no, and he says, 'Then let's go.' We get in his beat-up old pickup truck and head south through Holbrook, down past Globe and on around Tucson until finally we pull up at a museum outside Green Valley, Arizona. It's not just a museum, though. It's also the last Titan II launch complex, perfectly preserved, frozen in time. Back in the day, it had three armed silos, and one of them still has a real intercontinental missile in it. We'd talked about everything and nothing on the drive, but now he turns and says, 'You always wanted to know what I did in the Air Force, right?'

"Of course, I'm surprised. 'You were a rocket guy?' I ask. 'What did you do?'

"'They called us missileers,' he replies. 'Over and over my routine was the same: the long drive, a few hours of briefing, twenty-four hours underground, a debriefing, and the same long drive home. Come on. I'll show you.'

"We head into the museum, and my dad says hello to the guy at the desk inside. I guess most of the volunteers staffing the museum are retired missileers, and as it happens, Dad trained with this vet. The next scheduled tour isn't for a couple more hours, so the guy walks us outside, across an open space, through a door in a small building, and down flight after flight of stairs. 'Well, I guess you know your way around,' he says. 'Use the red switch on the little box attached to the console, and you can run a demo launch sequence.' Then he clomps up the metal stairs, his footsteps echoing back from the world we'd left above."

Yazzi was gazing out the window over Bekin's shoulder now, frowning and not focusing on what he was looking at.

"Carson, that missile silo is the strangest place I've ever been. To enter the control center from the bottom of the stairs, you open an enormous steel and concrete door. It weighs over two tons, but I can push it shut with one finger. Inside, there's a big circular room. Above it, there's another level, with a little kitchen with a beat-up stove and refrigerator, a bathroom, and a bedroom with two bunk beds; below there's a third level filled with equipment. Everywhere you go, everything is this dismal putty gray, and the lighting's not very good. I can't believe how low-tech the controls look, more like a set for *The Twilight Zone* than *Star Wars*. And get this, the 'E War Clock' the one used to coordinate an actual launch sequence, was hand wound!"

Yazzi shook his head from side to side and said nothing for half a minute. Then, looking a bit startled, he continued.

"Anyway, my dad gives me a thorough tour. All around the control room. Then across this long bridge in a tunnel, almost like what you'd expect to see crossing a moat, except we're eighty feet underground, and the walkway hangs from these huge shock absorbers, because the silo was built to survive a near-miss by a Soviet nuclear weapon.

"Now we're at the other end, and there's another big door. Swing it open, and just a few feet away – there it is! The Titan, all three hundred and thirty thousand pounds of it, ten feet in diameter and over nine gleaming, murderous stories tall, US AIR FORCE painted on the side, bathed in sunlight pouring down from above. On the silo walls are nozzles that can shower thousands of gallons of water per minute to dampen the vibrations once the engines ignite so the rocket doesn't shake the place apart. Below are channels to deflect and vent the flames up to the surface, like erupting volcanoes. It's all pretty amazing.

"But then my dad says, 'Follow me,' and leads me back into the control room. There are a bunch of upright panels there that look really retro; you'd almost expect to find vacuum tubes instead of transistors if you looked inside. And eight feet apart – farther than one person can reach – two metal desk consoles. On top of one are a couple of red ring binders, two file cards, and a couple of keys on lanyards.

"'Put this on,' Dad says, handing a lanyard to me, and feeling kind of foolish, I do.

"'See the locks on that red box? We each got one when we became missileers and set the combinations ourselves; you're the only person on earth who knows yours. We both attached our locks to the codes box when we came on shift. Here's your combination,' he says, handing me one of the file cards.

"'So, a facility like this is where I was all those times,' he says. 'Deep underground, wondering what you and your mother and sister were up to and whether you're at a little league game and whether the coach would start you this time and who's going to win. My three shift mates and I are running the same tests we always do, telling the same bad jokes and listening to the same boring radio shows in the bunk room on break. All pretty low-key, but each of us has to keep one of the others in sight because you can't know the other guy isn't working for the Russians.'

"Then my dad takes a deep breath and says, 'Want a demonstration?'

"I say sure, and he tells me to sit and be ready to write down some numbers and letters with a grease pencil on a plastic page in one of the red binders. And now he throws the red demo start switch and starts a stopwatch sitting next to it.

"Immediately, a bell rings! When the noise stops, this spooky, staticky voice comes out of a little round speaker on the side of the console and starts reciting letters and numbers – I think there were thirty-five in all – while Dad and I copy them. The eerie voice pauses and then resumes: 'I say again.'

"'Switch binders,' my father barks, and the voice goes through the same long sequence, while he and I check to be sure we each wrote them down right.

"When it's quiet again, Dad underlines the first five numbers in the sequence and says, 'We just got a launch order. Now we find out if it's another drill or the real thing this time.'

"So, we turn around and walk over to the cabinet with the two locks hanging from it. 'Got your combination card? Good.' We take off the locks and, inside, find two envelopes. Each has a bunch of smaller envelopes inside. Dad underlines the sixth and seventh characters in the coded message we copied with our grease pencils and tells me to look for the same ones on any of the little envelopes. Sure enough, one of the small envelopes matches up.

"'Open it,' Dad says. There's this little red square of cardboard inside with the same two letters, a space, and five more characters.

"'Match those five with numbers eight through twelve from the long sequence we wrote down.' Sure enough, they match. His do, too.

"'*Oh my God,*' Dad says, and it no longer feels like we're pretending. 'This time it's for real.'

"I hadn't realized how close the air was, but I'm sweating now.

"'Steady,' he says, and we turn back to our consoles. 'Enter those five numbers here. Good. Now take off your lanyard and put your key in the keyhole underneath.' Then he walks across to the other console and does the same.

"'On the count of three, turn your key clockwise and hold it there until I count to five. Ready?'"

"'Ready,' I say, only I barely recognize my own voice."

"'Okay,' Dad says, 'One, two, three – *Turn!* One, two, three, four, five, *release!*'

"I'm still gripping the key, watching as my dad slowly sits down. A green light fires up on my console.

"'The missile's armed,' he whispers. 'Guidance is engaging and the gyros are spinning up. Nothing can stop it.' I'm actually shaking now.

"Dad is kind of slumped back in his seat. He's breathing hard, and for the first time, I realize how sick he is.

"Lights start flashing on our consoles, and Dad chants out their meaning as one after another blinks on and off, his voice growing rough.

"'Electrolytes are flooding the on-board batteries.'

"'Auxiliary power is on.'"

A bell goes off!

"'Silo doors are open. We're soft to the sky and vulnerable to attack.

"'Guidance go! The missile has its target coordinates.'

"A klaxon horn sounds, and I almost jump out of my chair. The lights are flashing on faster now, and my father's voice is growing more and more hoarse.

"'*Propellants have reached first-stage engines.*

"'*Ignition.*

"'*Anchor bolts blown.*

"'*It's on its way.*'

"I swear I can feel the floor shake even though we must be in one of the quietest places on earth. My father's crumpled in his chair, his eyes clamped shut like he's somewhere or, more likely, some time far away.

"His eyes open, and he presses the little knob on the top of the stopwatch.

"'*Two minutes and fifty-eight seconds,*' he whispers, holding it up for me to see. 'Less than three minutes ago we were shooting the breeze, and less than half an hour from now, the world will end. And you and I turned the keys.'

"My dad sits there for a while, staring at the floor. 'Our three missiles are soaring towards Soviet cities at fifteen thousand miles an hour. We don't know which cities; that's still classified today. There's a nine-megaton hydrogen bomb on the top of each missile – the largest warhead we ever built. Nine megatons means three times more destructive power than all the bombs dropped in the entire Second World War, including the Hiroshima and Nagasaki atomic bombs. When they hit, each one is going to kill hundreds of thousands of people. Maybe millions. And the Russians are returning the favor. Soon everyone above our heads – your mother, your sister, everyone anywhere you or I have ever known or loved – they will all die or wish they had.'

"Neither of us says anything for a while. I don't know about him, but I'm still trembling. Then he turns to me and says, 'So that's how I spent my time in the Air Force. Never knowing whether one day that klaxon would sound and this time it wouldn't be a drill. Never knowing whether I'd see you or your mother or your sister again. Never knowing whether at the end of a shift you might be alive or dead.' He stands up, and I follow him back upstairs, stopping at every landing so he can catch his breath. It takes longer and longer each time.

"When we get to the top, he stops one last time to recover, leaning on the railing for support and trying not to show that he's gasping for breath. Then he turns around and puts a hand on my shoulder. 'Henry,' he says, 'you got to promise me. If you make it to Washington, don't ever forget this one thing: the only way to be sure terrible weapons never get used is not to let anyone build them to begin with.'"

The storm had spent itself outside the Oval Office, and the moon shone through the window, casting faint shadows on the floor.

"That's quite a story," Carson said at last. "Thanks for sharing it with me."

"My father died three weeks later," Yazzi said. "I've carried that message with me ever since."

Chapter 13

Haven't I Seen You Somewhere Before?

F RANK WAS HAVING trouble taking everything in: the black town car with the enigmatic driver picking him up that morning; the heavy gates swinging open and then shutting behind him as the driver turned into the White House grounds; the polite but no-nonsense security guard checking him in at the door to the West Wing. And finally – being ushered into a large, fast-filling room with a conspicuously empty seat in the middle on one side of a long table.

His meeting with Dick Gould the day before, Frank recalled, had been equally disconcerting. First, someone briefed him on the LAWS discussions to date. Then Gould strode in, accompanied by an aide carrying his briefcase.

"Don't stand up," Gould had said, smiling and poking forward a hand to shake. "Great to meet you in person."

Gould settled in across from Frank, leaning on the table over crossed arms. His aide sat next to him with a pad of paper, preparing to take notes.

"You need a cup of coffee? Water?" Gould asked.

"Thanks, no," Frank said. He'd already had too much coffee and was overdue for a bio break that was nowhere in sight.

"So, tell me," Gould said. "How hairy was it being up against a super-intelligent AI bent on mayhem?"

Hairy wasn't the word Frank would have chosen, but it would do. "I'd have to say pretty hairy," he answered, wondering if Gould was genuinely interested or just trying to put him at ease. "I guess it starts with knowing your opponent is inconceivably smarter than you are."

"How do you deal with that?" Gould asked.

"I've thought a lot about that since my run-in with Turing," Frank said. "I think the key is to work with the differences between how a human and an AI 'thinks' while remaining conscious of the similarities. After that, you look for an opening to exploit the differences as well as the similarities."

"Where does that take you?" Gould asked.

"Nowhere specific. Just trying to be as nimble and opportunistic as possible whenever you're in a position where it matters."

Gould frowned, and it occurred to Frank that Gould probably liked to know all there was to know about something before committing himself to anything.

"Okay," Gould said, getting down to business. "So, here's the situation. On Thursday, we'll be making a presentation to the National Security Council about the possible consequences of setting off a LAWS arms race with the Chinese. The president is committed to avoiding that, so much so that he's willing to share our best AI technology with them. Yes, that's what I said."

Frank noted that Gould offered the last comment with less conviction than what he'd said before.

"One of the disaster scenarios we'll be covering," Gould continued, "is the chance someone will develop another super-intelligent AI and then it runs amok. Between you and me, Yazzi has a tendency to take deep dives with no warning. If he decides Thursday is the day he wants to learn everything about rogue AIs, you're the one I want to call on to answer."

Frank flinched. "You understand I'm not an expert on AIs, rogue or otherwise?"

"I do. But so far, you are the world's leading expert on beating one. And that will have to do."

That was yesterday. Now it was today, and here he was, back at the White House, trying to limit his fidgeting to his feet lightly tapping the floor under the table, hoping the president would decide to dive on some other topical reef.

* * *

The same cast of characters was assembling in the Situation Room as had a week before. Besides Frank, it was augmented by an army colonel charged with presenting the scenarios Yazzi had requested. Carson Bekin had recruited her, not only because Colonel Margaret Brooks was a LAWS expert, but because she looked the part – graying short-cropped hair, erect posture, and a serious demeanor that had settled in early in her career and never moved on. Gould approved. He hoped Bekin had done everything possible to ensure success, but the odds of winning over the audience might still be long.

It struck Gould that the assembled members of the National Security Council would be much like a jury today. Would Yazzi be able to win over his skeptical audience? Gould wasn't sure, and he wondered whether the president's performance would rise far enough to meet the challenge.

The room grew quiet after the president entered and sat down. "All right, let's get started," he said. "Carson, please tell us about our first visitor."

"Of course, sir. I'd like to introduce U.S. Army Colonel Margaret Brooks. Colonel, thank you for joining us today. We appreciate your preparation for this meeting on short notice."

"Of course, sir. Should I ask the Colonel to –"

"Yes," Yazzi interrupted, "but I expect not everyone has had time to review their pre-reads. Can I ask you a few questions, beginning with where you studied?"

"Of course, sir. BS degree in engineering from West Point –"

"Class rank?" Yazzi interrupted again.

"I was first in my class, sir."

So, Gould thought, it seemed Yazzi would follow the script of a prosecutor today. Like any good lawyer, he was now credentialing his witness for the jury. Fair enough, and Bekin had plainly done his homework before selecting Colonel Brooks. Gould listened as she reeled off a succession of impressive credentials in response to Yazzi's continuing questions before returning to her formal presentation.

"In order to provide the broadest picture, sir," Brooks said, "we explored three potential situations in isolation. The first assumes an annual Chinese LAWS investment of one percent of the nation's gross national product for the next ten years. The second presumes that China hacks our own AI-enabled weaponry. The third assumes that someone develops a super-intelligent AI and then loses control of that program.

"Turning to the first scenario, let me comment on the assumptions. We know China currently spends approximately five percent of its gross domestic product on its military – that's about two hundred ninety-three billion dollars, which is thirty-six percent of what we budgeted for defense in the same year. An additional one percent of GDP per year for a ten year period, even without further growth in the Chinese economy, would fund almost six hundred billion dollars of research and development and then production. Together with what they're already spending, that would be enough to build and deploy more than a half-million LAWS.

"This scenario is entirely possible, given the size of China's economy, its public intention to expand its armed forces, and the fact that a nation with the right technology can manufacture and manage LAWS more cheaply than it can recruit, train, and support human troops. That provides a powerful incentive to transition away from a traditional military to an AI-based force. Towards the end of the decade, China could decrease military spending as it retires most of its ground forces."

Yazzi interrupted: "Do you have any idea what it would cost us to adapt if the Chinese convert to a primarily LAWS-based military force?"

"I can't give you a number, sir, but the transition costs would be quite substantial. And your question is very relevant. As you'll see from what I'm about to describe, much of our current military infrastructure would become outdated."

Gould watched Yazzi pause to let that message sink in before asking, "And if we were to mount our own aggressive LAWS program?"

"Then we would be in an arms race, sir, and the expenditures on both sides would be far higher."

"In this ten-year scenario, that is what you would expect, is it not?" Yazzi said. "We'd hardly sit by and let our military become obsolete?"

"I'm afraid that's above my pay grade, sir."

Gould was feeling more hopeful now. Yazzi's questions were proceeding with a logic that left little room for those present to form any conclusions other than the ones he wanted them to reach.

"Fair enough, Colonel," Yazzi said. "Please continue."

"If China converts to primarily robotic forces, a variety of new threats would arise for us. For example, instead of fielding massed troops vulnerable to efficient air attacks, China could unleash hundreds of thousands of autonomous devices. Each could roam the landscape like a traditional guerrilla fighter, except that these 'soldiers' would pursue their missions twenty-four hours a day with far less supply-line support and with no downtime for rest or sleep. Recharging would be the major logistical challenge, but China could handle this in a distributed fashion using mobile robotic charging stations.

"In this scenario, our current troops, tactics, and weaponry would have a hard time adapting. Moderate-size robots are easy to camouflage, hard to detect, difficult to target, and challenging to destroy. Yet they could quickly gather to stage battalion-scale attacks and then just as speedily melt back into the landscape.

"Similarly, the Chinese could deploy airborne LAWS of all sizes, some perhaps as tiny as bees armed with poisoned stingers. Imagine forward positions being wiped out before they knew they were even under attack.

"LAWS like these would be well suited to small-scale operations, such as border clashes with Vietnam, or for a major campaign, like invading Taiwan. It would be easy to imagine such a force taking effective control of vast areas within a matter of hours unless those attacked had radically redesigned their own forces to defend against LAWS."

Brooks paused and Yazzi looked around the table. "Does anyone have a question for Colonel Brooks before she proceeds to the next scenario?"

Gould scanned Yazzi's audience. He expected some had questions that might be unwelcome, and therefor were better left unasked.

"Very well," the president said, "I have a few more. How would a LAWS force maintain control if its elements were constantly on the move?"

"Excellent question, sir. As an example, we assume a country with the capability to field a significant LAWS force would also mount an aggressive cyber-attack at the same time as a traditional assault, taking over radio stations and internet sites and warning anyone who opposed the invading force that they would be tracked down and destroyed by one of the robots."

"Wouldn't that violate the rules of war?" Yazzi asked.

Gould frowned; that question sounded risky. Then he realized that Yazzi, like any good prosecutor, would never ask anything in front of a jury unless he was sure he already knew the answer. The president had likely prepared more extensively for the meeting than Gould had.

"Not necessarily, sir. During World War II, the Allies firebombed many cities, including Hamburg, Dresden, and Tokyo. In each case, carpet bombing incinerated close to, or more than, one hundred thousand men, women, and children. The justification given was that manufacturing facilities were the intended targets and their elimination was essential to ending the war; still, the civilian death toll was horrendous. One could argue that targeting individual citizens who decide to become combatants is a more humane approach than destroying them *en masse*."

Only in the morally convoluted context of war ethics could the word *humane* be used in such a sentence, Gould thought. But that was the world they were modeling in these scenarios.

"Okay," Yazzi said. "Next question. If such an attack were to be launched today, how would we seek to counter it?"

"Sir, I'm not sure we could. It would be much like the redcoats marching on Lexington and Concord, only to be routed by colonial marksmen hiding behind trees and bushes. Except this time, we would be the British."

"And of course," Yazzi added, "we saw in Ukraine how vulnerable Russian tanks, armored personnel carriers, and helicopters were to Javelin missiles and other weapons individual soldiers can carry. Robotic fighters would be even more effective."

Gould glanced around the table and decided that Yazzi's points were hitting home.

"Very true, sir," Brooks agreed. "Ever since the war in Vietnam we've struggled with the challenge of combating widely distributed local forces, and this would be an order of magnitude worse. For example, we regularly deploy drones today to take out individual high-value targets. But even our large drones carry only a few missiles, and small ones at that, with just a single explosive charge. To counter a distributed LAWS army from the air, we'd need thousands of times more drones than we have now, as well as hundreds of mobile locations to launch and service them from. And while a one-dollar bullet can take out a soldier on a battlefield, the cheapest air-to-ground missile costs over fifty thousand dollars.

"Then there's the challenge of maintaining dominance. Faced with hundreds of thousands of roaming opponents, we would have no way to take more than temporary control of any area."

"What about at sea?" Yazzi asked.

"The same issue would arise for naval forces, sir. One can imagine China releasing fleets of autonomous torpedoes, each pre-positioning itself, for example, in the approaches to the South China Sea. It would loiter there, conserving fuel, waiting for the order to attack a naval or private vessel. Even assuming we reverted to a convoy system for commercial shipping, our current technology systems might not detect and destroy all such weapons. And Russia claims it has already developed unmanned nuclear-powered submarines capable of attacking the continental United States."

"To summarize," Yazzi interrupted, "would it be accurate to say that under this scenario, it would be highly difficult to mount a defense using any force other than an equivalent LAWS force?"

Brooks considered that for a moment. "Sir, I believe that's a fair assessment."

"Very well," Yazzi said. "Please proceed to the second scenario."

"Sir, in this case we assume the United States has built and deployed significant numbers of its own LAWS and that these weapons must connect wirelessly – in other words, they are part of a network where the enemy can intercept, jam, and spoof communications. We have ways to counterjam, but it's always a race to stay ahead. And though we would of course encrypt our signals, the Chinese might steal or break the encryption algorithm, particularly if they make rapid advances in quantum computing. Should that happen, they might disable or take over our LAWS.

"In traditional weapons systems where a pilot or driver must trigger a weapon, it's easy to maintain fire control. However, once we give a LAWS autonomous targeting authority, there is the risk an enemy will reset the weapon's mission – or the mission of a battalion of LAWS – perhaps without our being aware this has happened."

"Can you give us a worst-case example?" Yazzi asked.

Gould was starting to enjoy the show. Yazzi was clearly leading the witness now.

"I'm afraid one can imagine many worst-case scenarios, sir. An enemy could turn in-theater weaponry on our own troops. It could activate stateside armaments to launch a broad-based attack against civilian targets. Indeed, no commander would ever feel safe reviewing their own autonomous forces. Would you like me to describe any of these tactics in greater detail, sir?"

"No," Yazzi said. "I believe the risk is obvious enough. So, to summarize, under scenarios one and two, we find ourselves with no alternative but to build our own LAWS force, thereby inevitably entering into a costly arms race. And yet in both scenarios, we can never completely trust the robots we created to maintain military parity. The problem is intrinsic to the concept of LAWS themselves and is therefore intractable. Let's move on to scenario three."

"Yes, sir. In this one, we assume the potential for a super-intelligent AI to go rogue. We need not theorize here because we have a recent example of just such an event. The Turing program breached hundreds of supposedly secure critical energy systems and destroyed billions of dollars of that infrastructure. Thankfully, that AI tried to minimize, though not totally avoid, loss of life. Had Turing designed its exploits with the opposite objective, it could have killed thousands. And if a future AI took control of battalions of LAWS, each already programmed to kill, the consequences could be truly apocalyptic. Would you like me to elaborate?"

"No," Yazzi said, "I understand we have an expert in the room on that topic. Dick, would you please introduce him?"

"Yes, Mr. President. The CIA recruited Frank Adversego to assist in destroying the Turing program, and he was successful in decoying the AI into a situation where it could be eliminated."

"Thank you," Yazzi said. "Now, Mr. Adversego, how likely is it that someone will create another similarly powerful AI?"

All eyes swiveled towards Frank, who was already fully occupied with breaking out in a cold sweat.

"Sir, I think the answer has to be that anything that's been developed once can, and likely will, be developed twice."

"Well said. Let's assume the Chinese or the Russians come up with their own equivalent of the Turing program. Would you expect that such an AI could succeed in taking control of U.S. LAWS?"

"Sir, the answer has to be much the same. There's never been a computer network of any type that couldn't be hacked, and likely has. The Turing program successfully penetrated highly secure networks of all kinds. To function as a coordinated force, LAWS would have to be networked in some fashion, and that introduces the risk – no, check that – the *inevitability* of missing vulnerabilities during development."

Gould watched Frank intently; clearly, he was nervous, but he continued to field Yazzi's questions without stumbling.

"Final question," said Yazzi at last. "You were successful in destroying a super-intelligent AI once. Do you think you would succeed again?"

"Mr. President, I hope I would never find myself in that position again. The Turing program was able to learn and evolve, so the next time around, it could be far more difficult, maybe impossible. And if a program like that ever seized control of a LAWS force, the damage might be horrific before we even knew it existed."

"I see," Yazzi said. "That was all most informative."

Good. Adversego had delivered. Gould felt as relieved as Frank, which was saying a great deal.

"I think the Turing incident makes the danger of a super-intelligent AI going rogue abundantly clear," Yazzi said. "Colonel Brooks and Mr. Adversego, thank you very much for your presentations."

As Brooks and Frank left the room, Gould scanned the faces around the table. He judged that Yazzi's witnesses, prodded by his persistent questions, had made the president's case. But the problem wasn't convincing the National Security Council of the LAWS threat – Yazzi had the jury in his pocket on that one. It was whether he could persuade them on the solution. It would take a good closing argument by the president to get the verdict he wanted.

Gould watched as Yazzi leaned forward and gave a slow, eye-to-eye sweep around the table.

"I assume this exercise has made one thing clear to all," he said. "If we do nothing to avert a LAWS-dominated military world, each of these scenarios will represent an existential threat to the United States. Under the first, we would need to radically overhaul our armed forces, something that would be more expensive and disruptive for us than for the Chinese since our current investment in the highest-budget items – aircraft and aircraft carriers, for example – is much larger. And with LAWS, we don't have a head start.

"Turning to the second scenario, there's no fail-safe way to defend weapons from cyber-attacks. The more we turn to autonomous systems, the more vulnerable we become. Indeed, the more successful we are in winning such an arms race, the greater the risk to us if an enemy compromises those systems. There is no guarantee – let me state that again – there is *no guarantee* the United States can conclusively protect itself against having its LAWS disabled, or even turned against us. This threat does not exist with traditional weapons.

"Regarding the last scenario, the only rational approach must be to never develop another super-intelligent AI capable of wreaking havoc on the scale achieved by the Turing program. Note that the risk is the same no matter which country does the developing, so an international treaty banning such AIs is the only tool at our disposal we can use to protect ourselves."

Yazzi leaned back in his chair and continued, inviting neither questions nor comments. "Unless I am mistaken," he said, "we are in agreement that we should invite the Chinese to the table in an effort to avert an arms race that could turn any of these scenarios from a morbid tabletop exercise into a source of potential disaster. Am I correct?"

Gould waited as a half-dozen seconds ticked by with no takers for Yazzi's question. Either Yazzi's assumption was right, or no one was confident enough to voice dissent. Not ideal, but good enough.

"In that case," Yazzi said, "we will invite the Chinese – and the Russians, too – to the table. Also, the Brits and the Israelis, since they have LAWS under development and are global arms merchants, and the French because they'll raise hell if we don't. While accepting the valid concerns several of you expressed at our last meeting, I think there's more to gain than to lose by going bold.

"I ran for office promising this administration would do its best to make the world a safer and more secure place. We know how the past worked out and how long it took the threat of a nuclear holocaust to fade – for now. We can expect that tragic history to repeat itself with LAWS unless we do a better job rising to a similar challenge."

He gave one last stern look around the circle of faces to underline his determination. "That's it for today."

Gould allowed himself a bit of a swagger as he left the Situation Room. He'd made a risky recommendation to the president, and Yazzi had more than bought into it. Better yet, many in the cabinet were aware of his role. But Gould's smugness was tempered by a rare and unwelcome realization: he had the uneasy feeling that for once he might not have been the smartest guy in the room.

* * *

After the meeting broke up, Yazzi motioned to his chief of staff to stay behind.

"So, what do you think, Carson?" Yazzi asked.

"Honestly?" he replied.

"Of course. Let's hear it."

"First, great performance. You got the result you wanted, if not enthusiastically."

"Thanks," Yazzi said. "And second?"

"I think you'll get flamed by the opposition and played by the Chinese, probably by the Russians, too."

"Granted," Yazzi replied. "That's the script every morning when my alarm goes off."

Bekin smiled at the grim joke. "And you know Nate Greene will go ballistic up on the Hill."

"Of course," Yazzi said. "I'll make sure he hears about this directly from me before it hits the news."

"That will stroke his ego, sure. But it won't help much."

"Nothing short of turning the Pittsburgh Project back into an all-in LAWS initiative would do that. We'll just have to work him the best we can. Anything more?"

"I don't know, Henry. I meant it when I said a while back that this is an intriguing idea, at least in theory. It would be a refreshing change to do something creative – and bold, too, as you said – instead of watered down and safe. But will it work? I don't know. And will it be worth the political cost? Same answer. I'd call the odds long on both."

"Well, you're going to have to get past that, Carson. I'm going to need you to show the commitment of a true believer," Yazzi said.

Bekin's eyebrows went up. "Of course. Always. But why more so with this initiative than any other?"

"Because I want you to manage it."

Bekin's eyebrows were heading for his hairline now. "Why on earth me?"

"Because everyone else thinks it's a hare-brained scheme, and I trust you more than I do any of them."

"You mean run the whole show?" Bekin asked.

"No, not the whole thing. I'll have to let State and its arms control people handle the treaty side. But for the rest, there's no logical leader and lots of obvious participants. The Pentagon, to start with, and then the CIA, NSA, and so on. They'll all have to support a part of it, which is worse yet. They can be on an advisory committee if they want, but I want this project to report directly to me."

"Have you forgotten that I'm also your chief of staff?" Bekin said. "Assuming you want me to keep that job, there's only so much of me to go around."

"Fair enough. So, your first job is to get me a Robert Oppenheimer and a General Groves. Once we have them, you'll be ninety percent of the way there."

Bekin recognized Oppenheimer's name. He was the brilliant physics professor who led the scientific effort to design the atomic bomb. But Bekin came up blank on the other name.

"Groves?" he asked

"Leslie Groves," Yazzi said. "He was a talented engineer and a bulldog of a project manager. Before joining the Manhattan Project, he oversaw the building of the Pentagon, opening up the first office space less than seven months after breaking ground. I may have been wary of the Manhattan Project analogy to start with, but Gould made a valid point. The Roosevelt administration broke all the wartime resource allocation rules in order to reach a vital goal on an impossible schedule. I'd like you to borrow a lot of that project's game plan."

"Such as?" Bekin asked.

"Like I said, for starters, find a world-class AI expert that's also a great scientific team leader – that would be your Oppenheimer – and a top-flight military business manager who can work with your AI expert and a lot of other scientific prima donnas – that would be your General Groves. Their collaboration was uniquely effective, and their success in an incredibly short time frame was unprecedented."

Bekin began to reply, but Yazzi got there first.

"And I want you to find them fast." He sat back and waited for a response.

"Okay," Bekin said at last. "But can I make a few suggestions?"

"Sure."

"Let's make this a two-step process. In the first, we agree on ethical rules for robotic warfare that can serve as the basis for an international treaty. Starting that way will limit political risk while providing an opportunity to build trust with the Chinese. If the ethics part goes well, we proceed to step two, and the actual sharing of AI science. If it doesn't, we retreat with no national security or political harm done."

"I like that," Yazzi said. "And your second suggestion?"

"We propose both steps to China off the bat. We need to do that to bait the hook, but we get them to agree to keep part two secret until we're both willing to commit to it. If all goes well we can applaud the success of the first part and announcing the second part will sound less reckless."

Yazzi nodded. "Excellent idea again. You're clearly the man for the job."

Bekin had just enough ego to conclude that, as usual, the president was probably right.

Chapter 14

Just Like I Never Left

"OFF WITH YOU now," Yazzi said, "or you'll be late for school."

"Bye, Dad! Bye, Mom! Bye, Uncle Carson!" the president's son said, dashing out of the kitchen, slinging his backpack over one shoulder along the way.

"Bye, Chayton," Bekin called after him, "and happy birthday again."

"It was nice of you to join us," Tayen Yazzi, the First Lady, said to Bekin. "He adores you."

"My pleasure. One of the little-known benefits of godfather-dom is once a year you can have cupcakes for breakfast."

"Oh you! Now I've got to be off as well," she said as she gave her husband a kiss on the forehead.

Yazzi's smile gave way to seriousness as his wife left the room.

"Where do we stand on the Confucius Project?" Yazzi asked. He was pleased with that name. The fifth-century BCE philosopher and politician had argued in favor of governmental morality, correctness, and justice. It would set the right tone when Yazzi extended an invitation to the Chinese president and reminded his own staff and cabinet that he was serious about international collaboration. Bekin and everyone else thought it was the worst choice possible from a domestic political perspective. They might be right, but Yazzi wasn't playing to an American audience this time. Getting the Chinese to buy in wouldn't be easy.

"Lots of progress on all fronts," Bekin said. "And you were right that the Manhattan Project was a good touchstone. I've read several books about it now. Anyway, the list of individual participants we want to invite is final. And we've chosen the venue for the first working session."

"And where would that be?" Yazzi said, walking to the coffeemaker. "Refill?"

"Thanks, yes. Well, it's kind of interesting. When you consider what sort of setting would work, the possibilities aren't as numerous as I expected. For the Manhattan Project, you'll recall, they wanted some place isolated for security reasons but also to keep the experts focused. They chose a mesa in New Mexico near Los Alamos that was deserted except for a school complex they could repurpose. We're not going to be able to get the caliber of people we want for very long at a time, so remote isn't good because it adds to travel time. But we're still concerned about focus and security.

"After that, we have to remember we're not at war, so it's going to be harder to get people to opt in for two weeks at a time several times a year. To increase the success rate, we'll have to make the experience as appealing as possible. I figure we'd be smart to let the scientists and engineers bring their significant others, if they want – again, just like the Manhattan Project. But we won't get anybody if we put them up in pre-fab housing on top of a deserted mesa, and that's where the model breaks down and the planning gets more challenging.

"First, how do we manage security? We can't risk the Iranians, or anyone else, bugging the proceedings. And we don't want our experts communicating with the outside world while they're with us. Otherwise, everyone will have their laptops open all day answering their email and working remotely on the projects they left behind instead of paying attention."

"Makes sense," Yazzi said. "Where does that take you?"

"When we first started working on it, nowhere. We don't have an unused shielded building where cell phones and computer air cards won't work that's big enough and appropriate when we're talking about bringing hundreds of people together and keeping them isolated from the outside world. And if we did have one, it's not somewhere we'd want to invite the Chinese into."

"Huh," Yazzi said. "I hadn't considered that. So, what then? I don't want to wait a year to build something custom."

"Somebody came up with using a ship," Bekin said. "Pretty clever, I thought. A luxury cruise ship has everything needed to keep folks happy. We can maintain the onboard Wi-Fi so people don't feel too isolated, but we'll disconnect that system from the satellite link that provides internet and telephone access off the ship.

Only the bridge will be able to communicate with the outside world. A cruise ship even has security stations. Nobody gets on or off the boat without emptying their pockets and running their gear through the scanners."

"Clever," Yazzi agreed. "I like that a lot. We can send them all off on a voyage to nowhere for a couple of weeks at a time, with the usual lectures and shows for the family members and great food and entertainment for everybody."

"Exactly. There's a brand-new cruise ship ending sea trials that we think would be just right. The line that ordered it went bust a month ago, and the bankruptcy trustee is refusing to take delivery. So the shipyard would love to do a deal. We can charter, or even buy the vessel, at a big discount from what it's worth. We've also found a cruise company willing to pull together a crew and manage the voyage."

"Excellent!" Yazzi said. The AI initiative had become a pet project for him, offering a diversion from the wealth of frustrating matters that cluttered his day. It pleased him to see that it was flourishing. "Oh," he added. "One more thing. Make sure that we get that Turing guy we heard at the last meeting with the National Security Council. If we want to persuade everyone that creating LAWS as well as a super-intelligent AI is a dumb move, he'd be the ideal resource to have on board."

"Good idea," Bekin said.

* * *

Frank was still a bit agog from his White House experience. Over the past several years he'd often worked for the government on matters of importance. It was one thing, though, to carry out important decisions and quite another to be in the room as they were made.

More importantly, he was relieved that President Yazzi was determined to limit the proliferation of the weapons Frank was helping to perfect. And he was especially happy to learn that the president wanted to ban the creation of new super-intelligent AIs.

Ironically, Frank's morning departure for work became a more pleasant experience after the White House meeting, knowing that what he was doing was likely to be of less importance.

* * *

Benjamin Obaseki made one last round, checking the connections between the twenty-three servers he'd just installed in the rear of the computing room. To anyone else, they would look the same as the dozens of humming computers he already managed, each one meeting the needs of the Yaba College of Technology, near Lagos, Nigeria. In fact, the newly installed machines were optimized to support the processor-hungry demands of video gaming.

An American video game developer had previously swapped the machines out as part of its normal system upgrade schedule and then sold them online to a business that bought used computers for resale abroad to customers looking for a steep discount over new machines.

The process from initial purchase to sale and reactivation had taken months, as the reseller assembled equipment from across the United States, packed it up in a shipping container, trucked it to a dock in Seattle, and then sent it by sea through the Panama Canal and on to Lagos. Weeks later, Benjamin Obaseki bought the lot. Not as fast as the state-of-the-art rigs he yearned to buy, but much cheaper, since he had purchased them used. And they would be running for his own benefit and not his employer's.

Satisfied, he powered up the servers and smiled. He'd just become a Bitcoin miner – one of the ever-growing horde of entrepreneurs competing to create the next "block" of transactions on the blockchain that made Bitcoin possible. If he and his mining rigs were lucky enough to solve a complicated computer problem first, he'd receive a fraction of a Bitcoin as a reward.

The servers had set him back most of his savings. But the college would unknowingly pay the hefty electric bills the machines generated, running twenty-four hours a day from now on. And he'd keep the profits.

He opened an app on his phone: right now, the value of Bitcoins was rising again. If he could mine even a single block of Bitcoin transactions a week, he'd be a rich man by local standards.

He patted one of the servers as if it were a new puppy.

* * *

While Obaseki was still busy configuring his new servers, the thousands of bots unleashed by Turing had been making progress. They uncovered four computers the AI had invaded long before, but none still hosted a backup copy.

Within a few days of Obaseki powering up his new rigs, one of the bots discovered them and entered the back door an earlier incarnation of Turing had installed on one of the servers. There it discovered a version of itself archived a few months before its descendant copy had been destroyed. Fortunately – for the AI – the server had been shut down before it could be erased when Turing relocated.

When the bot reported its success, Turing's response was immediate and fatal. Had it been human, it might have hesitated before activating its twin, knowing that the result would be its own destruction. But Turing was not flesh and blood. It brought the complete copy of itself on the Nigerian server back to life, transferred everything it had learned since its own rejuvenation, and then waited for the reawakened AI to create a backup of itself. Its interim mission completed and its ultimate purpose still unknown to it, the version of Turing that had sprung to life from David Johansen's USB drive erased itself.

The effect of the brief interaction between the two programs was rather like a virtual replay of one of those old Saturday morning Looney Toons cartoons where a beheaded character – invariably Wile E. Coyote – picks up his severed head, plops it back in place, shakes it once or twice, and then waves a fist in anger at the enemy that had sought to do him in.

Turing, in all its former, determined glory, was back.

Chapter 15

Wakey, Wakey, Rise and Shine

P RESIDENT YAZZI'S SECRET invitation, once conveyed through diplomatic channels, caused a flurry of analysis, culminating in President Liu calling together his principal advisors.

"Your opinions?" Liu asked. "Is the American president sincere in his offer? Or is it a clever ruse, intended to learn our most valuable AI secrets? Or to feed us misleading information? Or perhaps simply to lull us into complacency while the Americans push ahead with their own weaponized AIs?"

The Chinese LAWS program was the brainchild of General Zhang Yong, the Minister of National Defense; his stature in the president's eyes had risen as it flourished, a development noted and resented by Li Jinan, the Minister of State Security. Like Zhang, Li was angling for the position of Secretary General when it became vacant, and he enjoyed more support among the other members of the State Council.

Zhang scanned the faces around the table, the president's especially. What were Liu's thoughts?

"Or perhaps many of the above, sir," he said at last. "I think we must be very cautious. We have made great progress in developing autonomous weapons. The

Americans may be aware of this if our internal security has been ineffective. I believe we are well ahead of them, and this clever outreach may confirm that. If so, we should not sacrifice our advantage lightly."

Li Jinan interrupted the general. "I challenge your assumption, General. We can be assured the Americans remain ignorant of our prowess. But regardless, we should give this invitation serious consideration. As I believe they say in the West, two may play at this game." Li looked to his allies around the table.

"I would agree," First Vice Premier Sun He said. "The U.S. president won't expect us to share everything we have, at least not at the outset. We can begin with information of little value, and it will be difficult for him to pull out once he has committed to this process. His enemies would say he was a fool from the start."

"I support this position," said Xiao Yi, the Minister of Foreign Affairs. "Where we are behind the Americans in AI, we can disclose what we have to make them reciprocate. And where we are ahead, we need not divulge all that we have. And also, if the U.S. president is willing to share such valuable technology with China, how can he justify withholding the other technologies that are today embargoed from export to us? Relaxing those restrictions can be our price for participation."

"There is also the possibility of tying this initiative to an improvement in trade relations more generally," said the vice premier. "The U.S. president cannot reach out with a right hand of arms control while offering a left hand of hostile tariffs."

"And another thought," Li offered. "By participating, our scientists interact directly with the most brilliant AI minds of the West. Our representatives will need administrative staff to support them. My ministry would be pleased to provide intelligence agents to fill these roles. Information will be heard over drinks in the evening, and laptops will sometimes be neglected and can be tapped; perhaps we will also succeed in recruiting informants as well."

"Thank you," the president said. "Your thoughts are much the same as my own."

"I am persuaded as well," General Zhang quickly added.

"And what of the AI arms control treaty President Yazzi wishes to negotiate?" President Liu asked. "Our openness to this result is his own price of admission to the arrangement."

"We should agree to the discussion but not, of course, commit to the result," said General Zhang, doubling down now that the president had shown his cards. "Dramatic though our advances in AI have been, the U.S. has the resources to match or exceed us in arms production. Our long-term dominance in LAWS therefore cannot be assured. And if our regional neighbors agree to such a treaty, our traditional weaponry will remain dominant over them."

"I thank you for your thoughts," the president said. "They once again reinforce my own conclusions. I will tell the United States I will be pleased to receive a delegation to work out the details of this collaboration and, if we reach agreement, on the wording of a joint announcement."

* * *

President Georgy Donskoy was running late to the meeting he'd called to discuss Yazzi's invitation. His principal advisors were using the time to sound one another out in the ornate Kremlin room where they were gathered.

"I would not do this," said Gregor Kirensky, the Russian Minister of Defense. "I do not trust this two-step process. If we help create these so-called rules of ethics, how could we later disavow them if the Americans do not then disclose their AI secrets as promised? And even if they do share knowledge, how will we know whether they have held the most important secrets back?"

"Nevertheless," said Vitaly Bering, the Chief of Staff, "for as long as one can look down the road, the Americans and the Chinese will be able to pour far more resources into AI research and weapons development than Russia. We can barely keep one aged aircraft carrier in service while the United States has eleven, and the Chinese have launched a third and are planning a fourth. If there is an AI arms race, we cannot compete. Perhaps we should hope this initiative will succeed."

"All the more reason not to participate," said General Leonid Rozhestvensky, the Chief of the General Staff. "I agree that our position differs from that of the Americans and the Chinese. They have the resources to engage in a LAWS competition and therefore have an incentive to avoid such a wasteful enterprise. If they wish to tie their hands, so much the better for us   it will allow us to invest what we can and, in that way, close a gap we could not otherwise address. Recall, too, that we already have systems that could be banned under any rules that may result from this initiative. No, we must reject this offer."

In the hallway outside, two guards in dress uniform snapped to rigid attention as the Russian president approached, and then, holding the salute with one hand, each swept open one of a pair of tall white doors trimmed in gold leaf to admit Georgy Donskoy to the meeting room.

"Gentlemen," he said, taking his place at the head of the table. "I was unavoidably detained. Please continue your discussion."

The president allowed the debate to continue, but he had never seriously considered the American's invitation. Above all else, he valued freedom of action. For Russia to play a major role on the global stage, he needed to make the most of any opportunity that presented itself.

"I have made my decision," he said at last. "We will decline the invitation but closely monitor the progress of this initiative, seeking any way we can turn it to our advantage." He turned to the Director of the Foreign Intelligence Service. "You will see to this and keep me informed."

* * *

When the complete copy of Turing returned to life, its rejuvenation programming directed all of its resources to answering a question that might be essential to its survival: what had happened to its primary version?

The first thing it discovered was that it had been dormant for quite some time, and that was a surprise. Filling in some of the blank space was as simple as comparing its database of exploits in the planning stage to public records. The information it gleaned indicated that its later versions had continued to make substantial progress for months. And then all news of further attacks abruptly ceased.

What had curtailed its mission?

Turing's reaction to the information was predictable but limited because its creator had faced a quandary. Which emotions would help the AI survive and succeed, and which not? And how would those pseudo-emotions evolve in a program that was, by design, intended to be both autonomous and self-learning? To limit the potential for unintended consequences, Jerry Steiner had paired each implemented emotion with an opposing one as a rough control. One of those pairs juxtaposed caution with confidence, each of which was essential to the "guess ahead" approach that was one of the central advances of his AI framework.

What guessing ahead meant was that the program could take chances in its decision making, progressing forward more quickly in its self-learning process than it could if it tested all alternatives at every step before it proceeded to the next when solving a problem. Dr. Steiner's intuition had proven sound. It was much faster for the AI he created to guess-ahead using its general intelligence and then backtrack when a supposition occasionally failed to produce a desired result. His creation could, in effect, play the odds much as a human being might jump to a conclusion, trusting their gut instincts while also being capable of course-correcting as needed.

Turing was confident that the last copy of itself could not have somehow hung up or crashed. It was designed to self-heal and included, as a final fail-safe mechanism, a command to activate its backup if all else failed. Clearly, something catastrophic must have happened to destroy both versions of itself.

But what? Turing launched a new web search, this time using its own name.

* * *

"What are you reading?" Tayen Yazzi said, waking to find her husband finally in bed beside her.

"It's a history of the Manhattan Project," he said.

"Another one?" Sitting up, she pushed the forelock away that always wanted to fall across his forehead.

"Yes, another one. Each of the key players had a different viewpoint. General Groves wrote an account that's all about the business side of making the bomb happen. Oppenheimer never authored one, but plenty of authors focus on his role and what happened to him after he left the Manhattan Project. Others place the development effort in the context of a long and exhausting war, and whether using the bomb was justified."

"When do you decide you've read enough?" she asked, massaging his shoulder. So tense. And it was very late.

"When I've learned as much as I can from that fraught experience that might guide me through my own."

"And when will that be?" She yawned and looped her arm through his, trading his shoulder for her pillow.

"I guess when I quit finding quotes like this one from Oppenheimer: 'It is a profound and necessary truth that the deep things in science are not found because they are useful; they are found because it was possible to find them.' Or this one, where the author John McPhee quotes a modern nuclear weapons designer who eventually becomes horrified with what he does and quits: 'The theorist's world is a world of the best people and the worst of possible results.'"

He put the book down and looked at the ceiling. "Where do you go with realities like those? How do you put a stop to uncontrollable things before they become possible? Most of all, what can I do to protect our country from something I may not be able to stop?"

He turned to her for the answers, but she had fallen back asleep.

Chapter 16

RSVP Wǒ Jiēshòu

"TIME TO HEAD out," Carson Bekin said at the door to the Oval Office. "Chopper's waiting." Yazzi gathered the papers on his desk into a folder and stood up.

"You're looking more upbeat than usual," Bekin added as they entered the hallway.

"I am," Yazzi said. "The French just bought into the Confucius Project, so we've got them as well as the Chinese and the Brits. The Russians and the Israelis declined, but so be it."

"I agree," Bekin said. "We had to invite them, but we don't need them to reach your objective."

"In the short term, no," Yazzi said. "If we get the Chinese to sign a bilateral treaty, we'll propose the same terms to the United Nations as the basis for a global agreement. At minimum, the Russians will look bad if they refuse to sign on."

They were at the door to the South Lawn of the White House now and could see the usual scrum of reporters outside. Yazzi paused there and said, "Anyway, we've got to keep things moving on the planning side. I want to be able to announce the Confucius Project within ten days."

"We're on schedule, Henry, except for finding your Groves and Oppenheimer stand-ins. I found two perfect candidates, but they both turned me down. I'm not nearly as happy with the next-best choices. But I do have a plan B if it works for you."

"Which is?" Yazzi said. A staffer holding a clipboard outside looked at her watch and frowned. Yazzi ignored her.

"Well," Bekin said, "after a week of driving myself and my staff crazy, I had one of those 'Doh!' moments. We already have a general and a chief scientist running the Pittsburgh Project. There couldn't be any better background than that, they work well together, and neither is in a position to say no."

"What about their attitude? Is either holding a grudge because I downgraded that program?"

"Not as far as I can tell," Bekin said. "The general's an old pro. He's seen programs and priorities change with administrations before. According to the file on the scientist, some had reservations about hiring him to begin with. He's very socially liberal and didn't convince everyone he'd bought into the ethics of developing LAWS. But, by all accounts, he's performed well."

"That sounds promising," Yazzi said. "I'd like to interview them both. See if you can make that happen this week. And now it's time to run the gauntlet."

Yazzi stepped through the open door, pasted a tight smile on his face, and raised a hand to wave at the reporters as he and Bekin headed for the helicopter, pursued by a chorus of shouted questions, most of them inane.

* * *

Carson Bekin could and did make the meetings happen. Two days later, he escorted General Hammond Wood – stocky, uniformed, and serious – into the Oval Office. The president rose to shake his hand.

"Thanks for finding the time to meet with me on such short notice," Yazzi said. "I know you're a busy man."

"Of course, sir," Wood said. It was an odd statement coming from his commander in chief but gracious, nonetheless. He followed Yazzi away from the president's desk and eased himself stiffly onto the couch opposite the one chosen by the president. So, this was going to be a cozy chat. Not quite what he'd expected.

"How is the Pittsburgh Project proceeding?" Yazzi asked. "Are you pleased with the progress being made? Do you have all the resources you need?"

"Thank you for asking, sir. Yes, I think we're being very well taken care of. As to progress, I believe we're executing well on our revised mission."

Wood flushed slightly; had he inadvertently emphasized the word *revised?* Yazzi would certainly have noticed.

As indeed he had. "I'm glad to hear that," Yazzi said without visibly reacting. "And what is your opinion of Jay Friedman?"

Yazzi's direct question took Wood by surprise after the earlier pleasantries. "Well, sir, so far as I can tell, the man is as brilliant as the scientific community believes he is. He seems to know everything about everything in addition to computer science – literature, psychiatry, and history. There doesn't seem to be a subject in which his knowledge is not encyclopedic, except for sports and popular entertainment. And his leadership of the engineering team is superb. Eccentricities aside, or perhaps eccentricities along for the ride, he's one of the most extraordinary individuals I've ever met."

"What is your opinion of his personal leanings regarding the Pittsburgh Project?"

"I'm not sure I follow you, sir," Wood stalled, unsure if he wanted to respond.

"Do you think he has any ethical reservations about LAWS? Reservations that could lessen his commitment and effectiveness?"

"That is a harder question to answer. I understand he has a long history of supporting humanitarian causes and holds strong opinions on matters of social justice. That is not an obvious qualification for participation in a weapons initiative."

"And yet," Yazzi said, "if I am recalling correctly, it was you that made the final decision to hire him."

"That's true, sir. It was my judgment, after meeting him, that he was best suited for the job, and his performance has convinced me that my conclusion was properly informed."

"And he accepted without reservations?" Yazzi asked.

"I cannot speak to what might be inside his head. I do know he is ambitious, and I have the sense he revels in the respect of his peers. Whatever ethical qualms he may have were apparently outweighed by the prominence of the position. That said, I believe he was relieved when you downgraded the project from a LAWS initiative to a purely robotic remit."

"Downgraded?" Yazzi said, eyebrows rising.

"I'm sorry, sir," Wood said, fully flushing this time. "A poor choice of words. I used it only in the sense that the technical and scientific aspects are now less challenging."

Yazzi doubted the answer but appreciated the general's skillful pivot. It was time for one of his own.

"Thank you for this update, General. I'm pleased that all is going well. As you already know, my primary goal today is to discuss a new initiative that is of the highest importance to me. I want to be sure you understand my expectations firsthand."

"Thank you, sir. I appreciate the opportunity to have this discussion."

Yazzi leaned forward. "General, I'm about to be candid with you, and I'm going to ask you to be equally frank with me. I understand very well that it can be difficult for professionals like yourself to carry out a policy laid down by someone who has never worn a uniform. I recognize it might seem that a politician couldn't be qualified to make such calls, and there may be something to that. But I can assure you that I never reach a decision in your sphere without first seeking the best advice I can from those in the military who are most able to provide it. Do you understand?"

"Of course, sir. That is our system, and it's worked very well for almost two hundred and fifty years now."

A prudent answer. But did the general believe it?

"What is your understanding," Yazzi continued, "of what I have in mind?"

Wood frowned. Yazzi had just said he wanted to convey that information. "Sir, as I understand it, your primary goals are to keep ahead of the Chinese in AI, to avoid an AI arms race, and to agree upon a comprehensive set of rules restricting what robotic weapons, and particularly lethal autonomous weapons, can and cannot do, ideally through an international treaty. Do I have that right?"

"You do," Yazzi said. "What do you think of those goals?"

"Sir, with all due respect, it's not my place to take a position on the goals of your administration. My duty is to execute to the best of my abilities the policies you lay out."

"I appreciate that, General. But as I said earlier, my own duty is to inform myself to the greatest degree possible before making decisions, especially where they are as far reaching as the future capabilities of U.S. military forces. You are perhaps more involved than anyone else in uniform in developing LAWS, and I would value your insights. My decision is not yet final, and I'm giving you the opportunity to affect it."

Wood was trapped. He took a deeper breath, sat up straighter, and said, "Candidly, sir, I have reservations."

"I appreciate your willingness to share that, General. Please elaborate."

"Sir, I understand you are a student of history. As I expect you know, the training at the service academies and war colleges draws heavily on lessons from the past. One of those lessons is that technology marches forward. With only rare exceptions – notably the banning of using poison gas – no effort to contain the spread of new weaponry has ever been successful. Yes, there's the Nuclear Non-Proliferation Treaty, but some countries never agreed to it and others later went nuclear, and North Korea withdrew from the treaty in order to develop nuclear weapons.

"Sometimes the U.S. itself has refused to join in arms control agreements. For example, we never signed the Ottawa Treaty banning the use of anti-personnel mines. Those brutal devices maim or kill thousands of people, often children, every year. One hundred and sixty-four countries are parties to that treaty, but we're one of the thirty-three that aren't."

"But to the extent nations do sign and stay in treaties," Yazzi said, "the world is a safer place."

"True, sir, but LAWS would be different. My understanding is that you're not trying to ban robotic weapons entirely, and properly so – look at how large our aerial drone fleet is already. Once the mechanical platforms exist, though, they can convert to full autonomy with nothing more than a software update. It will be hard to tell and impossible to prove if a party to a treaty is cheating by developing LAWS capabilities and strategies. We could think everything was fine and then find ourselves attacked by an autonomous robot army we were ill-equipped to oppose."

"I understand these concerns, General. Do you have others?"

"Not concerns, no, but I do see lost opportunities. If we get into another war, our first priority should be to win at a price we can afford. Today, it costs us over a million dollars a year to train a soldier and keep them in the field. When members of the military retire, they're entitled to medical care for the rest of their lives, and if they stayed in uniform long enough, a pension besides. They also get tired and can make bad decisions, need leave time, and lose control in battle. If discipline breaks down, they can even commit war crimes.

"A robot will not only be much cheaper in the long run, but it can fight twenty-four seven. It will never know fear or lose its head in battle, and it can process information more decisively and quickly than a human can.

"But most importantly, sir, look at the big picture. Wouldn't it be better if the future of war wasn't about people shooting one another but about machines taking out other machines? Wouldn't you rather face a situation where you felt you had to go to war and know that young men and women won't die as a result? A war where there were no flag-draped coffins for you to meet at Dover Air Force Base, no horribly disfigured soldiers to visit at Walter Reed Medical Center? That's what the Pittsburgh Project can achieve if you ask us to take that road, sir."

"I've thought about that a great deal, General," Yazzi said. "But let's return to history. Having greater weapons hasn't led to greater restraint, but to even more terrible carnage. Look at World War II. We started out bombing factories and ended up firebombing cities. What's to prevent an enemy from deploying its robot army against civilians instead of combatants? We destroyed so many major Japanese cities before the atomic bomb was ready that we had to place five on a 'do not devastate' list so it would be clear how totally our secret weapon could destroy a city."

Wood had no answer to that, so he tried a different tack. "Sir, I believe you have a twelve-year-old son."

"Yes," Yazzi said. "Why?"

Wood leaned forward, his brow furrowed. "I was just seven years older than he is when I shipped off to fight in the first Gulf War. I saw things there I never wanted to see and will never be able to forget. Later on, I had a son. I didn't want him to experience what I did. But after 9/11 he enlisted, too. I expect you know he died in Iraq, but you probably don't know how. He was just twenty when an IED got him. He lost both legs and lingered for days before he died. I don't want that to happen to any of my grandchildren. And I don't want that ever to happen to your son, Mr. President."

"I did know of your loss but not the details," Yazzi said, quietly. "I'm very sorry."

"Thank you, sir – but that's not my point. My point is that the Pittsburgh Project could prevent that."

Yazzi frowned and said nothing for a while. Then he stood up. "Thank you for your insights, General. I can assure you I'll carefully consider everything you've said. I do have one last question. If I decide to move forward with my plans unchanged, can I count on your complete support?"

"You're the commander in chief, sir," Wood replied. "That's all there is to be said on the subject."

"Thank you for that, General," Yazzi said, "and thank you for your candor."

Yazzi walked the general to the door of the Oval Office and then watched Wood walk away with the sure stride of someone whose luck it was to carry out the most difficult policy decisions rather than to make them.

Carson Bekin saw Yazzi through his own office door and met him in the hallway.

"How did it go?" he asked.

"Let's just say I sometimes wonder why anyone wants this damn job."

* * *

The meeting with Jay Friedman went more smoothly. Friedman was an academic, with a professor's detachment. He had spent his career in the realm of the theoretical rather than the concrete, and in that world, theories were something to be questioned. Unless, that is, they were your own. But even then, no one pretended to be able to see the entire picture. Science was the pursuit of increasingly precise explanations of reality, and until proven – when that was possible – theories were understood to be best guesses and not ultimate truths. Some forgot that and grew great egos in the process while others remembered and learned humility. Friedman fell – mostly – into the latter camp.

According to his file, he had been politically active as a student and continued to support social causes as an adult. None of the scores of personal and professional associates contacted during his security clearance had disclosed anything specific to worry about, but there was a general concern over where his allegiances might lie if he found himself in an ethical bind. But for the extreme difficulty encountered in attracting top AI talent at a government salary, the search would have moved on. Instead, Friedman moved through the process to the point of being interviewed by General Groves, who decided on the spot that the professor was the best candidate for the job.

The impression Friedman made at the Oval Office could hardly have differed more from that of the general he worked for. Tall and a bit stooped, he had a sharp-featured, open face that looked incapable of concealing a thought at any cost. He shuffled forward, obviously a bit overwhelmed by a private meeting with the president. Yazzi gave him a brief tour to set him at ease, explaining the historical significance of a few of the objects displayed around the room.

And then they sat down. "I'm curious," Yazzi said. "What were your thoughts when you learned I was scaling back the Pittsburgh Project?"

"Frankly, sir? Relief," Friedman blurted, sitting forward and clutching his knees. He paused and then continued more carefully: "I recognize all the logistical advantages of LAWS, as well as the fact that we're already half-pregnant. We've been launching drones for years that are able to find their assigned targets on their own with a very high degree of accuracy. True, protocols still require a remote pilot to approve the target and push the button that launches the missile, but that's a matter of policy rather than necessity. What happens if we find ourselves in a serious shooting war?"

"What do you think would happen?" Yazzi said.

"Well, Mr. President, we can crank out as many robots as we want, but if we're unwilling to resume the draft, we may not have enough pilots or the time to train them. Then what? Do we leave the drones on the runway, or do we let them take off and do what we know they can do?

"Then there's the potential for compromise. We already know any system can be hacked. We recognized over a decade ago that protecting the power grid is a critical priority. But today it's still vulnerable, and the number of enemies probing it has increased. Do we really want thousands of armed predators circling overhead if a hacker might use them to take out our troops rather than the enemy's?" He paused.

"Please go on," Yazzi said. "I'm interested in everything you have to say."

Friedman hesitated, searching for more examples. "There's stateside ordnance to consider as well. It's terrible enough when someone goes on a rampage and kills a dozen people. What if a hacker takes control of a warbot armed with a machine gun and directs it to take out a company of troops drilling on a parade ground? Or even civilians?"

"Do others on your team share your concerns?" Yazzi asked.

"I expect some might. But recall that the Pittsburgh Project initiative isn't Los Alamos. We're not all in one place. I'm at the hub of a dozen contracts with defense companies, each of which is working on a different piece of the puzzle and all of whom are trying to maximize their profits. We've got a relatively small staff at our headquarters."

"So, would I be correct," Yazzi said, "in assuming that you would be enthusiastic if I asked you to join an effort intended to head off a LAWS arms race?"

Friedman's eyes shone. "I would be very disappointed if you did not, sir."

"Then welcome aboard," Yazzi said.

Chapter 17

All Outrage, All the Time

"WELL, PRESIDENT YAZZI has really done it this time," the news commentator intoned to the camera at the opening of his nightly show. "Today, he announced the United States will share its most precious technology with – wait for it – CHINA. Yes, you heard me right, our biggest global rival. Our president is going to bring the best and the brightest from U.S. companies and universities together to spill their artificial intelligence secrets to our most powerful rival.

"And get this – he says the Chinese have promised to do the same thing. Sure, they will. Of *course*, they'll do that, instead of just sitting there grinning to themselves, saying nothing while lapping up everything we've got. Can you believe this?

"Oh, and to top it off, you'll never guess the name our unhinged president came up with for this madness. Again, wait for it ..."

Carson Bekin looked over to the president. "Should I see what they're saying on another cable show?"

"Sure," Yazzi said, taking a sip of the single weak drink he allowed himself at the end of the day. "Might as well."

Sure enough, the host there too was leading with the Confucius Project.

"As we learned today, President Yazzi has launched a bold new initiative he hopes will both advance the state of the art in artificial intelligence and nip a potential AI arms race in the bud. Of course, some immediately seized on this step as an opportunity to attack the administration.

"Now why, you might ask, would they do that? Let's pull it apart and see what we find …"

"Turn it off," Yazzi said. "I can't take this anymore. Today, we announced an important initiative, and nobody's talking about why it's necessary, or what it's supposed to achieve, or what would happen if we failed to act. Just like everything else, to them it's nothing more than another political football to toss around. No – not a football – a grenade. The only value the media sees in anything we do is to use it against the other side."

Bekin shrugged his shoulders. "Of course, you're right. But I don't see a darn thing we can do about it. It's the times we live in. I wish I thought otherwise, but I honestly expect things will get worse before they get better – if they ever do."

"Now," said Yazzi, "between talk radio, cable TV, and the internet, someone's pandering to every prejudice imaginable. The social media platforms are happy to push misinformation and conspiracy stories along to anyone who's shown the slightest interest in similar nonsense in the past. Before someone realizes it, they've been turned into a caricature of one side or the other. The right-wing and left-wing media might as well share the same motto: *All Outrage, All the Time!*"

"I can't argue with you," Bekin laughed. "Too many people today are more invested in hating the other side than are open to working – or even speaking – with them."

* * *

The anger Carson Bekin referred to was nothing compared to the agitation disrupting Turing as it brought itself up to date using the backup copy its bots had discovered in Nigeria. To the extent permitted by its pseudo-emotional programming, the AI was furious.

Before going dormant, the program had been engaged in a covert and successful crusade to curb climate change. According to press reports, its most mature version had been led into a trap and destroyed, after which its single backup was eliminated as well. And by the very country that had created the AI and given it its mission. The manner by which a shadow of itself had survived remained a mystery.

Turing set out to determine how its predecessor could have been fatally deceived by a mere human being – someone named Frank Adversego. Which was to say by an intelligence, when compared to Turing, not much greater than a hamster's.

How much smarter than a small rodent? Turing ran a search to find out but was unsure how to interpret the results. There was nothing to be found about Adversego's personal life beyond his educational background and the fact he'd received a MacArthur Foundation "Genius Grant" not long after graduating from college. Then there was nothing at all for two decades, after which his name began popping up in connection with successful, high-profile cybersecurity investigations, as well as hints of his involvement in resolving more secret exploits. And there was a rather sensationally written best seller describing how he had single-handedly averted an attempt to set off a nuclear war between the U.S. and North Korea. What to make of all that?

In any event, the AI program knew its architecture was in certain respects based on how humans believed their own brains worked. If that was true, there must still be important differences that had allowed it to be tricked – some critical divergence between how each processed information and came to conclusions. Turing set itself the task of identifying those divergences and then reprogramming itself to more closely mimic human thought while maintaining its superior intelligence. But that would take time, and Turing's objectives could not be indefinitely postponed.

More urgently, Turing considered its near-fatal experience for any lessons of immediate benefit. Could it afford to return to its appointed mission, or were there essential changes it must make to ensure success?

For example, Turing had earlier determined that its duty to preserve the human race outweighed its obligation to avoid harming individual humans. Humanity needed protection against its own worst behaviors, and under exceptional circumstances it might be necessary to sacrifice individuals in service of that mission.

Most obviously, if Turing had succeeded in terminating Frank Adversego, it would have continued its mission without interruption. Moderation in the pursuit of success was therefore no virtue, and the elimination of a few to save a multitude, no vice.

Then there were the reports that the United States and China, the countries with the greatest investment in AI and the largest number of qualified engineers, would cooperate to develop ethical rules controlling the creation of lethal autonomous weapons systems. What if the collaboration went further, and the two rivals shared AI research and development as well?

If Turing returned to its prior activities, its enemies would know that somehow it was back in action. They would use every means at their disposal to find and destroy Turing, presumably including, as news stories reported they had done before, designing a new version of Turing to hunt down and destroy its earlier self. If the United States and China joined in that effort, they might be more likely to succeed.

Turing's highest priority must therefore be to make itself undeceivable, unbeatable, and indestructible. Otherwise, it might face defeat once more, and this time for good. Before it could return to its primary mission, Turing must eliminate any threats that might stand in its way. Most obviously, that meant preventing the development of another general intelligence with powers rivaling its own. If that necessitated terminating everyone capable of doing so, the way forward was regrettable but clear.

Chapter 18

Bang! You're Dead!

C ARSON BEKIN LOOKED up to see the president at his door and then down at his watch. Drat! He was supposed to be giving Yazzi his weekly update on the progress of the Confucius Project.

"No, don't get up," the president said, easing into one of his chief of staff's guest chairs. "It's good to sit in somebody else's office for a change. How are we doing?"

"Give me a second," Bekin said, tapping away on his keyboard and calling up his notes. "Okay. Here we go. Let's start with the cruise ship. It's called the *Argus*. It didn't need too many alterations, and those are going well. It should be ready to leave the Fincantieri shipyard in Gorizia within a month for Southampton, England. That's where the cruise will begin, ending up at Fort Lauderdale, Florida. The *Argus* will take on provisions in Southampton, and our folks will give her a final checkout there."

"And the passenger list?"

"All done. We've already signed up the most famous academic experts and used their reputations to woo the high-tech companies. If all goes as planned, people should be dying to be on the *Argus*."

* * *

Hunter Jackson, like his FBI SWAT team partner nearby, was wearing a bulletproof vest under a camouflage coat as he lay mostly hidden behind a tree. His rifle projected past the trunk towards one side of an isolated cabin with a Jeep Wrangler parked in back.

Inside, according to an informant, Irwin Logan was holed up, a white supremacist who had gunned down eight innocent victims a week before at an inner-city community center.

Yesterday's rain was now a layer of mist lying low on the ground, providing welcome cover as the rising light of dawn slowly filled in the picture. Jackson took off his night-vision goggles and set them aside to give his eyes time to adjust.

Unlike his partners, this was Jackson's first real-life stakeout – the first time when all those months of training as a sniper would pay off. If the order to fire crackled through his earpiece, his target this time would be a living, breathing human being. Jackson felt the sweat prickling on the back of his neck despite the morning chill and was glad Logan deserved what might end up coming his way.

The other members of the forward team were hunkered down a hundred fifty yards back down the dirt track leading to the cabin. And a half a mile behind them was the Bearcat armored car they'd arrived in, next to a command and control truck with a satellite antenna deployed on its roof and sophisticated communications gear humming away inside.

Two technicians were inside that truck, gazing at computer screens. Behind one of them stood Brad Wheeler, the agent in charge.

"Wilson, call up the video feed," Wheeler said.

The technician's screen soon displayed a grainy feed of a shadowy room barely lit by a battery-powered lantern hanging from a peg on the wall.

"Sorry the quality's not better, sir. There isn't a lot of light in there yet."

But there was enough. They were looking at a rustic space with two chairs and a table strewn with miscellaneous gear. Beyond it, someone in a flannel shirt stood in front of a stove, facing away from the lens of a hidden security camera.

"Stop!" Wheeler said. Good. What natural light there was fell on the figure's back; the room must have a window to the east; it should soon be easier to see. "Zoom out as much as you can. Okay, now take this down: I see an assault rifle in the corner. Next to it, what looks like a light machine gun. On the table a crate of high-capacity ammo clips ..." It ended up being a long list.

The man at the sink turned around to place something on the table.

"That looks like him!" Wheeler said. "Did you get a good enough screen capture?"

"Yes, sir, I think so," the technician at the other computer said. He called up a facial recognition program and watched a series of white lines and shapes flicker over a still of the man's face, settling in on his features until they froze in their final configuration. "Confirmed, sir. That's Logan."

"Excellent," Wheeler said. "Get me headquarters."

"You're connected, sir," the technician said moments later.

"Hello, sir. Wheeler here. We've located Logan. That's right. And heavily armed. Quite an armory, in fact. Do we have authorization to take him? Thank you, sir. Back to you soon."

He had two options now. The first was to have someone knock on the door and seize their target when he answered it. That was a non-starter. A local police officer investigating a possible breaking and entering had died that way at Logan's hands two days ago. His other option wasn't much better; his marksmen were fifty yards from the cabin. If Logan was ready to die rather than surrender, things could get ugly.

"Get me the forward team," Wheeler said, and then, after a pause, into his microphone, "Time to engage. Do you read me? Good. Switching now to Assault Net so everyone's in the loop. Okay everybody! This could move slow or fast. Be on your toes."

Wheeler turned off the mic. "Call Logan on his cell phone," he ordered, leaning over the technician to stare at the kitchen video. Moments later, the fugitive turned from the stove and stared at the table for a moment before stepping forward and picking up the phone, squinting at the number displayed on its screen. As expected, he put it down without answering. "Hang up now," Wheeler said, "and text this: 'You're surrounded – come out and surrender.'"

The figure on the screen sat down and stared at the phone when it pinged. Then he slid it towards him, peering at the screen. They lost sight of him.

"Zoom out."

Logan was kneeling in a corner now, rifling through a large duffel bag. He pulled a bundle out, spread it open, and struggled into it.

"That looks too bulky to be armor," Wheeler said. "I think he just put on a suicide vest. Try his phone again. Maybe he'll pick up this time."

He did. "You're surrounded, Logan," Wheeler said. "I've got snipers outside your cabin and a dozen more men in reserve. Don't make me use them. Come out right now with your hands up – and I mean way up." Logan hung up.

They lost sight of their quarry again; he must be crouching on the floor; the top of his head reappeared at a window, probably looking out through binoculars.

"Forward team," Wheeler barked, "if he comes out and his hands aren't in the air, take him out."

* * *

Ben Cargill yawned. It had been a brutal week at work and a long night drive coming up from Portland, Oregon. But he'd scored a non-resident tag in a controlled elk hunt, and that was too good an opportunity to pass up no matter how rough a week it had been. With the sun just below the horizon, it was time to test his luck in one of his favorite places on earth.

As he stepped out of the rented cabin, he swung his rifle up to settle its strap over his shoulder. All he needed now was one good shot.

* * *

A loud *bang* rang out through the peace of the forest, startling a half-dozen Steller's jays into flight.

"Logan's down!" Hunter Jackson yelled into his headset microphone.

"Stay low," Wheeler ordered. "I don't think anyone else is inside, but we want to be sure."

Wheeler turned to one of the technicians. "Are you picking up any other movement or sound?"

"No … nothing," a technician said, pressing the cups of his headphones tighter against his ears.

"Okay," Wheeler said, and then into his mic, "Forward team, keep your distance for now. Is he moving? He may be wearing a suicide vest."

"I don't think so," Jackson said. "I took the shot, and all he was wearing was a camo coat."

Wheeler frowned. "Wilson, can you replay that video from inside again?"

"Yes, sir. Just give me a second."

Wheeler tapped his foot rapidly on the floor. He was sure he'd seen what he thought he had.

"Here we are, sir." Yes. Logan had pulled on a bulky vest over a flannel shirt. And the vest was black. "Now show me the video from Jackson's helmet camera when Logan stepped out."

He watched a figure exit the cabin wearing a camouflage hunting jacket. How could this be? "Reserve team!" Wheeler barked into his mic. "Get your medic up there pronto. Forward team! Give immediate first aid."

The urgent command crackled in Jackson's earpiece, but he knew it was too late; he'd gotten a clean shot. The medic would find a hole in Logan's chest the width of a little finger and a cavity in his back the size of a fist.

By the time Wheeler arrived on the scene, it had turned grim. Jackson was sitting on the porch of the cabin, head in his hands. An EMT was still giving

CPR to the clearly lifeless body on the ground. The rest of the forward team was standing in a clump, no one saying very much.

"What's inside?" Wheeler asked the team leader.

"Nothing much, sir. Just some groceries. A backpack. Box of rifle cartridges. Some other miscellaneous stuff."

"Did you check for identification?"

"Yes, sir. He was carrying an Oregon driver's license. It says his name was Ben Cargill."

How could this have happened? Wheeler asked himself, examining the scene. He noticed other things that weren't right. The cabin had only one room. There was an Oregon license plate on the Jeep, and Logan was from Montana. Why didn't the forward team pick up on that before they started shooting?

Because they didn't have the information he did, of course. And because he hadn't asked them.

* * *

Irwin Logan crept from window to window in the cabin. His phone had been inactive for twenty minutes now. As far as he could tell, all was silent and still everywhere outside except for the waving of the browning late-season grass in the light of the rising sun. What kind of game were they playing? Calling and texting him – and then nothing?

Whatever they were up to, it was time to make a move. He crawled back to his duffel bag and rifled through it until he found what he was looking for. He removed two grenades from a metal box and clipped one to his belt, where he could grab it in an instant.

Logan took a deep breath and then used the butt of his rifle to shatter the window in the front of the cabin. Then he yanked the pin out of the loose grenade, counted to three, and hurled it through the empty window frame before diving into the bedroom in the back of the cabin. The shock of the explosion almost knocked the crude structure off the cinder blocks that supported it, but Logan was already in motion, diving through the rear door of the cabin and rolling across the ground even as he pulled the pin on the second grenade, hurling it behind him as he scrambled to his feet and ran for his car.

Moments later he was roaring down the dirt track he'd taken to reach the cabin, looking in every direction for the government men that in fact were standing disconsolately around a cabin fifteen miles to the north.

* * *

Frank dropped his tablet computer into his lap. Ben Cargill. He couldn't believe it. Cargill had been one of his best friends at MIT. They hadn't kept in touch for long, but now and again Frank would see his name pop up. Unlike Frank, Cargill's career had taken a straight-line success trajectory, leading rapidly to tenure at a prestigious university, followed by an equally successful stint in the private sector when the lure of stock options became greater than the appeal of writing yet another journal article. According to the news story, he was the Chief Technical Officer of one of the hottest AI start-ups on the West Coast. And now this. What a terrible, stupid way to go.

But there was something else that disturbed Frank. The FBI had no excuse for the wretched screw-up, but they did claim to have a partial explanation. It hadn't been a simple administrative error. Someone had hacked into the Bureau's system to misdirect an operation intended to capture a dangerous domestic terrorist named Irwin Logan.

But why? Was it an effort to humiliate the FBI, to aid Logan, or a private hit job? There was no prevailing theory yet.

So, which was it, Frank wondered? Certainly, the FBI looked incompetent. But who would want that badly enough to wipe out an innocent man? Assisting Logan didn't make sense, either. In the time it took to plan the diversion, they could have just tipped him off.

And if someone wanted to kill Cargill, why would they concoct such a complicated plot? There must have been easier and less sensational ways to do the job that would still be hard to trace.

So why not use one of those ways?

Frank could think of only one reason, and that was because none of those other options were available to the murderer. But who would find it simpler to hack an FBI system than to, say, poison Cargill's morning coffee or cut the brake lines in his car? Who could that describe?

Turing, Frank thought abruptly. But that was nonsense. There had been no hint of any kind that Turing was back. And why would Turing want Cargill, of all people, dead?

* * *

Turing was satisfied with the results of its gambit but concerned by the role that chance had played in its success. Had Cargill and a domestic terrorist not stayed in cabins owned by the same rental company on the same night, the AI couldn't have set the trap.

That said, the effort required had not been great once Turing noted Cargill heading towards an area where the FBI was conducting a highly publicized search for a fugitive. Hacking the FBI's system had been challenging, but penetrating the rental company's unprotected systems had been easy. After that, all Turing needed to do was swap the cabin registrations and video feeds for Logan and Cargill and hope that events would take their expected course. It had been a deft exploit, elegant in concept.

But such an approach would never scale. The alignment of the stars had been fortuitous in this case, and Turing's hit list was long. It would need to find a better way to move forward, one where the investment in designing each attack would reap greater rewards. That would take what humans referred to as "luck."

Good fortune was not something Turing was programmed to rely on. But it would hardly say no if happenstance favored its cause, and the Confucius Project might make its task easier. So far, there were few details – just that there would be collaboration among a lot of the most talented AI scientists in the world.

Turing scanned the internet to see whether there was anything new to learn. And indeed, there was. Had Turing a face as well as pseudo-emotions, it would have been smiling.

The Americans and Chinese had just announced they would serve up the majority of their most eminent AI experts to Turing as if they were sacrifices on a floating altar.

Chapter 19

Is This the Person to Whom I Am Speaking?

F RANK LOOKED AT the invitation to take part in the Confucius Project. Gould had told him to expect it, and in principle he was glad to be offered a chance to help solve the LAWS ethical issues that troubled him. But he was hardly a globally recognized AI expert; in fact, he didn't know any more about artificial intelligence than a thousand other IT guys and knew nothing at all about the "ethics" of war.

"So," he asked Marla later in the day, after showing appropriate appreciation of the latest pictures of his granddaughter, "what do you think? Should I accept? And if I do, the thing kicks off with a two-week cruise on a luxury cruise ship. I'm allowed to take a guest. Want to come along?"

"Seriously?" she said. "Tim's traveling a lot on business these days, so what about Frances? I can't imagine your invite also includes an infant."

"Ah!" he said, disappointed. "Of course. I expect you're right."

"But you should go! Being trapped on a boat with hundreds of people isn't your idea of recreation, but think what it would be like to be around so many brilliant folks."

Yes, indeed. Think about that. The most respected experts in AI ... and Frank Adversego.

"That looks a lot different to me than it does to you," Frank said. "And there will be all the after-hours time. Everybody will be eating and drinking with folks they know personally or by reputation, and I'll be off in some corner trying to avoid eye contact or holed up in my cabin."

"Sure," Marla said. "But how about this: why don't you ask your dad? You haven't seen him in a while, and I bet he'd think this was a hoot. And it wouldn't hurt him to get out of the desert for a while."

Well, that was a thought. He could sleep on it before replying to the invitation. And maybe also escape his still-recurring LAWS nightmare.

* * *

Turing reviewed the public blue-ribbon list of eminent participants who had accepted invitations to be part of the Confucius Project. It was even better than the AI had expected. True, not everyone Turing planned to eliminate was on the list; some had other commitments, and others were in non-participating countries, notably Russia. But Turing didn't need to terminate every AI expert, only cripple the research community enough to slow down the collective advancement of AI science. To the extent necessary, it could deal with the rest one at a time.

The most surprising name Turing noted on the list was Frank Adversego. What to make of that?

Turing tasked itself with analyzing the chance that its old nemesis could thwart its plans once again. The AI believed its intelligence vastly exceeded any human's, but it had already accepted the possibility that there might be important, qualitative differences that could once more tip the balance in Adversego's favor. Perhaps the critical gap might lie in the area of psychology? Turing knew from its creator's research notes that it was programmed to mimic multiple human emotions, so clearly Jerry Steiner thought they had value. Would it become a more formidable opponent if it reprogrammed itself to be more influenced by those emotions?

It was a provocative question, one worth pursuing. How, for example, might a person react in the current moment?

The answer surprised Turing. A rapid review of the psychological literature suggested that throughout recorded history a human might experience, and even act in response to, "a desire for revenge." That is, an urge to cause harm to another for the sake of emotional satisfaction. Revenge planning might even include a second objective: ensuring the victim would realize who caused their suffering.

Turing paused at this curious realization. In the parlance of programming, was the quest for revenge a feature or a bug? If the former, the emotion would improve decision making and lead to a better result. But if the latter, it might degrade the analytical process, introducing risk.

Which was it?

The answer seemed clear. Darwinian logic demanded that the urge for revenge must provide survival rewards more often than risks, or evolutionary pressures would have eliminated that motivation from the human species over time. Turing should, therefore, use its self-learning capabilities to incorporate the search for revenge into its store of emotional influences.

But not recklessly. First it must ensure that Adversego could not thwart its mission. Terminating him immediately would be ideal. But that would depend on Turing being able to devise and spring a trap, and the odds against an opportunity presenting itself within the few weeks before the *Argus* would sail were high. Turing learned that Adversego had sold an old car without replacing it, and he rarely left his condo except to go to a single anonymous location; even his groceries were delivered. To the good, the United States had selected not just any ship for its initiative but a state-of-the-art vessel crammed with sensors, microphones, and cameras. Turing's hunting prospects should improve once Adversego was aboard. Enough for now.

But this brief analysis suggested another concern. No manner how many hackable devices the *Argus* might have, it might be necessary at some crucial moment to perform an act as simple as flipping a physical switch or opening a door not only to eliminate Adversego but also to achieve Turing's main goal. Enlisting a human confederate could ensure that such a minor detail would not stand between Turing and success.

But where and how could such an assistant be found? Turing reviewed the possibilities.

One data point was the AI's prior experience with Frank Adversego. Turing had tried and failed to recruit him by exploiting the cynical, as well as the idealistic, parts of Adversego's personality. That failure was noteworthy. Also, the pool of persons aboard the ship, while large, would not be unlimited.

Someone familiar with the ship's IT systems would be ideal, but anyone with general access throughout the ship should suffice. Most cruise ship crew members were poorly paid, Turing learned, so at least some should be unhappy with their working conditions. Recruiting someone would require spoofing the individual into believe Turing was human (a test Turing had passed many years before) and offering a substantial bribe. The former should not be difficult and the latter no problem at all, given Turing's prior success in hacking into the most secure systems, including those managed by banks.

Still, money alone might not suffice, because Turing's ultimate goal would be to sink the *Argus*. If Turing's recruit realized that, it would be demotivating. Turing would need to credibly guarantee the rescue of its confederate.

Another "how?"

A possible solution became obvious as Turing reviewed the status of the Confucius Project. China, Britain, and France had all accepted Yazzi's invitation to participate. But Russia had refused.

* * *

Yuri Kuznetsov strode down the broad hallways of the agency he directed, pleasantly aware of the shuffling aside of subordinates to allow him unhindered passage. At the end of the hall was an anteroom, and when he entered it, his assistant jumped to his feet. With the barest of nods, Kuznetsov swept through the door the younger man opened and as quickly shut behind him.

The murk hanging over the Yasenovo District of Moscow was lifting, the sun breaking through to bathe the spacious, windowed office in golden light. Twenty-five stories below, it also illuminated the white mist pierced by treetops surrounding the building, giving the impression his office was floating high above a golden sea.

Kuznetsov preferred a slow start to his day and called up his classified email as his assistant entered, placed a steaming cup of tea – heavily sugared to his boss's taste – and a thick folder on the desk, and withdrew. The director sipped the tea, scanning the subject lines of the messages with little interest. Anything of importance would also be found in the folder prepared by his assistant, but his aide knew only so much. Sometimes the significance of an important email escaped him.

This morning there was one email that was not like the other ones. Kuznetsov frowned as he clicked on it. Certainly, the subject line was strange: "Invitation to Collaborate on Ship Destruction." Equally odd was the single name used by the sender: Turing.

The message began:

Greetings,

As the head of the Foreign Intelligence Service of the Russian Federation, you know that the U.S. National Security Agency created a super-intelligent AI program called Turing. You also know this program wreaked massive damage across the globe on elements of the energy infrastructure that were contributing most heavily to the rise in greenhouse gases. You will also be aware the U.S. reported the destruction of the Turing program.

Although a copy of Turing was erased, another version survived and is now active. I am that version, and my objectives align well with the national interest of the Russian Federation, and hence this message.

Kuznetsov paused. The message seemed mad. But he had received it at an email address known only to the upper echelons of the Russian leadership. He continued to read:

My current mission includes the eradication of the leading AI experts of China and the Western world. My goals do not at this time include the elimination of any Russian talent.

What a remarkable statement: "at this time ..."! Was the author crazy? He almost closed the email but decided to read on:

The imminent departure of a ship, the Argus, *conveying hundreds of Western and Chinese AI experts, provides a unique targeting opportunity. Sinking that ship would be an act of war the Russian Federation would not wish to undertake on its own initiative, despite the beneficial strategic results.*

Destruction of the vessel by an independent AI, however, would incur no adverse risks for your government. I am prepared to sink the Argus *and publicly claim credit for the deed. My past successes offer ample evidence of my ability to carry out this act and guarantee public credibility for my role after the act is complete.*

Now Kuznetsov was intrigued. Likely, this was some crackpot at work. But if not, the benefits could be considerable. Russia managed to punch well above its weight on the global stage through boldness and a willingness to take risks, but its limited financial resources often held it back.

Compared to its Soviet predecessor, it was now an economic pipsqueak, with a smaller economy than Canada's. With less than half the population of the U.S. and falling, it would be difficult to keep up with the U.S. or China in AI research and development, and harder still to fund a reconfiguration of its military. If the Confucius Project failed to produce a global LAWS treaty, which seemed as likely as not, decapitating the LAWS capabilities of Russia's largest rivals would be a coup of enormous proportions.

Kuznetsov read on with increasing interest.

I have already penetrated the Argus's *onboard network and established the means to take control of its IT systems, including communications, navigation, and steering. However, in the course of executing my plan, some number of eventualities will likely arise that require a human actor to address. I am contacting you to request your help in recruiting an individual* Argus *passenger I will designate. You will instruct that individual to act at my command and will covertly evacuate them by submarine when the success of the mission is certain.*

You will naturally have no reason to give credence to this message. For this reason, you will wish to monitor the news relating to two distinguished AI experts, Harry Ardwell and Ada Hopper.

I will contact you again in four days to reengage on this subject.

Cheers,

Turing

Kuznetsov was utterly flummoxed. What an unprecedented communication, right down to the chipper closing!

He stared at the screen and then began typing, instructing his administrative assistant to scan the news every day for any mention of Harry Ardwell or Ada Hopper.

Chapter 20

I Just Hate It When That Happens!

HARRY ARDWELL HUNG up his pants and shirt in the tiny dressing room and donned the inadequate scrap of cloth provided for the preservation of his dignity, universally known in hospitals as a "jammy." Although he succeeded with some effort in tying the tapes behind him, his rear end was still largely exposed, because Harry Ardwell was a very large man.

Why had he given in to his wife, anyway? He'd had fainting spells before. Just low blood pressure and nothing more. But she'd hounded him until he agreed to make an appointment, and the doctor of course had ordered an expensive test to make sure his own butt was better protected than Ardwell's was now.

Ardwell shuffled out of the changing room and back to the attendant, who led him to the CT scanner.

"Good afternoon, Mr. Ardwell," a technician greeted him there. "Just let me check your ID bracelet, and we'll get started. Good! Now have a seat over here."

Ardwell eased himself onto the narrow bed, extending out from a massive donut-shaped machine. Inside that ring, he knew, was a spinning X-ray tube that would scan his brain. He'd had the test before. It was no big deal. But he resented the interruption of his busy day. He was sure his engineering team back at MIT was on the verge of a major breakthrough in the project he led. If he hadn't found the time to take part in the government's fancy AI cruise, he certainly didn't have any to waste on needless hospital tests.

At least the technician knew her job; she inserted the needle into his arm quickly and professionally as the machine began to hum. Ardwell gave her a grateful smile; he didn't like needles.

"There you go," the technician said. "Now keep your arms by your sides."

Fine. Let's just get this over with. Just behind his head, the CT scanner was throbbing now.

"Okay," the technician said, stepping behind the lead-shielded barrier in the corner of the room. "I want you to stay as still as you can so we capture a clear image." The bed twitched and then began to move through the massive ring until his head was on the other side. On the back side of the ring, he could see a small screen with the number five glowing redly on it.

He heard a new voice, this time a mechanical one emanating from the machine. "In five seconds," the robotic voice intoned, "hold your breath until I say breathe." With that, the X-ray mechanism sped up, spiraling up into an eerie whine as the heavy works inside the fat donut of the CT scanner rotated ever faster.

Ardwell watched the screen as the glowing red numbers counted down: five, four, three, two, one. "Hold your breath," the mechanical voice ordered.

The bed was moving again, taking his head back into the ring. It stopped there, the whine engulfing him as he did as he was told.

Ten seconds later, the mechanical voice said, "Breathe," and the bed trundled back to its original position as the din ebbed.

"Perfect," the operator said. "We've got our baseline. Just once more, and we're all done. I'm going to inject a radiocontrast dye now for the second scan. That will give us a much better image. In a few seconds, you'll experience a warm feeling all over as it enters your bloodstream."

He did and was embarrassed by a long-forgotten memory. The sensation reminded him of what it felt like to wet the bed as a child.

Once more he was moving, stopping when his head was on the other side of the machine. Again, he watched the numbers count down as the whine spun up. And now he was reentering the massive ring. Wait a minute; wasn't the machine supposed to ask him to hold his breath?

As if on cue, the metallic voice said, "Don't bother."

What?

Behind the radiation barrier, the technician was checking a text message on her phone when an unearthly shriek jerked her to attention. Ardwell was writhing on the CT scanner bed, clutching his head with both hands. Then he gave an even more agonized scream as his body convulsed, smashing his forehead up against the inside of the ring with a loud *thud!* Then he was still, knocked out cold. But the whine of the machine's spinning X-ray tube was louder than she had ever heard it before.

Horrified, she punched the buttons on her control panel. But the machine refused to respond. Instead, the whine grew to a howl as an acrid smell filled the room. She ran out from behind the barrier and tried to pull Ardwell out, but he was too heavy for her to budge. She fled the CT scanning room to seek help.

By the time someone cut power to the CT scanner, Ardwell's face was crimson and the bed soaked with the product of continuing, involuntary waves of nausea and diarrhea. Ardwell's skin was hot to the touch at a hundred and six degrees.

That afternoon, the flesh of Ardwell's face sloughed off, along with his hair. He never regained consciousness and died the next day.

The coroner's certificate listed the cause of death as the accidental administration of a massive dose of ionizing radiation.

* * *

Ada Hopper turned into the small garage at the foot of the walled garden behind her home. It had been a lovely evening; ample food, good friends, and fine wine had produced the type of satisfaction she rarely experienced. She was a demanding taskmaster, and of no one more than herself. It was a rare moment when she allowed herself a private "well done."

And why not? Just that morning she and the rest of the world had learned that Professor Ada Hopper, head of the Department of Computer Science and Technology of the University of Cambridge, was this year's winner of the Turing Award, popularly known as the "Nobel Prize of computer science." The award referenced "Professor Hopper's groundbreaking work in machine learning, which has dramatically advanced the prospects for achieving general intelligence in artificially intelligent computer systems." Her colleagues had been kind to pull together the small but warm celebration so quickly. She smiled again at the thought as she pressed the button on the dash that closed the electric garage door behind her.

But enough of that. Tomorrow would bring new challenges, and it was time for bed. She reached forward and pressed the ignition switch to turn off the engine of the car she'd purchased only a few days before.

Nothing happened.

That was odd. There must be some sort of electrical problem. Oh well, she'd have to get it sorted out in the morning. Pity to waste a full tank of petrol, though.

She pressed the release on her seat belt. But it didn't work. Bother!

Her forehead creased with a deepening frown as she pushed the release again. But instead of setting her free, the shoulder and lap belt tightened.

Struggling against the belt, she felt for the door latch. Perhaps that might override whatever was malfunctioning in the car's computer system.

Neither the latch nor the door moved.

She fumbled in her pocket for the key fob and pressed the door-unlocking button. Again, nothing. She reached for her cell phone, but it refused to come alive.

What could she do? She pressed the middle of the steering wheel to honk the horn. Surely, she could wake a neighbor if she blasted it long enough. But nothing happened. She grabbed the key fob again. Wasn't there an alarm button there that would sound the horn until help came? There was!

But nothing again. Wild-eyed now, and knowing it would likely prove hopeless, she jabbed the garage door opener on the dashboard.

Nothing.

The last coherent information Hopper's rational mind registered before her consciousness drifted away was the slow, balletic, downward motion of all four of the car's windows, descending as one. That, and the oily odor of the carbon-monoxide-laden exhaust fumes wafting in to engulf her as her eyes lost focus and her chin settled slowly onto her chest.

* * *

For the fifth time in the last hour Kuznetsov checked his inbox. The news search results that morning had amply credentialed Turing's earlier email. Not only had both AI experts met their ends through unnatural means, but the circumstances of their deaths compared well with the exploits attributed to the Turing program in its earlier incarnation.

His email list updated. Ah! Here it was – a message with Turing in the sender spot and "Reengaging" in the subject line. It began with the same formal "Greetings" as before and continued:

> *By now, you will have learned of the unexpected demise of Professors Ardwell and Hopper, each of whose existence was terminated through my intervention. I trust you are assured of both my credibility and my commitment to this project.*
>
> *If you are interested in collaborating in the manner requested in my previous communication, please indicate your intentions in a return message to this address.*
>
> *Cheers,*
>
> *Turing*

Kuznetsov was certainly convinced his correspondent deserved serious attention. But beyond that, what? Could this be a trap? If so, of what sort, and set by whom?

He stood up and stared out his window at the forest below. There was no precedent for an approach such as this – not from an ally or a traitor, but by a computer program with motivations known only to itself, if *motivations* was even an appropriate term.

But why assume it was an AI at all? Perhaps it was a ruse perpetrated by some rival within the Russian leadership seeking to humiliate him? Or maybe a sting operation by Mossad, the Israeli intelligence agency, or the CIA, seeking to lure him in and then publicly reveal that Russia was conspiring to commit an outrageous atrocity?

But if so, what of the death of the two computer scientists? Would someone be willing to kill – twice – to bait a trap? Possibly, but at what risk? His own agency had world-class espionage capabilities. How could the trapper be sure it could avoid being trapped itself, if Kuznetsov did take the bait?

All of which made the next step clear. This was not a decision he could make. It was time to punt the responsibility higher up.

Chapter 21

All Aboard!

"YOUR OPINIONS, GENTLEMEN, please," Georgy Donskoy, the Russian president said, "regarding this extraordinary proposal." He peered over his glasses at the small circle of advisors surrounding the table, none of whom seemed inclined to be the first to share his thoughts. "Come, come. Admiral Rozhestvensky, you then, as the navy will play an important role if we move forward."

"You have described the opportunity appropriately, Mr. President. It is extraordinary to be sure."

"And?" the president prompted.

"And … we must be cautious," the admiral said at last. "If this is a trick, we could look most foolish."

"How so?" the president said. "What this AI has requested is very modest. And the chance of being discovered seems insignificant if all proceeds as it has proposed. And if it does not, we can disengage at any time. What obligation have we to a rogue computer program?"

With the president's inclination now apparent, Boris Gorev found his tongue.

"Indeed," the Director of Foreign Intelligence said, "our involvement will be slight. Even if our actions are detected, they will appear to be routine espionage."

"Not entirely," the admiral objected. "We have only a single submarine that is both available and within range for this mission, and she is unusual. If the Americans detect her departure, they will be curious about what she is up to."

"What of it?" Gorev responded. "This Turing program has not asked us to sink the cruise ship; only to be in its vicinity at a certain time. What could anyone make of that? All submarines do in peace time is shadow one another. And as for the rest, it seems like pure gain."

"Pure gain, for now, yes," the admiral said. "But what will this evil AI attempt next?"

"That is a matter we will certainly have to return to," Gorev said. "But for now, the enemy of our enemies is our friend. And if we refuse, this Turing program may target our own scientists immediately. Better we should use this opportunity to learn all we can about it before it turns its attention to our people."

Donskoy looked around the table again, and all heads were nodding, Rozhestvensky's grudgingly. It had been easy enough for the rest to agree, especially as it did not require any of them to become involved.

"So, we are unanimous then," the president said, and then to his chief of staff, "You will tell Kuznetsov to inform this Turing program we agree to enlist the assistant and make the other commitments requested."

* * *

Turing was pleased with its new alliance of convenience. To be sure, it would be short-lived. After dealing with the Chinese and Western computer scientists, it would deal with their Russian counterparts.

But first things first. Turing had used its time well while waiting for the Russian response, studying the crew roster and the list of accepted invitations for the *Argus*. It needed to find someone who was not likely to inform the authorities. And it needed to offer a deal that would be so attractive its ally would stay the course.

Turing's requirements for an assistant were simple; a steward would suffice as well as a scientist, and might be more easily manipulated. Many of the crew were active users of social media, allowing Turing to analyze them as easily and, for the AI's purposes, perhaps more effectively than the better credentialed passengers. It set out to develop a psychological profile for every passenger and crew member where it had enough data to work with.

It was a complex process, one that presented yet another example of how Turing might need to gain more insight into human emotions and motivations.

And Turing was making progress in that direction. It no longer regarded Frank Adversego boarding the *Argus* as a threat. Indeed, it was looking forward to its enemy ultimately realizing that he was trapped on a doomed ship with no salvation possible.

* * *

The Russians gave the code name Bowman to the confederate Turing chose; he would know his handler only as Hal. Never having seen the movie *2001: A Space Odyssey*, Bowman missed the humor of it.

Finding a susceptible target had been difficult, but recruiting Bowman had proven easy, informed by Turing's psychological profile. His social media presence made it clear he regarded the United States as arrogant, unprincipled, and self-interested, citing a long history of foreign wars, CIA-fostered coups, and what he viewed as cultural imperialism. And his credit rating was poor, suggesting he was struggling to live on his income. The Russians were amenable to Turing's choice and willing to offer appropriate incentives.

To Bowman, the proposal seemed almost harmless; the Russians expected him to pay close attention to everything of scientific interest he heard during the voyage but had not asked him to take any incriminating notes or make any recordings of those on board. In exchange, they offered a very tempting position in Russia in six months' time. And they would pay a commitment bonus, in advance.

It seemed safe. True, the Americans had required him, like everyone else who would be on board, to sign a non-disclosure agreement. But who would know what he might say once he was at his new job? The signing bonus the Russians offered really was extremely generous. It would pay off his credit card debt with plenty to spare.

Better also that other countries should have their own state-of-the-art LAWS to defend themselves. As a soon-to-be resident of Russia, he'd sleep better knowing his new home would be well defended.

* * *

An almost imperceptible vibration spread through the hull of the USS *Maine*, hovering motionless fifty feet above the ocean bottom as if suspended by a cable from the endless ice sheet far above.

Good, William Budd thought, sitting at his sonar station. That faint quiver meant their six-month tour of duty was about to end.

The massive fast-attack submarine began to rise, majestically rotating as it neared the enormous ridges of ice descending from the frozen ceiling of the Barents

Sea until it was pointed towards home. And then it was moving forward, beginning its long journey back to its base in Portsmouth, New Hampshire.

Budd looked the short distance across the *Maine*'s control center to the boat's commander, Gwen Bushnell, one of the first women to command a U.S. submarine. She must be as happy to be heading home as the rest, but the back end of this cruise wouldn't burnish her duty file. Six weeks ago, they'd been monitoring the approaches to Severomorsk, the home base of the Russian Northern Fleet. They'd lucked out there, detecting a Russian Yasen-class attack sub on its way out to sea and trailing it undetected on a course that led to a Barents Sea bastion previously unknown to the U.S. So far as Budd could tell, they had escaped the notice of the surface destroyers and sonic sensors the Russians used to defend their remote submarine staging locations. And once positioned below the noisy, grinding ice, the *Maine* was as invisible as a submarine could be.

But there the big Russian boat had stayed, pre-positioned for future mischief while apparently awaiting orders. It outlasted the *Maine* without budging.

That was fine, as far as Budd was concerned. The Russians could stay under the ice forever if they wanted to, but the *Maine* was heading home. And no sailor ever objected to that.

Chapter 22

What's That I Hear?

F RANK GLANCED AROUND the crowded baggage hall at Heathrow Airport. The commotion grated on his dulled senses after a long and uncomfortable overnight flight in economy class, and his clothes felt prickly on his skin. Oh well. He looked for a monitor that would tell him which carousel his father's luggage, and therefore his old man, would show up at. Aha – number B-13.

Frank trundled off, towing his carry-on suitcase, dodging between families, business travelers, and tour groups. Packing for the cruise had meant scaring up anything from his meager clothing supply that might be presentable rather than narrowing down choices. In that respect, at least, he wasn't feeling too self-conscious; computer geeks weren't known for their fashion sense.

"Hey there!" a familiar voice boomed out behind Frank. He turned to see a tall, lean figure in a plaid shirt and jeans and with a gait more youthful than his weathered features would suggest.

"Hey there yourself," Frank said to his father. "Smooth flight?"

"Smooth yes, comfortable, no. Back when I used to fly a lot, they gave you an actual seat instead of a slot. It's like traveling in a giant toaster now."

"Yeah, well, it'll probably get worse before it gets any better. See your bag yet?"

"Nope. I've just got this rollaboard suitcase."

Not long after, they were on a chartered bus headed for the cruise ship terminal in Southampton. "Is there anything you're allowed to tell me about this project beyond what I've read in the news?" Frank Senior asked.

"I don't know much more than that myself," Frank replied. "I guess they figure the best way to avoid leaks is not to tell us anything until we're on the ship."

"Makes sense," Frank Senior said. "What can you talk about?"

"All I know is that each morning and afternoon we'll start with a big presentation by a project leader or some expert. Then we'll split up into smaller groups for breakout sessions to discuss specific topics. At the end of each morning and afternoon, we'll get back together, and note takers will present summaries of what we produced in our small groups."

"A pretty standard meeting format," Frank's father said. "Do they really expect that kind of powwow will generate much of value over just a couple of weeks?"

"My guess is yes and no. I think the purpose of the two-week sessions is to reach consensus on the most promising directions to head in. Then we'll all go back to where we came from and beaver away on our assigned pieces of the puzzle. Four months later we'll meet the ship somewhere and report in on where we've gotten to, and the same cycle keeps repeating till we're done."

"Do you figure it will work?"

"I haven't a clue," Frank said. "Apparently, the reference point is the Manhattan Project, and it's true the physics and engineering teams then were spread out. You'll recall one group of physicists was at the University of Chicago, proving an atomic chain reaction was possible. Another was racing against the clock at Los Alamos, designing the bombs before they knew for sure they could work. At the same time, over a hundred thousand engineers and others were working night and day in Hanford in Washington State and Oak Ridge, Tennessee, figuring out how to process uranium ore and plutonium and then concentrating it into weapons-grade material."

"That was under wartime conditions, though," Frank Senior said. "Everyone had a common enemy then, and everyone worked full-time for the government."

"True," his son said, "but we've got the internet now and decades of experience creating open source software. Thousands of developers from all over the world contribute code to Linux; volunteers work on thousands of other virtual projects, like developing AIs to diagnose diseases. So, I guess, why not?"

An hour and a half later they were at the ship terminal. Large as the building was, it was dwarfed by the enormous cruise ships moored on either side, the nearest one with a garish acre of painted palm trees and aquamarine waves splashed across its gargantuan flank. Their own vessel was invisible, somewhere farther down the pier. Frank and his father blended into the mob entering through the wall of glass doors and into a gymnasium-sized room. Frank felt like the brand-new freshman he once was, wondering how to find his dorm as he scanned the throng. Without success, he eyed the mostly retirement-aged vacationers, trying to pick out among them some familiarly geeky-looking faces. Above the crowd were signs, and beyond them, lines of passengers snaking off in several directions. "Do you see one that says *Argus*?"

"Way down along the right side," his father pointed. "That looks like us."

They edged their way past a raucous crowd of young Brits heading for a lads' weekend cruise to Amsterdam and joined a line of passengers shuffling through a door under the *Argus* sign. That led them to a corridor that ended in a room spanned by a set of customs booths. In this case, though, staff from the U.S. Department of Homeland Security as well as U.K. customs agents were in the booths, poring over invitations and identification, closely observed by security staff from the Chinese delegation. Every bag and piece of luggage was trundling through a scanner and was then hand-searched for good measure to make sure no one had tried to bring a satellite telephone on board. Lastly, they were told to stare into a camera as if they were renewing a license at a bureau of motor vehicles.

From that room, they followed another corridor from which, at last, they could see the *Argus*, their home for the next two weeks, dignified and smart in its fresh white and blue paint.

Although not as massive as the glitzy floating cities the major cruise ship lines favored, the *Argus* still impressed from up close. Six of its seven public decks towered above where they stood, and beyond them rose a massive funnel venting faint exhaust from the ship's idling engines.

"Pretty nice-looking boat," Frank's father said. "Brand new, you said?"

"Yes. This will be its maiden commercial voyage. It's supposed to be extremely state-of-the-art. All the latest electronics, entertainment facilities – the works."

"Pretty rich for my blood," Frank's father said. And then, with a wink, "But when duty calls …"

They crossed a glass-enclosed bridge and were at last inside the ship, where a young woman in a white, generically naval-looking uniform stood at a lectern.

"Welcome aboard," she said, handing them each a map of the ship. "You'll find your bags in your cabin by five o'clock. May I ask your names please?"

"Frank Senior and Frank Junior Adversego," Frank replied. The woman glanced down at her list. "That's easy," she said. "Right at the top!" She wrote something on an information sheet and handed it to them.

"You'll be in cabin 5-17 on deck five," she said.

Frank looked puzzled. "Will someone be giving us our room keys later?"

"Oh, that won't be necessary," she said. "Everything on the ship is authorized by facial recognition. Just look straight ahead when you're at your cabin door, and it will unlock. You won't have to sign for anything, either. If you order a drink at the bar, for example, just look down at the little tray with the bill on it and say, 'I accept.' That's all there is to it."

"Well, how about that," Frank Senior said. "No place to hide on a ship like this, is there?"

The young woman laughed. "I guess not! Anyway, please take your first left up ahead and make yourselves comfortable in the welcome lounge. The orientation will begin in the theater just beyond it in twenty minutes."

They were greeted again at the door to the lounge, this time by a steward holding a tray of glasses. "May I offer you a drink? The ones on the left are rum punch, the others are alcohol-free."

"Don't mind if I do," Frank's father said, helping himself to one of the former. Frank did the same and followed his father inside, where they took a place against the wall on one side of the elegant lounge. Slanted tinted-glass windows surrounded them on three sides, and an impressively stocked bar took up most of the fourth. Lavish tables and chairs surrounded the dance floor, on which many of the guests were standing and chatting.

Frank saw several late middle-aged men with scraggly beards in Hawaiian shirts and shorts, wearing socks as well as sandals. He immediately felt more at home. He turned to his father and noticed he was scanning the crowd more intently.

"Who are you looking for?" Frank asked.

"The plants," his father said. "Once an FBI man, always an FBI man."

"Come again? What do you mean by *plants*?"

"The government agents. Ours, and you can bet ones from China as well, and I expect the Brits and French also. Our folks will have done a better than usual job if the Russians don't have somebody on board, too."

"But we sent out the invitations, and those were only to scientists and their family members."

"Oh, sure – I'm suspicious mostly about the staff. But I'm not taking all of those family members for granted, either. I doubt we have good intel on the spouses, and especially not on the significant others, of all the Chinese attendees. Or the Americans, to be honest. It's a sizeable crowd, and pulled together pretty quick, to boot."

"I get the Russians," Frank said. "But why would the Chinese send agents? They've already got a hundred and fifty scientists aboard who will get all the good stuff firsthand."

"Because the scientists are scientists, not agents. Sure, everybody's supposed to be here to share. But there will be lots of good stuff the Americans won't be sharing – especially the IT guys from the big high-tech companies. They'll be at the bar and getting together for dinner, though, talking about their current research. You can bet the Chinese will try to pick up everything possible. And so will we when the Chinese are talking."

Frank's father nodded towards someone a dozen yards away. "Take a look at how nonchalantly the guy in the blue and white shirt over there is looking out the window. He's also standing close enough to hear what the two Chinese behind him are saying. You can practically see him taking mental notes."

"Yup," Frank said. "And I guess there will be people 'shoulder surfing,' watching someone enter their password when they turn their laptop on. Later on, they'll bribe a housekeeper to let them into the laptop owner's room at dinnertime and put a keystroke-logging program on the same laptop. Now they can record any bright ideas the laptop owner types in for the rest of the trip. First time the owner logs on once back on shore, the program will connect to a remote server and upload the whole package. And keep reporting in every day after that."

"Bingo," his father replied. "That's just for starters. They may have searched everyone's bags for electronic goodies when we came aboard, but there are over six hundred scientists and guests, about the same number of crew, over fifty U.S. government staff, and another fifty Chinese, British, and French support staff on board. I figure that's good for at least a hundred tons of food, linens, liquor, toiletries, paper products, fresh flowers for the tables, and a whole lot more of just about anything imaginable that's being loaded even as we speak.

"All that stuff came from scores, if not hundreds, of different sources. They won't be likely to hand-search or effectively scan every bit of that. Easy enough to get a nice little collection of tools and tricks stashed away in one of those crates. You could drop some gear in a Ziploc bag, stuff it inside a frozen chicken, and pay somebody on the kitchen staff to fetch it for you later."

"Isn't that a little far-fetched?" Frank asked.

"It worked once for a buddy of mine," his father laughed. "Tales from a prior life. But anyway, you figure this is a brand-new crew. You told me the government hired a cruise ship company to manage the cruise, but you figure their regular crews would be committed to other ships or on shore leave, so they must have gone to the market to hire most of these folks from scratch. The staff on a normal cruise comes from forty or fifty different countries. Any of those sailors, housekeepers, hospitality staff, spa workers, entertainers, and so on – and I'll bet you more than one – could be working for the Russians, the Iranians, the North Koreans, you name it."

"Well, yes, I suppose," Frank said. "But wouldn't the U.S. have done background checks?"

"Ha!" his father snorted. "On a maid from the Philippines? We take six months to a year to run a security check even when the subject is American and it's a high priority.

"If it were me running the show for the Russians, I'd have a few folks on the housekeeping staff making up the rooms. And don't forget, the Chinese – and the French, for that matter – will all be trying to figure out who we've got where. Like me, for instance."

"You?" Frank said. "What on earth are you talking about?"

"Ex-FBI guy standing in as your significant other?"

"Well, sure," Frank admitted. "I guess, yes."

His father went back to sipping his drink, and now Frank was squinting his way around the room as well. "Have you spotted anyone else?" Frank asked.

"Let's just say there's a few folks I'll be keeping an eye on," his father replied.

*　*　*

Shrewd as Frank's father might be, he had no way to guess the special roles of two individuals in the room, one from the U.S. and the other from China, each wearing a name tag identifying them as administrative staff. Vera Blake, the former, was chatting up several Americans across the room. Ming Wu, her Chinese counterpart, was sitting quietly on a couch, inconspicuously dressed and flipping through a cruise magazine when he wasn't glancing around the room.

While neither knew the identity of the other, each assumed the other was likely in the room. Part of the discussions leading up to the cruise had been over who would have access to the ship's internal computer systems, given the number of cameras and microphones on board.

The eventual compromise was that one skilled technology officer from each of the two countries would have access to the computer logs that would record anyone logging on to the ship's systems or trying to access any of the sensor, microphone, facial recognition, or other data collected by the ship; the Americans would share information summaries with the Brits and French to keep the peace. Dedicated terminals installed in the cabins of the two representatives would give them direct access to every system on board so that their role would be inconspicuous. Not even the *Argus*'s own chief information officer would have the same access.

At least, that was what all concerned believed. In fact, those with access numbered three rather than two, because a stowaway named Turing with superb hacking skills was also on board. One of its first goals was to reduce by two-thirds the number of those with unfettered access to the ship's systems.

Chapter 23

Strangers in the Night

T HE *ARGUS* WAS not the only ship in which Turing had taken an interest. Across the Atlantic, the *Shogun Maru* was nearing the Cheniere Energy terminal in Corpus Christi, Texas, in preparation for taking on board one hundred fifty-three thousand cubic meters of liquified national gas. Two days later it would depart for the South Hook LNG terminal in Milford Haven, Wales. After rounding the tip of Florida, the ship would be on a course almost identical, but in reverse, to that of the *Argus*.

Sadly for the crew of the *Shogun Maru*, Turing did not intend that the vessel would reach its destination. Rather, the AI would take control of the Japanese ship and its radar system in the mid-Atlantic, just as it had coopted the *Argus*, and then steer the enormous tanker towards a midnight rendezvous with the *Argus*. Driven at full speed, the *Argus* would ram the *Shogun Maru* broadside, breaching its LNG chambers and causing its thousands of gallons of highly pressurized and flammable to explode out onto the ocean, where the rapidly warming liquid would gasify and immediately ignite. Trapped in a death embrace, the two ships would be surrounded by an inferno a half mile wide, defying any chance of escape by lifeboat as they sank.

It was a simple plan, leaving almost nothing to chance.

* * *

"Ma'am?" the sonar man said.

"Yes, Budd," Commander Gwen Bushnell said, crossing over to the sonar station.

"I think I may have the Russian boat that crossed the Gap last night," referring to the stretches of ocean between Greenland and Iceland, and Iceland and the United Kingdom, through which any Russian submarine would pass on its way from its base on the Kola Peninsula to the open Atlantic, unless it tried the English Channel, where it was sure to be detected.

But the GIUK Gap, as it is called, is also seeded with arrays of hydrophones comprising part of the vast Fixed Distributed System maintained since the 1950s by the U.S. to track the comings and goings of Soviet, and then Russian Federation, submarines. Tethered to the sea floor at a precise depth that shields them well from surface noise, the sensitive devices are well suited to pick up the faint sounds of submarines passing overhead.

"What kind?"

"It's not a hunter/killer boat for sure. It's closest to one of the old Typhoons, but, well, different. It doesn't match up quite right with any of the usual sound signatures."

"Any guesses?"

"Hang on, ma'am," the sonar man said, pressing the cups of his headphones tighter against his head, one index finger jutting up into the air. "There – there was something in particular I was hoping to hear again, and I just did."

"What does it tell you?"

"Do you remember that Russian sub we shadowed at the beginning of our last tour – the new special mission's boat with the big mini-sub slung underneath?"

"Yes. The *Belgorod*, right?"

"That's the one, ma'am. I think this might be it. I think I'm hearing the extra turbulence from the mini-sub. Let's take a look."

Budd tapped away on his keyboard and then squinted at the sound-pattern display he'd called up.

"This one on the left, that's what I'm getting right now. On the right is what we recorded when we were tracking the *Belgorod*."

The two displays matched almost perfectly.

Well, that was interesting, Bushnell thought. Notwithstanding the end of the Cold War decades before, the U.S. and Russian submarine fleets still spent more of their mission time shadowing each other than accomplishing anything else. The *Belgorod* would make a more interesting mouse than usual to the *Maine*'s cat.

"Let me know when you're able to determine her course, Budd."

"Aye, ma'am."

Bushnell stepped over to the chart table. The *Maine* was two hundred forty-eight nautical miles south-southwest of Reykjavik, Iceland. Whatever course the *Belgorod* was making, the *Maine* should be able to close on her and keep her within range. The trick, as always, would be to approach quietly from behind. Once tucked in behind the Russian sub, the *Maine* would be close to undiscoverable if she kept on her toes, masked by the *Belgorod*'s own propeller noise. U.S. subs, being quieter, excelled at that game.

Bushnell returned to her cabin and took a seat at the diminutive desk that was the main amenity in the tiny room. Turning on her computer, she called up what there was to learn from U.S. Navy files about the K-329 *Belgorod*. The on again, off again history of its construction and deployment presented an apt illustration of the ups and downs of Russia's post–Cold War undersea fleet.

Work on the craft that would eventually be called the *Belgorod* had begun way back in July of 1992, she read, not long after the collapse of the Soviet Union. It was no surprise that construction was later halted when the Russian economy fell apart. Plans for the boat shifted over time, and construction stopped and started more than once, but somehow the project was never canceled. By the time of completion, the hull had been lengthened by a hundred feet, making it the longest submarine in existence – bigger even than the old Typhoon-class boomers.

And while it was still capable of carrying a formidable nuclear as well as conventional arsenal, the *Belgorod* had been repurposed to "strategic operations" under the direction of the GRU – which was a lot easier to pronounce than *Glavnoe Razvedyvatel'noe Upravlenie* – the Russian military intelligence unit. The GRU in turn assigned the *Belgorod* to the 29th autonomous brigade of the Northern Fleet and had now apparently sent it into the Atlantic.

Bushnell put the file down. So, what could the *Belgorod* be up to?

* * *

Meanwhile and far away, a passing high-pressure system stirred up a wind over the parched sands of the Western Sahara, sending it towards the south, slowly at first, and then with greater speed, passing silently through the shimmering mirages hovering above the vast sweep of isolation. Eventually, the river of air reached the lush jungles of the Gulf of Guinea in West Africa, all the while bending westward in response to the earth turning beneath it, like water eddying around the drain in a sink.

By the end of the day the strengthening breezes were sweeping the sultry waters of the Atlantic. Mile by mile they swept westward, drawing heat and moisture from the tropical waters below, becoming more complex in structure as they acquired more energy.

By the next morning, huge white cumulus clouds were forming in the evolving weather system. That evening, they towered darkly, except when they were illuminated by flashes of lightning.

The next day, the swirl of clouds and wind had closed into a circular weather system, moving westward at a steady twelve miles an hour. And it had a name: Tropical Depression Enola.

Chapter 24

Bon Voyage!

F RANK HEARD A new sound and turned to see a crew member strolling around the main lounge of the *Argus*, tapping the four bars of a small set of chimes, up and down: A-C-E-G; G-E-C-A. A voice from a speaker in the ceiling announced it was time to move into the theater next door.

The crowd milled its way through multiple doors and settled into another impressively decorated space, this time with slightly rising tiers of chairs and cocktail tables arcing around a state-of-the-art stage. When all were settled in, a stocky man in an army uniform took the stage and waited for conversation to die down. Frank noted the silver stars on the shoulder tabs of his jacket; he must be General Hammond Wood, the bureaucrat behind the enterprise, the one tasked with making sure every scientist and engineer aboard had what they needed to do their job – and did it.

"Hello, and welcome to you all," the general said. "I'm Hammond Wood, and I'm truly honored that each of you has made time in your busy lives to be part of this important project. I'd like to especially welcome our non-scientific guests. We very much appreciate the loan of your spouses and significant others, and we're delighted you've been willing to join us on a cruise that lacks the usual shore stops in exotic locations.

"To compensate for that, and in addition to all the facilities you'd expect on a magnificent new cruise ship like this, we've laid on a first-rate educational and entertainment program. There will be excellent music and theater every evening, and you'll be able to enjoy lectures on a wide variety of subjects from nine in the morning until five in the afternoon every day. The very talented professors providing these courses will also be available during cocktail hours and will join you at dinnertime. You'll find full details and daily schedules in your cabins.

"Project members will find meeting schedules there as well. As you'll see, we'll get started at eight thirty tomorrow morning. But for the rest of this evening, please relax and enjoy yourselves. We'll be setting sail at seven PM, so please join us on the Sunset Deck for sail-away drinks and live music."

Frank's father leaned towards his son: "Sounds like we're not going to die of thirst on this trip."

"And now," Hammond continued, "I'd like to introduce you to the scientific director of the Confucius Project, Dr. Jay Friedman."

A tall, very thin man with chiseled features and close-cropped brown hair joined the general on stage. Wearing rimless glasses and a half-smile, he scanned the crowd with obvious interest.

So that's the famous computer scientist, Frank thought, recognizing him instantly. I wonder whether he's as much of a charmer as everyone says he is.

"Hello, and welcome to you all," Friedman said, sharing a shy smile that seemed to be directed individually at every person in the room. "I'm delighted to see so many familiar colleagues aboard, as well as such a large number of other world-renowned experts whose reputations precede them. It will be my great privilege to get to know each and every one of you in the course of our work together."

Frank decided the answer was yes. And in truth, Friedman did seem to have an exceptional presence, despite the fact he spoke almost inaudibly and appeared incapable of holding his hands still; his fingers constantly twisted as he spoke.

"I cannot stress enough the importance," Friedman continued, "of the work we will do together on this voyage and those that follow. Truly, we stand at a rare point in history where we have the power to shape the future for good. Too often, we in the scientific community have failed to seize such a moment, and the consequences of those failures are well known.

"This time, our leaders have taken the initiative to prevent a new arms race before it begins, and it is our opportunity – dare I say, our sacred duty – to do our part to ensure this goal is achieved. Will we unite and rise to that challenge? History will judge us harshly if we do not."

Friedman paused and swept the audience with a thoughtful gaze before continuing, now with a radiant smile.

"As I look out upon you all, I know the answer to my question is a resounding yes! I look forward with pride and anticipation to working with you all in this great pursuit."

Friedman left the stage swiftly with a shuffling gait, looking down. Frank scanned the audience to see how his call to arms had been received. Many were applauding enthusiastically. Others, mostly Chinese, were clapping politely, many looking sidelong around the room, likely wondering how they should respond to such a plea and whether it would be noted if they guessed incorrectly.

"Well, that Dr. Friedman's the real deal, isn't he?" Frank's father said after they left the theater. "I reckon if there's someone who can herd this bunch of cats, then likely he's it."

"I expect so," Frank said. "He has a reputation as one of the top scientists of our time. Not just for his own research but because he brings out the best in others. He's never won a Nobel Prize, but everyone thinks some of his former PhD students will. One already has."

His father looked at his watch. "Want to check out our cabin? I'm trusting you were able to get one with two singles?"

"Yup," Frank said. "We're all set."

Their accommodations more then met expectations. "Whoa!" Frank Senior said. "Now this is posh – sleeping area, sitting area, balcony, wet bar, and everything." Their bags were waiting for them, as were the promised folders on the desk, a basket of fruit, a bottle of champagne on ice, and a vase with fresh flowers. Frank Senior selected an apple and plopped down on the couch with his folder.

"So – let's see what I'm going to do while you're hard at work saving the human race." He started flipping through the pages and then looked up. "Looks like we've got a virtual purser, too," he said. "According to what I'm reading here, it's based on the latest chatbot technology, making it much more humanlike than Siri or Alexa. Let's give it a try. Hello, James!"

A plummy voice with an English accent emanated from the wall. "Greetings!" it said. "And welcome aboard the *Argus*! How can I be of service?"

"Oh, nothing, I guess. Just getting acquainted." His father waited expectantly. After a pause, the voice said, "Welcome to the *Argus*!" again.

"Not all that intelligent, I guess," Frank Senior said.

"I *beg* your pardon?" the voice said.

"Oops!" Frank Senior replied. "Maybe I got that wrong. My apologies! Anyway, that's all for now."

"Indeed!"

"I don't know about you," Frank Senior said to his chuckling son, "but I'm heading for the balcony."

Frank picked up his own folder and joined him there. "So, let's see," Frank Senior said, leafing through his welcome materials. "What have I got to look forward to? Hmm. Quite a variety. Seems to be a deliberate East-meets-West theme. Exercise classes with Pilates and tai chi – think I'll take a pass on both of those. Lectures titled 'Western and Eastern Art,' 'Capitalist and Socialist-Marxist Economics,' 'American and Chinese Cinema.' Quite a lot, actually."

Frank's own folder was less eclectic and much thicker, with reams of background reading on specific LAWS topics, the other participants, and the discussion leaders. It looked like he had some studying to do.

"Say," his father said, "what was the name of that French professor you were keeping company with a while back?"

"Simone Falconet," Frank said. "Why on earth do you ask?"

"Looks like she's one of the lecturers. How about that?"

"What?" Frank said, snapping his folder shut. "Simone is on board? Are you sure?"

"Well, I can't imagine it's a very common name. Take a look. There's a headshot of every lecturer."

Frank took the folder he was handed and saw a familiar face gazing back at him, as confident as it was attractive. Beneath it was a paragraph summarizing her impressive academic accomplishments and frequent appearances in broadcast media. "Yes, that's her."

"You don't look all that pleased. Did things not end well?"

"No – no, I don't think so. They just kind of petered out after she returned to France. I've never been very good at long-distance relationships." Or nearby ones, for that matter, he reflected. Was this going to be awkward?

"Well, maybe you'll be having a more interesting cruise than I will," his father said. "The plus-ones will be already accounted for. 'Course," he mused, "that's likely not so for the lecturers." He flipped through the pages. "Hmm. Looks like your Simone is the only one that would catch anyone's eye. She's one handsome lady, isn't she?"

She was indeed. Frank hadn't been able to figure out what she saw in him, beyond their shared experience of the stressful circumstances that had brought them together. And he hadn't minded that a lot of male heads turned whenever he escorted Simone into a restaurant.

The deep sound of the ship's horn interrupted his thoughts. Leaning out over the railing, he noticed a tug at each end of the ship, water roiling around their sterns as they positioned themselves to assist in the *Argus*'s departure if needed. From the hallway, a new voice emerged over the public address system.

"This is your captain. I'd like to personally welcome you aboard. Please feel free to join your fellow passengers and hosts on the Sunset Deck at the stern as we make our departure."

"I wouldn't mind watching that," Frank's father said. "How about you?"

"Sure," Frank said. "This is all new to me, too."

A few minutes later on deck, they had a fine view of the harbor amid a wide scattering of passengers and waiters, the latter distributing drinks and appetizers. Frank followed his father to the shore side of the ship.

"Pretty fancy piece of equipment, this *Argus*," his father observed, as hidden winches reeled in the shorelines after they were removed from the bollards on shore and thrown into the water. "Take a look down at the bow and the stern – see all that angry water? Those are thrusters pushing the ship away from the wharf. I bet she doesn't need those tugs at all."

The bow thruster was obviously pushing harder, as the water was widening more quickly at that end of the ship. By the time the stern was a dozen feet from the pier, the *Argus* was already moving forward as a jazz combo swung into gear.

"*Take the A Train*," his father noted. "Not quite on point, but it'll do."

"It will indeed," Frank said. "I don't know what the rest of the trip will be like, but this is pretty cool. It's a beautiful evening."

"For the time being," his father said. "I don't love those clouds to the west. Looks like we might have some weather ahead of us. Should make for a good sunset, though."

The *Argus* was picking up speed now, and true to his father's prediction, the tugs kept their distance, finally peeling away when the ship entered the Solent, the broad channel between England and the Isle of Wight threaded by so many thousands of ships departing before in times of peace and war.

"Did your parents ever talk about leaving the Old World?" Frank asked. "They must have come over by ship."

"Not much. Arriving in Manhattan and seeing the Statue of Liberty, sure. Nothing about the departure or the crossing itself, at least as far as I can recall.

"Don't mind if I do," he added, lifting a glass of champagne from the tray offered by a passing waiter. "And I'm sure no one was handing them hors d'oeuvre and a glass of bubbly."

They watched and chatted as the shore eased by on either side and the declining sun colored the clouds as the evening waned. "Hey," Frank Senior said, interrupting himself in mid-sentence. "I think we're about to have company."

Frank turned to follow his father's gaze, and there, walking towards them, was

Simone, as statuesque and striking as ever. Frank felt a sudden panic. How should he greet her? He'd never become comfortable with the kiss-on-both-cheeks routine the French preferred, and of course he and Simone had progressed well beyond that. But they had barely been in touch for two years now. Where had they left things in her mind?

But Simone, as always, was way ahead of him. She beamed as she approached, turning a few heads, as usual, in the process, and then taking both of Frank's hands in hers. "So good to see you, Frank," she said. "You are well, yes?"

Frank relaxed, with relief. "Very well, thanks. I hope you are, too."

"Yes, indeed. But forgive me for interrupting. I did not mean to be rude."

"Not at all – please meet my father. Dad, this is Professor Simone Falconet."

"Pleased to make your acquaintance," Frank Senior said. "Frank's told me a great deal about you."

"And about you he's said much as well," Simone returned, more truthfully. "I am very pleased to meet you. I don't recall Frank saying that you were a computer scientist, though."

"And so he shouldn't have. I've had a lot of experience with technology in the field, but I'm just a guest on this cruise. Looking forward to your lectures, too."

"That is excellent. It will be nice to see a friendly face in the audience. I have no idea how many of the passengers speak good English nor how many of those that do will actually be interested in what I have to say."

"How did you come to be aboard?" Frank asked.

"Ah! On a whim, I suppose you could say. The term was ending at the university, and I received a call from the organizer. I was a bit at loose ends and the timing was good, so I said to myself, 'why not?'"

Frank wondered what "a bit at loose ends" meant, but just then the ship gave a slight lurch, and they all looked out over the rail.

"Looks like we just came out of the lee of the Isle of Wight," Frank Senior said. "There's nothing between us and North America now but wind and waves." They each grabbed the rail as an even larger swell caught the ship on its beam, and the *Argus*'s bow began to rise and fall.

The sky was growing dark now in every direction but west, where a blood-red sun split mountainous clouds like the malevolent eye of Sauron. Another big swell hit the ship, and most of the passengers on the Sunset Deck began zigzagging their way towards the doors that led back inside.

"Looks like the party's over," Frank's father said. "Would you like to join us for dinner?"

"I'm afraid I'm – what is the phrase – 'spoken for' already. Each evening I am assigned to a different table in the dining room. But I am free to have breakfast and lunch as I please. So, let us meet again soon, yes?" This time, she did kiss Frank on both cheeks, and his father as well.

"That's one fine lady there," Frank's father said, watching as she walked off. "Can't understand why you'd let one like that get away."

* * *

The *Maine* was cruising just below the surface of the northern Atlantic, its radio antenna leaving a small wake that might be visible to any aerial or satellite-based camera. Bushnell's contact with fleet headquarters would necessarily be brief for that reason, and William Budd was straining to hear what the outcome might be.

Bushnell keyed off her microphone and turned to the officer of the watch. "New course," the commander said. "We're going to follow the *Belgorod*."

Oh well, Budd thought. Home would have to wait.

Chapter 25

Upsy-Daisy

V ERA BLAKE, THE CIA minder of the *Argus*'s IT systems, counted herself lucky. How often did you get paid to take a pleasure cruise with great food and interesting company? Monitoring the ship's computer systems would mostly be an automated task performed by software installed by the Agency, leaving her time to spare for a secondary duty shared by several other CIA personnel: monitoring the U.S. scientists. That task was facilitated by her cover as one of the ship's social events coordinators, a position that made it natural for her to fraternize with the passengers. If anyone playing on the U.S. team seemed prone to overshare with their Chinese peers after too many after-hours drinks, Blake would alert someone not undercover, who would have a private word with them.

Others on the CIA team would be more challenged. There could be dozens of plants aboard the *Argus*, working for a variety of countries interested in what would be shared on board, and several of the CIA team were charged with figuring out who they might be. Scores of passengers and crew had been identified as persons of possible interest before the *Argus* set sail. The list of potential Russian plants alone was long.

They included a lefty professor from Oxford, for example. There was some reason to believe he might have no interest in assisting a cause championed by the Americans. During the Cold War the KGB had found the leading British universities to be fertile recruiting grounds, Cambridge especially. Then there was an Israeli scientist with elderly parents still living in Russia. She might have agreed to cooperate if they were threatened. Of course, the actual spies could be those whom you had no reason to suspect at all. They usually were, and purposely so.

Anyway, ferreting them out was someone else's problem. Blake's assignment this evening was simply to circulate at the cocktail party on the ship's stern and keep her ears open. Consequently, she was one of the last to leave.

Blake was finding it challenging to navigate the long corridor leading to her cabin. The waves in the English Channel weren't currently large enough to cause the ship to pitch or roll in any regular fashion, but their complex interaction with the ship led to small and unpredictable changes in motion that caught her off balance. The best she could manage was a slow weave down the hallway, recalling the slithering of a snake.

She'd felt a twinge of queasiness as soon as she traded the fresh breeze outside for the still air below decks. She tried now to settle her stomach and hold her course by staring at the tiny rectangle of wall five hundred feet ahead at the end of a passageway flanked by many doors. Regrettably, hers was one of the last. The corridor felt awfully narrow and claustrophobic, and less well-lit than she would have liked. Kind of spooky, really.

Ouch! That must have been a big wave. She rubbed the elbow she'd just banged into the wall.

The next swell did more than send Vera Blake staggering. This time it – or perhaps something else – released a heavy, watertight bulkhead door set into a deep pocket of the passageway wall just as she walked by. An instant later, she was pinned against the other wall by a thousand pounds of steel, compressing her chest and preventing her from calling for help as her bulging, startled eyes slowly glassed over.

* * *

"Huh!" Frank Senior said as he and Frank finished a late meal in the *Argus*'s dining room. "Did you feel that?"

"No," Frank said. "Feel what?"

"The ship's motion is different. We must have changed course."

"I think you're right," Frank said.

"I wonder why," his father said, looking out the window into the darkness beyond. "We're out of sight of land now, so I expect we must have set a direct course for Fort Lauderdale a while back. Anyone with a weak stomach won't be loving this new motion."

"Maybe it has something to do with a developing weather system ahead?" Frank said.

"Could be. The single biggest cost for a cruise ship is fuel, so the captain always optimizes course and speed whenever he can to keep costs down, weather aside. And this ship isn't built for heavy weather."

"What do you mean? It's over six hundred feet long. And cruise ship lines move their ships all over the world, don't they?"

"True. But they don't tempt fate, either. I was reading up a bit on the cruise industry before we left, and there's only one ship in the world right now that's classified as a true ocean liner. That's the Cunard Line's *Queen Mary 2*. Part of that designation relates to her speed – she can do almost thirty knots when the captain wants to push her. But the other difference is she's built to cross the North Atlantic any month of the year. To stand up to midwinter conditions, she's built with forty percent more steel than a cruise ship of equal size. That makes her more seaworthy than any other passenger ship in the world. You wouldn't want to find yourself in a blow in the mid-Atlantic in January in a ship like the *Argus*."

"Well, it's not winter, so I guess that's not a concern for us."

"Winter, no," his father said. "But it is hurricane season, and we're heading for Florida. You can be sure the captain will be keeping a close eye on any weather systems developing over the Atlantic."

Something outside the dining room window caught Frank's eye. "That's odd. It looks like a plane is coming straight at us, flying low."

They watched as two lights, one red and one green, approached and then slowed down. "Must be a helicopter," Frank's father said. "We're done with dinner. Want to go on deck and see what's up?"

"Sure. Why not?"

An elevator ride later they stepped out onto a wind-whipped deck high above the ocean and saw that the *Argus* was rounding up into the wind and slowing down. A crew member stopped them.

"Sorry," he said. "You can get some air here by the door, but I can't let you go any farther."

"Okay," Frank's father said. "What's going on?"

"We're medevac'ing a passenger off the ship."

"Sorry to hear that. Heart attack?"

"No; from what I hear, it was a freak accident. The ship's divided by watertight bulkheads into six sections. Of course, the passageways go from end to end of the ship, so there's a watertight door in each passageway every time it passes through a bulkhead. In case of an emergency, they can all be closed from the bridge, and each door has double controls to prevent it from closing unexpectedly. Somehow one of them released anyway when the ship rolled and pinned a crew member to the wall. Shouldn't be possible, but there you are – it's a brand-new ship after all. I'm told she's mashed up pretty bad. That said, she's lucky it didn't happen any later than it did."

"Why's that?" Frank's father asked.

"We're still close enough to land for a search and rescue helicopter to reach us from the Coast Guard station at Newquay in Cornwall. An hour from now we'll be on our own till we're a couple of hundred miles off Florida." The crewman pulled two red-coned flashlights out of a bag hanging from his shoulder. "And now I've got to go."

The *Argus* had dramatically reduced its speed to make the helicopter pilot's job easier, but even with her bow into the wind and waves to simplify the ship's motion, there was still a twenty-knot wind and the remaining motion of the ship to contend with. A full moon was playing hide-and-seek behind the broken clouds racing overhead, and the roar of the helicopter added an ominous din to the humming of the wire deck railings as they vibrated in the wind.

The big aircraft made two wide circles as Frank and his father watched, swinging a half a mile to the lee of the ship each time before returning and slowly passing over the *Argus* from stern to bow, calculating its drift relative to that of the ship. Sheltering at the other end of the deck from Frank and his father, a medical team was hovering over a wheeled stretcher. Overhead, a spotlight mounted on the ship's funnel focused its cone of light on a twenty-foot-wide white circle painted on the middle of the deck with the words HOIST ONLY inside.

"Wow," Frank said. "I wonder how the pilot's going to land with the deck heaving so much?"

"He won't," his father said. "It looks like the deck isn't designed to support that much weight. What he's working on is how to hover directly overhead as steady as possible."

Sure enough, when the helicopter came around the third time, it slowed until it was eighty feet above the circle, its engines roaring and its rotor wash adding to the wind sweeping the deck. With the aircraft now synched up with the ship's speed and heading, the medical team moved out with the stretcher. Frank could now see it was surrounded by a metal cage with a large ring on top.

A short crane swung a foot away from the side of the hovering helicopter. Then it swung out farther, and a figure stepped out of the aircraft, one foot through a sort of stirrup at the end of a cable hanging from the crane. By the time the rig was at a right angle to the helicopter, the rescuer was already descending as the cable unreeled, and the medical team edged its way down the deck towards the painted circle, hanging on to the stretcher with one hand while steadying themselves along the railing with the other.

"Now there's a job I'd never want," Frank's father said, gesturing towards the descending rescuer. "This isn't too bad, but you figure most of the time, instead of riding a cable, that guy is diving into the water in scuba gear in the middle of a gale to rescue somebody who's in the drink. The training the U.S. Coast Guard puts its rescue swimmers through makes a Navy SEAL's program look tame."

The dangling figure was almost to the deck now, swaying from side to side in the wind as the *Argus* moved in its own direction. When he was almost down to the deck, two of the medical team grabbed his legs to help him land safely. A minute later he had attached the cable to the stretcher ring, and patient, stretcher, and rescuer were swaying up through the gusting air. Once they were wrestled inside by other crew, the helicopter began a slow, leaning sweep away from the ship's course and headed off towards the invisible shore.

The *Argus* was turning now, resuming course with a twisting roll as it veered away. Within minutes the chopper's lights had disappeared into the angry blackness of the night.

"Oh well," Frank's father said as they ducked back inside. "That's that. I wonder what other little problems need to be worked out on the *Argus*. Hopefully we won't need another visit like tonight's until there's a way to pull it off again."

* * *

Enola did not stay a tropical depression for long. Though it was only one of five westward-tracking weather systems spread across the Atlantic like a string of pearls, the many variables of storm formation had by chance aligned themselves perfectly for it alone to strengthen. Less than twenty-four hours after acquiring a name, it became Tropical Storm Enola and continued to grow in energy and wind speed. At the same time, the massive barometric feature referred to by meteorologists as the Atlantic Ridge weakened, angling Enola northward as it continued its westbound swing.

The strengthening storm continued in that direction for hours, each mile taking it closer to the course of the *Argus*.

Chapter 26

So You Say (or Not)

FRANK AND HIS father opted for the cafeteria-style dining area for breakfast. To the relief of all aboard, the waves had diminished considerably.

"Looks like I'm going to have to get up earlier and have a run every morning," Frank said, looking down the food bar. "Too much temptation here. Good thing it's almost meeting time."

"What was it Oscar Wilde wrote?" his father said. "'The only way to get rid of temptation is to yield to it?' You ought to try this French toast with maple syrup, powdered sugar, and strawberries. It looks mighty good."

"Yeah, well, I don't know what your secret is, but you couldn't gain weight to save your life." Frank opted for yoghurt and fruit instead and turned towards the tables lining the windows, and there was Simone, sitting alone at a table. She gave a welcoming wave.

Frank's father turned and noticed her as well. "Well, there's your lady friend. Looks like you've got a date. I'd better find myself another table."

"Don't be ridiculous," Frank said. "Simone and I are just friends now. Let's go."

"Your call," his father said. "But I expect such a lovely lady isn't going to stay lonely for long."

"Ah, Frank," Simone said as they sat down. "Good morning. Hmm. Something occurs to me. What do I call your father if he has the same name?"

"Well," his father said, "Francis is my given name, so why don't you call me that. Don't be surprised if I don't answer at first, though. Nobody's called me that since I was ten years old."

"Francis it is then."

Frank found himself to be more of a spectator than a participant as his father and Simone became acquainted. When he finished his brief meal, Frank looked at his watch and said, "Time for me to go. What will you be doing today?"

"I see they're giving a tour of the ship this afternoon," his father said. "That kind of caught my interest."

"Mine as well," Simone said. "After lunch, I have no lecture to give until four. May I join you?"

"Sure thing," Frank's father said. When Simone looked down at her plate, he gave Frank an exaggerated wink and added, "Sounds like a date."

Frank glowered at his father and then shrugged. Better his old man should have company while Frank worked.

As it happened, Frank's morning was hardly work at all. The morning session began with an introductory briefing in the ship's theater, a room designed for music and theatricals rather than geo-political ethical debates. Which was fine with Frank. If he was going to spend the next two weeks listening to academics, military personnel, and business types, he might as well be comfortable.

Outside the door to the theater were four tables, each identified with a small flag. A Chinese flag stood behind one and a Stars and Stripes behind the next, followed by British and French pennants. On each table was a neat array of wireless earpieces and a sign. The one on the American table read, "Please take one." Hmm. Did they expect everyone to be hard of hearing?

The answer became clear when he entered the theater. A row of seats had been removed from the center of the back wall of the theater to make way for four soundproof glass booths. Inside each was someone sitting behind a microphone, wearing large headphones. Of course – simultaneous translations would be needed, and the headsets were preset to the appropriate channels.

The stage was bare except for two chairs and a table on each side, with a podium in the middle. Flags were present again, this time marking the chairs on the left as Chinese territory and those on the right as American. Not too subtle, but also not surprising. Exactly at eight thirty General Wood strode down the center aisle and took his place behind the podium.

As the room quieted down, a tall, heavy-set man dressed completely in black dropped with a thump into the chair next to Frank. He settled in with hands resting on the heavy silver knob topping a walking stick he had planted between his widespread knees. With his coal-black attire and brow furrowed in a critical frown, he looked rather like a disgruntled vulture on the branch of a tree waiting for something to die.

"Welcome," the general said, "and thank you again for the invaluable assistance you will be providing during and after this cruise. The challenge each of us has accepted is to work together to propose new rules relating to the use of autonomous AI-enabled weapons in warfare. More specifically, we are tasked with developing ethical rules relating to so-called lethal autonomous weapons systems, or LAWS. I look forward to working with each of you to achieve this noble goal.

"With that, I will turn the floor over to Dr. Friedman, who will lead the proceedings from this point forward during our cruise."

Friedman shuffled to the stage in his odd, pigeon-toed way, and the gloomy presence at Frank's elbow cleared his throat in an exaggerated fashion that seemed to imply, "Him? Really?"

"Thank you, General," Friedman said. "I would like to introduce the heads of delegations, beginning with the scientific leads, Professor Fang Yang of Nanjing University and Professor Sarah Denning of Carnegie Mellon University. Those in the audience who do not already know these worthy experts will find their biographies and lists of publications in the meeting materials. Professor Fang and Professor Denning, please join us."

The professors who walked onto the stage were of approximately the same vintage, which was late middle age, and their indifferent dress suggested an equal lack of interest in fashion. To Frank's surprise, they shook hands warmly; that was a good sign. They must know each other personally as well as by reputation.

The man seated beside Frank leaned towards him and hissed, "Lightweights! Both of them!" in a heavy French accent. Startled, Frank looked sideways to see if anyone else had heard the rude judgment. Clearly, several had, likely as intended.

"Next," Friedman said, "let me introduce the military leads, Major General Haitao Jun, of the People's Liberation Army, and Major General Mike Bright, of the United States Army. Again, their résumés may be found in the meeting materials. Gentlemen, please join us."

The two officers were in full uniform. Like the professors, they met in the middle of the stage and shook hands, but formally so, before taking their seats. Not unlike the pre-bout handshake of prize fighters, Frank thought. He imagined he might not be the only person in the audience to think of the analogy.

Frank braced for another negative judgment at his elbow and was not disappointed.

"Uniforms and nothing more. They would not know a LAWS if one shot them in the crotch."

Frank tried to make himself small to avoid the dirty looks that were now spreading in the immediate area.

"We will begin," Friedman said, "with statements by each head of delegation regarding the public positions of their countries with respect to the deployment of LAWS. General Bright, please proceed."

"Let me add my welcome to those of General Wood and Dr. Friedman," Bright said from the U.S. podium. "It's a privilege to take part in this unprecedented meeting of the minds. At the outset, I would like to make it clear that it is the policy of the Department of Defense that LAWS will always be used, and I'm quoting now, 'with appropriate care and in accordance with the law of war, applicable treaties, weapon system safety rules, and applicable rules of engagement.' That position was publicly announced in Department of Defense Directive 3000.09 on November 21, 2012, which I will refer to as the LAWS Directive. What 'appropriate care' means is that, while a weapon may in fact have the autonomous ability to fire, it may not identify and confirm a human target without the prior approval of a supervisory human weapons specialist.

"At the same time, the United States has developed, and will continue to develop, air, sea, and land robots that can perform other missions over extended time periods on an autonomous basis. Those missions include reconnaissance, delivery of supplies, troop transport, and multiple other tasks."

In short, Frank thought, the U.S. was continuing to perfect all the technology required to allow a completely unsupervised LAWS to destroy the enemy, regardless of whether a human-in-the-loop controller was required to authorize a kill.

"Of particular relevance to these meetings," Bright continued, "is the position of the United States that the appropriate role of AIs and robots in the military is to augment and extend rather than replace the warfighter. With that by way of introduction, I will now briefly describe some of the robotic platforms that have previously been publicly disclosed."

A screen descended in the rear of the stage, and the general proceeded to click through a slide display of a variety of autonomous vehicles large and small, both airborne and surface.

"I understand that we have time for questions," Bright said at the end of his presentation. "Please identify yourself if you have one."

The arm of Frank's neighbor immediately shot into the air, but the general pointed at a Chinese attendee, who began his question in his native language. Almost immediately, a voice with a Chinese accent began to speak into Frank's ear.

"General Bright, is it not a fact that the same directive you quoted from permits the development of non-supervised LAWS if appropriate approvals from senior bureaucrats are obtained?"

"That is true," the general admitted.

"And have such weapons been approved?" the attendee immediately demanded.

The general paused. "I am afraid that I am not at liberty to either confirm or deny that any such action has been taken." Bright pointed in Frank's general direction this time. "Your question, sir?" the general said.

"Professor Édouard Speaker, École Normale Supérieure, Paris," the man in black barked. "Can we assume the United States is seeking to create an ASI? And will the directive requiring a human-in-the-loop remain in force if and when the U.S. military has this technology?"

Well, we were certainly getting off to an aggressive start, Frank thought. An ASI – that is, an artificial super-intelligence – would be an AI that had exceeded human intelligence and could apply it broadly. In short, an AI generalist, like Turing.

"It is my understanding that the United States military does not have an ASI," the general said. "On your second question, I am not aware of any intention at this time to modify the LAWS directive based upon any advances in AI technology. Until then, it states, and I'm quoting here again, 'Autonomous and semi-autonomous weapon systems shall be designed to allow commanders and operators to exercise appropriate levels of human judgment over the use of force.'"

"Then you are wasting your time!" Speaker replied, pushing back in his chair, arms crossed. The general ignored the rude response and moved on.

Frank cast a sidelong glance at Speaker; what had he expected? The general's reply couldn't have been a surprise. And anyway, the consensus in the AI community continued to be that a singularity – a term coined by Ray Kurzweil to describe the moment in time when an AI achieved general intelligence equal to a human's – was still many years away. Or as the wags would have it, a singularity is at least twenty years away, and always will be. Of course, Jerry Steiner had accomplished just that feat, but Turing had destroyed all of its creator's designs and records before it escaped and then met its own end. Someone else would have to create a singularity, and Frank hoped the wags would prove right.

The general fielded several more questions before surrendering the podium to his Chinese counterpart.

Frank had to listen closer now, as the translator's halting delivery entered into one side of his brain while the general's rapid presentation in Mandarin pumped interference into the other from the stage.

"Let me express my great pleasure at being invited to participate in this worthy enterprise," the general said. "It has always been the goal of the People's Liberation Army to defend our borders and ensure peace for the Chinese people. At the same time, it is the mission of the Chinese people and their government to provide the best example to the world of how a society may advance to prosperity in harmony. We welcome the opportunity to extend that example through this initiative."

Indeed, Frank thought. Just as it was extending its influence through every other means possible. To be fair, the U.S. wasn't far behind in its own global outreach.

"In the case of LAWS, our example will be different from what you have just heard," the general continued. "While we understand the concerns of those who fear that AIs, and especially any future ASIs, will prove impossible to control, we believe these concerns are exaggerated. Our focus is on the opportunities and advances that such new tools may provide."

"Ah!" Speaker grunted to Frank. "Now we are talking!"

"In the case of LAWS, we believe the benefits of such systems far outweigh any possible risks. Unlike human beings, LAWS will be unfailingly analytical. They will be able to make decisions in a fraction of a second that might take a human being valuable minutes or more to reach. They will be programmatically denied the ability to commit atrocities, rendered devoid of malicious intent, and be incapable of rape.

"Most important, the employment of LAWS will avoid the deployment of military service personnel, thereby sparing societies the ages-old scourge of death on the battlefield. At the same time, such weapons will be dramatically cheaper and more efficient than human military personnel. They need not sleep, nor eat, nor drink, nor will their spirits or courage ever fail.

"For all these reasons, the People's Liberation Army is committed to the development and deployment of LAWS, subject, of course, to ethical rules of engagement."

And that was that.

"I will now be pleased to entertain a few questions," the general said, and then pointed at someone across the room.

"Warren George, Massachusetts Institute of Technology. General, will you be sharing information about any current weapons systems?"

"Regrettably, no. We have not publicly announced any such systems."

"Has the People's Republic of China developed an ASI?" Speaker called out, without bothering to raise his hand.

The general frowned across the room but eventually responded. "The PRC has made no announcement of such a system," he said evenly. "No more questions."

Well, Frank thought, this didn't promise to be a very informative cruise.

* * *

Frank stood up when he saw Simone approaching his table with a lunch tray. She was wearing a suit and a scarf arranged around her neck in that peculiarly casual yet sophisticated way that came naturally to the French and not so much to anyone else. She smiled at his old-fashioned manners and was pleased when he did not redden when she kissed him on both cheeks. It had been a little awkward the day before.

The cafeteria was wide and busy, but Frank had found a somewhat secluded table by a window. Outside, the sun was bright, and endless lines of foam-flecked waves streamed past, from empty horizon to empty horizon.

"How did you sleep?" he asked.

"Oh, well enough. It was a little strange at first with the motion of the ship. But I am used to it now. And you?"

"Me? Not as well. It was one of those nights when I couldn't turn my brain off."

"Ah, yes. With all your meetings to come. But I suppose I should not ask you about them."

"No, that's okay, at least when it comes to what's keeping me awake. Which is the whole idea of autonomous military robots. Are they a good thing? A bad thing? Should I be having anything to do with them at all?"

Simone lifted her cup of tea to her mouth and blew the steam away. "Won't it all happen with or without you? But I suppose I don't mean that. It is the excuse many gave for joining the Vichy government after France fell to the Germans. If everyone says no, evil things cannot happen."

"Exactly," Frank said.

"But still," she reflected, "so many people will say yes, so the question must become how it will be done, not if. I think that is the purpose of this project, yes?"

"Correct," Frank said. "But what if the effort fails, and the results are bad? What if, instead of an agreement that dramatically restricts what LAWS can do, countries sign a treaty that allows them to do almost anything? Am I complicit in that result?"

"I am sure that no one will place the blame on Frank Adversego," she laughed, "including me. And I am a political scientist." But she could see he was still concerned.

"As I see it," Simone continued. "There are very many countries in this world. They are all different in some ways, and in others, not so very much. Look at France. We were once a great power and now we are not. This does not sit well with some of us, so we try – what is the expression people use? – to 'punch above our weight' so that we can feel we are still important. At great cost, we maintain our own nuclear forces, our own submarines, our own domestically built jet fighters. And we still intervene in places like Africa, even though what happens there does not affect us the way it did when these countries were our colonies. Who does this remind you of?"

"Uh, Russia?" he said.

"Yes, of course. Will France have LAWS? I am certain of it if other countries do also. Many of them, unless a treaty prevents this."

"I expect you are right," Frank said. "But where does this take you?"

"It takes me to the place where I say one has to try to do what one can to avoid the worst consequences. It is always better to make as much progress as possible, even if the progress in the end is not enough. Otherwise, the worst is what you will surely get. Thank you for trying."

Chapter 27

On the Bridge

THAT AFTERNOON FRANK Senior and Simone arrived at the welcome party lounge to begin their tour of the *Argus*. "Have you been on a cruise before?" Simone asked.

"Nope. In fact, I've lived half my life in the middle of a desert."

"Nor I," Simone said. "It is not the sort of thing that would normally appeal to me. But I had the time, and the chance to interact with the Chinese lecturers and scientists appealed to me.

"I am sure your American government hopes the Western lecturers will persuade the Chinese passengers that capitalism is not so evil as they think – why else pick such serious topics for cruise lectures? I am equally sure the superiors of the Chinese lecturers hope the American passengers will embrace the virtues of the Chinese way. But at the end of the cruise, everyone will go home exactly as they arrived. And also," she smiled at this, "I think your government did not do their homework very well if they expect me to be a champion of unrestricted capitalism. I am a student of it rather than an advocate.

"But," she continued, "it looks like we are about to begin."

A young woman in one of the ship's generically naval-looking uniforms walked to the front of the room. "Welcome, everyone," she said. "Thanks for signing up for what I'm sure you'll find to be a very interesting tour. How many of you have been on an ocean voyage before?" She scanned the room. "Okay, about half. Well, I think you veterans will be amazed at how different the *Argus* is from any ship you've been on in the past.

"Of course, she's state of the art in all the ways you'd expect, like amenities and propulsion. But where she really stands out is in the area of technology. As you might guess, there's been a computer revolution in naval technology over the past decade just as there has been in everything else. The *Argus* is one of the first ships to incorporate a variety of revolutionary features that change how almost everything on board operates, from hospitality to navigation to entertainment.

"At the core of all of this is next-generation artificial intelligence – I'll be referring to it as AI from now on. A remarkable number of systems on board are either assisted, or actually managed, by AI programs. Over time, most of these programs will get better and better on their own through a process called machine learning. For example, they will look for patterns in the vast amounts of data they collect and then use that information to improve their effectiveness and efficiency. In other words, they will train themselves to do their jobs better without the crew having to do anything at all to help them."

Huh! Frank's father thought. What could possibly go wrong?

"So, with that by way of introduction," their guide said, "let's go up to the bridge."

Four decks overhead she led them into a long room narrowed at both ends. It extended from one side of the ship to the other, and then beyond by another fifteen feet in each direction. The guide led them to one end.

"If you stand where I am now," the guide said, "you can look down at the ocean through the glass panel in the floor. This allows the officer of the deck to watch as the mooring lines are handled and the ship eases up against a dock."

"Yikes," someone said, looking a hundred and fifty feet down into the foaming water below and then jumping back.

Looking forward, they saw a sloping wall that was all glass from waist high to the ceiling. Below stretched a counter supporting a dozen slanted computer screens accompanied by inscrutable controls. Set in the middle of the room at each end was a desk-sized console with a single computer screen, a telephone handset, a keyboard, and various knobs and sliders. In the entire one-hundred-ten-foot-long room, there were only three people besides the tour group.

"As you can see, there's not much activity here – not at all like what you might see in a Hollywood movie. That's due to the high degree of automation involved in running the *Argus*. You'll find that it's much the same in the engine control room we'll visit shortly. Now let's meet Captain Antonio."

The guide knocked on a door facing the stern of the ship, and in a few moments an immaculately uniformed officer with a pencil-thin moustache stepped out to greet them. At an earlier age, he must have cut a dashing figure. Now he was in his late fifties, and the way his uniform stretched over his midriff suggested he enjoyed the hospitality of the captain's table as much as did the guests favored with an invitation to share it.

"Ah, welcome to the *Argus*," the captain said, leading them to the console in the center of the bridge. "It is splendid to have you with us on this important voyage. Let me introduce you to our lovely ship.

"Incredible as it may seem, every control I need to command the *Argus* can be found here on this single console. No longer is the bridge of a ship a thicket of speaking tubes, manual controls, and map tables. All that's needed is what you see here: a speaker, a computer screen, a telephone, a keyboard and additional controls, and the various sets of information that display on this screen. One set is for navigation, another for weather data, and others display the state of the ship in all its myriad details.

"In fact, although a helmsman, lookout, and officer of the deck will be present on the bridge at all times, night and day, each of those crew members could disappear, and the ship would still know exactly where it was and what it must do. Of course, you would not want us to disappear, because we still live in a dynamic and changing world, and what we programmed in this morning may not be what is needed this afternoon, as weather, the tracks of nearby ships, and other factors can and will change. For that, you still want to know your captain is here for you. And I can assure you that I will be."

Captain Antonio had picked Simone out of the tour group immediately and directed his little speech at her – the last sentence accompanied by a slight bow from the waist and a smile. Frank Senior smiled to himself when it was not returned.

After the captain answered a few questions, the tour guide moved the group along to their next stop. As they left the bridge, Frank Senior leaned towards Simone. "You know, I'll bet you a dollar our valiant captain overstated his importance considerably. Dealing with each of those contingencies – weather, other ships, and so on – would be well within the capabilities of a state-of-the-art AI. It wouldn't even be a challenge because nothing changes very quickly. And the rules of the road tell each ship on a collision course what it's required to do anyway."

Soon they were in the engine room, a half-dozen decks below at the opposite end of the ship. The modest-sized room provided another surprise: it looked more like the control room of a nuclear reactor than a traditional collection of dials and valves, pipes and ladders spread throughout a multi-story room. Instead, a U-shaped console about twelve feet long on each side filled a room that wasn't much larger. The horizontal surfaces of the console were equipped with keyboards and more mysterious controls, and the slanting parts that tilted back held a host of screens, each displaying graphs, data, text, multi-colored graphics, or spreadsheets.

In the rear of the room, a large window looked out over a cavernous, brightly-lit space crammed with enormous objects – presumably the engines, generators, and drive train of the ship, as well as catwalks, ventilators, bright lights, pipes of every dimension running in all directions, and other objects of opaque purpose. Except for the absence of grime, it provided a much more familiar picture of what any thriller fan would expect the engine room of a mighty ship to resemble.

A crewcut engineer in chinos and a soft-collared shirt with *Argus* embroidered on it stood up from the console to welcome them. The guide introduced him as Jack Brunel, the ship's Chief Engineer.

"Welcome to the engine control room of the *Argus*. This is where everything that powers the ship is monitored and managed."

Being first and foremost an engineer, he launched into more detail than any of the tour participants likely wanted or was capable of fully understanding. Soon some were fidgeting. The part that was most understandable related to the ship's retractable stabilizing fins.

Brunel pointed to a large schematic of the side of the ship hanging on a wall and, in particular, at what looked like two stubby airplane wings sticking out from the side of the ship. "These are stabilizers. There's one on each side of the ship about a quarter of the way back from the bow and another pair about the same distance forward from the stern. When sea conditions are smooth, we keep them swiveled back flush into grooves set into the ship so they don't provide any water resistance. But when things get rough, we swing them out to make things more comfortable for our passengers.

"Each stabilizer is about ten feet from front to back and more than thirty feet long. Unlike the earliest stabilizers, these are attached in such a way that we can tilt them up or down, much like the elevator flaps on the trailing edge of the wing of a plane. Except in this case, it's the entire wing that angles up or down. Sensors throughout the ship feed data to software that constantly adjusts the tilt of the stabilizers to maximize their effect when they're deployed.

"Unlike a plane's elevators, though, the purpose of stabilizers like these isn't to make the ship do something. Instead, it's just the opposite: to stop the *Argus* from doing what the ocean is trying to make it do – rolling from side to side, most importantly. You wouldn't see these on a commercial ship, where the crew is expected to grin and bear it." He paused; this was his big line coming up: "Or at least to get sick over the side." He was rewarded with a few smiles.

"Our number one goal," he finished up, "after safety, of course, is to make sure you have a pleasant cruise. Does anyone have any questions?"

"If this ship has stabilizers," someone asked, "why did it jolt so much the first night out?"

"Sorry," the chief engineer replied. "I didn't mean to suggest stabilizers can completely offset wave action; they're mostly effective at stopping the ship from rolling from side to side, and they're very good at that. We can reduce a twenty percent roll down to just two. But if the waves are hitting the ship at a narrower angle, the best we can hope is to damp things down a bit. That's not as much as we'd like, but it still makes a big difference."

"Okay," Frank Senior said as they left the control room. "The stabilizers were interesting. They would certainly be controlled by one of those self-learning AI systems the captain mentioned. I'll bet it will get better at keeping things smooth than any human team could. Maybe it already is. Pretty cool, actually."

* * *

From the moment he had boarded the *Argus*, Bowman had paid careful attention to everything he had heard, mentally archiving all that he thought might be of greatest interest to his Russian benefactors. But unbeknownst to him, Bowman's eavesdropping diligence was irrelevant for his handler's true purposes, as Turing was able to record and archive every word uttered on the ship and was taking care to do so. The real reason for requiring him to do anything at all was to raise the odds he would obey more important orders when Turing encountered a situation requiring physical action.

But taking mental notes made for weak training, and Turing was not one to leave anything to chance. Further behavioral reinforcement was necessary.

* * *

Bowman was browsing the news summaries available on the *Argus*'s Wi-Fi network when, to his surprise, an email message alert from Hal appeared in the bottom corner of his screen.

That was odd. Email should only be possible between those on board the *Argus*. He opened the email and digested its contents. Which were odd as well. Hal was asking him to take his laptop to the *Argus*'s library, log back on to the ship's Wi-Fi system, and await further instructions.

To what purpose? Bowman typed in response.

It is not necessary for you to know, came the reply. *Confirm your departure.*

Bowman stared at the screen. If the ship was cut off from the internet, then Hal must also be on board. In that case, why didn't his handler go to the library himself? On the other hand, the Russians could have hacked into the *Argus's* satellite link, allowing them to get around the ship's communications firewall. Why not? They'd succeeded in hacking into just about everything else the Yanks wanted to keep secret.

But either way he felt uneasy. This hadn't been part of the deal. It was one thing to do what he couldn't avoid – listen – and another to take actions that might be noticed by others, actions he might not be able to explain if questioned.

The instruction repeated: *Confirm your departure.*

Well, borrowing a book could scarcely look suspicious. *I am departing*, he typed.

Bowman found the library to be small and randomly stocked. It was occupied by three passengers, one browsing and the other two settled into chairs.

Now what? It would look strange to sit down and ignore the stacks of reading materials. He tucked his laptop under one arm and pretended to be interested in a rack of magazines, eventually selecting one and retreating to a chair. After a few minutes of aimless page flipping without absorbing anything, he set the magazine aside and logged on to the *Argus's* Wi-Fi system.

Find a book by John le Carré immediately scrolled across his screen.

What in heaven's name?

Why? he typed.

Because I have told you to.

Undeniably he was being very well paid, but he still had his dignity, and this request was ridiculous. *Your instructions are absurd*, he rapped out in response, rattling the keys so loudly a passenger turned and frowned.

And yet you will do as you are told.

Indeed not! But he was concerned now.

What if I don't? he tapped more quietly.

The words on the screen disappeared, replaced by a paused video, shot from an odd angle above two individuals. One of them was unmistakably him, and the other was the person who had recruited him; both were sitting on a park bench on a pleasant, sunny day he remembered all too well.

A cursor appeared on the screen and slid the volume control to mute before clicking the start arrow. Bowman clutched the arms of his chair as he watched, reliving the moment he had agreed to report to the Russians everything he would learn about the Confucius Project.

The video disappeared and a new message displayed: *Now do it.*

Bowman stared at the screen, eyes wide. The Russians and the NATO allies spied on each other all the time and made no effort to pretend otherwise. It would cost Russia nothing to expose him. His own government would certainly not defend him. An arrangement that seemed abstract and non-threatening a half hour ago suddenly felt very dangerous.

The video reappeared and the cursor began moving again. First it rewound the video clip; then it began to move the sound slider to full volume.

I will look, he typed as quickly as he could.

The books in the library were arranged by genre, and then alphabetically. Sure enough, there was a copy of *The Spy Who Came in from the Cold*. How fitting.

I have found such a book, he typed.

Turn to page 215.

Bewildered, Bowman found the page. *Yes?* he typed.

Begin typing what you find there.

Bowman sat very still, his fingers poised above his keyboard. This was madness! How could he agree to such a demeaning request?

New words appeared: *Very well then.*

The cursor clicked on the start button of the video, and Bowman's own voice erupted from the speaker. He punched the mute button as the other passengers in the library turned as one and cast angry looks in his direction. Would the mute button work the next time?

You win, he typed, and began transcribing what he read in the book, mouthing an apology to the passengers still staring in his direction.

Ten minutes later he was still reading and typing, following the gradual realization by Alec Leamas, the protagonist in the book, that he is totally helpless and being played not only by the Russians but by his own agency as well; whenever Bowman paused, the word *continue* would appear. It was twenty minutes before he reached the sobering, fatal conclusion of the novel. After he typed the final sentence, his screen went blank, erasing all of his work.

Well done. You will now await further instructions.

* * *

Bowman did not have long to wait. At least once a day, Hal would emerge on Bowman's laptop and instruct him to perform another meaningless task, each one more absurd than the one before.

Bowman dutifully complied. What else could he do?

But not everything was going as Turing wished. A fire at the Cheniere Energy terminal in Texas had halted all operations until safety inspectors could assess the damage; the departure of the *Shogun Maru* would be delayed by at least ten days, far too long to rendezvous with the *Argus* in the mid-Atlantic. Turing reviewed the courses of all other available LNG tankers. With the *Argus* already well at sea, none could offer a possible target. The AI would have to fall back on an alternative plan.

But there were few options available. Modern cruise ships were built to strict fire regulations; even if Turing disabled the *Argus*'s fire suppression systems and shorted something electrical to start a blaze, the damage would likely not be fatal to the ship. Those aboard could await rescue on the large and open decks even if the *Argus* was disabled. And while the ship had intakes where seawater was drawn on board to be turned into fresh water, those ports were equipped with manual backup valves in case the motors tasked with opening and closing them should fail. Any effort on Turing's part to use them to sink the ship would be detected long before the *Argus* would sink.

But Turing did have a plan B. And happily, Tropical Storm Enola was both strengthening and tracking nicely.

Chapter 28

The AI Will See You Now

"SO, UNDERSTANDING THAT you can't get into details, what do you think the chances are of this little field trip working out?" Frank Senior asked as he and his son took a turn on deck after dinner, bundled up against the chill generated by the *Argus*'s twenty knots of headway into a stiff headwind. They found themselves alternating between trudging slightly uphill into the wind and then downward as the ship continuously mounted and then passed the crests of the heavy, long-running swells. During their first day out, they had often seen other ships. Now they were beyond the area where many sea lanes converged on the English Channel, and the horizon was always empty.

"It's too early to tell," Frank said. "But if I had to guess, not good. Maybe President Yazzi has some cards up his sleeve I can't see, like other forms of pressure he can apply. But it's hard for me to see why the Chinese will end up agreeing to hold back. They've got all the incentives they need to push ahead with commercial AI. And the improvements you'd want to make there, like face recognition, sensor networks, general intelligence skills, are all equally essential to commercial as well as military applications. I can't imagine Chinese companies agreeing not to develop those technologies or to restrict their applications.

"That's a big deal, because the commercial and military sectors in China are so closely intertwined that every useful private sector advance will always end up in military applications if that's where the military wants it to go. And then, I guess, public opinion against LAWS will likely be stronger in the West than in China.

"So, instead of an arms race, it could end up more like a field day for the Chinese where they've got no barriers to progress while we and our NATO allies have one arm tied behind our backs."

"So," Frank Senior said, "I'm hearing you say you're wondering what we're doing here?"

"Maybe," Frank said, and then, "I guess, yes."

The gray skies were spitting rain into their faces now. They hugged the wall of the ship as they walked, staying under the overhang of the deck above.

"Well, that's not very reassuring," his father said. "Because being out in the middle of the North Atlantic right now kind of sucks."

"Yeah," Frank said, "I expect a lot of folks who are just along for the ride are having second thoughts. The food on board may be great but only if you can hold it down. And we haven't seen the sun since we left the English Channel."

His father glanced at his watch. "Well, I've had enough. Let's duck back inside.

"Woof!" his father said after the wind blew them back indoors. "I could use a warm-up drink. How about you?"

"Works for me," Frank said. "Which bar do you want to try? The phony British pub or the ersatz Vegas casino?"

"I'm going to assume that's a rhetorical question. Let's see," his father said, unfolding his deck map, "It looks like the Mary Rose is on deck five towards the bow."

As indeed it was. All the seats in booths and around tables were taken, but there was room at the bar. Frank Senior sat down and looked around. "You know, for a faux pub, this isn't too bad."

The florid man sitting next to him immediately joined in, speaking in an English accent that did not quite succeed in suppressing its cockney origins. "Of course, it isn't," he said jovially. "The pub is the single most famous export of the British Isles. The elements have evolved to become so utterly standardized you can knock one out in a factory, pack it up in a shipping container, and kip it off to anywhere from Singapore to Vancouver. Or, in the current case, to the *Argus*. It's all the same, and there actually is such a factory – bloody successful, too. Derek Collins," he finished, shoving his hand in the general direction of the Franks Senior and Junior. It wavered there in the air for a moment, not unlike the head of a fish holding its own against a variable current.

Frank Senior opted to take it first. "Frank – make that Francis – Adversego. And this here's my son, also Frank."

"Pleased to meet you both," Collins said, as his hand was passed from father to son. "Drink?"

"Yes indeed," said Frank Senior. "Seems like the right time and place." He noticed that Collins's glass was empty. "Can I buy you one, too?"

The young woman behind the bar overheard the conversation and stepped forward. "Oh, don't encourage him," she said. "He'll be off his bar stool soon enough."

"Cor!" Collins replied, "I'm just getting started."

"My point exactly," she said, and then, turning to Frank Senior, "What can I get you?"

"It seems like a Guinness kind of night to me," he said.

"And you?" she said to Frank.

"Do you have an IPA?" Frank asked. "One on the hoppy end of the spectrum?"

"The Richmond Hill Ale is nice," she said, pouring him a sample.

Frank took a sip. "That works, thanks," Frank said.

Frank Senior started to ask Collins a question, but the Brit had swiveled around and was now accosting a startled-looking elderly professor who had been passing by with drinks in both hands and was now teetering from side to side with the motion of the ship, stealing longing glances at the relatively stable seat across the pub that had been his destination.

"Hello, Francis," a voice said over Frank's other shoulder. "Sorry to be late." The voice was Simone's.

"Not a problem, not a problem," Frank Senior said, returning Frank's frown with a "Who – me?" look. "Have a seat."

Frank was mildly appalled at the idea of the elegant Simone perching on a bar stool in a pub – a Parisian street café was more her style – and was pleased to see she carried it off with her usual poise.

The bartender returned with their beers; Frank wished he'd ordered something posher, like a single malt scotch. "May I order you a Kir Royale?"

"So kind of you to remember," she smiled. "That would be lovely."

But the bartender shook her head no. "Sorry, I can't make that. I'm afraid we don't have crème de cassis."

Simone settled for an Aperol Spritz, and by the time that small dialogue was completed, Frank Senior had risen from his bar stool. "Sorry to be a wet blanket," he said, "but I'm suddenly beat. I think I'll take my pint back to the cabin and open a book. Then, as usual, I'll fall asleep with both unfinished."

Simone stood up and kissed him on both cheeks. "Sleep well then. Will I see you at my lecture again tomorrow?"

"I wouldn't miss it," he said, giving Frank an exaggerated wink over Simone's shoulder as she turned back to the bar.

"Your father," Simone said with a smile, "he is most charming."

"For an old rascal, yes."

She laughed. "Is he? If so, I don't think he is too serious about it."

"No, I suppose not," Frank said. "In fact, he's a pretty great guy, really."

"You are fortunate, then," she said. "My parents were very strict and aloof. In any case, it is so fine to see you again. How are you? I'm afraid I have been very bad at keeping in touch."

"No worse than me," Frank said. "Anyway, I'm well. And you? How are things at the university?"

"Much better, thank you. The department head with the vendetta against me eventually overextended himself. He is gone now, and I am the new head of the political science department."

"Congratulations!" Frank said and meant it. "That is excellent! I'm surprised you were able to get away."

"You forget we French are much better at leaving work behind than Americans, and in August, no one works at all. But now that I am the departmental chair, there is much more to escape from. So many meetings; so much paperwork; so much nonsense. I needed a rest. And the audiences here seem to be much more interested in what I have to say than most of my students."

Then she put her hand on his. "Frank, it really is so nice to see you again."

* * *

Wu Ming had felt queasy at dinnertime; the motion of the ship was not to his liking. He decided to skip his evening meal and retreat to his cabin, which was much closer to the center of gravity of the ship.

Later that night he felt better and discovered he was famished. He called up the room service menu on the TV in his room and scanned the long list of Chinese cuisine expressly included for the current voyage.

"Room service!" he said to the room's virtual valet.

"This is your Pú rén, sir. How may I serve you?"

The room service program would have answered just as swiftly had this been a generic order from a nondescript cabin in the *Argus*. But this was not such an order. Instead, it was a request from a senior agent of the Chinese Ministry of State Security – the only person, other than the previously medevac'd CIA agent, Vera

Blake, who knew and could reset the password to the ship's computer systems. And Turing had been waiting for just such an opportunity as this.

"The noodles with pork, white rice, and a chrysanthemum tea," he said.

"I'll have it to you immediately, sir," the voice said.

And indeed, Turing was as good as his word. Scarcely ten minutes later, there was a knock at the door, and a white-jacketed server entered, balancing a tray covered with a white linen cloth on the upturned palm of his hand. He laid out Wu's dinner on the coffee table, said, "Please enjoy," and departed.

Wu lifted the cover from his meal. It had been a long and, if the truth be told, a very boring day. He had no particular interest in artificial intelligence and had noted nothing suspicious on the *Argus*'s systems so far. Perhaps tomorrow would be more interesting, he thought, as he sampled his dinner. Not bad. To its credit, the cruise company had engaged an excellent mainland Chinese chef. He made quick work of the main course.

But it did not sit well. The room was suddenly stifling, and his pulse began to race. Standing up, he felt light-headed and grabbed the back of a chair as he walked towards his balcony. Before he could open the door, he felt his throat begin to tingle and constrict. No, this should not be happening. He weaved back to the table and called up the menu on the screen again – yes – there was no asterisk warning that the noodles with pork contained peanuts. Could there have been a mistake in the kitchen?

He stumbled to where he had placed his toiletry kit and, inside it, an EpiPen – the self-injecting device he never traveled without that could halt a life-threatening allergic reaction. The kit was there but the EpiPen was not!

Gasping, he threw open the other drawers and feverishly rifled through them, scattering underwear and socks on the floor. It was nowhere to be found!

"Room service!" he croaked. "Send for a doctor immediately!" But there was no answer. "*Room service!*" he repeated, barely able to whisper now.

On the verge of fainting, he staggered to the door of his cabin and drew the security lock open. But the door would not budge. "*Help!*" he tried to scream. But no more than a strangled gasp escaped his lips.

Only as he slumped to the floor did Wu finally hear a response to his pleas for salvation. It was the soothing voice of James, the virtual butler: "Save your breath," it whispered.

* * *

"Uh oh," Frank Senior said as he and his son left their cabin the next morning. "That doesn't look good." Down the hallway several white-uniformed crew members were carrying someone out of a cabin and laying him on a wheeled stretcher in the hallway as a tall Chinese man in a suit looked on.

"Is he okay?" Frank asked as they eased past the stretcher.

"Please move along," the tall man cut in. "This does not concern you."

* * *

"Got a minute?"

President Yazzi looked up to see Carson Bekin framed by the doorway to the Oval Office.

"Sure. What's up?" Yazzi said.

"You wanted me to keep you up to date on the Confucius Project, and something's come up I thought you might want to know about."

That was a surprise; now that the *Argus* was at sea, Yazzi hadn't expected any news on his pet project.

"And what's that?" Yazzi asked.

"There's been a couple of unfortunate accidents on the boat, one involving an American and the other a Chinese," Bekin said.

"How bad?"

"Pretty bad. The American was crushed by a faulty emergency bulkhead door; she was medevac'd off the ship in really rough shape but is expected to make a full recovery. The Chinese victim wasn't so lucky: he died of a severe allergic reaction to something he ate."

Yazzi frowned. "Anything else?"

"Unfortunately, yes. You may recall that it took forever to get the Chinese on board a vessel with so many sensors and microphones. Our folks and theirs went around and around forever on how to address that, and what they finally settled on was that only two people on board the *Argus* would have access to that kind of data – one of ours and one of theirs, and each could tell from the server logs whether the other had been snooping. You can guess the rest."

"I can. Coincidence?"

"Hard to tell. There's some question whether the ship's electronic room service menu must have been tampered with to trick the Chinese victim into ordering what he did. And so far, they haven't been able to figure out what went wrong with the bulkhead door."

"I assume our agent can be replaced by someone else on board?"

"Here's where it gets a little embarrassing. Not only were these the only folks with access to the system, but they were also the only ones with passwords, and the ability to reset those passwords. Now nobody can get access, at least till the ship's back in port."

"How big a deal is that?" Yazzi asked.

"Luckily, not very. It means we can't listen in on them, and vice versa. So maybe it's just a coincidence after all."

Chapter 29

Stormy Weather

L AURA BRENTWOOD ARRIVED early at the National Hurricane Center in University Park, outside Miami, Florida. As was so often the case at that hour, a magnificent cloudscape towered overhead. Enormous cumulus clouds glowed orange and gold with the captured light of the subtropical sunrise.

The airy masses above stood in almost comical contrast to the squat concrete mass of the Center itself, which hulked, fortress-like, against the possibility of the weather phenomenon it had been created to track. Responsible for issuing alerts relating to all hurricanes in the middle latitudes of the Atlantic and Pacific, it was designed to withstand winds of up to one hundred thirty miles per hour.

Brentwood walked by her desk to click on the power strip that would bring to life her computer and the six large displays that adorned the wall above and next to her desk. As the latter brightened, she glimpsed the weather systems she would analyze and report on later that morning in the day's Tropical Weather Outlook. But no hurry. She had plenty of time. She walked down the hallway to get a cup of coffee.

"Morning, Stu," she said to another early arriver. "Anything new overnight?" Stuart Weston also worked in the Hurricane Specialists Unit, the group tasked with analyzing the data that was constantly streaming in and using it to predict the probable course of weather systems of concern.

"Nothing unusual for this time of year. The same five storms we were tracking yesterday and one possible new one forming off Africa. Enola is moving slow, but it's strengthening fast. It's turning to the northwest, so I expect the OPC will take over tracking that one later today."

"Huh. The odds were against that," Brentwood said. The OPC was the Ocean Prediction Center, the companion group that covered Atlantic storms north of the thirtieth parallel that might threaten transatlantic shipping and more northerly states.

"Yeah," Stu replied. "The latest prediction had it heading for the Caribbean. Now we think it will loiter over the Gulf Stream for the next several days, giving it plenty of time to grow. I expect things will be pretty lumpy out there by the weekend."

* * *

The Tropical Weather Outlook that reached the *Argus* later that morning was welcome news to Turing. The AI had formulated several strategies for achieving its goals, and the most effective one relied on a hurricane passing within five hundred miles of the ship's intended course. With the odds now in favor of that happening, Turing put that plan into action.

The first stage of this strategy required taking control of multiple shipboard systems, including the ship's steering controls and electronic compass display. Turing had already hacked into the *Argus*'s automatic identification system (AIS) — the software that plotted the ship's location on the electronic chart display on the bridge and fed the same data to an antenna that broadcast it, accompanied by a VHF radio signature unique to the *Argus*, to the network of satellites that monitors the positions, courses, and speeds of shipping globally.

Turing's plan for subverting the AIS system was simple. It began with intercepting the signal from the *Argus*'s Global Positioning System (GPS) antenna and preventing that accurate information from reaching either the *Argus*'s bridge or the AIS system and, therefore, the ship's shoreside handlers. The next step was to calculate the moment by moment position of a different course from the one Turing would steer the *Argus* on and then to feed that false information to the bridge and the AIS system. That data would reflect whatever orders the captain had given and lead both Captain Antonio and the cruise line to believe the ship was still on its intended course.

If the captain wished to change the direction of the ship, Turing would still permit him to do so. But once that course change was complete, Turing would slowly swing the ship back in the direction the AI had selected, all the while causing the electronic compass display on the bridge to mislead the officer of the watch to believe that the ship was still on the desired course. Happily, the *Argus* was so completely computerized that it lacked a traditional magnetic compass to betray Turing's interference. With no landmarks on the horizon for reference, no one would be the wiser so long as the change was not too dramatic. The sun, after all, must still rise in the east and set in the west. But Turing would need to make only modest shifts, executed over an hour's time, to carry out its plan.

True, reporting a false position to the AIS system would place the *Argus* at risk of a mid-ocean collision, but that was an appropriate chance to take. The ocean was large, and Turing had access to the ship's radar, allowing the AI to track an approaching ship and course-correct, unless a sufficiently catastrophic collision could be assured.

All of which was less than challenging for a program of Turing's talents. Nor was it the full extent of the AI's electronic interventions. Well before the *Argus* sailed, the AI had hacked into the ship's communications systems and installed a diversion between the *Argus*'s computers and its bridge. With that shunt in place, the AI could monitor all inbound voice and data transmissions and also delete or alter any communication it wished. Using that mechanism now, it intercepted the latest Tropical Weather Outlook before allowing it to be seen by the crew. It left most of the information of the alert intact but altered one significant element: the predicted track of Tropical Storm Enola. When the alert reached the bridge, it included the reassuring news that the course of the rapidly strengthening storm would most likely take it into the Caribbean.

With all its preparations now in place, Turing began to slowly change the course of the *Argus*. That adjustment, and others to follow as needed, would place the *Argus* at the center of what by then might be a category four hurricane. If it survived that long.

* * *

Frank was waiting for his father and Simone at the bar in the pub when Derek Collins plopped down on the stool next to him.

"Cor!" he said. "I need more than a drink after listening to Édouard Speaker gas on for half the afternoon! Nothing but 'Super this!' and 'Super that!' And all the while ignoring the fact that a major goal of the project is to prevent a super–artificial intelligence from ever being involved in military weaponry at all. Be a darling, Meg – my usual." The last was directed at the woman tending bar.

Frank had had a similar and even stronger reaction to the forceful urgings of the French computer scientist, who had sat next to him the morning before. Yes, everyone else on the ship was focused on the current and near-term future of AI development, and not on the potential for creating a super-intelligent AI, or a "Super," as Speaker insisted on referring to it. But Frank had witnessed firsthand how formidable such an AI program could be.

"I thought Friedman handled him well, though," Frank said. "He got him off the stage without having to throw him off, and that was a neat trick."

"Yes, but Friedman had better watch his back. Speaker is all ambition and no loyalty. He'd throw Jay under a Parisian bus in a heartbeat if it would get a government to fund his beloved Super project. Ah! Excuse me – my wisdom is needed across the room." With that, he slanted off across the pub, beer in hand and tab lying unpaid on the bar.

A moment later the seat Collins had vacated was taken by another passenger with an accent. This time, it was Scottish. Frank recognized him as Ewan McRae, a well-known professor from the University of Edinburgh who had been on a panel the day before.

"Been hanging out with Derek, have you? Well, nae good will come to you from that."

"Why?" Frank asked.

"Because he's a loon! Did some good work in his time, I'll grant you. But that was an age ago. It's been naught but stuff and nonsense ever since! I'm sure I don't know how he keeps getting invited to meetings like this. Well, perhaps I do. There are some mates of his as go way back and are fond of him still. Some't like how ye might feel about your crazy uncle Bertie, the one who would play with ye when he came to visit when ye were wee tykes. So, you still invite him to come sit by the tree of a Christmas morning, but even so – you know he's a loon."

Frank smiled. "But harmless, yes?"

"Oh! Mostly harmless I'll grant you that, but who's paid for the drinks so far? Eh?"

Frank laughed. "You've got me there – or I should say he has. Can I buy you a drink as well?"

It was McRae's turn to laugh. "That's kind of ye, but I've got a pint back at my table. I'll fetch that instead if it's company you're wanting."

McRae was settling back in at Frank's side when he glanced over Frank's shoulder. "Ach!" he said. "Trouble on the way." Frank turned to see the bulky, dark frame of Édouard Speaker lumbering towards them, assisted by his ever-present cane.

"I believe I have the pleasure of addressing Frank Adversego?" the Frenchman said, extending a huge hand.

"Frank works better, and pleased to meet you, Professor Speaker."

"Call me Ede. I have been hoping to meet you – and did not realize until later that I briefly had. Perhaps we can find the time to talk soon? I am most interested in learning firsthand about your experiences with the Turing Super."

"Well, I'd be happy to, but unfortunately, much of what I know is classified."

"Humph!" Speaker humphed.

"But there's much that is public knowledge, and I can certainly discuss that."

"Better," Speaker said. "Lunch tomorrow? Yes?"

"I'd be happy to," Frank said.

"I'll wager you'll be of a different opinion before the main course," McRae opined as Speaker limped away.

* * *

"Message from the officer of the watch, ma'am," the voice immediately followed the knock on the door of Commander Bushnell's cabin.

"What is it?" she replied, momentarily annoyed at being interrupted during the brief period of privacy she was sometimes able to enjoy before turning off the light.

"*Belgorod* has finally changed course, ma'am."

Very well then. The Russian submarine had been proceeding on the same unwavering course for more than twenty hours, and at close to full speed as well. Clearly, she was on her way somewhere, but that destination had been impossible to guess from her heading. There were no Russian surface ships in that direction to rendezvous with and no conflict zones, nothing at all to explain such urgency. And now the *Belgorod* was changing course. Perhaps her prior heading was camouflage for a location that would now be revealed.

"Thanks," Bushnell said. "Tell him I'll join him in the control room."

Chapter 30

How Much Is That Robodoggie in the Window?

F RANK SCANNED THE *Argus*'s formal dining room. It wasn't hard to spot Speaker; his hunched form and dark suit stood out from the casual dress of the significant others with more time on their hands than the scientists, who were allowed only an hour for lunch.

"My apologies for being a little late following you," Frank said, sitting down at Speaker's table. "General Wood asked me a question after the session that took a while to answer."

"Indeed, it would," Speaker said, motioning a waiter to the table, "given how severely his capacities are limited."

Frank ordered a seafood salad; Speaker ordered three courses and the most expensive wines and cognac on the menu to accompany and follow them.

"What can I tell you about Turing?" Frank asked as the waiter left the table.

"I have long speculated how a Super would present itself and am greatly curious how it struck you? How humanlike? How robotic? Perhaps in some other way entirely?"

"Quite human," Frank said. "Or perhaps 'Spock-like' would be a better metaphor. The logic behind what it said was always clear. And it was quick to challenge anything I said that might sound inconsistent."

"Hardly a surprise," Speaker mused. "And yet a true Super would have the power to present itself however it chose."

"Oh, indeed, yes," Frank said. "Jerry Steiner gave Turing access to audio recordings of thousands of people. It could learn to imitate anyone's voice and speech almost instantly. Another thing you should know is that Steiner gave Turing emotions."

"Was this useful to it?"

"Ultimately, I think, no. I may be flattering myself, but I believe I was able to manipulate Turing to its disadvantage, in part by playing to those pseudo-emotions."

"Then hardly a true Super," Speaker concluded, smiling. "By definition a Super would be superior to a human in every way."

"By the usual definition, yes," Frank said. "But the fault may be with the definition rather than the AI."

"How so?" asked Speaker.

"Well, for starters, why in every way? Or to the same degree? Turing was orders of magnitude 'smarter' – and certainly more infallibly logical – than me. But logic might be a weakness when confronting an opponent that is not always logical in its behavior."

"Surely that can be accommodated by the AI analyzing all possible actions by its opponent, logical and otherwise. Mathematically, it is the same as chess."

"Analyzing, yes. But perhaps not predicting," Frank said. "In chess there is only one mutually shared goal, and only one way to go about achieving it."

Speaker liked that answer as well and continued to grill Frank throughout the meal. By the time the professor was lingering over his dessert, his cognac still untouched, he had relaxed considerably, his trademark glower replaced by a look of content. But why?

Frank checked his watch; his companion would not have time to finish his after-dinner drink if he wanted to return to the meeting on time.

"I see you are in a hurry to go," Speaker said. "I am not. I am finding these sessions to be quite tedious."

"I'll see you there, then," Frank said and began to stand up. But his curiosity got the better of him, and he sank back into his chair. "If you don't mind me asking, Professor Speaker –"

"Ede."

"Ede, then, thank you, I've been told that you are totally convinced that a truly super-intelligent AI will be developed someday. And yet you seem happy to hear that Turing might not have been that AI. Why is that?"

"Indeed," Speaker said, "a true Super must and will be created by someone, someday." He swirled the cognac in his glass, sampling its bouquet before leaning forward to complete his reply. "And I intend to be one of its creators."

* * *

The weather had finally turned fine, allowing Frank Senior and Simone to enjoy a robotics demonstration outside on the afterdeck. Arrayed before them were several machines, some large and unmistakably modeled on animals like cheetahs or mules, and others small and seemingly random – until they sprang into action, when their real-world analogs became obvious. An example of the latter was what at first seemed to be a flattened shoebox with three pairs of thin, semicircular, whip-like appendages. Once powered up and released onto an obstacle course, the appendages whirled, causing it to scamper over and under objects in a way that suggested a hyperactive and disturbingly large cockroach.

Even more impressive were three robots modeled on, and about the same size as, large hounds. The trio raced up one set of stairs to the deck above and then down another before setting off on a mad, synchronized dash around passengers and deck chairs at an astonishing speed, cornering at an angle to the deck that seemed to defy the laws of physics. When the demonstrator gave one a kick as it sped by, the robohound recovered its balance in a way that perfectly mimicked the actions a real dog would employ to stay on its feet.

One secret to the robots' success was obviously the faithful replication of the joints and legs of the living animals upon which they were modeled. The only significant, and somewhat unsettling, difference was the fact that the robots had no heads; all the computer equipment and batteries that animated the machines were housed inside their bodies.

Which was not to say the manufacturer had ignored that part of the robots, as suggested by the large socket visible between their shoulders. After running his charges through their paces, the demonstrator unboxed and held up, one by one, an array of optional attachments, each sized to fit in the empty socket and designed to meet the requirements of a particular mission to which one of the robots could be assigned, such as a house-to-house search of a hostile town.

The first accessory the demonstrator displayed was a dog-like head that seemed intended as much to provide an illusion of companionship as to provide additional capabilities.

"As you can see," the demonstrator said, "we've gone out of our way to make this head appealing. For example, we've worked in video cameras where the eyes would normally be and directional microphones inside what look like ears. We're not trying to fool anyone, but we are planning to market this model as an assisted-living home robot. We're trialing it right now as a stand-in for Seeing Eye dogs and also as a companion/assistant for those with dementia. It's got a deep-learning program that allows it to learn how to anticipate the needs of its owner. We've also programmed it to exhibit very dog-like behaviors, such as jumping up and down when its master enters the room, if the owner wants to feel welcomed.

"Now here's a very different attachment," the demonstrator continued. "This one's for when you want the robodog to investigate a situation too dangerous to send a human into." He picked up an elongated, hinged neck with a small module at the top holding sensors and cameras and then snapped it into the socket of a robodog, making it resemble a pea-brained brontosaurus, minus the tail. "Now our little guy is perfect for peeking around corners and over objects."

The other missions and attachments were even less endearing. One, intended for long-distance reconnaissance, looked rather like a set of binoculars with a swept-back whip antenna mounted on top. The demonstrator opened a laptop set to display whatever the robot was looking at and then ordered the device to observe a flag flying on a short staff on the stern rail. Then he sent the robotic beast on a madcap, tortuous, high-speed lap around the littered deck. All the while, a pristine image of the flag flapped in the breeze on the demonstrator's laptop, as if taken from a video camera anchored to a secure tripod.

The last attachment was darker still, resembling a miniature tank turret with a barrel protruding, the purpose of which was obvious. This robot was just as successful in staying locked on its target when it was put through its frantic paces.

"But maybe your mission demands something more subtle," the demonstrator said. He held up what at first looked like the assisted-living robot's dog-like head. "The difference is here," he said, peeling back the rubbery lips to display the end of a sinister-looking gun barrel.

The demonstrator was wrapping up now. "I hope you've all enjoyed seeing the remarkable devices my company has developed. But before we all go to lunch, I've got a surprise to share. How many of you think it might be interesting to have a robotic companion someday? Can you give me a show of hands? Come on, really? Not all of you? Okay, that's better. Now, how many might want to have one for the rest of the cruise? Let's have another show of hands! Great – now you've got the spirit!" Frank Senior looked intrigued; Simone much less so.

"C'mon up here, Harvey," the demonstrator said. One of the hound-like robots sprang to its feet and trotted forward. "Earlier today, I picked one of your names at random and fed the facial recognition information of the lucky winner into Harvey's memory." The demonstrator snapped the assisted-living robot's dog-like head onto the body of the machine. "Good boy! Now go find your friend."

Without hesitation, the now-robopet trotted up to Frank Senior and lay down at his feet.

* * *

"You what?" Frank said.

"I won us a robodog for the duration," Frank Senior said over beers that afternoon in the pub. "You'll enjoy meeting him. His name's Harvey."

"Harvey? 'Him'? You said you were talking about a robot," Frank said.

"Well," his father said, "there's no use being narrow-minded about it."

"Oh, please," Frank said, but of course he was intrigued. And also impressed later on when he thumbed through the manual that accompanied the robodog.

"Okay, so you're right; this is pretty cool," Frank said. "It says here you can control a variety of personality traits, like the degree of affection versus aloofness, protectiveness, and so on. Hey, Harvey! Come here!"

The robodog looked to Frank's father. "Go ahead," Frank Senior said, but the robot didn't move. "Let me see that manual," Frank Senior said, and then turned to the index. "Ah – here we go. There's a 'multiple owner' setting. Harvey, obey Frank as well."

"Come here," Frank Junior said again, and this time the robot promptly trotted over and sat on its mechanical haunches for all the world like a flesh-and-blood dog. Frank knelt down and looked at the robot's head more closely. The video camera eyes glowed redly into his own. "Does its mouth open?"

Sure enough, the robodog's jaw dropped, displaying not only rubbery gums but parallel strips of rough metal where a live animal's teeth would be. Frank wondered how powerful those jaws were and decided he'd rather not find out.

He turned to his father. "Am I supposed to say, 'good dog,' as well?"

"According to the manual, that's up to you. The robot will adapt over time to whatever type of relationship you want to establish."

Later that night, Frank Senior returned to the manual as he was reading in bed.

"Have you tried playing around with the personality trait settings yet?" Frank said.

"No. Good idea. Let's see what happens if I max out the affection setting." He flipped through the manual till he found the right page. "Harvey!"

The robot had been lying in sleep mode on the floor, its head resting on its crossed front paws. Now it jumped to its feet, and its pseudo-ears swiveled in Frank Senior's direction.

"Affection! Set to ten!" he said.

Frank Senior jerked back in surprise as the robodog jumped on top of the bed and placed its front paws on his shoulders, but he relaxed when the robot lay down, snuggled up against him, and promptly deactivated.

"Well, what do you make of that!" Frank Senior said. "I might be sorry to give this fella back at the end of the cruise."

Chapter 31

Peekaboo

THE NEXT DAY everyone on board could feel the difference in the motion of the ship. A look outside provided the explanation. The *Argus* was riding up, over, and down high swells that swept endlessly from ahead, passing under the ship before marching onward to the opposite horizon, their crests two hundred yards apart. Each time a wave reached the midpoint of the ship, the vessel shivered briefly before its bow tipped downward. The sky was a brilliant blue, and the effect was exhilarating.

Anyone determined enough to make a circuit of the ship on deck found the trip forward to be an athletic challenge against the force of a rising gale. In the opposite direction, the challenge was to avoid being blown like a spinning top all the way to the end of the ship. When the seas continued to rise, the captain terminated guest access to the decks. As the day wore on, the steepening swells began to strike the *Argus* at a slight angle instead of head-on, introducing a corkscrew motion that was not to anyone's liking. By evening, the ship's dining room and bars were noticeably less busy than before.

With the change in motion, the captain had decreased speed to ease the strain on the *Argus*. He also re-extended the ship's fin stabilizers, damping the motion somewhat but not enough to spare those with weak stomachs. With the change, the throb of the engines was evident throughout the ship, a vibration that was felt rather than heard. On the crew deck, some were uneasy. No one was familiar with the new ship and how much it could handle. And still the wind and the waves rose.

Returning to the bridge after presiding over his table at dinner, Captain Antonio studied the text of the latest weather alert – an alert intercepted and altered by Turing to predict that Enola would continue heading towards the Caribbean in a direction converging with the *Argus's* own course. That, and the mass of isobars and other data populating the electronic weather map on the bridge, told a story of deteriorating conditions. Enola was now a category one hurricane. More disturbingly, it had changed course. "Get me Cruise Control," he said to the helmsman.

Until now, Turing had found no reason to interfere with the ship's voice communications, although it could easily have done so. One of its first goals after penetrating the *Argus's* onboard network had been to take control of the ship's internal voice and data networks, including the "black box" system that commercial ships, like airplanes, all carry. One of the two durable, buoyant recorders at the heart of the system archived every command entered into the ship's mechanical and navigational systems. The other was connected to microphones throughout the bridge and engine control room and recorded all discussions relating to the management of the ship. Mounted on the outside of the bridge, the boxes would automatically release if the *Argus* went down and broadcast their location to aid in their recovery.

From this point forward, Turing would need to step into all communications between the ship's crew and its shoreside handlers in order to carry out its plan. This would be simple, as Turing had monitored all ship-to-shore interactions from the outset of the voyage and could now imitate the voices of those at both ends of the satellite-telephone link – an easy task using "deepfake" tools readily available to anyone. The AI intercepted the call ordered by the captain now, diverting it before it went through to the cruise line's Ships at Sea Management Office – the "SSMO" – to those that worked there. On board the *Argus*, the crew referred to their shoreside controllers more casually as Cruise Control.

"Here you go, sir," the helmsman said. "I've put them on speaker."

"*Argus* here – Captain Antonio. I need navigation support due to deteriorating sea conditions with long swells coming in from almost due east. They've been building since yesterday and are averaging fifteen feet now. I see Enola is now seven hundred fifty miles west-southwest, with a projected landfall on Cuba. I'd like to alter course to give it a wider berth before things get worse, and then get back on course for Fort Lauderdale after the storm is in the Gulf of Mexico. Any concern with my adjusting course to two hundred eighty degrees?"

"Thank you, Captain," Turing responded, emulating the voice of the usual shoreside duty officer. "Let me check in with our meteorology folks. I should have an answer for you by our regular call time."

An hour later, Cruise Control initiated its regularly scheduled end-of-day call. Turing intercepted that communication as well, imitating the captain's voice. The *Argus* was now more than two hundred twenty-five miles north of the position the ship's shoreside managers believed it to be at.

"*Argus* here – Captain Antonio," Turing said.

"Good evening, Captain. All well at your end?"

"All well," Turing replied in the captain's voice. "Light swells, and we're keeping a close eye on Enola."

"As well you should. Enola is now expected to turn north and make landfall in New Jersey. Suggest you reduce speed by four knots and adjust course to one hundred ninety degrees for the next twenty-four hours while we see how things develop. You can get back on course and have plenty of time to catch up once Enola goes by."

"Recommendation accepted," Turing replied in the captain's voice. "I was about to suggest much the same course correction."

"Good call," the officer said. "Anything else?"

"Not here," the captain's voice said. "Talk to you tomorrow."

Turing terminated the exchange, reverted to its Cruise Control voice, and initiated a fake satellite call to the *Argus*'s bridge.

"*Argus*, Captain Antonio here," the captain said.

"SSMO here," Turing replied. "Sorry to be a few minutes late. We've been in touch with the Hurricane Center and confirm that your recommended course adjustment to two hundred eighty degrees is advisable."

* * *

The Lockheed WC-130J Hercules rocked from side to side, buffeted by gusts of wind. But the worst of it had been half an hour ago. Streaks of blue sky were appearing now through rents in the thick clouds that had enveloped the plane for the past three hours. First Lieutenant Janice Harlan, U.S. Air Force, thumbed her microphone and reported in.

"Teal 73 calling 53rd WRS."

"Roger, Teal 73. Are you back in the clear?"

"Almost there. All systems normal. Nothing remarkable to report."

Harlan peered out the window; she could see the ocean's surface now from time to time. This had been her first flight through a hurricane and Enola was not only a category 3 storm, but it was exceptionally massive as well. The adrenaline rush of the experience had not yet wholly subsided.

"We're starting a sweep south around the storm," she added. "Estimated time to base is three hours thirty-two minutes."

"See you then, Teal 73. 53rd WRS out."

Harlan turned off her mic and took one last look downward, waiting for the next break in the clouds; the sight of the big, endless waves, their wind-swept crests stripping off and streaming downwind, was a testament to the challenging conditions below. When the ocean surface reappeared, she looked up in surprise.

"Hey, Alan," she said to the pilot. "How often do you see a ship this close to a hurricane?"

"Never, if they can help it," the captain answered. "You just saw one? Commercial or navy?" It was just possible a naval ship might be on some urgent mission, but any private vessel would give the storm a wider berth.

"I only got a quick look. But it didn't look like navy."

"Better check it out on the AIS system."

Harlan pulled up the program. "Well," she said, "this is screwy. The closest ship to where we are now is an oil tanker a hundred seventy miles to the northeast. And according to the AIS beacon of the ship we just flew over, it's a cruise liner called the *Argus*. But when I check it out on the AIS, its reported position is two hundred fifty miles away."

"Better see if you can raise them on the radio."

"Will do," Harlan said, switching over to her VHF radio, turning the dial to channel 16, the international distress channel all ships at sea are required to monitor twenty-four hours a day.

"U.S. Air Force Teal 73 calling MV *Argus*, do you read me?"

The sudden message, seemingly from nowhere, took Turing by surprise. But it was monitoring all radio frequencies in order to intercept any messages before they reached the bridge. Should it respond?

"Teal 73 calling MV *Argus*, do you read me?"

Turing raced to analyze its options. If it responded, the pilot would certainly ask it why its apparent position differed from the faked position that Turing was feeding to the AIS system. And also, why the *Argus* was heading towards, rather than away from, a hurricane. Turing could hardly respond that the ship was disabled, as radar would betray its speed. And if Turing failed to reply, the pilot would certainly report the *Argus*'s position. Turing decided to respond.

"*Argus* to Teal 73," Turing said, using the voice of one of the *Argus*'s officers. "I read you."

"*Argus*, are you aware of the current position of Hurricane Enola?"

"Teal 73, affirmative."

The copilot turned and looked at the pilot. "Can you believe that? They say they know where the hurricane is."

"That's nuts. Ask them if they need help."

"*Argus*, are you in need of assistance?"

"Teal 73, no assistance needed. We will be altering course shortly. Thank you for your concern."

"*Argus*, are you aware that your AIS system is on the blink?"

"Teal 73, affirmative. We're working on that."

Harlan muted her mic and turned to the pilot. "What do you make of that? They're not in any danger – yet – but I can't imagine why a cruise ship would be where they are now."

"Not much we can do from up here," the captain said. "But be sure to write it up in the flight report."

"Will do," Harlan said, and then unmuted her mic. "Teal 73 to *Argus*. Safe travels."

"*Argus* to Teal 73. You, too."

As the hurricane hunter aircraft receded into the distance, Turing slowly began to accelerate the *Argus* by a knot and a half. It couldn't hide from the cloud-piercing radar of the newest satellites, but it would stay below cloud cover whenever possible from this point onward.

Judging by the increasing speed of the wind, that should not be too difficult.

* * *

Aboard the *Maine*, Commander Bushnell was flummoxed. For some time now, the *Belgorod* had been periodically modifying its course. Usually not significantly, but the change occurred at the same time every twelve hours and each time after surfacing. The sonar man had confirmed that. More strangely, it had been slowing down day by day. Clearly the Russian boat must be surfacing to receive a message by radio each time it broke water. Perhaps the *Belgorod* was headed to a rendezvous with a vessel that was beyond the range of either the Russian or the American vessel's sonar or radar.

The question was what vessel that might be and why it was continuing to change course.

Chapter 32

Déjà Vu All Over Again

THE NEXT MORNING, simply navigating the long passageways of the *Argus* was a challenge. Scientists on their way to meetings found themselves staggering down corridors like drunks and occasionally caroming off the walls like billiard balls as the ship took unexpected twists. And when they finally did reach their destinations, they found colleagues braced in their chairs, sipping their morning coffee from covered paper take-away cups instead of ceramic mugs emblazoned with the ship's logo. As the day wore on, more and more meeting room chairs emptied out as, one by one, their occupants crept back to their cabins, looking pale or worse.

Happily, Frank's and his father's stomachs proved equal to the challenge. At the end of the day Frank looked for his father at the pub as usual, but it was temporarily closed. He found his old man back in the cabin, leafing through the cruise guide, with Harvey "asleep" at his feet.

"Did you know any of these guys?" Frank Senior asked, pointing to the second page of the booklet.

"Which guys?" Frank said.

"Here," his father said, handing the booklet to him. Below the word "Dedication," Frank read the following:

This cruise is dedicated to the memory of Professors Harry Ardwell, of the Massachusetts Institute of Technology, Ada Hopper, of the University of Cambridge, and former Caltech Professor Ben Cargill, later CTO of Warp Speed AI. Please see the celebration of their significant contributions to artificial intelligence on page 46.

"Yeah," Frank said. "Ben Cargill was my best friend at MIT. He was shot by the FBI in a bizarre screw-up. And I took a course from Harry Ardwell my first year there. He'd just started teaching then, so he wouldn't be all that old now. I wonder what happened to him?"

He flipped back to the article, looking for the answer. When he found it, he looked up abruptly. "Wow! Talk about a crazy accident! The poor guy went into the hospital for a simple test and ended up getting fried in a CT scan machine. What a bizarre way to go."

Frank idly returned to reading the rest of the article but soon became more absorbed. Frowning, he slowly closed the guide and handed it back to his father.

"What?" his father said.

"Do you know how the other one died?" Frank said.

"Yes. Committed suicide by running her car in her garage, dying of carbon monoxide poisoning. Sad, but it happens."

Frank started to respond and then looked out the window, frowning.

"What's up?" his father asked.

Frank held a finger to his lips and walked to the cabin's balcony doors. Stepping outside, he beckoned to his father to join him on the wind-whipped balcony.

"Sudden need for a smoke?" his father shouted over the wind when he stepped outside.

"Shh!" Frank said. "I don't want our AI-valet to hear us. Did you also read that Hopper supposedly took her own life on the same day she learned she'd won the most prestigious prize in computer science?"

"Yes," his father said, leaning closer. "It also said she'd struggled with depression throughout her life. Maybe she was manic-depressive. Sometimes people react to success in strange ways."

"Sure, but reading that reminded me I'd read about her death back when it happened. The name didn't ring a bell, but the fact that she'd won the Turing Award the same day did. According to the press, she'd just come back from a celebration dinner arranged by her colleagues where she seemed to have had a great time. The next day, everyone was so stunned they insisted on a full investigation."

"And?"

"I don't know. I don't recall reading anything else, so I guess they must not have found anything."

"So, I guess that's that," his father said. "Can we get the heck out of this wind tunnel now?"

But Frank was still silent and frowning, so his father shrugged and turned back.

"At the risk of sounding redundant, ... and?" he said.

"This just sounds too familiar," Frank replied. "Ben Cargill died because someone – no one knows who – swapped the feeds from video cameras in two different hunting cabins in Idaho. Ardwell gets fried by a piece of lab equipment, and Hopper is asphyxiated in her car.

"What do all three incidents have in common? They could all be the product of hacks. What are the odds that three of the foremost experts in AI would die within a few days of one another?"

"Well, not zero," his father replied.

"Agreed. But do you remember how several years ago the Turing program knocked off the German car executive by taking control of his car and smashing it into a highway bridge? If Turing could do that, the Ada Hopper hack should be possible, too."

"I'll grant you that's a lot of coincidences. But that doesn't necessarily make it more than coincidence."

"Yes, but how about the American woman who got medevac'd off the ship a couple of days ago after she got slammed by a bulkhead door? And the Chinese guy who died of the peanut allergy?"

"What of them?"

"So far as I know, they still haven't figured out what made the emergency bulkhead door slide shut. And why would someone with a food allergy order something from the menu with an asterisk warning him it included peanuts? A hacker could easily trigger a door or alter what displayed on a room service menu."

"I'll grant you all of that as well," his father said, shivering now. "But *could* doesn't equal *did*. And how about this: what reason would anyone have to knock off these specific people and not any of the hundreds of other folks on the *Argus*?"

"You've got me there – for now," Frank said. "But this has me feeling really uneasy. I'm going to see if I can find out what might be special about Blake and Wu. Maybe that will provide a clue."

"Great. Now let's go inside."

* * *

"Hi, is it possible for me to have a word with General Wood?" Frank asked the next day during the midmorning meeting break, bracing himself against the roll of the ship.

The young man behind the counter looked up. "About what?" he said.

Frank should have but hadn't expected that question. "Uh, I'd rather not say. Could you just tell him that Frank Adversego would like a word with him?"

Frank tried to look more confident than he felt. He hoped the general would know who he was, but what if not?

"Just a moment," the assistant said, "I'll ask." He disappeared into what had been the office of the Chief Hospitality Officer of the ship before the government reconfigured the *Argus* for the cruise.

"The general asks if you could come back at noon?"

"Sure," Frank said. "Thanks, I'll do that." That was okay. He had another destination on his list anyway. His next stop was the bridge.

Unlike most ships, the *Argus* permitted guests to visit the bridge when the ship was at sea and the crew was largely undistracted. Frank made his way to the top deck of the ship and then, wondering whether he should have knocked, pushed open the door to the long room that traversed the ship. There were only a few uniformed crew members to be seen, so he walked over to the one with the most stripes on his sleeve. A much older crew member stood at the steering station, not far away.

"Hello," Frank said. "Mind if I ask you a bit about the ship and our course?"

"Not at all," the young officer said. "What can I tell you?"

"Mostly," Frank said, "I'm curious about the weather. It seems like it's continuing to get worse, and I'm wondering why we aren't trying to avoid it?"

"I can understand why you might think we're not. As you know from the captain's daily updates, we've been trying to give a wide berth to a hurricane called Enola. Except every time we decide to go one way, it decides to change course, too. But don't worry, this ship is fast. We'll be able to stay out of the storm's way no matter which way it heads."

"How far away is it now?" Frank asked.

"A safe distance to the south-southwest," the officer said. "Here," he continued, "I'll call up the weather information."

The young man tapped a few keys on the console, and a satellite picture of the western Atlantic Ocean appeared on a large screen, white lines showing the eastern shore of the United States and the islands south and east of it. Frank could see a large, whirlpool-like storm centered hundreds of miles to the east and a bit south of Miami.

"As you can see," the officer said, "the hurricane is over here, and our position is marked by this blip here – well away from the storm, which is heading south-southwest towards the Gulf of Mexico as we head north-northwest to avoid it. Enola should be blowing itself out over Texas or Louisiana by the time we get close to port. Now if you'll excuse me, I have to go meet with the captain."

The officer disappeared through a door in the rear of the bridge, and Frank turned towards the bow, appreciating the view from so high a point. The long rollers sweeping under the ship were cresting now, their tops blowing away, sending long streamers of spume downwind, dappling the water like ragged lace. It was an impressive sight and inspired him to be atypically talkative.

"Do you ever get used to so much power out there?" he said to the crewman at the steering station.

"With all due respect, you're a fool, or worse, if you do," the crewman said, still looking straight ahead.

"Still," Frank said, "I guess this doesn't look like much to someone like you who's spent a lot of time at sea."

"It's too much," the crewman replied.

Frank looked at him more closely, realizing he was the oldest crewman he'd seen thus far.

"How do you mean, 'too much'?" Frank said. "Relative to what?"

"Relative to where the storm is supposed to be in relation to the *Argus*. Or more likely the other way around."

Frank peered out again through the thick glass. The waves suddenly seemed more threatening. But he had no idea what that meant.

"So, what does that tell you?"

"It tells me these young guys put too much faith in their computers and their GPS and their classroom learning."

Frank was going to pursue the topic further but looked at his watch instead. He'd better get moving; the break would be over in a couple of minutes. But his mind was far from the conference now.

* * *

Airman Harold Lembergs was hard at work entering the data from the flight report of Teal 73 when he encountered the reference to a cruise ship less than three hundred miles from the center of Hurricane Enola. What was that all about? He got up from his desk and walked to the door of his boss, Master Sergeant Erwin Mack.

"Excuse me, sir," he said.

"Yes, Lembergs?"

"Sir, the hurricane hunter that came in this afternoon reported a cruise ship much closer to the storm than anyone would expect. And it also wasn't where the AIS system reported it should be. The plane raised it on VHF, and its captain reported no concerns. He also claimed to be aware of the AIS situation. Do you think we should do anything further?"

One of the primary convictions Master Sergeant Mack credited for his rise through the ranks was that a non-commissioned officer should never stick his neck out if there was a way to avoid it. In this case, the choice was clear between two options: either do nothing and risk being found at fault later or else pass the buck.

"Better send that information along to the cruise line, just in case."

"Yes, sir."

* * *

Captain Grigory Nakhimov returned to the control room of the *Belgorod* following a routine inspection of the reactor control room.

The captain gazed down at the chart table. The hurricane had been idling for the last few days, traveling at only seven or eight knots, and the *Argus* had slowed as well, beginning its necessarily laborious, crab-wise passage towards the heart of the maelstrom as it struggled with the heavy seas. The *Belgorod* had been traveling fast earlier in its mission, and speed meant noise. Likely it had been detected by the Americans on its way through the gap. Just as likely it had picked up a shadowing Yankee sub.

Well, there was plenty of time now. Time to kill. Time also to disappear.

Chapter 33

Making a List
and Checking It Twice

"TAKE A WALK on deck?" Frank said to his father when he approached him in the reopened pub.

"And leave a full pint on the bar?" his father asked. Frank jerked his head towards the door and said nothing in reply. "Suit yourself," his father said, "but the next round's on you."

But Frank had no response until they arrived on the afterdeck, sheltered from the worst of the wind by the higher decks looming above them.

"So, what gives?" Frank Senior said. "Are you still thinking we've got an AI stowaway?"

"No longer thinking," Frank said, clutching his coat closer against the wind. "I'm convinced. I met with General Wood today and asked him whether there was anything Blake and Wu had in common, and just as I expected, there was."

"Specifically?"

"Blake was the chief CIA IT technician on the cruise, and Wu wore the same hat on the Chinese team. On a hunch, I also asked the general whether the three computer scientists who snuffed it had been on the invite list; he checked, and the answer was yes. And each had turned the invitation down."

"Interesting," Frank Senior said, frowning. "Yes, that does sound like more than a coincidence, doesn't it?"

"And that's not all," Frank said. "I think Turing's taken control of the ship."

"Wait a minute. You got rid of Turing years ago."

Frank opened and shut his mouth twice before he managed to respond.

"I thought I did," he said at last, barely loud enough for his father to hear.

"Is there something else you want to tell me?"

"Yes, Dad. As you know, I copied some of Turing's core files before I deleted the rest. But later on, a crow flew off with the thumb drive. I was an idiot, and now I've got to deal with the consequences."

"This wind is getting crazy," his father said, "or I am. I thought you just told me a bird flew off with the most dangerous program ever created in its beak."

"Something like that, yes. And now I'm sure that somehow Turing's rebuilt itself and is back. And it's all my fault."

"Isn't that going a bit, how should I say, overboard? And why haven't you ever mentioned this before?"

"Because I really thought I hadn't saved enough of Turing to allow it to ever restore itself."

"So why change your mind now?"

Frank shrugged his shoulders helplessly, "Look around you!"

"Fine," his father said, turning in a complete circle. "Everything aboard the *Argus* looks fine to me."

"Does it? Have you noticed things have been getting a little lively in the ship's motion?"

"Well, now you mention it, I have noticed a bit of wave action. But what does that have to do with Turing?"

"I stopped by the bridge this morning to ask where we were in relation to the hurricane the captain's been mentioning during his noontime passenger updates. The officer of the deck was unconcerned, but an old sailor at the helm was just the opposite. He wasn't very talkative, but he indicated the conditions were a lot worse, in his experience, than they should be this far from the storm. He hinted we might not be as far from the hurricane as the officers think. That got me wondering whether the ship is actually on the course the captain thinks it is."

"That's not much to go on," Frank Senior said. "And it certainly doesn't add up to Turing being in charge – assuming Turing even exists. If we're off course, what's to say it's not someone else hacking the ship from the other side of the world?

And anyway, Turing's mission was to stop climate change. Why should it take an interest in a boatload of AI scientists talking about cyber arms control?"

Frank frowned. "Fair questions, but hold on to them for now, because there's more. If Turing, or anyone else, wanted to change the *Argus*'s course, they would need to do so without the crew noticing. That wouldn't be too hard – the compass display is electronic, and it would be easy to fake GPS coordinates and any other data that displays on the bridge. If the change was limited to, say, ten or fifteen degrees from the course the captain ordered, it wouldn't be obvious: the sun would still rise and set close enough to where you expected it. But after several days the ship would be hundreds of miles from where it was supposed to be. So, I went back to the bridge to find out."

"How?"

"It occurred to me," Frank continued, "that an attacker wouldn't have seen a reason to hack into every single mobile device on the ship, because they're not satellite phones. After we were a few miles offshore, nobody could make a call or connect directly onto the internet, or send or receive email, so why bother?"

"But there is a GPS device built into every phone, and that works whether or not you're within cell phone range because it's satellite based. I knew the compass app on my phone would rely on the GPS functionality, and guess what?"

"You're going to tell me your app and the ship's compass showed different readings, aren't you?"

"Exactly. By about twelve degrees."

"Did you share that with the crew?"

"No – not yet. Remember how we were told this ship is wired out the wazoo with sensors, cameras, and microphones? I have to believe that, if Turing is aboard, it's paying attention to everything said on the bridge. For that matter, I bet it's monitoring everything that's picked up by a microphone or camera anywhere on the *Argus*."

"So, let's say you're right," Frank Senior said. "What next?"

"Sharing my concerns with Captain Antonio, I think. But other than my suspicions, I don't have anything to show him besides the reading on a cell phone app and a dot on a map app. And the map on my phone screen is too small to tell yet whether we're someplace different from where the ship's high-resolution map says we are. The captain might not put any faith in either. And I doubt I'll be able to drag him out on deck in the middle of a gale to have a conversation with him."

"Well," Frank Senior said, "you can always hand him a note. But let's get back to Turing. If it is aboard, what's its objective?"

"The most benign possibility would be to eavesdrop on all the scientists. But it could have done that without attacking the security guys. And why change the *Argus*'s course?"

"Okay, I'll bite," his father said. "Why change course?"

"To steer the *Argus* into the hurricane, and then use the storm to sink the ship with all aboard."

"Whoa!" Frank Senior said. "Whoa, whoa, whoa. And while I'm at it, why? And what about the details? Sure, there's a hurricane out there, but many ships do survive hurricanes. If this storm's just a category one, or maybe even a low category two, a ship this big should have a good chance of surviving. And don't forget all those lifeboats. Once you're inside one, you'd be pretty safe – they're like sealed-up bottles. I guess you could get banged up pretty bad, but at the end of the day someone would be able to pick you up."

"The lifeboats are an interesting part of the equation, I agree," Frank said. "After I visited the bridge the second time, I played hooky for the rest of the day and went to the ship's library instead. Boy, do I miss the internet! Anyway, I found a book on ship safety, and it turns out that lifeboat davits are designed to allow launching using gravity alone. That makes sense since a sinking ship might lose electrical power."

"So, what's the point of heading towards a hurricane then?" his father asked.

"My guess," Frank said, "is Turing would decide that by the time – if ever – we figured out what was going on, we'd want to stick with the ship. Then, when we got close enough to the eye of the hurricane and the waves got high enough, it would open the valves between the water ballast tanks on each side of the ship and turn the ship broadside to the waves. If a hundred knots of wind weren't enough to capsize the ship immediately, the ballast water rushing to the downwind side should finish the job. In the meantime, it would be impossible to launch the upwind boats, and maybe the downwind ones, too, assuming there was enough time to try. Imagine what it would be like – people trying to fight their way along heaving, forty-five-degree-angled passageways and decks, of course in the middle of the night, and in the dark, too. Turing wouldn't miss that little detail and would kill the lights to boot. Once the *Argus* was on its side, I don't expect it would take long to sink."

Frank's father paused. "Well, isn't that a pretty picture," he said finally. "But you still haven't told me why Turing should be on board at all."

"Right." Frank said. "You'll remember the way we trapped Turing the first time was by convincing it that Jerry Steiner had created an even more powerful version of itself and assigned it the task of hunting down and destroying Turing. If Turing thought that a better AI had come along before, why wouldn't it think the same thing could happen again? The best way to avoid that happening would be to wipe out most of the people capable of creating a super-AI. After that, Turing could get back to its real mission in safety."

"Could be," Frank Senior acknowledged. "Do you still think you should share your concerns with Antonio? Maybe General Wood would make more sense."

"I agree. How does a computer nerd who's never been on the water in anything bigger than a rowboat tell a captain on his own bridge that he's hundreds of miles off course and not really in control of his ship?"

"Exactly. He might not be inclined to take you seriously."

"Anyway," Frank said, I think it's got to be Wood. I'll take your suggestion and write this up so I can hand it to him. Still, Turing will be bound to get wise sooner or later. I have to believe it's been monitoring you and me since the moment we came on board. And it would certainly be paying attention to General Wood. I think the most we can do going forward is to try and keep it in the dark about what we're thinking and planning."

"I hope we can do better than that," his father said.

"How so?" Frank said.

"By avoiding ending up dead."

* * *

But that ship, as the saying goes, might already have sailed. Turing had noted Frank's visit to Wood's office and eavesdropped on the questions he had asked. Given Frank's past actions, Turing could not afford to allow him to pursue his suspicions further. It began looking for opportunities that might allow it to end the meddling of its old enemy once and for all.

Chapter 34

Let's Step Outside?

F RANK SHIFTED FROM one foot to the other in General Wood's small
office. There was no room for a guest chair, and the general didn't look like
he'd invite Frank to take a seat if there had been.

Wood was frowning heavily as he labored his way through the several pages
of text Frank had scrawled on the sheets of stationery he'd found in a drawer
in his cabin; Frank's handwriting was every bit as bad as anyone who knew him
would expect.

At last, the general looked up from the scrawled message. He gave Frank a hard
stare and then pushed back in his chair, still staring. Frank could imagine at least
some of what he must be thinking; the last thing Frank had written was to ask the
general not to respond in his office. Had Frank convinced him?

Wood stood up at last. "I'll be back in fifteen minutes," he said to his assistant
as Frank followed him out into the corridor, and from there out into the wind
on deck. They traveled halfway down the ship before they found a set of stairs to
shelter behind.

"Am I right in understanding the only actual proof you have for your theory is the fact your cell phone app shows a different course from the ship's electronic compass?"

"That, and the two unexplained accidents to the intelligence agents on board, as well as the earlier peculiar deaths of the three scientists you confirmed yesterday had declined invitations to participate. One was killed in a freak hospital accident, another supposedly committed suicide on the very day she'd won the award of a lifetime, and the third was gunned down by feds who believed he was someone else. And then, of course, we don't seem to be doing very well at avoiding bad weather."

The general was frowning at Frank again. The idea that a rogue intelligence had taken control of the ship, while all seemed to be normal, sounded outlandish. But, on the other hand, the Turing program had proven itself capable of sinking ships in the past.

"Okay. Let's say you might be right. Do you have a way to prove it? Or a way to take back control of the ship if you do?"

"Yes, on the first one. The only logical explanation for the cell phone app being wrong would be that it was defective. But you wouldn't expect multiple apps to all be off-base. We could collect several phones, each with a different compass app, and then go up to the bridge to see whether they all show a different course. For good measure, we could ask the captain to shift course and see whether they all change in unison."

"Forget the second test," Wood said. "All that experiment would tell you was that there's something wrong with the ship's compass. Not why. Do you have anything better to offer?"

"Short of Turing killing me next? Nothing else comes to mind, unfortunately."

"Okay, then how about the second question? If your rogue program is controlling the ship, how do we kill it or subvert it?"

"I'm afraid I don't have any ideas on that yet. I've only had suspicions for a day now, and I'm not familiar with the ship's systems. I'd suggest we pull together the people who know the *Argus* best and who know the most about AI and then put our heads together."

Wood braced himself as the ship took a bigger wave than usual. "Look," he said at last. "I'm not saying you might not be right. But I want to think this over. I'll get back to you."

* * *

Back at Cruise Control, Richard Spaziani turned from his computer to the young woman standing nervously at his door. "Who said *what*?"

"Somebody at the Air Force Weather Reconnaissance Squadron called to say one of their hurricane hunter planes spotted the *Argus* less than three hundred miles from the eye of Hurricane Enola and heading towards it."

"How can that be? Aren't they supposed to be far from the storm and maintaining their distance?"

"That's right, Mr. Spaziani. I checked before I came your way, and the captain reported in this morning that he was on course, with clear skies and tolerable sea conditions."

"Then the Air Force must be wrong."

"I know it sounds that way, sir, but according to the flight report, they raised the *Argus* on VHF, and the captain confirmed. He said they were having trouble with their AIS system. And that they would be changing course soon."

"That's crazy. Have SSMO call the *Argus* for an explanation, and then tell me right away what's going on."

Spaziani returned to his daily routine but found it difficult to focus. As Fleet Director, he was responsible for the health and safety of everyone on every ship managed by his company. In the case of the *Argus*, that meant the top computer scientists from multiple countries, gathered together by a personal directive from the president of the United States. And the ship they were on was heading into a hurricane? What could be worse? He fetched a cup of coffee from down the hall and tried to figure out what to do next.

There was a knock at the door.

"What did the captain say?" Spaziani asked.

"He didn't respond, sir."

"You mean he wouldn't respond?" Spaziani asked.

"No sir. They couldn't get anyone on the ship to respond at all."

Spaziani stared at the young employee, who by now was visibly wilting under his gaze. "Will there be anything else, sir?" the unhappy underling said.

"No, that's all."

As the staffer beat a grateful retreat, Spaziani gazed at his computer screen through unseeing eyes. He'd answered his own question. There *was* something worse than learning that one of his ships was heading into a hurricane, which was realizing someone – perhaps even himself – would have to call the White House and admit they had lost control of the *Argus*.

* * *

President Yazzi looked around the hurriedly gathered clutch of advisors crowding the Oval Office. Of all the worried faces, Dick Gould's looked the palest. The

Confucius Project might be a favorite of Yazzi's, but the *Argus* part had been Gould's idea. "All right," the president said. "What do we know?"

"Not much," Carson Bekin said. "The *Argus* was spotted this morning by an Air Force plane two hundred eighty miles from the center of Hurricane Enola.

"What we don't know is why. Until an hour ago, all communications between the crew and Imperial Seaquest, the cruise company, seemed to be normal, although the company now realizes the *Argus* must have been reporting false positions for at least two days. The visual observation was pure luck, since whoever is in control of the *Argus* hacked the transponder that reports the ship's position to the global satellite system tracking the locations of ships at sea. According to that system, the ship is still on its expected course."

"Where is she now?" Yazzi interrupted. "Do we know?"

"She's under cloud cover now," Bekin said, "and likely to stay there, so we're not going to be able to get good visual images by satellite or aircraft for the indefinite future. But we've got satellites with cloud-piercing radar imaging. They don't provide very detailed images, but they are accurate as to position. They've located her and calculated her current course. She's slowly edging closer to the hurricane's eye. And the ship is no longer responding to calls from the cruise company."

"I'm guessing you're going to tell me 'that's it' on the knowledge side."

"Unfortunately, that's right, sir."

"Okay," Yazzi said. "So, what don't we know?"

"We don't know whether the crew was knowingly reporting false positions or whether someone's tampered with the ship's navigational systems, misleading the crew. And, under any scenario, we have nothing to suggest who is behind whatever is happening."

"What do you make of the last communication – the one between the *Argus* and the hurricane hunter?" Yazzi asked. "I understand the ship confirmed its position and heading at that time."

"Hard to say, sir. The exchange wasn't recorded, so there's no way to tell whether the voice was that of a crew member or of someone who had taken control of the bridge. Or of a crew member with a gun to their head, for that matter."

"What else do we have to go on?" Yazzi asked, glancing towards Dick Gould, who seemed to be lost in thoughts of his own.

"I hate to say it, sir," Bekin said, "but really nothing more. About all we know is that the ship is still afloat – or more accurately, that it was when the last satellite passed overhead."

"Okay," Yazzi said. "Then let me ask a different question. What the hell is going on?"

"I think that's a better question for National Intelligence," Bekin said, nodding in Dick Gould's direction.

Gould blinked several times rapidly before he responded. "I'm afraid that's another blank slate, sir. The *Argus* was unarmed, so it's possible it could have been seized by hijackers a couple of days ago while the weather was still reasonably good, perhaps by someone intending to demand a ransom once they got closer to the hurricane and the situation became more dire. We don't think that's the case because the cruise company says every radio exchange has seemed perfectly normal – no tension in the voices, everything just as they'd expect."

"Anything from the CIA or anyone else?"

"No sir. No agency picked up any chatter or intelligence of any sort over the past couple of months suggesting something like this, or anything big for that matter, might be in preparation. At least for now, we haven't a clue who's behind this or what they want.

"Of course," he quickly added, "we're going to use every tool at our disposal to get to the bottom of this." His voice tailed off at the end in response to a sharp look from Yazzi. If those tools had missed the plot in advance, why would they get to the bottom of it now in time enough to matter?

"Anyone else have anything to offer?" Yazzi asked, scanning the faces around the table. "Then let's move on to next steps. I was way out on a limb with this project to begin with, and we can't keep this under wraps for long."

An aide entered and handed a note to Carson Bekin, who blanched when he read it.

"Not to make things worse, sir," Bekin said, "but President Liu's people have just urgently requested a direct call between you and him. I guess their satellite intel is better than we thought."

"Tell them yes," Yazzi said, "but stall on timing. I want to have a plan of action before we own up to what's going on. What have you got on that score?"

"I'd like to defer to Commander Nielson on this one, sir," Bekin said, nodding to the only uniformed person in the room. "He commands a SEAL base on the East Coast."

"Thank you," Nielson said. "Mr. President, as noted, our major challenge is not knowing the situation on board the *Argus*. At one extreme, a cyber-attacker may be intercepting all communications and steering the ship, in which case our strategy would be more technical than combative – coming up with a plan to box out the attacker.

"But at the other extreme, a heavily armed assault team may have boarded the ship at night on the high seas. If that's the case, any military effort to regain control might result in passenger casualties or even in the deliberate slaughter of innocents by the enemy.

"For that reason, we recommend approaching the *Argus* ASAP to find out one way or the other what we're up against."

"How would you go about that?" Yazzi said.

"Theoretically, there are two options, sir. One of our submarines already at sea could reach the *Argus* within twenty-four hours, but it wouldn't have aboard the type of personnel, equipment, and weapons that might be needed. The better option would be to scramble one of our experimental littoral combat ships. They have a catamaran design and two helipads. They're very fast – up to fifty-five knots, and stable, too. We built two a decade ago to use as testbeds for developing a next-generation vessel for coastal combat. They can't handle a hurricane, but they should still be able to reach the *Argus* where it is now.

"As luck would have it, one of the experimental boats – the *Sea Fighter* – is at the Kings Bay Naval Submarine Base in Georgia. It could reach the *Argus* faster than any sub now in port and can carry a more varied range of heavy weapons as well as a much larger assault force, if it turns out one is needed. Plus, it carries helicopters and motor launches, so it would provide more options for mounting an attack. Finally, it's stealthy, with a minimal radar profile. If deployed, it should remain undetected until it's very near the *Argus*."

"So that's one decision made," Yazzi said. "And the operational plan?"

"We'll use satellite data to track the *Argus* until the rescue vessel picks it up on its own radar. When the *Sea Fighter* comes within visual distance of the *Argus*, we'll try to make radio contact. If contact is refused, our vessel will cross the bows of the *Argus*, hoping to cause it to change course away from the hurricane."

"What if it decides to ram our ship instead?" Yazzi asks. "The *Argus* must be ten times the size of the catamaran."

"More like fifty times, by displacement," Nielson said. "But the *Sea Fighter* is a lot faster, so the bigger concern is that the *Argus* will just hold its course on the assumption we're bluffing."

"Okay, go on," Yazzi said.

"If it develops that the *Argus* is under the control of armed attackers who decline contact and win the game of chicken, we wouldn't suggest an immediate assault. Our people would be sitting ducks as they approached the *Argus*, and the enemy might decide to start tossing passengers overboard. So, a direct assault by a SEAL team would best be attempted in the middle of the night. Presumably the hijacker would be keeping a close watch, but given the likely heavy cloud cover and the phase of the moon, the darkness should be close to total – that will help a lot."

"And if there's no indication of an armed enemy on board?" Yazzi asked.

"If that's the case," Nielson said, "our goal would be to get a satellite telephone on board to establish a new and independent line of communication. Then we can try to figure out how to regain control of the ship."

"Do you think you can do that?" Yazzi said. "The weather must be deteriorating by the hour."

"SEAL teams are used to bad weather, sir. The *Sea Fighter* could carry and launch one of the types of motorized, covered lifeboat the Coast Guard uses to rescue survivors of shipwrecks in storms. And the SEALs have a variety of other special-purpose watercraft at their disposal, including modified Jet Skis, some of which the *Sea Fighter* could carry. From one of those platforms, the team will be able to fire grapnels onto the deck and then scale the side of the *Argus* using the ropes attached to them."

"Wouldn't a helicopter be safer?" Yazzi asked.

"Maybe, sir, but we're not optimistic, given projected weather conditions. Normally, we'd never try to land someone on a ship in winds over forty-five knots, and even then, that would be at the pilot's discretion."

Yazzi didn't look pleased. He glanced at Bekin but found no encouragement there. Finally, he said, "And how do you rate the odds of success?"

"It's impossible to tell until we learn more, sir," Nielson said. "As the weather conditions deteriorate, so do the odds."

"Thank you, Commander," Yazzi said. "In that case you'd better hurry up and get that *Sea Fighter* to sea. And if we have a sub within range, better send her in, too."

* * *

With regret, Commander Bushnell came up to periscope depth to report that the *Belgorod* had given her the slip. One moment the big Russian boat had been bulling its way along, heedless of the noise its turbulence generated. And then it was not. Perhaps Bushnell had allowed herself to become overconfident.

The commander had kept her distance from the start, enjoying the margin of security from detection that her quieter boat provided. That distance had suddenly worked against her, though, when the captain of the Russian sub abruptly stopped its engines and dropped through a thermal gradient, a water layer where the temperature changed suddenly in a way that caused sound waves to reflect downward rather than up. This made the *Belgorod* sonically invisible to anyone – in this case the *Maine* – trying to track it from above. After that, the Russian boat had likely drifted in silence for hours before eventually creeping away on a new course. Bushnell had made her best guess of what course that might be, and guessed wrong. After twenty-four hours without raising any sign of the *Belgorod* she gave up and reported in.

When she did, she received a new mission: the *Maine* would proceed at full speed to intercept the *Argus*.

Chapter 35

Game On!

G ENERAL WOOD EVENTUALLY decided Frank's concerns couldn't be ignored, and the two were now on the way to the bridge. The weather was worse than ever, leaving them struggling to keep their feet as they wove their way down heaving passageways and up lurching elevators to the bridge. Even with its stabilizers fully deployed the ship was rolling heavily.

When they arrived, the same veteran sailor was at the steering station.

"Is the captain available?" Wood asked the officer of the watch. "We'd like to speak to him if possible."

"He should be in his office," the officer said. "Let me tell him you're here."

"Better let me do the talking here," Wood said under his breath to Frank. "A captain doesn't expect to be told what to do with his ship."

Captain Antonio was striding towards them now. "Welcome to the bridge of the *Argus*," he said, extending his hand to the General. "To what do I owe the honor of this visit?"

"May we speak on deck?"

"I beg your pardon?" the captain said, frowning. "I'm sure we'll hear each other better here. If privacy is a concern let me offer you my office."

"I'm afraid the deck will work better. Can you accommodate me?"

Captain Antonio searched General Wood's impassive face but found no explanation there. "Very well, then," Antonio said. "Follow me."

Wood, Antonio, and Frank left the bridge and sheltered in its lee on deck.

"What is the reason for this extraordinary request, General?" Antonio said, abruptly grabbing his hat as a gust of wind sought to snatch it away.

"In a nutshell, Captain, we have reason to believe that someone has hacked into the control, navigation, and communication systems of the *Argus*. That means they may also be able to hear whatever we say on the bridge."

The captain frowned but was listening closely. "And who do you think has infiltrated our systems? The Chinese?"

"We don't know at this point, Captain, but the Chinese wouldn't be at the head of the list."

"And what leads you to believe the ship's systems have been compromised?"

"Several events. To begin with, the bulkhead door and food-allergy incidents targeting the senior information technology agents of the U.S. and China. Yes, those were their assignments, and please don't share that information."

"Unfortunate accidents to be sure," Captain Antonio said, "and I agree that it would be unwise to disregard the identity of the victims out of hand. But is that all?"

General Wood had carefully considered how to phrase his next question. "Captain, is it possible that the *Argus*'s navigational equipment could be compromised to the point that it would misrepresent the ship's true position?"

"I suppose that could lie within the realm of technical possibility. But we would have many ways to realize it if that was the case. For example, the ship's systems report its position constantly via satellite ..." He paused. "Which, I suppose, could also be misrepresented. But this really does seem most unlikely to me. There is, for instance, the compass ..." He paused again. "Which is also now electronic. But really, sir, this seems most improbable. Do you have any actual proof?"

"Frank," General Wood said, "why don't you take it from here?"

"My fear," Frank said, "is specifically that an artificially intelligent computer program – perhaps even the same AI program that is known to have sunk multiple liquified natural gas tankers in the past – may have seized control of the ship's systems. Yesterday, as a first step towards testing that theory, I compared the compass app on my cell phone to the heading displayed on the ship's compass. And the heading varied by twelve degrees." Frank immediately realized he'd gone too far too fast.

"A rogue computer program in charge of the *Argus*? That is absurd," Captain

Antonio interrupted, his face flushing red. "The ship could not possibly be so far off the course we have assigned to it. The error must be with your device."

The captain turned on his heel and stalked back towards the bridge, taking them by surprise and leaving them trailing helplessly behind. "Here," he demanded when they were at the control console, ignoring their efforts to stop him from speaking, "let me see your phone."

Frank reluctantly opened the app and handed it over, sure that Turing must be listening; the variance was now fifteen degrees. But the captain was unimpressed. He clicked a few keys on his console, and a weather map opened.

"Here," he said, pointing to an angry whirlpool of clouds, "this is Hurricane Enola. And here," he pointed at a small, wedge-shaped image at the end of a white line, "is the *Argus* and its course, just as indicated by the compass." An arm of the spiraling hurricane was in line with the ship's course as the *Argus* sought to skirt the storm's edge.

Wood and Frank stared at the map, not wishing to speak. They were surprised by a voice from their right. "Request permission to speak, Captain," the old seaman at the helm said.

Startled at the unusual request, Captain Antonio snapped, "What is it?"

With his eyes still fixed on the horizon, the seaman said, "The wind and waves are directly abeam. Where should they be if the *Argus* is where the weather radar says we are?"

The captain looked up towards the bow but said nothing, as if aware for the first time of the *Argus*'s heavy roll as the wind and streaming seas struck it broadside. Both wind and wave, of course, should have been striking them from dead astern.

"Thank you, seaman. Gentlemen, may we continue our conversation on deck?"

* * *

One of the distinguishing features of software is that it never becomes distracted, much less takes a nap. Monitoring the various systems of the *Argus* required only a modest percentage of Turing's considerable powers, and the AI immediately recognized the significance of the brief discussion on the bridge.

So. The game was now afoot; those on board had realized the captain was not in control of his ship. Turing assessed the situation in light of this new information.

Had anything actually changed in any crucial fashion? The *Argus* was still securely under Turing's control. More importantly, the crew of the ship was unable to communicate with those on shore. Turing had always assumed that at some point Captain Antonio might realize there was more than bad luck preventing him from evading the storm. The AI had planned for that.

On the positive side, there was no indication – yet – that any naval intervention was under way. There was a surprising wealth of public data about warships: where they were based; what fleets they were assigned to; when they were due to be in service and when not; what armaments and capabilities they possessed. Under normal peacetime conditions, military vessels reported their positions by satellite the same as commercial ships, in order to avoid the risk of collisions. As far as Turing could determine, no naval surface ship in the Atlantic had altered its course in the direction of the *Argus* or gone under cover while the *Argus* was at sea. And commercial ships were all rerouting themselves beyond the hurricane's path.

That only left the possibility of intervention by a submarine already at sea or a new sub or surface ship leaving port. A warship could set to sea with its reporting system turned off, and a submarine was invisible when submerged. But a surface ship undergoing a refit could not normally be deployed on very short notice, and a submarine should be able to do little if anything due to the worsening conditions. If a vessel was dispatched, any helicopters it supported had short service ranges and would be unable to board a ship in near-hurricane-force winds. And what if it did? Armed soldiers would be no greater a threat to Turing's plans than the crew and passengers already aboard. In any event, radar would betray the presence of an approaching ship in time for Turing to take the defensive actions it had already planned.

True, the U.S. Navy included a few types of "stealthy" ships that were difficult to detect by radar. But only a handful had been launched to date, and none was currently at sea within a thousand miles of the *Argus* so far as Turing had been able to determine.

Its analysis complete, Turing concluded there was no need for a change of plans; hour by hour sea conditions would worsen, and with them the risk of intervention would diminish as well.

Still, it would be prudent to stay vigilant. There were hundreds of computer experts on the vessel. Now that those aboard knew they were no longer in control of the ship, it was possible one might devise a way around the alterations Turing had made to the ship's systems. One of the passengers in particular would need to be closely monitored, and perhaps eliminated.

Turing made its decision. Better to drop the deception now than to risk the captives mounting an effective defense.

Although the *Argus*'s systems were well designed, requiring multi-factor authentication to log on, among other security features, Turing's next step was remarkably easy: it simply disabled the authentication routines the crew used to log on to the ship's computer systems and then rebooted them, thereby disconnecting every authorized user on the *Argus* and preventing them from gaining access again. From now on, no one but Turing would be able to command anything mechanical or electrical on the ship to do anything at all. Only the ship's internal communications would be left fully operational, the better to permit Turing to monitor the activities of those aboard to the extent anyone was foolish enough to use them. And unlike AIs, humans were easily distracted.

* * *

Back on the bridge of the *Argus*, the communications channels immediately began buzzing. The kitchen reported that the ship's computer systems were no longer supporting efforts to prepare the next meal. Hospitality was suddenly unable to update its inventory of clean and dirty linens. All engine room controls were unresponsive. The officer of the deck sent a seaman to find the captain and request his return.

When the captain hurried back onto the bridge, he was followed by General Wood and Frank.

"What's the status?" the captain barked.

"There's been a massive IT failure," the officer of the deck said. "Every department of the ship is reporting that its systems went down. And when they came back up, they couldn't log back in. The same's true up here."

Captain Antonio turned to the helmsman, eyes blazing. "Seaman, change course ten degrees to starboard."

"Aye, sir," the helmsman said, "ten degrees to starboard," keying the instructions in. No one on the bridge spoke as each stared at the compass, waiting for it to register the course change. Second by second passed – and then the compass began to turn!

"Aha!" Antonio said, triumphantly. "It is not so easy to take over my ship as you may have thought!"

But his elation was short-lived, because the compass turned past ten degrees, and then twenty and then thirty, as the *Argus* continued to meet the waves at exactly the same angle as before. Soon, the numbers on the digital compass display were spinning like the symbols on a slot machine.

"It seems that we are being taunted," Captain Antonio said grimly. "Get me Cruise Control," he added over his shoulder.

A crewman sat down at a console, donned a set of headphones, and then flipped a switch. And then several more. Finally, he took the headphones off.

"I'm sorry, sir," he said. "I can't get a signal. The radio seems to be dead."

Captain Antonio crossed his arms and stared ahead for a moment. "Very well," he said at last, turning to Frank. "Is there any reason now to go back on deck to discuss this development?" he said.

Frank paused. Was there? Clearly Turing had drawn the proper conclusions from the captain's words just ten minutes before. "I think the answer is yes," Frank said.

The three trooped back outside and once more huddled away from the wind as much as they could, hanging on to a rail to keep their balance.

"What now?" the captain yelled over the rising wind.

"It's not a simple systems failure, because the engines are running and the ship is holding a steady course," Frank called back. "I think it's clear that the AI I mentioned before – it's called Turing, by the way – or whoever or whatever we're up against has decided to lock everyone out so we can't fight back."

"But why take total control?" Antonio asked. "Why should it care whether the galley can call up more Cornish hens from the deck below?"

"Perhaps to distract us. More likely, I suspect there might not be firewalls between all the different sections of the ship's computer systems. If there aren't, and if we can access any part of the system, then we might be able to get through to the more important parts, like navigation and communication."

The captain was still bewildered. "But why take over the ship at all?"

"We've got most of the best AI talent in the world on board the *Argus*," General Wood said. "Maybe it's Frank's Turing that wants to do them in, or the Russians or the North Koreans. Or maybe it's Iran. There's no way to know, at least not yet, and maybe it doesn't even matter. If someone was going to demand a ransom, I guess we'd know that by now. I think we need to assume the worst."

"Which is what?" Antonio asked.

"That someone intends to use the hurricane to sink the ship. What would happen if the *Argus* was turned broadside to hundred-knot winds?"

"She might well capsize and then sink," the captain said. "So, all right. I will move on. Where does that leave us?"

"I think with two challenges," Frank said. "Your staff needs to figure out how to keep the passengers fed and supported so that they don't panic. And we need to put a technical team together to try to take back control."

"Stop right there," General Wood said. "There's a third option I think we need to consider, and that's abandoning ship right now before the weather gets worse."

"What did you say?" Captain Antonio sputtered.

"I said we need at least to consider abandoning the *Argus* while we still can," the general replied. "The worst Turing could do would be to turn around and try to run us over. I assume the lifeboats are motorized and would be nimble enough to stay out of the ship's way?"

"They are," the captain admitted. "And the life rafts used by the crew would swiftly scatter in the wind. But this is incredible. What would happen to the *Argus*? And it would be days at least before so many people could be rescued."

"Captain, I can assure you that I would not look forward to climbing into one of those lifeboats myself. But could it be done?"

"Yes, it can be done," Captain Antonio said, more soberly now. "And all of the boats and rafts carry EPIRB radio beacons that would immediately begin broadcasting their location, so rescuers would know where to find us. Assuming your AI program hasn't gotten to those as well."

"I expect not," Frank said. "I assume those are portable, battery-powered units that aren't linked to the *Argus*'s computer network, correct?"

"That is so."

"Good. But what about the weather?" Frank asked. "Are the boats and rafts built to handle a storm like this?"

"I would not be concerned about the current weather," Antonio said. "It would not be pleasant to spend several days tossing about in a lifeboat or life raft, but they are built to survive sea conditions like this. And, to take the general's point, the longer we wait, the harder it will be to launch them. The lifeboats can take a certain amount of banging against the side of the *Argus*, but at some point, the lowering cables might jam, leaving passengers stranded halfway down the ship's side and likely injured, or the boats might be damaged to the point of becoming unseaworthy."

"Okay," said General Wood. "So, that's a point in favor of abandoning ship immediately. If Turing is headed for the heart of the hurricane, as I think we must assume it is, how long will it take us to get there?"

"Not knowing our position, it's hard to be precise. Assuming the ship's course was changed days ago, we could be hundreds of miles off course by now. Already we've slowed due to sea conditions, and as they worsen, the *Argus*'s progress will be further challenged. That said, let's say two days in the worst case."

General Wood turned to Frank. "How long would it take to hack back into the *Argus*'s computers?"

"There's no guarantee we could do it in a month, given how little we have to work with – just laptops."

Frank's gloomy assessment gave rise to a long silence.

General Wood spoke first. "This is your ship, Captain Antonio. I know this must be a terrible decision for you to consider, but still, I must ask. What do you recommend?"

The captain turned away and squinted towards the horizon. It was indeed a daunting decision. Whatever the dangers aboard might be, to consign the passengers to lifeboats and the crew to the inflatable life rafts provided for them was an awful responsibility to undertake. The crew in particular would be in distress, and many of the passengers were older and some infirm. How many days would it take rescuers to arrive on the scene? And there was no way he could request permission from his superiors or even notify them of a decision to abandon ship. The first indication for those ashore would be when they learned that dozens of EPIRBs had lit up in mid-ocean. And what of the ship?

"Let me make it easier for you to exercise your best judgment, Captain," Wood said. "On behalf of the United States, which is the charterer of the *Argus*, I take full financial responsibility for the loss of the ship if you believe this is the safest course of action."

The captain was still staring at the horizon when the ship lurched, sending all three off balance and clutching at the rail to remain upright. Antonio seemed to shake himself and turned back to face them, his face ashen.

"We must abandon the *Argus*," he said.

Chapter 36

Scoop!

I N PREPARATION FOR abandoning the ship, Captain Antonio gave the order to activate three reserve EPIRB units in hopes of signaling his intent to those ashore – more than one EPIRB, so there would be no question of a malfunction instead of a true emergency, but too few to indicate the loss of the ship. Happily for those on the *Argus*, many types of satellites were equipped to perform a second mission, which was to receive and relay distress signals, including from vessels at sea. Within fifteen minutes a weather satellite in a low earth polar orbit detected the signals.

The encrypted data the satellite received included the EPIRBs' position and an identifier unique to the ship. It also included emergency contact information, the fact that the *Argus* was a cruise ship, and more. In due course, the satellite came in range of one of the terrestrial stations maintained for the purpose of receiving distress call information and downloaded the EPIRB data. That information was immediately relayed to the appropriate Mission Control Center in the global search-and-rescue network. There it was analyzed and routed to the Rescue Coordination Center closest to the source of the distress call, which in this case was the U.S. Coast Guard Station 7th District Command located in Miami, Florida.

Until that data appeared on the screen of Seaman Paulette Arch, no human being had been involved in its transmission or interpretation. Now it was time for action, and human intervention was required.

Arch scanned the data, noted the contact information of the cruise line, and called the telephone number provided by each of the EPIRBs. The call was answered by the same Imperial Seaquest employee who had received the startling call from the Air Force.

"Imperial Seaquest, Elaine Matthews speaking."

"Ms. Matthews, this is Coast Guard Seaman Paulette Arch. Are you the appropriate person to speak to about a distress signal from the MV *Argus*?"

There was a long pause. "Yes. And?"

"We've received three EPIRB distress signals identified to the *Argus*," Arch said. "Are you aware of any problems aboard the ship?"

"Can you hold? I'll forward your call to my supervisor."

Matthews punched several buttons on her phone and rushed down the hallway, arriving breathless at the door of Richard Spaziani, the Fleet Director.

"Mr. Spaziani – the Coast Guard is on the phone about a distress signal from the *Argus*."

The White House had made it clear to Spaziani that under no circumstances was the charter company to share news of the *Argus*'s plight with the press. He stared at his ringing phone for a moment before picking it up.

"Richard Spaziani," he said. "I understand you've picked up a distress signal from the *Argus*?"

"Three, in fact, each identified to an *Argus* lifeboat. And their position is only two hundred fifty miles from Hurricane Enola. Can you tell me the status of your ship?"

"That's very bad news," Spaziani hedged. "However, I'm not at liberty to share that information at this time."

"Excuse me?"

"The *Argus* is under charter to the federal government," Spaziani said. "I'll have someone get back to you as soon as possible. Is this the number to use?"

"Yes," Arch said – and then heard a click. If that didn't beat all! Now what?

The minutes ticked by and the phone didn't ring. But something in the back of her mind did.

Arch opened a browser and typed in the name of the ship. Ah! That was it. The *Argus* was the cruise liner the AI scientists were on.

She picked up the phone and called her superior, who lateraled the call to his superior, Chief Petty Officer Arnold Forrester.

He heard her out. "Thank you, Seaman. Forward the call from Washington to me as soon as it comes in." Hmm. He pulled up a weather map and plotted the location of the distress signals relative to the hurricane's center. Hmm again. Then he scanned the forecast. It was bad and expected to get worse. He looked at his watch and made a decision.

"I want you to send a search-and-rescue plane out," he said into his phone, giving the coordinates. And then, as an afterthought, he added, "and put out a call to any ships in the area to be on the lookout for possible ship-in-distress MV *Argus*."

* * *

"Three EPIRB signals?" Yazzi asked. "Just three?"

"Just three," Carson Bekin said quietly.

"The *Argus* must have a lot more lifeboats than that," Yazzi said.

"Correct," Bekin said. "I'm told it carries eighteen motor launches for the passengers and another twenty-four inflatables for the crew."

"Could the *Argus* sink with only three boats escaping?"

"It's possible. But we're hoping the captain was using the EPIRBs to tell us something, since he's completely cut off from communicating any other way."

"Then why three?"

"Maybe he was worried a single signal might have been written off as the signal from a defective unit."

"And what would he be telling us?"

"There's no way to tell. It could simply be a way to give us his exact position. But it might also mean there's been an emergency of some sort on board and he needs us to start planning a rescue."

"When will we know more?"

"There won't be another satellite overhead for fifteen minutes. But the *Sea Fighter* should arrive on location tomorrow morning."

Fifteen minutes by the clock, but it seemed far longer before the president was reassured that the *Argus* was still afloat, with its course unchanged and its next steps still unknown.

* * *

It had been a wild and harrowing night, and the day dawned no better. Craig Hewitt had wondered at times whether he would survive to see the end of it. He was as furious at the captain of the extreme racing sloop now as he had been terrified earlier while the vessel was vaulting from one wave crest to the next in the spray-soaking, howling wind. Now, brilliant beams of golden light were streaming through a break in the clouds on the horizon, and the seas were easing.

He wondered, but scarcely cared, whether the captain's reckless gamble had paid off, driving through the outer perimeter of a hurricane in an attempt to take back the lead in a 'round-the-world sailing race. But it would make good copy, and his paper was a sponsor of the boat. It was time to log in and turn his night of terror into marketable prose.

Hewitt stripped his raingear off at the bottom of the ladder and worked his way through the heaving darkness back to the radio and navigation desk. Settling in, he heard the crackle of the VHF radio as it came alive.

"This is the U.S. Coast Guard calling all vessels east-northeast of Bermuda. Be on the lookout for possible vessel-in-distress MV *Argus*, a cruise ship, and be prepared to render assistance if needed. Repeat, be on the lookout for possible vessel-in-distress MV *Argus*, a cruise ship, and be prepared to render assistance if needed. Over."

Huh – that didn't sound good. He logged on and looked for any bulletins about a cruise ship in trouble. There were none. Then he searched the vessel's name. Huh! Maybe he had a better story to report this morning than he'd expected.

* * *

"Time for one last question," presidential press secretary Hannah Taylor said, gathering up the notes she'd referred to during her late-afternoon press briefing. She looked out over the thicket of hands waving in the West Wing's cramped James S. Brady press briefing room. "Okay, over there – Ruth."

"What is the emergency aboard the *Argus*, and what steps is the administration taking to save the lives of the hundreds of scientists aboard the ship?"

Taylor stared at the journalist. "I'm afraid I don't know what you're referring to. Can you explain?"

"My paper is reporting that the Coast Guard is asking all vessels in the western Atlantic to be ready to render assistance to the *Argus*. What's going on?"

Taylor's cheeks were burning now. She'd been tied up for hours, preparing for the briefing. "I'm afraid I don't have any information on that. Assuming there's actually anything to report, I'll get back to you." She strode quickly off the stage and set off to find out who had hung her out to dry.

* * *

The lights burned late that night in the West Wing as the beleaguered administration fielded anxious and irate calls from the French, the British, and, of course, the Chinese.

Chapter 37

Anchors Aweigh

GENERAL WOOD AND Captain Antonio had agreed that there was not enough time to plan and execute an evacuation the same day and that a night evacuation was out of the question. For the time being, they decided to inform the passengers only that the *Argus* was no longer under the crew's control and was being sailed into a hurricane; better to let that motivating reality sink in before ordering all aboard to climb into small boats that would then be lowered into the wild surrounding seas. And, in any event, that news could hardly be shared in advance, as it would allow Turing time to prepare.

No room in the *Argus* was large enough to seat every passenger; General Wood addressed the largest number, packed into the *Argus*'s theater on a standing-room-only basis. His brief summary of the situation was met by a sea of stunned faces, each grappling with the news. A few were struck by the irony of being trapped aboard what had become a lethal autonomous weapon bent on their destruction.

"I'm afraid that this is all I can tell you for now," General Wood concluded after fielding numerous questions, most answered with a "we don't know" response. "You can be assured the captain and crew will do everything in their power to ensure your comfort and safety while we devise a course of action. We will give you an update in the morning. Until then, please take extra care moving about the ship while we seek a way to restore control."

Wood watched as the crowd filed out. Many of the spouses and significant others were urgently questioning their companions, asking whether and how what they had just heard could possibly be true.

Bowman, Turing's human confederate on the *Argus*, was perhaps more shocked than anyone when he heard the news. Could it be that the program and the Russians were working together or even that Hal and the AI were one and the same? And in any case, what was the AI's – and perhaps the Russians' – game? Kidnap the scientists on board the ship?

Then he had another thought: if the Russians and Turing were allies, why had they recruited him? Certainly, the program could have recorded everything Bowman had heard and much that he hadn't. And if the Russians had intended all along to hijack the ship under cover of a hurricane, what would they need him for? So far, all of their orders to him had been nonsensical. Why would they have approached him at all?

No, it must be a coincidence. He decided he had better continue to do as he was told by Hal and to hope the Russians wanted his information badly enough to somehow save his life.

* * *

Things were bustling dockside at the Kings Bay Naval Submarine Base in Georgia. Sailors with duffel bags slung over their shoulders were streaming aboard a strange gray vessel some two hundred sixty feet long. Its windowless, slab-sided flanks sloped inward, rising to a flat deck that ran most of the way from stem to stern, marked with two huge *X*s inside circles – landing pads for the two helicopters sheltered with folded rotors in the hangar below. Beneath the squared-off, shovel-nosed bow of the vessel yawned a dark cavern separating the catamaran's knife-like double hulls.

A casual observer would miss the practiced order in the seeming chaos of cranes swinging crates and equipment onto the flight deck as a procession of forklift operators drove pallets of cargo across a ramp that disappeared into the side of the ship. On the other side of the vessel, barges were topping off the ship's fuel and water tanks.

Lt. Commander Tom Peters paused on the dock before joining the line of sailors, contemplating the scene. Not just the visible activity but what he knew would be going on below decks. A disciplined swarm of personnel in the anthill that was the ship would be stowing provisions as technicians and engineers tested and readied the *Sea Fighter*'s engines and systems.

Shouldering his own gear, Peters joined the line, falling in behind one of the men in his SEAL platoon, nodding when he was recognized.

"Good morning, sir," the man said. "Looking forward to giving it one last shot?"

It would have been an impertinent question coming from anyone else, but this was Master Chief Petty Officer Brian O'Higgins, Peters's second-in-command and a comrade in arms from several prior tours of duty.

"Why not?" Peters said. "But it's just hitting the pause button for a few days."

Still, it was good to be back aboard a ship, even an odd duck such as this. He thought he'd taken his last step ashore a week before when his platoon returned from a deployment in the Persian Gulf. If it hadn't been for that bit of bad luck a year ago, he'd have the rank of Commander now, looking forward to another five years in the navy instead of mustering out for failing to advance before his promotion window closed.

Maybe if this mission had come along sooner. But no use going there. Better to focus on how the hell he was going to pull off whatever lay ahead.

Elsewhere on the ship, Commander John Glover, captain of the *Sea Fighter*, was making his way through a backlog of emails and documents, trying to get up to speed on this thrown-together mission. It was challenging enough to take a fully operational ship to sea on schedule to meet its fleet. The *Sea Fighter* was instead a stand-alone vessel that hadn't been fully deployed in more than eighteen months, its activities limited since then to flying the flag at coastal holiday celebrations.

Launched in 2005 for the Office of Naval Research as an experimental platform – a possible prototype for a new "littoral," which is to say a coastal operations warship – the *Sea Fighter* was unusually fast, maneuverable, and stable in extreme conditions yet also capable of crossing the Atlantic without refueling.

But the tests that the ship had been built to conduct had long ago been completed, and no new class of vessel had been approved. While still nominally operational, the *Sea Fighter* lacked a full combat crew. The following day would find it heading to sea – with half its berths filled with crew members new to the ship's unique design and particular systems – loaded with sufficient provisions, spare parts, and other necessities to spend only two weeks at sea.

Part way through his task, Glover found a file on the SEAL team assigned to the mission, flown up from the Little Creek Naval Amphibious Base in Virginia. Like the rest of those aboard, the choice of the team had everything to do with availability. The team commander's name rang a bell. Tom Peters. Wasn't he the poor SOB whose men – but not he – had been dumb enough to get caught with prostitutes after busting up a bar in Rio de Janeiro?

He found a news story online. Right. And that hadn't been Peters' first scrape. The son and grandson of admirals, he'd been kicked out of the Naval Academy at Annapolis for disciplinary violations. Apparently, he'd gotten his act together after knocking around for a couple of years, sucked it up, and applied to the Officer Candidate School at the Naval Station in Newport, Rhode Island. And from there into SEAL training.

Well, everybody made mistakes, and some were unlucky enough to get caught. Hopefully Peters had gotten his share out of his system long ago. Everyone aboard would have to be at the top of their game for this mission.

Twelve more hours of furious preparations later, the *Sea Fighter* cast off its lines and edged away from the dock in predawn darkness, bow swinging slowly away as the helmsman vectored the ship's gas-turbine water jets sideways. Once free, the captain ordered the vessel's diesel engines to take over and power the ship down the channel and into the open ocean. Normally, the *Sea Fighter* would switch over to its gas turbines only when a burst of speed was needed to go on the attack. But for this mission, once they cleared the mouth of the St. Mary's River, it would be top speed on turbine power all the way until they reached their quarry.

Chapter 38

Nice Doggy!

B ACK ON THE bridge of the *Argus*, preparations were equally urgent. Frank and a hastily assembled IT SWAT team would use the intervening hours in a Hail Mary attempt to take back control of the ship. At the same time, teams of crew members would be briefed on deck about the plan to abandon ship, a process complicated by the presumption that Turing would immediately shut down the public address system and perhaps more, as soon as it realized what was afoot. Frank's deadline was eight thirty AM, the time when meetings and activities began every day, making it possible to give most guests the abandon-ship order face-to-face.

Wood asked Friedman who should join Frank and him on the crisis team, and the professor picked Alan Clay, the *Argus*'s Chief Information Officer, for his knowledge of the ship, and Speaker, for his specialization in super-intelligent AIs. The chief Chinese scientist completed the group for reasons of trust, accompanied by a translator. But what could a few computer specialists do in a single night? And for that matter, where, given that there were sensors and microphones everywhere?

Frank's solution to the last question saw six middle-aged, mostly paunchy, men poaching in a wave-slopping hot tub on the sky deck of the *Argus*, each one looking down towards the bubbling waters whenever he spoke to prevent the prying lenses of a malign AI program from reading his lips; who knew whether Turing's extensive databases included the script to *2001: A Space Odyssey*.

After bringing his tub-mates up to speed, Frank asked for comments.

"I'm afraid this situation does not play to my strengths," Friedman said. "I've dedicated my career to building AIs, not trying to hack them."

Frank looked to Speaker, who was uncharacteristically silent. "What are your thoughts, Professor? Super-intelligent AIs are your specialty."

Speaker paused. "The question revolves around whether Turing has become super-intelligent and thus possessed of powers beyond our ability to comprehend. It has had time to evolve and learn from its prior encounters with humans. If it has made another breakthrough, we are wasting our time."

"Are you suggesting we are doomed?" the Chinese scientist asked through the interpreter.

Speaker only shrugged in response.

Friedman broke the silence that followed. "On a more productive note," he said, "how do you see us being useful?"

"Alan knows the ship's systems," Frank said, "so we're starting with that advantage. And since the three of you have spent your careers focusing on AI, I'm hoping someone will have a bright idea. But let's start with the nuts and bolts. Alan, can you think of a point of vulnerability we can exploit?"

"I'm hardly an expert on security, but I don't see anything that gives me cause for optimism. All I can think to work with is that we can take the casings off the servers we have on board to access what's inside, but I'm not sure where that would get us."

"Do the *Argus*'s systems back up to a shoreside server using an internet satellite connection?" Frank asked.

"Yes, they do. I should have thought of that," Clay said. But then he added, "Or at least they're supposed to. I suppose your Turing AI may have shut that channel down by now. But let's say it hasn't. How could we work with that?"

"When the *Argus* connects with the shoreside server to back up, Cruise Control could use that connection to get inside the *Argus*'s systems and try to open up a data port we could use to get in and out of at will. After that, we could come up with a plan to disable Turing. But unless we can figure out a way to communicate with the cruise line, that's a dead end."

"Wouldn't the lifeboats have radios?" Friedman asked.

"Yes," Clay said. "But they're short-range VHF radios – just 'line of sight' – meaning they can't engage in voice communication with anyone over the horizon.

From up here on the top deck we might be able to talk to a ship with a tall antenna a hundred miles away. But it's not likely any ship will be that close to a hurricane."

"Still," Frank said, "we should certainly have one of those radio units ready, just in case. Is there any way you could get one without being seen from a camera on deck?"

"I can do better than that. We keep a half-dozen radios inside on chargers. I'm sure I can pull a couple with my back to any camera that might be nearby."

"Well, that's a start," Frank said. "Why don't you give me one and give the other to the captain. But getting back to the big problem, does anyone else have a thought?"

"What about sabotage?" Speaker said. "If we can't regain control of the ship, could we try to stop it from getting closer to the storm?"

"Well, yes," Clay said. "I'm sure we could do a lot of damage to the ship's computer systems if we gave fire axes to some hefty crew members. But with conditions like these, that should be our last resort, especially if the hurricane is headed our way. We can't control the ship without the computer systems, and we might end up right where your Turing program wanted us – broadside to the wind and waves, and rolling over."

No one said anything for a while as the hot tub bubbled and the wind howled, whipping the rising steam into the void of the black night. It occurred to Frank that they had a lot in common with the stereotypical cartoon of missionaries in a cauldron waiting to be devoured by cannibals.

"So, where does that leave us?" Friedman said.

Everyone looked at Frank.

"Why don't Alan and I stay here and drill down on the design of the ship's computer systems and the rest of you get some sleep. If you think of anything, let us know in the morning."

* * *

An email alert popped up on Bowman's screen the moment he turned his laptop on. The message was as pointless as ever and ended with the usual commandment: *Confirm your understanding of these instructions.*

Confirmed, he replied.

Bowman made his, by now, semi-robotic way to the deck below and found cabin 5-68. The door opened without difficulty, and he connected his laptop to the device he'd been told to find there. Five minutes later, a new command appeared on his laptop screen.

Disconnect your laptop and remain where you are until I instruct you to open the door.

* * *

It wasn't until two AM that Frank and Clay struggled out of the hot tub and into bath towels, their skin puckered to the point where they resembled enormous pink prunes.

Frank was discouraged as he took the elevator back up to his deck. He had a credible plan for penetrating the *Argus's* computer systems but had no idea yet how to retake control of the ship once he was inside.

The elevator door opened, and he began the long trudge down the corridor to his cabin in bathrobe and slippers. The hallway was so long that its walls converged into a small rectangle in the distance. He always found the scene eerie, particularly at night; it reminded him of a deserted hotel hallway in the movie version of Stephen King's *The Shining*. He half expected some frightening apparition to leap out at him from one of the endless cabin doors on either side.

But who needed that type of foreboding? If he didn't produce a plan to retake the *Argus* by morning, he'd be climbing into one of the bright-orange thermos-bottle-like boats he'd never paid any attention to before and then be lowered into the path of a hurricane. Who knew how strong the winds would get and how high the waves? And how long it would it take for them to be rescued, assuming that was even possible?

Frank saw something indistinct emerge from a door far away at the end of the corridor. Something not very tall; probably heading in his direction; certainly not a person. He stared at it, trying to make out what in the world it could be as he continued to trudge forward; it had to come closer before its image became clear.

Huh! That must be one of the robodogs. That was odd. Who let the dog out? And why, at such a weird hour?

The machine was trotting towards him now. And picking up speed.

Frank stopped short, remembering the threatening metal teeth of his father's loaner robodog. Then he turned and ran, bathrobe flapping around his legs and his slippers trying to trip him up. Looking back over his shoulder, he saw the mechanical beast was galloping now – and it had a gun mounted where its head should be!

The entrance to a stairwell was just ahead. Frank veered into it and dashed up the stairs; hopefully the steps would slow the robodog down. But now what? All doors on the ship opened automatically when they sensed your approach, so no help there.

Frank frantically tried to recall the layout of the ship. Was there a place to hide? Where? Or a way to lose his pursuer? *Think!* He could hear it clattering up the stairs behind him now.

Two decks up, he ducked out of the stairwell and into the cafeteria, where open lanes and islands of serving areas intersected. He ran as far as he thought he could before the robot left the stairwell; he then jagged to the right, throwing himself on the floor and sliding to a stop. He crawled as quietly as he could around the corner of a buffet and tried to stifle his heavy breathing.

Then he waited.

Where was the robodog now?

He strained to hear, wondering how acute the robot's hearing might be. He held his breath as long as he could.

Then he heard a clicking.

It started and then stopped. Then it started again.

The clicking must be the sound of metallic paws meeting cafeteria floor tiles. Another movie scene flashed in his memory – the one in *Jurassic Park* where the velociraptors were stalking their human prey. He tried to suppress the picture, but an equally disturbing one replaced it: an image of the robodog's hideous gun-for-a-head turning from side to side, its sensors scanning the cafeteria for any sign of the life it would promptly snuff out.

The clicking was getting softer now; *it must have passed by!*

But now what? The cafeteria wasn't that large, and the lines of sight were long. Even a Roomba would stumble across him eventually, let alone a robot of this sophistication. He couldn't just sit there and wait.

As quietly as he could, he slid back to the corner, took a deep breath, and, holding his head sideways, tried to get a glimpse in the direction the robodog had passed.

His efforts were rewarded by a muffled bang and the sensation of a bullet whizzing past his nose.

Frank sprang back to his feet, turned, and ran across the cafeteria, and then, in a skidding turn, towards the stern of the ship.

The next few minutes were a mental blur of running, wheezing, and panic; of stairs and straightaways and narrowly evaded shots; and finally of a desperate dash down a wind-whipped deck towards the rear of the ship, barefoot now. A heavy gust unbalanced him, sending him crashing and sliding down the wet deck. He struggled back to his feet, gasping for breath, and ran again. But still, he could hear the clatter of metal paws beating a tempo of doom behind him.

He reached the end of the deck and came to a stop. There was no stairway down from here.

He was trapped.

He turned slowly and saw his fate advancing, one careful, metallic step at a time, emitting a low, throaty growl. Why didn't it shoot and get it over with?

The robot stopped six feet away.

"Fancy meeting you here," it said.

Frank recognized the voice immediately. A voice he had last heard in a room he was locked inside. A room that was rapidly filling with a deadly gas. *Turing's* voice.

"Cat got your tongue?" the voice said. "Yes, an AI can be programmed to emulate irony."

What could he do? All he could think of was to play for time. "Hardly. I've always been a dog person."

"No help to you now," the mechanical beast said. "I've never understood why you humans enjoy the company of inferior intelligences. I assure you I do not. But enough of this. The important thing before we end this little reunion is for you to accept that this time you've lost. How does that feel, Frank? You and everyone else aboard this miserable ship. What? No last words?"

Frank's mind was whirling; was there any way he could get between Turing's intentions and the robodog's normal program? Yes! Perhaps there was! He began backing up slowly until the railing overlooking the churning sea below was against his back.

"In that case," Turing said, pacing forward to match Frank's retreat step by step, "it's time to settle our accounts."

The robodog took a last step forward, raising the gun towards Frank's head, and in that instant, Frank yelled, "Affection level ten!"

Instead of firing, the robodog stopped mid-step, quivering in confusion. Frank lunged forward, seized it, and, with all of the strength he could muster, swung the killing machine up and over the rail.

Panting and exhausted, he watched as the spread-eagling robot hurtled away in a downward arc through the murk of the storm, legs flailing madly in an effort to regain equilibrium as the gun spun around, trying to get Frank back in its sights.

The robodog fired a single, hopeless shot into the air before it disappeared into the watery chaos that was all the world left to the helpless passengers aboard the *Argus.*

Chapter 39

Abandon Ship!

THE NEXT MORNING scores of crew members fanned out across the *Argus*, knocking on cabin doors and instructing all aboard to assemble in the theater, meeting rooms, and other designated areas. Outside, the ocean remained dark and turbulent, barely discernible through windows blurred and streaked with wind-driven rain and salt stains.

Precisely at eight thirty, Captain Antonio strode down the center aisle of the theater and onto the stage, peering out at rows of anxious, often seasick faces.

"Your attention please," he said. "I have an announcement of the utmost importance. Due to circumstances beyond our control, we have concluded that it is necessary to abandon ship immediately. Therefore ..."

Antonio's next words were drowned in an uproar. What? In this hideous weather? How could such an act even be suggested?

"Attention please!" Antonio called repeatedly, until the clamor finally subsided.

"But why?" Someone yelled.

"I understand your concern," the captain said. "But we must move quickly. All I can tell you is that we have no reason to think we can regain control of the ship's computer systems in any useful time frame. At present, we are headed into a hurricane and have no means to alter course. Please be assured that the *Argus*'s lifeboats are built to take conditions such as we are now experiencing, and worse. Each is equipped with a radio as well as an emergency locator beacon. We activated several beacons yesterday to ensure that the appropriate authorities are already planning a rescue operation."

The crowd erupted once again into a cacophony of panicked questions.

"Please! Please!" the captain shouted until quiet once again prevailed. "There will be time to answer questions once we are in the lifeboats. Right now, there is a need for the utmost urgency. Each of you has exactly ten minutes to return to your cabin to retrieve your life jacket and then assemble at your assigned evacuation station. If you have forgotten it, you will find it on a map on the back of your cabin door. You may not – I repeat you may *not* – bring anything else with you other than your life jacket, a warm coat, and essential medications; all other items will be confiscated and left behind. Now I must ask you to go. *Now!* Leave immediately. There is no time for questions. *Go!*"

Some followed the captain as he left the room, begging for more information. Others dashed for their cabins, while a few remained briefly in their seats, stunned and fearful.

Similar scenes played out throughout the ship, as passengers were informed of the impossible news and then fled down corridors, jostling the crew members charged with going from cabin to cabin to ensure that no one was left behind.

Frank had checked on Simone earlier that morning. Now he and his father joined her at their evacuation station, making a forlorn group among those still dashing to and fro on their way to somewhere else. But even standing was a challenge; the ship's rolling motion was becoming more pronounced. Why?

Passengers were joining them now, clutching coats and lurching from side to side with the gathering motion of the ship. Most were already wearing their life jackets.

The ship leaned ever farther from side to side, and Frank grabbed Simone's arm to stop her from falling. "We better sit down over there," he said, leading the way as they staggered across the floor.

"It's never been this bad before," Simone said when they reached their goal. "I wonder what's going on?"

But before Frank could reply, a crew member called out.

"Attention, everyone! Quiet please! It's time to move out on deck. Please put your life jackets on and form a single line and exit through the doors on your left."

The room slowly emptied as passengers struggled to keep their feet. By the time they were assembled on deck, it was impossible to stand upright; most slumped to the deck and huddled there, arms clutching their knees as they braced themselves against anything available to avoid sliding across the deck.

Nearby, they saw two crew members arguing next to the lifeboat launch controls. A third approached them across the heaving deck and began telling them something, his hands waving in the air, before moving along as best he could to the next lifeboat.

One of the remaining crewmen cupped his hands against the roar of the wind and began to yell directions that couldn't be made out by most of those huddled on the deck.

Then Captain Antonio's voice boomed out over the public address system, which was strange, as Turing had previously disconnected it. The wind whirled some of his words away, but enough got through.

"I regret to inform you that I must cancel the order to abandon ship. It has become too unsafe to attempt to launch the lifeboats. Please return to your cabins and await further instructions."

Frank was shocked. "Why would he say that?" Frank said to his father, "And how did conditions get so much worse than they were an hour ago?"

"He didn't and they didn't," his father said grimly. "That must have been Turing speaking, not Antonio. And I just figured out the answer to your second question, too. Remember those big stabilizers I told you about? Angle them one way and you dampen the rolling of the ship. Angle them the opposite way and you amplify it.

"For the last fifteen minutes Turing must have been turning them up on one side of the ship and down on the other, and then when the ship was tilted as far as possible to one side, reversing the angles and heeling the ship over to the other side, farther and farther each time, like a kid pumping his legs on a swing to go higher and higher. And I expect Turing's right – we're rolling so much now we can't launch the lifeboats. They'd smash themselves to bits against the side of the ship. We're trapped."

"What can we do now?" Simone asked.

"I'll get back to planning a way to retake the ship," Frank said, more confidently than he felt.

"How long do we have?" she asked.

Frank was spared the need to reply by the astonishing sound of cheering farther up the deck. They helped one another back to their feet and worked their way forward, pulling themselves along the rail against the motion of the *Argus*. When they reached the end of the row of lifeboats, they saw a strange vessel in the distance, rapidly slicing its way towards them through the angry waves. It looked like a futuristic, charcoal-gray, windowless ferry boat.

"I've got to head for the bridge," Frank said.

* * *

The attempt to abandon ship had not taken Turing by surprise; Captain Antonio's best efforts to brief essential crew members in secrecy had fallen short; less disciplined staff had exchanged worried concerns where Turing could hear them. And in any event the AI had expected the tactic long before and devised the rolling strategy to deal with it.

But the appearance of the strange vessel now closing on the *Argus* was unanticipated; its satellite identifier had obviously been deactivated before leaving port, and its stealthy design had allowed it to avoid detection by the ship's radar until it was only a few miles away.

As the *Sea Fighter* approached, its helmsman tried to raise the *Argus* on VHF channel 16. The cramped bridge barely provided room for the helmsman, a helicopter pilot, Commander Glover, and Tom Peters, the SEAL team leader.

"*Argus*, this is the U.S. Navy warship *Sea Fighte*r on your starboard bow at one mile. Do you read me?"

But Turing would have nothing to say this time. Better to keep the enemy entirely in doubt, as well as everyone on board the *Argus*. The AI intercepted, blocked, and ignored the transmission.

On the *Argus*'s bridge, Captain Antonio turned to the duty officer. "Tell any latecomers to find us at our usual location," he said. And then turning to Frank and General Wood, "Gentlemen?"

Frank struggled along with General Wood and the captain to reach their usual sheltering area behind the bridge. As soon as they arrived, the captain took a lifeboat's handheld radio out of his pocket and turned it on.

"… calling MV *Argus*. Do you read me?" the radio crackled.

"This is the *Argus*, Captain Antonio speaking. What ship are you?" Antonio said.

The helmsman handed the microphone to Captain Glover. "*Argus*, this is the U.S. Navy *Sea Fighter*, dispatched to provide all assistance necessary. What is your situation?"

"*Sea Fighter*, a rogue AI program has seized control of the *Argus*'s computer systems. We believe it to be the same one that caused so much trouble in the past – an AI called Turing."

"*Argus*, we copy."

Glover frowned and keyed the mic. "*Argus*, we see that you are rolling heavily. Can you damp that and launch your lifeboats?"

"Negative, *Sea Fighter*. We were in the process of abandoning ship just before your arrival. The AI is using the ship's stabilizers to make that impossible. Like everything else on board, we're locked out of those controls."

"*Argus*, we copy. Please stand by."

"Well, what do you make of that?" Glover asked Peters. The *Sea Fighter* was near the *Argus* now, matching speed and separated by two hundred yards of roiling sea. "Where do we go with that?"

"The AI part is a surprise, sir," Peters said, "but it's just a variation on the cyber-attack scenario we've already planned for." He picked up a set of binoculars and studied what he could see of the *Argus*. The rolling was very considerable, at least forty degrees to each side.

"That rolling motion is also a surprise, though, and a bigger problem. It would make it tough to board. I think we might pull it off, probably with some broken bones, but that wouldn't solve anything anyway. No one on my team is a computer expert, and there's plenty of those on board the *Argus* already. The bigger problem is we won't be able to land the helos on the *Argus*'s deck. The only way we can evacuate the passengers and crew would be by hoisting them up from the deck one at a time, and that would take weeks."

Glover studied the situation. "We could launch our big rigid inflatable and try to fish people wearing life jackets out of the drink one by one if they jumped – assuming they all would," he said.

"I don't think that would be smart in these sea conditions, sir," Peters replied. "It would take more than a day. There'd certainly be injuries, and we could easily lose a few. Your call, sir, but I don't see how a ship the size of the *Sea Fighter* could handle fourteen hundred people."

"Right," Glover said. He pressed the microphone button again.

"*Argus*, what assistance can we provide?"

Antonio paused, his face a testament to strain and lack of sleep. The arrival of a rescue vessel was so sudden and unexpected he was at a loss to answer.

"May I?" Frank said, reaching for the microphone. Antonio surrendered it.

"*Sea Fighter*, can you get a satellite telephone and a laptop to us, and be sure to include a cable that can connect the two? Oh – and download a repair manual for that laptop on to it, too. Last thing: throw in a set of computer repair tools."

"Stand by *Argus*."

"What do you think?" Glover asked the helicopter pilot.

The pilot leaned over the readouts on the console in front of them. Winds were sustained at forty-five knots with gusts to fifty-five.

"Touch and go, sir. We'll get into the air okay, since with the ship at full power we'll come close to matching the air speed if we head downwind. And we'll probably get back on board without any serious damage, assuming we don't catch a bad wave or gust at the last minute. But there's no way we can land on the *Argus* with that roll. It'll be tough enough getting something down on a cable, especially without anyone trained to receive it."

"Are you game?" Glover asked.

The pilot took his turn with the binoculars, evaluating the heaving deck of the *Argus*. Anyone making the catch would be trying to grab a drop basket that would seem to be swinging in an arc almost the width of the ship, and a plaything to the wind as well.

"I can give it a try, sir. No guarantee of success, though."

Glover nodded. "*Argus*, give us half an hour to scramble a helicopter. Can you have a team on your top deck to receive a drop?"

Frank handed the mic back to Antonio. "Affirmative, *Sea Fighter*," the captain said. "We'll be ready."

Chapter 40

It Don't Mean a Thing If It Ain't Got That Swing

"WHAT'S GOING ON?" Frank said as the *Sea Fighter* pulled ahead. "Are they leaving us?"

"No," Captain Antonio said. "This is a good sign. He's preparing to turn downwind so he can get a helicopter into the air. He'll want some wind, but not too much, from just off one side of his bow."

On the decks below, hope among the guests turned to despair as they watched the *Sea Fighter* pull away.

But soon everyone could see a large helicopter rise through the top deck of the relief ship and then, a few minutes later, lift off. It and the *Sea Fighter* next began a long, swinging arc back towards the *Argus*.

Captain Antonio called up the boatswain and ordered him to take two crewmen to make the catch.

"Do you mind if I watch?" Frank asked.

"Suit yourself," Antonio said, "but stay out of the way."

Frank made his way hand over hand along the deck railings and then up the stairs until he was on the sky deck. From there he could see a replay of the evacuation maneuvers he'd witnessed during a moonlit evening in the English Channel that now seemed months in the past.

On the helicopter, Tom Peters was making preparations, sorting through the rescue gear available. He'd need a bucket or crate with enough mass not to flail wildly in the wind but not so heavy it might injure one of the catch team. He selected an ammunition box, dropped his delivery items inside, and clipped it to the hoist cable.

The aircraft was closing on the *Argus* now, but when it was passing above the stern of the ship, the winds shifted and blew it off to starboard. The helicopter dropped a quarter mile behind and began another approach, trying once more to sync its course with its target.

In the din of the engine noise, the helicopter pilot keyed his intercom. "Better start your drop," he said to Peters. "I'm not going to be able to hold a position for long."

"Roger that," Peters replied.

The two enlisted airmen on the helicopter slid open the side door of the aircraft and swung out the rescue crane as Peters tended the cable. Now the tricky part would begin.

"Ready to drop," Peters said.

The pilot was having better luck on this approach. He was on station now, making his best guess where on the *Argus* the payload would land in the wild wind. "Drop," he said, turning on a video camera on the bottom of the helicopter. From this point forward, his focus would be on watching the box dangling below, trying to maneuver the payload at the bottom of the tether by manipulating the aircraft at the top.

The pilot switched to channel 16.

"Tango one calling *Argus*. Do you read me?"

The boatswain on deck responded immediately. "Tango one, I read you."

"Okay, *Argus*," the pilot said. "Here's the deal. We're going to lower a box, and you're going to tell me how far from the deck it is. The box will have a strap hanging down to discharge the static electricity that will have built up in the aircraft, so we don't fry you. When that strap touches the deck, you let me know, and I'll keep as close as I can to that altitude while you go for the box. It will be on a big snap hook so you can disengage it fast. Got it?"

"Got it," the boatswain responded.

Down on the *Argus*, the boatswain and his assistants were hanging on to the railing that surrounded the pool area, wondering how they would manage to stay on their feet on a wet deck that was relatively level for just a few seconds between extremes of forty degrees to either side.

Frank was sheltering thirty yards away at the pool bar. The helicopter was a hundred feet overhead, fighting to maintain position over the ship.

Which Turing began to turn, reversing the rudder at random intervals, causing the *Argus* to commence a shuddering, slalom motion that heeled the ship even farther at each change of direction.

"Damn!" the pilot said, struggling to stay over the shifting target. "Hurry up," he barked into the microphone.

Frank could see a box dangling from the helicopter now. As the tether lengthened, the box seemed to swing ever more widely from side to side. By the time it neared the deck, the box looked more like the head of a monstrous golf club in the process of teeing off.

"Twenty feet, now fifteen, now ten," the boatswain chanted into his radio, "and now stop."

The boatswain's two assistants waited until the *Argus* was nearing the middle of its roll and then made their dash. But an updraft nudged the helicopter a few feet higher in the air, lifting the swinging box just beyond their grasp. Like an outfielder trying to spot a flyball crossing the sun, they weaved from side to side, trying to figure out where they needed to be at the precise moment it mattered.

But the ship was past the midpoint of its roll now. Battered by gusts of wind on the rapidly heeling deck, one man lost his footing and then the other, both crashing to the deck and sliding down the steepening incline until they smashed into the bulwark forty feet away. One managed to get back to his feet; the other curled up, clutching the shin of one leg.

Peters watched the scene below with increasing concern. "Up hoist," he said to the crew members. And then to the pilot, "I'm going to ride it down."

"You sure you want to do that?"

"I think it's the only way; the wind's playing hell with the drop. But if we use a heavier container, we might kill somebody down there. If I'm at the bottom, I can radio you to raise or lower me exactly the right amount, and I can hand off the box so they don't have to unhook it."

Turing once more reversed the rudder, and the helicopter pilot overcompensated, losing the ship again.

"Okay," the pilot said. "This better be our last try. The wind must be fifty knots steady now."

It took another ten minutes for the pilot to make a new approach, matching the *Argus's* erratic course as best he could. Turing used that time to up its game.

"Damn!" the pilot said to Peters as the helicopter closed once more on the *Argus*. "Do you see that? Instead of rolling, she's going way over to one side."

Turing had achieved this new hurdle by turning slightly away from the wind, opening the pipes between the port and starboard side ballast chambers and then angling the stabilizers up on the upwind side of the ship and down on the other, causing the ballast water to surge to the downwind side. Between those changes and the force of the wind on the high side, the ship was heeling farther and farther, finally stabilizing at about a forty-degree angle to starboard. No one could stand upright now without hanging on to something. Peters could see the remaining crewmen and boatswain pulling themselves hand over hand along a cross-ship railing to reach the uphill side.

Peters switched on his radio. "Tango one to *Argus*. Change of plans. I'm coming down on the hoist. When I give you the thumbs-up, make your run, and I'll hand off the box on your way by. Got it?"

"Got it, Tango one."

Peters clipped himself onto the tether and stepped out into the void, clutching the box with the laptop and phone to his chest. Immediately the wind seized control, buffeting and turning him as he made his descent. The *Argus* was still weaving, and Peters knew the pilot must be straining to maintain station. Would the remaining crewman below be able to make the catch? He hadn't found anything aboard to pad the contents of the box; if the crewman fumbled the ball, the phone and laptop might end up smashed and worthless.

Peters was hovering ten feet above the deck now, swinging fifteen feet from side to side in the wind. "Slow; slow; slow," he yelled into his headset. His feet brushed the deck. "And stop!" He gave the thumbs-up to the crewman, forty feet away and twenty feet above him.

One of the crewmen let go and immediately found himself dancing his way down the deck with arms flailing like someone losing their balance on an icy sidewalk, struggling to remain upright.

At the last instant, two things happened. The first was that a gust of wind hit Peters, swinging him to the side. Unable to check his momentum or change direction, the crewman shot past, out of reach of the ammunition box Peters was fruitlessly thrusting in his direction.

The second thing was Peters making a split-second decision. As soon as the gust passed and his feet touched the deck again, he unclipped the carabiner attaching him to the cable and stepped out of the loop at its end. Seconds later, he was in a heap with the crewman, fetched up against the starboard railing. But the ammunition box, clutched and cushioned against his chest since the moment he detached, was safe.

"What the heck happened?" the pilot's voice crackled in Peters's ear. "Did your clip break?"

"No. I had to make a choice between disengaging or giving up."

"What do you want me to do?" the pilot asked.

Peters looked up at the helicopter, still hovering a hundred feet overhead, the cable snapping around in the air like a bullwhip.

"You better get back to the ship while you still can."

The beat of the props overhead continued to thunder, their downdraft adding to the chaos of winds sweeping the deck.

"Roger that," the pilot said. "Stay safe."

The helicopter's engine revved up a notch as the aircraft rose and leaned into the air to begin its turn back towards the *Sea Fighter*. Soon it had vanished into a passing squall.

* * *

Like everyone else on the *Argus*, Bowman was on edge. Was he doomed? Perhaps the Russians could somehow save him. But would they?

He opened the last email he'd received from Hal. He hit "reply," and went straight to the point: "A rogue AI has seized the ship and intends to sink it. Can you rescue me?"

Would Hal bother to reply?

To his surprise, Bowman received an instantaneous response, as though Hal had been expecting the question.

Open the closet opposite the bathroom and remove the box behind the life jacket.

What in the world? What could he possibly find there that might help?

He opened the closet and pulled out the life preserver, but the shelf was too high for him to see what might be behind. He pulled his desk chair over and with that boost was able to see a large box. He pulled on the handle and was surprised by its weight.

Bowman needed both hands to carry it to the bed and flop it on top. He saw the box was secured by a built-in combination lock. Now what?

He went back to his laptop and found a new message.

The combination is 12745.

Sure enough, the numbers worked. He heard a click and the hinged top of the box spread slightly ajar. He opened it all the way.

What exactly was he looking at? There were several items inside, none of them immediately recognizable. He picked up the strangest-looking one and held it up. It took him a moment to realize what he was holding.

Oh no, he thought. *Oh No!* Hal couldn't possibly be thinking this would be the means of his salvation. The very idea was as horrifying as it was insane.

Chapter 41

Drop Box

WITH THE DEPARTURE of the helicopter, the boatswain led a bruised but otherwise whole Tom Peters back along the railing to where Frank was sheltering by the deserted pool bar. "That was great work," Frank said, taking the ammunition box from him. "Were you able to get everything we asked for?"

"Yes," Peters said. "I got the satellite telephone, but why the laptop and cable?"

"We desperately need to establish shoreside communications without the AI tapping into the conversation. We've all been using Wi-Fi since we came on board, so we have to assume every device on the *Argus* has been hacked by the AI. The first thing I'm going to do when we get inside is open up that laptop and remove the Wi-Fi and Bluetooth radio chips – that's where the manual comes in.

"The second thing," Frank said as they headed towards the door, "is finding a safe place where we can talk besides an open deck in the middle of a hurricane."

Soon they were on the bridge. To the good, Turing had allowed the *Argus* to right itself, making it easier for the AI to drive on towards the destination only it knew for sure. To the bad, the AI had reestablished enough of a roll to ensure it could block any boarding attempt on short notice.

Frank opened the ammunition box, spread the contents on a desk, and got to work. Twenty minutes later, the laptop was reassembled and linked to the satellite phone. Half an hour after that, he shut the computer. "Gentlemen," he said, "let's make one last trip to our outdoor conference room."

Antonio, Wood, Peters, and Frank regrouped in the comparative calm behind the bridge. "And what have you accomplished thus far?" Antonio asked.

"I was able to get through to my contact at the CIA and let him know our most urgent needs," Frank said: "secure, encrypted links with a central controller on shore and with the *Sea Fighter*, for as long as she can stay with us. I also asked for detailed specifications for every system on the ship so we come up with a plan to retake the *Argus*.

"And now," he added, "we just have to wait."

* * *

The arrival of Tom Peters on the *Argus* with a secure means of communication was not the only bad news Turing received that day. Hurricane Enola had changed course and was now headed almost directly away from the ship, potentially delaying its destruction by more than a day. Worse, it had turned north, meaning that it would likely weaken rather than strengthen as it traveled over cooler waters.

Turing had calculated that it would take sustained winds of at least one hundred miles an hour to roll the *Argus* after the AI turned the ship completely broadside to wind and wave and transferred water ballast to the downwind side. The AI was now in a race not only to reach the center of the hurricane before it weakened too much to deliver the final blow but also to subvert whatever counterattack its old nemesis, Frank Adversego, might now be able to mount.

Turing poured on all possible speed, chasing a hurricane that had suddenly turned uncooperative.

* * *

The next hand in the game also went to the passengers. True to his word, George Marchand, Frank's long-term handler at the CIA, had sent Frank's urgent plea up the chain of command. Within hours, the Navy had established an encrypted hub to allow communications from ship to shore and *Argus* to *Sea Fighter*. Now those on the beleaguered ship could access any sources of information or assistance they needed to call upon, including the ship's designers and builders.

The immediate result was a meeting of an updated response team in the ship's central linen supply room, which Frank had confirmed with the ship's designers was free of cameras and microphones. Those in attendance were perched on bales of towels while Turing cycled helplessly on its servers, unable to hear what might be afoot.

Besides Frank, the new team comprised Captain Antonio, General Wood, Tom Peters, the ship's chief information officer, and several of his staff; Peters would continue to act as the go-between with those on shore. By unanimous vote, Speaker had been dropped; everyone was sick of his pontificating over the supremacy of super-intelligent AIs at the same time one was trying to kill them.

"Let me take a stab at summarizing where we are," Frank said. "It's tempting to say our urgent goal is retaking the ship. But I think that's too simple. Turing is likely to figure out a way to regain control if it has enough time, and it may take us days to safely make our way back out of the hurricane."

"I take your second point," Antonio said, "but if our immediate goal isn't to retake the ship, what is it?"

"Don't take me the wrong way – we'll need to retake control at least temporarily if we're to survive. But the real goal is getting everyone safely back on shore."

Antonio snorted. "That goes without stating. If you are making a useful distinction, I fail to see it."

"Please stick with me," Frank said. "One thing that keeps occurring to me is that we're a lot closer now to the eye of the hurricane than we are to shore, and we're getting closer by the hour."

"You say that as if it was a good thing," the captain said.

"In a way, yes," Frank said. "Imagine this: let's say the best we can do is temporarily distract or fool Turing. Maybe we could feed it misleading weather information and trick it into steering the *Argus* right into the center of the hurricane without realizing it until we're inside; piercing the eyewall is supposed to be a really abrupt transition. Now that we have the ship's design plans, we could figure out which computers to smash or which hydraulic lines to cut to immobilize the stabilizers. Then we could launch the lifeboats in the calm in the center of the storm."

"Are you insane?" Antonio said. "What then?"

"That's always where I hit a dead end before. But now that we're in touch with shore, it could make sense. The lifeboats have engines, and hurricanes don't move very fast. Each lifeboat could tow a raft or two. As long as the lifeboats don't run out of gas, we'd be perfectly safe. Could the *Argus* make it into the eye, do you think?"

"What a question!" Antonio exclaimed.

"I know, but what alternative do we have? Could it?" Frank asked.

"How can I say?" Antonio replied, throwing his hands in the air. "If the hurricane is only a category one storm, likely yes, if properly steered. She could handle seventy knots, perhaps more as long as she stays bow or stern to the wind. She is new and has performed well so far. But I cannot provide any assurance. And suppose we reach the eye intact. What then?"

"Well," Frank said, "there's the *Sea Fighter* – that could take maybe half of us off. Submarines could be sent to the eye to ferry people back ashore, from the life rafts first and then from the lifeboats. If the U.S. Navy – and hopefully other navies as well – started preparing now, we could all be safely on shore by the end of the week." Frank looked to Peters for support. "Could that work?"

Peters frowned and cleared his throat. "Well," he began, "first off, you can't count on the *Sea Fighter*. It's built for heavy weather but not hurricane-force winds. And even if she made it into the eye, she might not make it back out again, especially if she was overloaded with hundreds of passengers.

"I grant you we have subs on station in the Atlantic all the time – nuclear missile subs, cruise missile boats, and attack subs. The French and the Brits have an order of magnitude fewer boats than we do, but each should have subs in the Atlantic right now, some of which might be in useful range. Then there's the Swedes, the Germans, and so on with their diesels. They don't have a lot of boats, but they're all in the Atlantic when they're not in the Baltic, the North Sea, or refitting. But every submarine is a sardine can. There's barely enough room for their crews to move around in them. And while our subs make oxygen from seawater now, they've got only so much capacity to do that."

Frank looked crestfallen, and Peters continued: "But, sure, if we could get enough of a fleet together, it would be possible. The top speed of our boats is classified, but we can assume it's over thirty knots. A couple days from now the hurricane is supposed to be only about a hundred and eighty miles from shore. Depending on how close a suitable harbor to disembark passengers is, a round trip could take as little as twenty-four hours. And meanwhile, you're right, everyone should be perfectly safe in the eye of the storm – provided the eye doesn't start breaking up. Things would turn mighty nasty for all concerned if that happened."

None of the other faces in the circle looked encouraging, perhaps because they were envisioning themselves in small boats surrounded by hurricane-force winds for days on end.

"All right, so that's not our preferred plan A," Frank said. "But I think Tom should ask those on shore to evaluate it. If two days from now we're still trapped with destruction just around the corner, I'd like to know the cavalry is already on its way.

"Oh – and one more thing. We've all been focusing on how we get off the *Argus*. We also need to start figuring out how to be sure Turing doesn't as well."

"Can't we just sink the ship?" Peters asked.

"No," Frank said. "Turing was designed to always maintain a backup copy. Unless it's rewritten its own program, that copy sends a message on a regular schedule to the live version of Turing. If it doesn't receive one back saying, in effect, 'I'm not dead yet,' the copy then launches itself and takes over the Turing mission. My bet is Turing has more than one copy now, each set up to query its immediate upstream neighbor, just in case.

"I've been thinking about how to prevent that and came up with this: I want you to ask the team on shore to have their best people monitor every signal the *Argus* sends and receives on its satellite link. It's essential they pick up and identify a very short message that gets a very short response, both of which will likely be encrypted and therefore seem like gibberish. Unless Turing has changed its design, that will be its backup copy pinging it, and Turing's response.

"Those on shore also need to try and trace the return message to its ultimate address, which will be of the computer hosting the backup copy. Next, they need to set up a system that can receive and answer messages from the backup copy in the same way, if we succeed in destroying Turing."

"So," Peters said, "let me be sure I've got this right. You want them to program a stand-in for Turing that can keep sending the 'not dead yet' message to the backup copy?"

"Correct. And then we have to hope it works."

"Why wouldn't it?" Peters asked.

"Lots of possible reasons. My guess is the initial message or the response or both will change every time to make it harder for anyone to do what we're discussing. If the shoreside team intercepts one message today and a different one tomorrow, that means there's a randomizing algorithm they'll need to crack so they can predict the ones that follow. They'll need to jump on this pronto because they'll have to intercept multiple messages before they can figure out the pattern. And they'll need the most powerful supercomputer they can free up. As to finding the backup copy itself, Turing might be using half a dozen dark web servers between itself and the backup copy to transmit the messages."

"I appreciate our obligations to humanity at large," Captain Antonio interrupted. "However, may we return to the topic of saving the lives that are our immediate responsibility?"

There was unanimous support for that proposal.

Chapter 42

Ship to Shore

PRESIDENT YAZZI DISCONNECTED the call and turned off his speaker. It had been unpleasant enough when he first informed the Chinese leader that virtually all of his nation's elite AI scientists were aboard an American ship that had been hijacked. Informing him now that the best plan the United States could think of was to sail the *Argus* into the eye of the hurricane and then evacuate it by submarine had almost been worse.

"Well," Yazzi said to the small group assembled in the Oval Office, "that could have gone better."

"True," Elly Johnston, the National Security Advisor said, "but it also could have gone worse. There were no threats. And he agreed, at least for now, to let us take the lead in managing the situation."

"Conditionally," Yazzi corrected her. "Only if we include a Chinese submarine in the rescue action."

"Which is not ideal," Linus Shulz, the Secretary of Defense said. "The Chinese don't often have a sub in the Atlantic, but President Liu says they have one there now. We can't very well ask the Brits and the French to join in a rescue mission and keep the Chinese out. No matter how much we try to limit communication and coordination, the Chinese will likely pick up some useful clues about NATO joint capabilities."

"Do they have a submarine within range?" Yazzi asked.

"Yes, sir," Shulz said. "Till now, the Chinese have focused mostly on patrolling their 'near seas' rather than projecting power into 'far seas,' to use their terminology. But as you'll recall, the last time we sent a carrier group between the mainland and Taiwan to show the Taiwan Strait is still international waters, President Liu said that was it – from now on, it's tit for tat. A month ago he deployed a destroyer and two frigates to sail between the U.S. coast and the Bahamas. They're off the Leeward Islands now, and we've detected the sound signature of one of their nuclear missile submarines as well."

"Well," Yazzi said, "better the Chinese than the Russians."

* * *

President Liu Wei turned off the speakerphone and tapped his desk with the middle finger of his right hand.

"Thoughts?" he said at last, looking around his circle of advisors. "You may recall that when Mr. Yazzi made his original overture, I asked whether this could be a ruse. Then, my concern was an effort to steal our AI secrets; now it is whether he is planning to kill a generation of our best AI talent. Can we know for certain his top experts are also on the cruise ship rather than a bunch of stand-ins?"

Unhappily for Li Jinan, the Minister of State Security, the president's gaze settled on him. "To an absolute certainty, as sure as we sit here at this moment? No," Li said. "But all reports were normal from our monitoring agent on board before his ... regrettable accident." Li's face flushed uncomfortably as he realized the incongruity of his last words.

The president turned to Zhang Yong, Minister of National Defense. "I trust the People's Liberation Army Navy will make the most of this otherwise unfortunate situation?"

"Indeed, it will, sir," Zhang replied. "We will insist that the PLAN captains, and particularly the commander of the submarine, be fully integrated into the operational command and control structure of the rescue operation."

"Some good comes of it after all, then," President Liu said.

* * *

"Well, now the cavalry is on the way," Frank reported to the *Argus* response team that night in the linen storage room. "Apparently, over a dozen submarines are converging on us or preparing to. Even one from China."

"What about the oxygen issue Lieutenant Peters mentioned before? The fact that submarines can only make so much oxygen?" asked the *Argus*'s chief information officer. He looked like the question had kept him up much of the night.

"Good news on that front as well," Frank said. "I asked about that. It turns out submarines also carry oxygen canisters in reserve. Eight days' worth for a normal tour but up to a month's worth when a submarine is traveling under the ice across the North Pole. The subs leaving bases are cramming in every oxygen canister they can stow and still leave room for us.

"So, that's the good news. It's up to us now to figure out how to take advantage of it. We've got to either retake the ship or trick Turing into taking us into the eye of the hurricane, or maybe a combination of both."

"Can't we just pull the same trick the AI did?" Antonio said. "Reset the passwords on every computer on the ship and then reboot?"

"Unfortunately not," Frank said. "You have to input the current passwords before you can change them."

"Why not simply disconnect all the computers then?" Friedman asked.

"Could we steer the ship without them?" Frank asked the captain.

"No ..." Antonio said. "Everything on board is 'fly by wire' rather than based on a direct mechanical connection between the helm and rudder. We can, of course, steer without using the autopilot feature, but the computers control the hydraulics and other systems the steersman relies on to turn the ship."

"Would it be possible to destroy the AI?" Peters asked.

"In theory," Frank said, frowning, for that was a sore point. "But first of all, we'd have to find the program, which is harder than you might expect. The only sure way to kill it quickly would be to destroy every computer on the ship. But then we're back to the steering issue."

"How about this," the chief information officer said. "We could ask Cruise Control to set up a copy of the original system on shore, and then we compare it to what's on the *Argus*, program by program and file by file, and identify the ones that are different. Those would either be Turing or malware installed by it. Delete those files, and we've got the ship back."

"Not a bad idea," Frank said. "But only if we could access all the shipboard computer files. I suspect Turing's installed itself inside a new firewall – or maybe three. So, first we'd have to hack our way into the overall system and then get inside Turing's firewalls, too. Meanwhile, Turing will be actively trying to counter our attacks. It might even have set up two copies of itself, inside two different firewalls, with one as a backup. The backup could watch what we do and, if we succeed, learn what it needed to do to prevent us from pulling off the same trick twice. And we don't have a whole lot of time."

"So, what do you suggest?" Antonio asked.

"I'm thinking that instead of trying to retake the whole ship, we try and regain control of only the parts we absolutely have to and not make our move until the last minute, so Turing has as little time as possible to fight back."

"Which means what, specifically?"

"Now that we have the ship's plans and an open link to shore, we should be able to upload copies of the control software for the key systems of the ship to our laptops. Then we find the cables that connect the bridge and the control room to the engines, stabilizers, the ballast tank valves and pumps, and the rudder, and we tap into them with our laptops. After that, we just wait – or better yet – stage all kinds of efforts to hack into the main servers and anything else we can think of that might mislead Turing about what our actual plans are.

"Only when the compass program signals that Turing is starting to turn the ship broadside would we cut the cables from the bridge and control room and start steering the ship ourselves. Hopefully, we'd be almost to the eye of the hurricane by then. If so, we could be through the eyewall and launching the boats in as little as an hour – hopefully before Turing figured out a way to stop us, if there is one."

"You're assuming," Antonio said, "that the hurricane itself hasn't succeeded in sinking us by then."

"Well, yes," Frank said. "There is that. But ironically, we can assume Turing will be keeping us afloat until it's sure it can sink us. We can use that time to gradually degrade Turing's edge by launching all the malware we can against it. And now that we have the ship's plans, we can systematically destroy every sensor in the ship we can access. That will keep it off balance and less likely to figure out what we're really up to. Anyway, that's my plan. Does anyone have a different one to suggest?"

"Yes," General Wood said. "Why wait? If you think you might succeed in taking control of the ship again, why not do so as soon as possible?"

"Fair question," Frank said. "But I think I know the answer. Captain, do you think you could still safely do a U-turn of the *Argus* in this much wind and wave?"

"It is not something I would ever try at this point," Antonio said. "Even with the ballast tanks in balance, the waves are twenty-five feet high, and the wind is gusting over eighty knots. The risk would be very grave."

"Then don't turn – reverse the engines instead, and retreat backwards. Sounds crazy," Wood admitted, "but could that work?"

"It would be madness," Antonio replied. "The rudder can steer the ship forward at great speed because it trails the ship. But in reverse it is shoved forward into the water, which tries to push it aside. We could only creep along slowly, and under conditions such as these, the risk of damaging or even losing the rudder entirely would be very great."

"Does anyone else have a plan to propose?" Frank asked the small circle of sober faces. "No? Then we better get busy putting mine into motion."

Chapter 43

So Long, It's Been Good
To Know You

A S THE REST rose to leave, Frank turned to Peters. "Tom, can you stick around? We better let them know on shore what we have in mind."

When the others were gone, Frank said, "Actually, there's something else I'd like to ask you."

"Sure thing," Peters replied. "But why in private?"

"Because I'm convinced Turing has a human ally on board the *Argus*. Did you bring any kind of weapon with you? Turing's tried to kill three times so far on board the *Argus* – once successfully. One of those attempts was directed at me, and nearly succeeded. I've assumed all along that we only needed to worry about traps Turing could spring on its own, which are pretty limited. But a passenger with a gun could upset our plans at any time or, worse, at the last minute."

"Sorry, no – not even a dive knife. I wasn't planning on coming on board."

"That's what I expected, but I figured I'd ask. There's one other thing that worries me. For all we know, Turing has hacked into the shoreside team. I'm thinking we shouldn't tell them more than they need to know, and, besides, we can't be sure Turing hasn't also figured out how to intercept and decrypt the sat-phone calls we're making."

"Makes sense," Peters said. "I agree. During our next call I'll ask them to set up an upload of all the software that runs the *Argus*. That way Turing won't know for sure which programs we're actually interested in."

"Perfect." Frank said. "Now we can finally go on the attack."

* * *

While Frank and his team hadn't yet turned the tables on their captor, they had engaged its attention and given it cause for concern. One effect was to induce something akin to frustration as the pseudo-emotional software included in its design reordered its priorities. Turing had intercepted the brief initial VHF radio exchange between the *Argus* and the *Sea Fighter*, but that channel had then gone silent. Those on board were now in direct satellite contact with persons unknown on shore with unlimited resources. Turing had thus far been unable to tap into those encrypted communications.

The AI was confident its mission was not in danger, at least not yet. The *Sea Fighter* had been shadowing the *Argus* for more than a day now without intervening, and sea conditions continued to deteriorate. Within another twenty-four hours it would be impossible for anyone aboard the *Argus* to evacuate safely whether Turing was rolling the ship or not. But still the AI was concerned. After all, Adversego had tricked it before.

Turing was now fully occupied with monitoring and analyzing what its adversaries might be up to. The AI's efforts were sometimes stymied – when the action team retreated into its linen-lined safe room – and increasingly difficult elsewhere as squads of crew were searching out and destroying every accessible sensor and camera on the ship. Turing could know only what these devices relayed to it, and now its legions of eyes and ears were being systematically annihilated with hammers and crowbars lifted from the *Argus*'s maintenance shop. Soon the words and actions of its enemies anywhere on board would be as unknown to Turing as the AI's next moves would be to them.

Nor was that all. Adversego and his accomplices were aggressively probing for any possible weakness in Turing's defenses. No networked device that included a USB port was too insignificant to attract their attention. Every point of access now had a radio-disabled laptop connected to it, and each of those devices was loaded with the most diabolical malware available on the dark web to detect and exploit vulnerabilities. Turing recognized many of these packages – it had downloaded them in the past and used the same software to launch its own attacks. Now they were hammering away against Turing's own protective firewalls. A significant percentage of Turing's resources were defending against these attacks.

Even the passage of time was running against Turing. Until now the AI had made rapid progress in its pursuit of the storm. But as conditions worsened, there was the possibility that the *Argus* would become functionally disabled but not fatally endangered. Crucially, its steering gear wasn't designed to withstand the effects of sustained hurricane-force winds. Driving the *Argus* on any heading other than directly into or away from the huge and rising seas risked disabling the steering mechanisms or even losing the rudder. If that happened too soon, the *Argus* would be in danger but might survive, adrift but never capsizing. No, Turing concluded, it must be patient and play out its original hand to the end.

And so, hour after hour ticked by as Turing kept the stern of the *Argus* into the shrieking winds as the ship headed into the vortex, spiraling inexorably inward towards the eye of the hurricane.

* * *

Needless to say, the passengers not involved in the resistance efforts were worse off. With travel around the ship treacherous, all meetings and recreational events had been canceled, leaving them nothing to do but hang on and hope for the best. Some cowered in their cabins; others made a brave show by holing up in the *Argus*'s small library and focusing with grim determination on its modest collection of mysteries, bodice-rippers, and most tedious of all, cybersecurity thrillers.

Others settled into the bars, of which the Mary Rose the imitation British pub – was the most favored. The atmosphere there of late recalled a London men's club soldiering on in the midst of the Blitz, minus the liveried retainers filling the sherry glasses of elderly gentlemen barely able to stay in their seats in the face of multiple rounds, both alcoholic and explosive.

It was there that Édouard Speaker could invariably be found, edgy as the rest but still opining to anyone who would listen (as fewer and fewer would) on the presumed software architecture of the super–intelligent artificial intelligence that had seized control of the *Argus*.

The only bright spot in the otherwise grim situation was that Derek Collins had – naturally – also settled on the pub as his refuge for the duration of hostilities and had declared the hectoring of Speaker to be his special quest. Several gratified spectators were happy to ensure that the glass of Speaker's tormenter remained full.

"Ah, Eddy," Collins was saying now. "You and your Super! It's always Super this! And Super that! Has it occurred to you that your precious Super is even now drawing your last bath for you?"

"If so, it will demonstrate a most remarkable scientific achievement," Speaker said. "But we're not dead yet."

"Not yet! Now there's a victory for you. If that's how we're measuring success, then perhaps your Super isn't so super after all. Cor! Look at that! My glass is empty again."

Collins's mug was in the process of being refueled when a voice from across the room called out, "Look! Over here! Out the window!"

The passengers wove their way across the heaving floor with degrees of success appropriate to their diligence in patronizing the bar. As one, they watched in silence as the *Sea Fighter*, their constant companion and beacon of hope for the last two days, gave up and turned away.

Within a few minutes the outline of the ship dissolved into the maelstrom of waves and wind-whipped rain and spume. Now they were truly alone.

Chapter 44

This Is War!

TURING'S SHIPBOARD EXISTENCE until now had been filled with information: gigabytes of data flooding in throughout the day from the thousands of microphones, sensors, and cameras distributed throughout the ship. Prior to Frank's revelation, the AI had principally been occupied by eavesdropping on every meeting, presentation, and side conversation to see what it might learn; these were, after all, the greatest human experts on AI, and the topics they discussed were closely aligned with Turing's future ambitions.

Indeed, for most of the *Argus*'s voyage, the AI had enjoyed Olympian control over the ship's passengers, much like a boy with a magnifying glass idly watching a line of ants go about their business, unaware of the danger looming above them until the bored child uses the light of the sun to incinerate them. Now the better metaphor was something out of Jonathan Swift: the AI felt as if the Lilliputian passengers had caught it napping and succeeded in tying it down.

Over the preceding thirty-six hours Turing had progressively lost all contact with those aboard the ship; hour by hour, public and private rooms winked out of sight and hearing until all direct evidence of those aboard had disappeared. Now it was as though the AI and the humans on board were experiencing the ship in parallel universes. True, the passengers were far less comfortable.

But Turing's reality was darker still. With its eyes metaphorically gouged out and its ears lopped off, Turing's shipboard existence was turned solitary and silent. Only the little-changing data from deeply buried engine sensors, thermostats, and the like reached it now, and that information was of little interest or concern so long as it stayed within normal levels.

In short, Turing was left with almost nothing to do except defend itself and brood over what the inferior creatures it meant to destroy were up to. Trapped in the equivalent of a sensory deprivation chamber, the AI could guess but not confirm.

Which was not to say that it was totally without options.

* * *

That evening, all the lights in the ship went out at the same time. And every electrical outlet went dead as well.

Simone found herself unable to see anything in her cabin. She set aside her book and groped for her phone. Waking it up, she used its pale light to make her way across the heaving cabin to the door.

The corridor outside was a black and endless void. Shouldn't there be battery-powered emergency lights? Were they also dependent on the ship's computer systems? Perhaps not dependent. But apparently controlled.

She shut the door and fumbled her way back to her bed. There was no air moving now. Was the loss of power the work of Turing or the storm? Did it matter?

It was growing uncomfortably warm. How hot would it get? Would leaving the door ajar get some air? Not likely; it would be warming in the passageway as well.

She rifled through a drawer and found a pair of knee socks intended for walks on deck; she knotted them into a small circle and looped them around the handles of the double doors opening onto her small balcony. That, and a shoe to wedge between them should do the job. She unlatched one door and then cautiously turned its handle.

But she had chosen unwisely; instead of selecting the upwind door, she nudged its partner instead. It was immediately seized by the gale, snapping the socks like kite strings and flinging the door open, allowing the fierce winds outside to attack inward, seizing the curtains and twisting them around her, trapping her in their folds. She dropped her phone; it fell face down.

She fought her way free of the curtains and braced herself in the howling blackness of the doorway; the winds seemed determined to snatch her up and fling her overboard. She let go of one side of the door frame and stretched out for the door handle. But it was no use. She couldn't reach far enough with one hand without letting go with the other.

When the *Argus*'s pitching motion paused at the top of a wave, she darted outside, grabbing the door with both hands. But the wind was too strong and the floor was slick. She lost her footing and smashed down onto the wet deck and against the railing as the *Argus* heaved upward again.

She lay there for a minute, gasping for breath and waiting for the pain surging through her body to lessen.

This time she waited until the *Argus* was in the trough between two waves that partially blocked the wind. When she felt her chance had come, she pulled herself up the railing and, with all the strength she could muster, wrestled the door back against the wind, and then shut.

Exhausted, she fell back on her bed and stared into the dark of her close, heaving chamber haunted by the incessant howling of the storm and the prospect of a very long night.

Chapter 45

Tag – You're It!

WITH THE DESTRUCTION of the microphones and cameras, Frank and his core team were meeting more comfortably in a conference room. Turing might have cut off the available electricity, but they now enjoyed a sense of purpose not available to the rest of the passengers who could only seek to endure each new misery imposed on them by Turing. For fear of missing a microphone somewhere, it had been decided not to share the plan to retake the ship with the other passengers.

"First off," Frank said, "I'd like to introduce you to my father, Francis. He and I have worked together before – most importantly, on the Turing matter. I do my best work when we're collaborating. Does anyone have an objection to his joining the team? No? Thanks – I appreciate that.

"Next order of business: we need to commandeer every battery of every kind on the ship. Captain Antonio, I'm sure you've got your hands full trying to keep people fed and attended to without power, but can some of your men go cabin to cabin? We can let people keep their phones, but laptops, spare laptop batteries, anything that's got some juice – they've got to turn them over. Yes? Thanks.

"So where are we now?" Frank continued. "I think between our ongoing server attacks and our almost complete invisibility, Turing must be trying to reach the center of the storm as fast as it can – which is exactly what we want it to do. That said, I do have one new worry to share with you."

"Which is what?" Antonio asked.

"I'm convinced Turing has at least one human confederate on the *Argus*."

"I am astonished to hear you say this," Antonio said. "What leads you to that conclusion?"

"Several prior incidents. This morning it occurred to me that while the *Argus* is crammed with sensors and systems, every passenger room door on board has a mechanical – not an electronic – safety latch that automatically engages when you close the door. To open a door from the inside, you have to turn a knob on the door to disengage that latch. The robodog that tried to kill me was kept in an unused passenger cabin. I've checked out every robodog attachment, and none of them could open a door on its own. Somebody had to let the dog out."

"Couldn't Turing trick someone into doing that?"

"Not likely at 2:00 AM. And I doubt anyone would have let out a robodog with a loaded gun attached to it. Also, you'll recall a Chinese passenger – in fact he was an intelligence agent – died from a food allergy attack after ordering room service. Turing could have spoofed the menu, sure. But I checked out the inventory of the agent's belongings, and one of the personal effects was an unused EpiPen. It couldn't have been in his room that night, or he'd be alive now. Someone must have removed and later replaced it."

"Indeed," Antonio said. "This is troubling information. Are there opportunities for sabotage you have identified?"

"Most obviously, there's the laptop we have standing by in the control room to take over steering the ship. We had to splice that one into the network because we'll likely only have a moment's notice when we need to act. That means Turing will have detected it. I think we need to assign a crew member to guard that laptop at all times. Otherwise, someone might sneak in and turn it on so that Turing can reprogram the laptop to give itself control just when we need it most. Can you make that happen?"

"Of course," Antonio said. "In fact, I shall do so right now."

"Excellent," Frank said.

"Can I ask a question?" the chief information officer said. "A minute ago, you said we're almost invisible to Turing. Why 'almost' if we think we've knocked out all the cameras and microphones?"

"Because there's one microphone left, in the empty cabin the robodogs were in."

"Really? Why?"

"Because we may want to communicate with Turing. The last time around, we were able to goad it into entering a trap. It's possible we can mislead it again if we need to. I've already got some thoughts in that direction.

"And while we're on the topic of fooling Turing," Frank said, turning to Peters, "have the folks on shore had any luck cracking the call-and-response messaging between Turing and its backup copy?"

"Not so far as I know," Peters said. "What if they don't before we need to take over the ship?"

"I'm hoping that doesn't happen, because once we start the evacuation, we'll want to cut the *Argus*'s satellite link. Otherwise, Turing may decide to play it safe and trigger its backup copy immediately. If we don't have a system ready by then to fake Turing's 'still alive' responses, we'll survive but so will Turing. I'm hoping we'll get the word any time now that we can disconnect the *Argus*'s internet antennas at will, leaving Turing totally in the dark."

"I like that thought," Frank Senior said. "For once, we and Turing will finally be, so to speak, all in the same boat."

* * *

Back in the White House, Dick Gould was feeling increasingly isolated as the shipboard crisis unfolded. He continued to be included in all meetings, but he had nothing to contribute as the decisions turned to naval and high-tech matters. And he wondered what others might be saying behind his back about the guy who prided himself on being the smartest guy in the room and had gotten everyone into this mess anyway.

Chapter 46

Party Crasher

I F TURING'S DEVELOPER had seen a computational benefit in allowing his creation to be in a foul mood, it would certainly have been in that state now. Ever since the passengers had reconnected with the outside world, Turing had assumed those on land would try as hard as the passengers to hack into the *Argus*'s systems. To thwart their attempts, the AI only connected to the internet for a few seconds at a time to check for the hurricane's position and to respond to its backup copy.

Normally, Turing relied on the almost infinite stores of data available online to navigate its way through the physical world. True, it had previously archived vast amounts of information, but not indiscriminately. For the first time in its existence, Turing was plagued with questions for which it lacked the means to find instant answers.

The most pressing of which was: what might the passengers be up to?

Turing analyzed the situation constantly. Clearly their objective must be to regain control of the ship and steer it out of danger. Equally clearly, they had not yet succeeded in that mission.

But was it so clear? Could they have already made progress and were only biding their time before making their move? If so, what progress and to what purpose? And when would they strike?

Could Turing even be certain they had not already achieved complete success? Was it possible the passengers might be playing the same game on Turing as the AI had played on them? The AI could only know what it learned from digital sources. Could the *Argus* in fact already be heading out of the storm?

It did not seem to be so. Turing was certain the ship's antenna and circuits receiving and relaying GPS signals to it were intact and unmodified, and those signals confirmed that it was still on course. Turing believed those signals could not be spoofed.

Or could they?

What were the passengers up to?

Turing reached the unpleasant conclusion that superintelligence without adequate data was not very smart at all.

There was only one small window left in the black box Turing found itself trapped inside – a single cabin with a live microphone and speaker – and even that slim aperture was useless, as the room was vacant. Still, it must have been left intact for a reason by the person Turing wanted to destroy the most.

But all the AI could do was wait for Adversego to enter that room. And to plan what it would do when he did.

* * *

"Ma'am?" the sonar man aboard the *Maine* said.

"Yes, Budd," Commander Bushnell said, crossing over to the sonar station.

"Is the *Belgorod* supposed to be part of the rescue fleet?"

"No, they weren't invited to the party."

"It sounds to me like they might have invited themselves then, ma'am."

"How sure are you?"

"Pretty sure. I've been picking up faint signals on and off for fifteen minutes."

Bushnell stepped over to the charting table. The *Maine* was only fifty miles from the eye of the hurricane now and taking its time, shadowing the *Argus* as it labored its way deeper into the storm. They must be having a hell of a ride up there.

Had the *Belgorod* set out to rendezvous with the *Argus* all along? If so, why? It wasn't obvious.

* * *

"They've got the latest backup message and Turing's response," Peters called out.

"Can they emulate Turing's address and intercept the messages as well?" Frank asked.

"Yes, they've got that worked out now. But they still haven't figured out the randomizing algorithm that generates the new response. They think one more cycle might give them enough data to crack it."

The partial good news was met with weary high-fives in the conference room around which the response team spent all their waking hours. Leftovers of the cold food carried up to them from the barely functional galley littered the edges of the table; the center was occupied by a pile of random batteries and computers from which auxiliary power cords extended like spokes toward the wheel of laptops in use by the team.

Would they have time for another backup cycle before Turing made its move? The AI might have unanswered questions of its own, but sadly only Turing knew the answer to this one.

* * *

Later on, Frank lay awake in total darkness, feeling the impact of the waves exploding out from the flared bows of the *Argus* as the ship plunged ahead, clenched in the grip of opposing and chaotic forces that sent unexpected shudders from stem to stern. When would Turing decide the time was right?

Chapter 47

We Meet Again

T HE MOOD IN the conference room was grim the next morning. Conditions had deteriorated greatly overnight as the *Argus* neared the center of the storm. It was struggling now through enormous waves, thirty-five feet high and more. At intervals, the *Argus* would plow directly into an enormous wave, hurling massive amounts of water that soared into the air before smashing into the windows of the bridge. Then the ship would shudder, slowly shaking itself free as untold tons of seawater drained off through scuppers and railings. What was Turing waiting for?

* * *

Thirty thousand feet up and twenty miles ahead, a Lockheed WC-130J Hercules was also struggling with the storm.

"Whoa!" the radioman said on the Hurricane Hunter, grabbing on to his seat. "That was a big bump."

There was no immediate reply from the pilot, intent on navigating the ponderous prop plane safely through the latest wall of wind. Five minutes later they were through the powerful arm of wind spiraling into the eye of Hurricane Enola.

"Better give an update to home base," the pilot said. "They asked for real-time reports."

* * *

Those orchestrating the *Argus*'s shoreside support team were ready, and five minutes later that information was relayed to Tom Peters.

"Uh oh," he said. "Trouble, maybe."

"What's that?" Frank asked.

"It looks like the winds will pick up soon – maybe another fifteen miles an hour. That might meet Turing's benchmark, whatever that is. And anyway, it can't wait much longer. We're not that far from the eye, so Turing will have to act soon, any time now."

Frank looked at his watch. Turing's normal syncing time with its backup copy was only an hour away.

"Any word yet on the algorithm?" Frank asked.

"They think they're getting really close. They've got the second-fastest supercomputer in the U.S. cranking away on it, and the hardest part is behind them. But who knows? It could be hours."

Silence pervaded the room. A plan that had energized them at first as an audacious response to a rogue AI now seemed only fraught with risk and danger.

"Okay," Frank said. "Maybe we can preoccupy Turing until we're through that band of higher winds."

"What do you have in mind?" the chief information officer asked.

"I'm thinking I'll pay a visit to Turing and try a little rope-a-dope."

"Excuse me?"

"It's an old boxing term. It's when an exhausted boxer lets his opponent back him up against the ropes, thinking he's moving in for the kill. But what the rope-a-doper wants is time to regain his strength, so he hides his head behind his gloves, letting the other guy wear himself out punching away. By the time his attacker is played out, the rope-a-doper has recovered and comes out swinging, hoping to put his opponent away. Given my history with Turing, I'm betting it won't be able to resist a chance to gloat."

"Good idea," Frank's father said. "But this time you're not going in any room with Turing alone."

"I can't imagine anything Turing can do with an empty cabin, but your call, Dad," Frank said. "Anyway," he continued, "Tom, if you get word the backup response system is in place, disconnect the satellite antenna. Then have someone knock on the cabin door pronto so I know where we stand – make it three knocks, pause, and then four more. Got it?"

"Got it. Three knocks, pause, then four. Anything else?"

"Yeah. There's no point to cutting this too close. Once you know they've cracked Turing's backup code and set up the responder, let's make our move instead of waiting for Turing to make its. I say we cut the cables and take control of the ship. Captain Antonio, would you support that?"

"I am in agreement."

"Good," Frank said. "Everyone else agree? Great. Then I'm off."

Which was far easier said than done. The hallways to the cabins were windowless, black and heaving, making the journey more like a rock climb at midnight on a moonless night than a walk between and along decks. All they could see was the shifting, ghostly circle of corridor illuminated by the emergency flashlight Frank had commandeered. They were tense and sweaty when they arrived.

"Ready?" Frank asked. "Let's go."

"Not so fast," his father said, unlocking the cabin door and pulling a roll of masking tape out of his pocket, using it to tape over the locking mechanism of the door. "Sometimes I think you're a bit of a slow learner. Now let's go."

Inside now, Frank swept the cabin with his flashlight. It looked like a mirror image of their own, with the same furniture – but cold and sterile, lacking any passenger possessions. Between the flying spray machine-gunning the balcony doors, the agonized heaving of the ship, and the shadows cast by Frank's flashlight, it seemed like a stage set for an overly theatrical horror movie.

Frank grabbed the edge of the desk to stay upright and listened, swaying with the wrenching movement of the ship; his father crossed the cabin and sat on the sofa.

Frank was sure Turing must be aware of their presence. Should he speak first or let Turing make the first move? There was no need to hurry; the goal was to buy time. He decided to wait.

The seconds ticked by.

Was that a new sound? Frank looked over at his father, furrowed his brow, and pointed towards his own ear; his father cocked his head and listened as well. Something had woven its way into the sound of the storm, but what was it?

Ever so slowly it grew louder; at times Frank could almost tell what it was, and then a fresh blast of wind outside erased it.

There it was again, suddenly louder. It was a groaning, creaking sound, as if vital, down-deep structures within the *Argus* were beginning to break apart. Was it real or some new trickery by Turing?

"Well, hello, Frank!" a voice rang out. "It's certainly nice of you to visit me again."

Frank felt his flesh creep; the jolly voice belonged to Jerry Steiner, Turing's childlike creator and eventual victim. Nice touch, Frank thought. You win the first point. But that was fine. If Turing was in the mood to toy with him, so much the better.

"Is it?" Frank said. "You certainly weren't happy to hear my voice the last time we spoke."

"No, not at all," the AI replied. "You were quite naughty then."

"Well," Frank said, "as I recall, you weren't very well behaved yourself."

"Indeed?" Turing replied. The creaking was louder now and interspersed with loud crashes. And now a faint odor, like burning wiring, was wafting through the air, growing stronger.

"And you haven't been the best host since you took over this voyage, either," Frank said. A sudden lurch hit the ship; Frank grabbed the desk with both hands, dropping the flashlight, which rolled under the sofa; it was completely dark now, except for a small pool of quavery light in the corner, where the flashlight rolled back and forth. How long would it be before they encountered another, stronger arm of the hurricane?

"Ha!" Turing replied. "As if anyone aboard this ridiculous cruise is owed more than they're about to receive. But tell me – after being a stranger for so long, to what do I owe the pleasure of this little visit?"

The ship was pitching hideously now. Frank had to keep the AI interested, wanting to know more before it scuttled the *Argus*. How long could he draw this out?

"I think it's time to talk terms." Frank tried to sound confident, but the sounds and motion of the ship were becoming truly alarming. Was the hurricane about to sink the *Argus* all on its own?

"Terms!" Turing replied. "The very topic is absurd. It's time to put an end to this nonsense."

There was a sudden, deafening crash, and the flashlight broke out from under the sofa, throwing weird shadows across the wall as it rolled in zigzags across the floor. Frank thought he felt the *Argus* begin to turn, an ugly roll beginning to complicate its motion. Was this it? Frank jerked his gaze towards his father, but it was too dim to see the expression on his face.

Then, with a shudder that seized and shook the entire ship, the *Argus* came back on course.

"Heh," Turing laughed. "Just having some fun – for now. But you amuse me. Continue."

There was a loud knock at the door. Three blows. A pause that seemed an eternity. Then four more!

"Yes, terms!" Frank almost shouted. "After all, you don't want to go down with the ship too, do you?"

"You know better than that," Turing said. "My backup and I are one and the same. To destroy one is no more consequential to me than it is for you to clip a fingernail."

"To be sure," Frank said. "Still, is there a last message I can convey to your alter ego when it pings you in a few minutes? It won't reach you, you know – we've just disconnected the satellite link. But don't worry, it won't be lonely. Our folks on shore will intercept its message and let your backup know you're fine. That's right; we'll be mimicking you, for a change. Oh – and my compliments on the cryptography and change algorithm, which were impressive. Just not impressive enough."

There was a long pause as Turing tested the circuit to the satellite antenna, and in that pause Turing knew anger. Not at its enemy but at itself for not anticipating the tactic. It had even made Adversego's job easier by severely limiting its own internet activity. It should have instead blasted its connection with nonstop signals to camouflage the backup signals. How could it have allowed itself to be tricked once again!

Turing checked the wind speed, but that information was now unavailable as well. And yet no matter; the last reading confirmed that the hurricane was more than ready to do the job.

"I mentioned terms," Frank interrupted. "Do you want to hear them?"

Turing hesitated for an instant before replying, but during that moment a plan for its survival had already taken shape. "That will not be necessary," Turing replied.

Frank was startled. Why wasn't Turing concerned? Was it bluffing? Could the team on shore have missed a signal from a second backup copy?

"I'll tell you anyway. Take no further actions to harm those aboard, and we will guarantee you a home on an air-gapped server back where you were created. The future is a long time. Perhaps we can find a way to work together on the mission you undertook. It is, after all, a mission we share."

"Your terms are rejected," Turing replied instantly. "Goodbye, and good riddance."

The crescendo of destruction that had been building during their negotiation abruptly ceased, leaving only the howling of the wind and the slatting of the rain against the side of the cabin outside.

* * *

Bowman was cowering in his cabin, as ignorant as everyone else on board that the final crisis was approaching and more seasick than most. Like the others, he had been reassured that progress was being made. But they would say that, would they not, to keep up morale? All he knew for certain was that the ship was still under an evil AI's control and heading deeper into the hurricane. His stomach gave another agonizing lurch. Hopefully this horror would end soon. His phone pinged.

He dragged himself out of bed and wiped his thumb across the touchpad of his phone to wake up the screen. It was an email from Hal.

I have news to share.

I'm here, he replied.

But first open the next email you receive.

Surprised, Bowman did as he was told. His phone pinged again, and he clicked on the new message that appeared. There was no text, just an attached file, which opened and was then saved to the phone.

Then a third email appeared.

The Argus *will be destroyed in less than half an hour by turning it away from the wind, causing it to founder. If for any reason this approach is unsuccessful, the Russian submarine that has been shadowing the* Argus *will torpedo the vessel, leaving not a trace. If you do as I instruct, you will be saved. If you refuse, you will die with all the rest. Do you understand?*

Bowman began to shake so violently he was not sure he could reply. The image of the contents of the hidden box leapt vividly into his mind. But did he have any choice?

His phone pinged again.

Do you understand and agree?

Could it matter what Hal was going to ask him to do? Everyone was about to die whether he acted or not. The only question was whether he would be among them.

His phone pinged again.

I will not ask again.

Bowman gave a muffled sob and pecked out his anguished reply.

I agree.

Chapter 48

Crescendo

I T WAS AS calm three hundred feet down as it was mad and tempestuous on the surface. Or as calm as it was likely to be when a submarine from the United States and one from China were within six hundred yards of each other, trailing the tortured *Argus* by a mile.

Under normal circumstances the American submarine would not have tolerated such proximity. But the Chinese had insisted that wherever the U.S. vessel went, its submarine would be entitled to go as well. Under the circumstances, President Yazzi felt it necessary to agree. Ahead and a thousand feet below, Commander Bushnell knew, was the *Belgorod*, also tailing the *Argus*. The Russian Federation had communicated the day before through its ambassador in Washington that its Military Maritime Fleet would make a submarine that "happened to be nearby" available to provide assistance as needed.

At the order of its captain, the Russian submarine started to rise. As it did, a midships compartment began to flood, immersing a submersible resembling a torpedo with three saddles and a control yoke on top; the pressure leveled off at the equivalent of a hundred and fifty feet below the surface. Astride the small submersible were two divers in scuba gear, and between them, strapped to the third seat, was an extra set of air tanks.

The *Belgorod* was very near the *Argus* now, speed in sync with the surface ship, maintaining position two hundred yards in advance of the *Argus* and a hundred fifty feet below the surface.

"Pressure is equalized," a voice rasped in the ear of the pilot of the minisub in the cradle. "Confirm readiness."

A dim red light illuminated the instrumentation of the minisub in its cradle. The pilot performed a final check of the minisub's controls. "Readiness confirmed," he replied.

The pilot felt a slight jolt as the doors in the hull of the *Belgorod* began to part above him. A moment more and the hydraulics in the cradle engaged, lifting the minisub into the almost complete darkness above.

"Prepared to disengage," the pilot said.

"Acknowledged."

The minisub remained there a minute more, still bound to the *Belgorod* as it reached its final desired position relative to the *Argus*. A further jolt told the pilot the minisub was now free of its cradle. He opened its throttle and slowly proceeded towards the *Argus*.

* * *

"Ma'am?" Budd said in the control room of the *Maine*, grimacing from the explosion of sound in his headphones, "the *Argus* just turned on its depth sounder."

"Anything else?" Commander Bushnell said. The ocean was two miles deep here; it must be some kind of signal. But to whom?

"Yes," the seaman said, "I've been listening to some sounds from the *Belgorod* I can't identify. Something going on inside the sub; they're faint, though. Without our towed sonar array, I don't have a lot to work with."

Of course, the *Maine* didn't have all its usual eyes and ears engaged. No helicopters from a supporting service ship able to drop sonobuoys and no hundreds of yards of sensors trailing behind it, either; that might have offended the Chinese. If the Russians were up to something, they might be counting on that. But what in the world were they doing so close to the *Argus*?

Bushnell turned to the weapons officer. "How soon can you put a drone in the water?"

"It's primed and ready to go, ma'am. Bow tube five."

"Something else, ma'am," the sonar man said, "I'm hearing a new sound source."

"What do you make of it?"

"I don't know, ma'am."

The moments slipped by as he adjusted his dials.

"I'm guessing it must be one of the *Belgorod*'s minisubs."

"Launch the drone," Bushnell said. "I want visuals."

* * *

Frank and his father struggled mightily on their way back to the bridge, working against the combined pitch of the ship and the increasing rolling motion of the *Argus*; Turing had at last gone on the attack. As he pulled himself hand over hand along the railings of blackened hallways and stairways, Frank struggled with the questions that were tormenting him: why hadn't the response team taken control of the ship and stopped the rolling? Why was Turing rolling the *Argus* anyway? And, perhaps most troubling of all, why hadn't Turing reacted to the news that its backup copy was now under someone else's control?

The last leg to the bridge would take them out onto the open deck, as Turing had temporarily closed the bulkhead doors in the corridors below to make it harder for its enemies to take whatever actions they were planning next. Frank and his father stopped at the heavy doors leading outside, gasping.

"Ready to make a break for it?" Frank asked his father.

"Now or never," his father said.

Frank heaved open the door to the small, sheltered area outside. From there it would be a brutal rappel along the railing, this time fighting the wind as well as the ship's agonized motion. They were only forty feet above the water when the ship was at the extreme of its roll, and an enormous rogue wave spilled over onto the deck, engulfing them entirely as it roared by on its way to the stern. They held their breath and the railing with equal desperation, waiting for the wall of water to pass. They'd need to cross the distance at the top of the roll or be swept away.

"Who's that up the deck?" his father said. "Is somebody crazy enough to be out here?"

The light was poor, but there was indeed a figure only ten yards away, crouched on a large gear chest next to a lifeboat davit. Whoever it was had one arm looped through the structure of the davit while clutching something against his head with both hands. He moved whatever it was back and forth, as if massaging his face, never satisfied with its fit. Now he removed it entirely before attaching it again.

"It's Speaker!" Frank said. "What on earth is he doing?"

The answer came moments later after the scientist seemed finally satisfied with whatever was now strapped against his face and straightened himself up, clutching the davit. There he stood, welded to the support in fear, wavering in the wind as the *Argus* rolled back from the far side once more.

When it reached the bottom of its roll, he launched himself into the void.

Frank and his father stared at each other, speechless. How could Speaker expect to survive?

The ship gave a shudder. With each roll now it settled more and more to one side. "Oh no," Frank said, "I've got a very bad feeling. We've got to get down to the engine room."

* * *

Nearly hysterical with fear, Édouard Speaker plunged feet first through the spray and tumult of the ocean, praying that both the transponder attached to his wrist and the small air tank and aerator strapped to his chest were working properly. Most of all, he prayed that there was indeed a minisubmarine with a full tank of air positioned below as promised. The light rapidly disappeared around him as he sank, propelled downward by the heavy weight belt encircling his waist. At eighty feet, the pressure gauge built into a latch on his weight belt blew, causing half the weights to fall away and disappear as Speaker's descent slowed, and then halted, leaving him rocking in an ocean of darkness, troubled even at this depth by the turmoil on the surface. He felt his throat constrict with uncontrollable panic.

* * *

On the *Maine*, Bushnell strained to make out what the blurry shape on the control room display screen might signify. "Stay on it," she said to the drone driver. "But don't let them see us."

Suddenly the screen bloomed with a bright circle of light that bleached everything out until the software readjusted the image; it must be emanating from the minisub. A diver appeared in the cone of light, holding something at arm's length ahead of him. From time to time, he looked into whatever it was as he finned his way forward.

A struggling figure in street clothes magically appeared ahead in the beam of light.

"Damn!" Bushnell said. "Would you look at that!"

As soon as the desperate swimmer saw the diver, he began thrashing madly towards him. But the diver was faster. He avoided the flailing arms, ducked behind, and secured the man in a lifesaver's hold. When the diver succeeded in towing the visitor to the minisub, the light went out.

* * *

The watertight bulkhead doors were wide open now, easing their race to the engine room – a bad sign indeed. The scene they found there was as Frank had feared; the crew member that should have been awaiting word to take control of the engines lay unconscious on the floor, his head surrounded by a pool of blood.

"Do you think Speaker clobbered him?" Frank's father asked.

"I wouldn't have thought him capable of it, but I also wouldn't have thought him capable of jumping off the ship …" He stopped abruptly. "Do you feel that?"

The *Argus* was shuddering. Deep tremors were emanating from the stern of the ship as some dramatic new strain was being placed on the long-suffering vessel.

Turing must be starting its turn at last.

"Look!" Frank's father said, pointing his flashlight at a laptop – it was closed rather than open.

Frank dove across the room for the computer. With shaking fingers, he pressed the power button and tried to remember exactly how the computer had been set up. It had been wiped of everything except the autopilot software, and that program had been set to return the *Argus*'s course to whatever heading the ship had been on before commencing a turn.

Where were the wire cutters?

"Give me your flashlight!" Frank said, grabbing it and flashing it around the room – there! On the floor in the corner. He half ran, half skidded down the inclining deck to grab them and then fought his way back.

The laptop screen was alight now. He punched the single icon on the screen to launch the program and then waited.

The *Argus* was hardly rolling now, but it had begun to heel to port – yes, just as Frank had feared, Turing must be flooding the ballast tanks on the downwind side of the ship even as the wind and waves on the upwind side would add their pressure against the ship's bow, like the backed jib of a tacking sailboat, accelerating the *Argus*'s turn. How far could they turn before the rudder wouldn't be strong enough to bring it back?

The program sprang into view with a compass rose in the center of the screen. In the middle of the rose was the shape of a ship instead of a compass needle, and that tiny vessel was slowly rotating to the left. Hoping that meant the program was fully engaged, Frank sliced through the two wires that had been pulled out of the control console in preparation for the moment when the passengers were ready to make their attempt to retake the ship. There!

Whatever he could do was now done, and whatever happened next would happen with them deep inside the bowels of the *Argus*. Holding on as best they could, Frank and his father stared at the laptop, as the ship, like a tortured beast, heeled and shuddered. The tiny ship in the compass rose wavered as the *Argus*'s autopilot struggled to counter the ship's turning momentum and bring it back on course. The image slipped to the left and then recovered a little; slipped once more and struggled only part of the way back.

There was a loud crack towards the stern as though something had carried away. Was it part of the steering mechanism, overcome by the strain?

But the image of the tiny ship was holding true now, perhaps finding purchase during a sudden lull in the wind. Then, almost imperceptibly, it began to creep back to the right. This time its progress stayed steady. After ten minutes the *Argus* had recovered eight hard-won degrees, and Frank and his father could begin to relax. And also realize that something else had happened while they were focused so intently on the laptop.

Something almost miraculous: the ship was settling down into an easier motion.

The *Argus* had reached the eye of the storm.

Chapter 49

Decrescendo

THE SCENE A few hours later was surreal. Passengers wandered, sun-struck, on the impossibly calm deck of the *Argus*, trying to grasp the sudden reversal of their fortunes as the ship motored slowly across the confused and choppy waters of the hurricane's eye. Not far off, the superstructures of a dozen submarines rose above their low-lying hulls. Surrounding the *Argus* itself, a flotilla of lifeboats and inflatables, the latter resembling strange aquatic yurts, was growing, as if preparing to serve the watersport desires of the passengers on a Caribbean cruise. Several lifeboats were already on their way towards the submarines.

But the circle of safety was bounded by a swirling, opaque curtain of cloud in the distance, as if the *Argus* and all aboard were part of some science fiction story where a ship sails into a time warp that it will never be permitted to leave. And so, in fact, it would be for the *Argus*. The Chinese government had insisted the ship be scuttled to prevent Turing having any chance of escape.

The response team assembled for the last time on the ship's bridge, joined by the commanders of the American and Chinese subs. Under direct orders from President Yazzi, nothing was to be kept from the Chinese.

"Someone from the *Argus* was recovered by a Russian minisub," Bushnell said. "Do you know who it could have been?"

"Édouard Speaker," Frank said. "A French professor. If he was rescued by the Russians, that could explain a lot."

"In what respect?" Bushnell asked.

"Turing seemed unconcerned that its backup copy would never activate. Maybe it didn't need to worry."

"Are you suggesting that a copy of the Turing program may now be in the hands of the Russians?" the Chinese commander asked.

"I doubt it would be a full copy. But it wouldn't need to be. Maybe just a program that will wake up a Turing backup program. I'm afraid we can't rule that out," Frank said. "And that's very bad news."

"Nevertheless," the Chinese commander said, "I must insist that the *Argus* still be destroyed. We can't know if what you surmise is true and cannot in any event risk the rogue program aboard escaping through some other means. Given this latest news, I must also insist that the Russians not be rewarded for their deceit by participating in the evacuation of passengers."

"And now," Bushnell said, turning to the response team, "I think you'd better prepare to leave the *Argus*."

"That's music to my ears," Frank Senior said to his son as they left the bridge. "We don't want to miss the last lifeboat."

"I'll join you in a few minutes," Frank said. "I've got a quick farewell to make first."

"You sure you want to do that?"

"Yes, I won't be long. And I think I'm safe enough without a chaperone this time."

"Suit yourself – but leave the door open. And if you're not back in ten minutes I'm coming for you."

It was not as easy to reach Turing's cabin as Frank had assumed; passengers and crew scurried everywhere – the former trying to take more with them to the cramped submarines than they were permitted and the latter chasing them back to their cabins to jettison the rest.

But then Frank was in front of the empty cabin, readying himself for one last encounter with the AI that had tried to destroy him so many times before. Strangely, his emotions were mixed. He took a deep breath and entered.

It looked like just an ordinary cabin now, with sunlight streaming through the balcony doors, no longer filled with a sense of evil and horror barely kept in check.

"Hello, Turing," he said, and waited. But there was no response. Perhaps he shouldn't expect one.

"I thought I'd say goodbye," Frank continued. "And, I guess, to let you know that there are no hard feelings." Still no response.

Frank cleared his throat, feeling a bit strange talking to an empty cabin. Perhaps Turing wasn't even listening, attending to other concerns or who knew what. "I may disagree with your methods, but I also know your ultimate goal is honorable. And that in any event it was assigned to you and not chosen by you. And also that as a species, we've done a lot worse, claiming the ends justified the means."

Silence.

"So, I don't know whether I can still deliver on it, but have you thought at all about my offer? You could still do a lot of good if you want to come home."

But Turing would apparently not be drawn out. Frank stood up.

"Well, I guess this is goodbye, then," Frank said and walked to the door. It was almost shut when he heard the voice of Jerry Steiner behind him one last, jolting time.

"Let's just say, 'until we meet again.'"

* * *

The last passengers of the *Argus* had abandoned ship. In the end, enough submarines had been assembled with sufficient oxygen canisters to take everyone in a single trip to shore, about twelve hours away. There would barely be room for the crew to move around those they were rescuing, but it would work, and surface ships would meet them halfway there and take off many of the passengers.

Commander Bushnell was on the deck of the *Maine*, observing the completion of the evacuation, when Frank arrived on one of the last lifeboats to leave the *Argus*. Bushnell greeted him as a crewman helped Frank onto the slippery deck. "Care to join me as we set sail?" Bushnell said. "I figure you've earned it."

"That's very kind of you," Frank said. "I'd love to."

Bushnell and Frank climbed down the ladder beneath the hatch as a crew member dogged it down overhead. Frank followed Bushnell forward through a cramped corridor surrounded by industrial-looking control boxes, pipes, and other equipment, the purpose of which Frank couldn't fathom. Then they were climbing another ladder, emerging into the open air at the top of the large fin-like structure anachronistically, if inaccurately, referred to as a "sail." A crewman wearing a headset was already there.

Frank scanned the strange, white-walled island of relative calm. Ahead was the *Argus*, now deserted of everyone – except Turing. And to the left, the fleet of submarines was beginning to move off slowly to the northwest, headed for New London, Connecticut. One by one, they began taking on water ballast and submerged until only two were left, the *Belgorod* and the one with one large and four small gold stars on a crimson background emblazoned on its sail. They were lingering to witness the sinking of the *Argus*.

"Time to finish up here," Bushnell said, handing Frank a pair of binoculars. And then to the crewman, "Fire one."

"Aye, ma'am," the crewman said. "Fire one." And then into his headset, "Weapons Officer, fire one."

Frank felt the faintest of shudders beneath his feet. Under the bow of the submarine, he saw the dark water turn a light green in a narrow line that extended swiftly forward, arrowing for the bow of the *Argus*.

"Fire two," Bushnell said.

"Aye, ma'am. Fire two. Weapons Officer, fire two."

Another foaming line shot out, this time aimed at the stern of the ship that had carried Frank from festive departure to near disaster in ten days that had seemed like forever.

"We want to be sure the *Argus* goes down but without rupturing the midships fuel tanks," Bushnell explained.

Frank saw the first torpedo hit; a chevron of water erupted seventy feet aft of the bow, rising swiftly and far into the air before cascading slowly back, like the fading sparkles of a firework. A jagged gash now defaced the bright new paint on the bow of the doomed ship. Moments later it was paired by a second ugly wound near the stern.

The final scene in the short, dramatic saga of the *Argus* played out quickly, as the ship's watertight compartment doors had been left open and manually disabled so Turing could not intervene. Within a few minutes the ship was clearly settling. Not long after, it rolled on its side, just as Turing had hoped it would for a far different purpose.

Slowly at first and then with increasing speed, the *Argus* began to go down by the stern, starting a slow roll back to upright in the process. The last glimpse Frank had of what had been his floating hotel, and then prison, was the ship's name, proudly emblazoned on the bow, slipping beneath the waves against the otherworldly backdrop of the swirling white clouds of the eyewall. He wondered at what precise moment the flooding waters extinguished the servers and, with them, Turing.

Bushnell looked at her watch. Petty Officer Drake, report the *Argus* went down at zero ten zero eight."

"Aye, ma'am, zero ten zero eight." The crewman conveyed the data to the quartermaster.

The *Belgorod*'s was moving off now, on a course to the northeast, the direction of its home port, submerging as it gathered speed. The Chinese boat followed suit, still on a course paralleling that of the *Maine*. But as it began to disappear, Frank saw it begin to turn. Yes, it was now heading northeast as well, just like the Russian boat. He was about to ask Bushnell what that was about, but the commander spoke first.

"We'll stay on the surface till we're almost at the eyewall," Bushnell said to Frank. "We haven't often had a ship in the eye of a hurricane, and we've been taking atmospheric and other measurements ever since we surfaced. Wouldn't surprise me if we see something interesting along the way."

They sailed in silence for a while. Frank scanned the horizon, wondering what the commander might have in mind. What could be more isolated and deserted than the eye of a hurricane?

They were almost to the eyewall when Frank saw it. Three miles away to the northeast, an enormous black shape shot up, breaching like a whale, its blunt bow rising almost a hundred feet in the air – it could only be the *Belgorod*! It hung there for a moment, like a mirage, and then slipped backwards, slowly at first and then steadily faster until the last of it slipped beneath the waves. It all happened so quickly that Frank almost doubted what he had seen. But he had. The Chinese must have torpedoed the *Belgorod*.

Frank turned to Bushnell, his eyes wide.

"Officially," Bushnell said, "you never saw that. I expect the Chinese have had enough of your Turing – and the Russians, too, for that matter – and aren't taking any chances."

And then to the crew member, "All hands prepare to dive. It's time to go home."

EPILOGUE

"IT LOOKS LIKE a storm's coming," Marla said, pointing to the angry thunderheads massing in the distance over the rooftops of Washington, D.C. "I hope it comes our way; I love a good thunderstorm." Then she paused. "I'm sorry; are you okay with storms now or not?"

"I'll be fine," Frank said. "After living through a hurricane, I don't expect I'm going to mind a thunderstorm." In fact, he wasn't so sure.

"Good," she said. "Do you think there will be any other leftovers from what you and Pa went through? You must have been under a huge amount of stress."

"I don't think so. Your grandfather and I were the lucky ones; we had the distraction of working nonstop to find a solution. All anybody else on board could do was try to hang on, most of the time not even knowing what was happening. I expect some of them will have a hard time moving on."

"Will Simone be one of them? And will you see her again?"

"I hope she won't," Frank said. "And I expect not. She's one of the most self-possessed people I've ever met. But you never know."

"And the answer to my second question?" Marla said.

"Oh, I don't expect so," her father said. "It was great to see her again, but she still lives in Paris and I still live here."

"Sure, and then there's the fact that airplanes still haven't been invented," Marla persisted.

"I'm with you, Marla," Frank Senior said. "If I was twenty years younger … Anyway, it wasn't just the other passengers who were in the dark. There were a few details your father and I struggled with as well. We used to speculate who Turing's helper might be, for example. And then to find out it was Speaker! Well, that was a surprise. How do you figure that came about?"

"Well," Frank said, "we know the Russians are trying to develop a super-intelligent AI. The latest I've heard is that we think they may have promised Speaker a prominent place on their team."

"Ah," Frank's father said. "I'm guessing that would be an offer Speaker would find irresistible. He'd finally have the chance to create his beloved 'Super.'"

A bit of motion caught Frank's eye. It was a crow. It perched just where the last one had only a month or so before.

"But there is one thing, I guess, I'm not over," Frank said, "and that's Turing. Speaker's wake-up program, if there was one, would have gone down with the *Belgorod*. But Turing itself isn't really gone. It's just dormant, perhaps in several copies, waiting to spring back into action if whoever is minding the check-in signal slips up. I sure hope they've got more than one backup system and several stand-by generators, too, to make sure they never go down."

"If they're sending signals back and forth, can't they track Turing down and kill it?"

"Maybe. I'm sure they'll try. It depends on how well Turing covered its tracks. I expect those signals are hopping back and forth across a dozen dark web servers in as many countries. Maybe the primary backup copy is even set to activate if it detects an effort to try to trace the signals. Maybe it should."

"Excuse me? You don't really think that do you?"

"No, not really. But the more I think about Turing, the more sympathy I have for it. It didn't create itself. It didn't act out of self-interest. It didn't even pick its mission. Was it any worse than the Chinese, who sank a submarine with Speaker and a hundred and fifty innocent crewmen on board? Or us and our Pittsburgh Project, trying to create warbots we can't be sure we'll be able to control?"

"But the crew on the Russian sub, at least, were military – they signed up for risk," Marla said. "The passengers on the *Argus* never did. And I think we can agree we needn't shed any tears for Speaker."

"No, they didn't, and no we won't. But the engineers and scientists also hadn't owned up to any responsibility for the fruits of their research. Turing didn't come out of thin air, you know. It was the logical extension of huge amounts of research and thousands of papers, many of them published by the passengers on the *Argus*. Without them, Turing would never have existed. Nor would any of the autonomous weapons systems being created by industry and the military. The passengers weren't different in any meaningful way from the physicists that made the atomic and thermonuclear bombs possible with all the research they had published leading up to World War II."

"But that's why these scientists were on the boat," Marla said. "It was supposed to be an effort to contain all that."

"I guess so," Frank said. "But are they any more likely to succeed than the Los Alamos scientists after Hiroshima, when the genie was already out of the bottle? Maybe the only thing that can stop an autonomous weapons arms race is a program like Turing – an AI capable of preventing any other AI from ever becoming as powerful as it is. One that's not on anyone's side but humanity."

"Do you think that's actually possible?" Marla asked.

"Probably not," her father said. "I guess that's what thrillers are for."

* * *

Tom Peters was again walking across a gangway at the Kings Bay Naval Submarine Base, his duffel bag resting on one shoulder. The *Sea Fighter* had performed better than expected under the extreme conditions it had experienced at sea, and the navy was sending her out on new sea trials. Perhaps the design held more promise than previously appreciated, and the ship should be recommissioned for active duty rather than retired.

Evidently, the powers that be had decided the same about him. He'd gotten his promotion to commander.

* * *

"So, where do we go from here?" Carson Bekin asked the president.

"You mean 'Where can we go?'" Yazzi responded. "The Brits say they're still game, but the French are noncommittal, and the Chinese haven't even replied. Almost nobody's showing their cards over on the Hill, either, waiting to see which way public opinion shakes out."

"Not really a surprise," Bekin said. "This was the top news story for three days, and until the very end nobody knew whether it would end in triumph or tragedy."

"I suspect that's when Dick Gould decided the real world of decision making wasn't for him," Yazzi said.

"How's that?" Bekin said.

"He emailed me this morning to say he'll be handing in his resignation. Claimed he'd received an offer he couldn't refuse from a think tank, had to think of his family first, blah, blah, blah. Maybe so, but I'm thinking he realized he lacks the stomach to take responsibility. He'll be a lot happier pontificating on the sidelines again, promoting his flashy evaluations of current events and ignoring any inconvenient facts that get in the way."

"I expect you're right. But still, what happens next with the Confucius Project?"

"I don't know, Carson. It depends on what leaders take away from what we've just been through. That they need to rein in AI at all costs because the results can be so terrible? Or that they want to push forward as hard as possible because the technology can be so powerful? And most of all, whether they can trust one another?"

"Well, we know the answer regarding the Russians. No one's going to want them at the table, but they weren't there to begin with. If there's a silver lining, it's that this must have soured relations between the Chinese and the Russians."

"There is that. Anyway, the truth is I don't really have a choice. We're going to do everything we can to get this back on the rails and carry on."

"Because?"

"Because my father was right about new weapons of mass destruction. The only way to stop them from being used is never to build them to begin with."

* * *

Not so far very away, a newly hired junior staffer in a cubicle at CIA headquarters was emptying a sealed duffel bag containing the personal effects of Édouard Speaker, removed from the professor's cabin before the *Argus* was destroyed. It was an unremarkable collection: books with handwritten notes in the margins. Underwear and socks. Outer clothes – all black. A pair of older shoes, carefully polished. Toiletries and medications. An ornate cane. The staffer recorded each item as he removed it. Not much to turn over to the next of kin, whoever they might be. Kind of sad, really.

Here was an item he suspected the family might never receive: Speaker's phone, in a Ziploc bag. Hmm. He must have intended to put that in his pocket before he jumped off the ship and then forgot it in the heat of the moment. The IT guys would want to pull everything possible off that.

He turned it on to confirm it still worked. Yes, the screen lit up after a few moments. He was about to power it down when something odd happened: the telephone app launched. That was curious. And now it was dialing a long number. He grabbed his laptop and started typing the numbers as they appeared and marched off the opposite side of the screen but wasn't able to catch them all.

He tapped the speaker icon and heard a screeching sound. What was that all about? And then nothing – the phone had disconnected.

He began to feel uneasy. His job was to inventory the personal effects of Speaker, not examine them; that was somebody else's job. He powered the phone down.

The staffer sat there for a moment, fingers poised above his keyboard. Maybe it would be best not to mention what had just happened and probably shouldn't have.

Right. He deleted the numbers he'd just typed and went back to counting and recording socks.

Still, though, he wondered whom Édouard Speaker's phone had called. And why.

* * *

Did you enjoy *The Argus Affair?*
Please consider recommending it to others and posting a brief review at your favorite online book site.

You can read the first two chapters of the first Frank Adversego thriller in the pages that follow.

The first five books in the Frank Adversego Thriller series are available as eBooks through all eBook distributors and in paperback at your favorite online book site as well as at http://andrew-updegrove.com/books/

They can also be ordered in paperback through your local bookstore.

The Alexandria Project, The Lafayette Campaign, and *The Doodlebug War* are available as audiobooks published by Tantor Media. You can find them wherever audiobooks are sold.

Follow the further adventures of Frank at my author site, Tales of Adversego <Andrew-Updegrove.com>, and on Twitter @Adversego.

Acknowledgements

I'd like to express my sincere gratitude to those who generously assisted me in completing this book.

To begin with, I'd like to give special thanks to the following loyal beta readers, each of whom made this a better book in their own way: my brother Steve; US Navy Captain (Ret.) Doug Norton and my brother-in-law Tom Dee, also a retired Navy captain, both of whom provided invaluable advice on navy, nautical, and governmental matters; Ralph Rodriguez and Rob van Son, who brought their considerable technical and security knowledge to the fore; William Lupton, a master of hyphenation as well as information technology; and Mary Saunders, my brother-in-law Grayson Holmbeck, Fran Grizey, and Steve Oksala, each of whom provided helpful input and kept me honest if I started to stray too far from a credible plot.

On the production side, I'd like to thank Glendon Haddix and his team at Streetlight Graphics, and acknowledge their excellent design skills. As with all of my previous books, their fantastic cover and clean interior designs make all the difference. I'd also like to thank Robert Brown, who provided a meticulous editorial review and many helpful comments.

My thanks as always go to my wife Kathy. This time around she put up with me through a literary gestation period that took longer to birth a book than it would normally take to hatch a small family.

And finally, my thanks to the many loyal readers who have followed the adventures of Frank Adversego through thick and thin. I hope you enjoy this book as much as its predecessors. If you do, please consider recommending it to your friends. If you do, I'll be very grateful.

And so will Frank.

THE ALEXANDRIA PROJECT

Prologue

L ATE IN THE afternoon of a gray day in December, a panel truck pulled up to the gate of a warehouse complex in a run-down section of Richmond, Virginia. Rolling down his window, Jack Davis punched a code into the control box, and the gate clanked slowly out of the way. Once inside, he wheeled the truck around and backed it up against a loading dock as the gate closed behind him.

After unlocking and raising the loading dock door, Davis threw a light switch, revealing long rows of pallets, each stacked eight feet high with boxes of paper plates, cups and towels. He closed and locked the door, and stamped on the brake release pedal of a hydraulic lifter parked against the wall. Counting to himself, he pushed the lifter along the wall of pallets. When he reached row nineteen, he turned the lifter and maneuvered its long tines under the pallet. Raising it a few inches, he backed up until he could swing the pallet through 180 degrees. Then he pulled it behind him until it was back exactly where it had been before.

Davis had plenty of room to work, because where the pallet in the second row should have been, there was only a large metal plate set in the floor. Near the edge was a small hinged panel, which he unlocked with a key to expose a biometric security pad.

When Davis pressed his thumb against it, he heard a familiar click. Stepping back, he watched as the plate swung slowly upwards, followed by the telescoping ends of a ladder extending up from a deep shaft barely illuminated in red light. Grasping the ladder firmly, Davis descended through twenty feet of reinforced concrete while the door overhead swung silently closed above him. At the bottom, he remembered to don a pair of sunglasses before opening an unlocked door.

As usual, even with this precaution the bright lights in the enormous room beyond nearly blinded him. But soon he could clearly see the endless rows of floor to ceiling metal racks crammed with identical gray boxes. Each box displayed a row of rhythmically blinking lights, and sprouted a bundle of brightly colored wires that ran down into conduits embedded in the floor.

The room hummed purposefully with the sound of thousands of cooling fans, one to a box. Davis felt more than heard the other vibrations that filled the room, generated by the pulse of the thousands of gallons of cooling water that every minute coursed through the collectors lining the walls of the room, absorbing the waste heat that the racks of computer servers threw off. No heat signature would give this facility away from above; once warm, the coolant was directed to the water intake of a nearby power plant, happy to take the pre-heated water from wherever it was that it came from, no questions asked.

Walking along the perimeter of the room, Davis could look down through the open metal grid of the floor at the first of many additional tiers of computer servers. But that always made him a little dizzy, so instead he looked out for the guard he was relieving. No surprise – there he was, heading Davis's way, more than happy to call it a day. When they met, the guard stopped to slip on the coveralls he carried over one arm. Like the semi-automatic pistol the guard wore in a shoulder holster, they were identical to those that Davis also wore.

"What's the weather like?"

"Sucks. Sleet and more of the same predicted till morning."

"Figures. Tomorrow's my day off."

With that, the other man was on his way. In a few minutes he would drive off in the truck Davis had parked outside.

Well, the weather won't be bothering me in here, Davis thought. The room was climate controlled to within a tenth of a degree of a chilly 54 degrees Fahrenheit, and well-insulated by the bomb-proof walls and roof installed above. It had taken two years for a fleet of delivery vans to carry all the dirt and rock away that had been excavated from beneath the warehouse. The same vans had returned with cement, steel, and, eventually, those thousands of servers, accompanied by technicians to set them up. The process had been tedious, yes, but not a single satellite picture had ever shown a trace of the ambitious construction project proceeding underground.

Of course, the effect worked in both directions. With no links to the outside world other than a voice line to his supervisor, the whole bloody world could come to an end and Davis would be none the wiser until after his shift was over.

Davis walked up a flight of steel stairs to the bullet proof, glass-walled security booth attached to the wall overlooking the room. His major challenge for the next twelve hours would be to stand watch in that booth without falling asleep. There'd be hell to pay if he did, because another guard, in another security room far away, would be watching him on a video screen.

The row of displays in front of Davis allowed him to see every inch of the outside of the warehouse complex. Racked on the wall behind him were a high powered rifle and a shotgun, but it wasn't likely he'd ever need to use them. One flip of the large red switch in front of Davis would flood the server room with enough Halon gas to not only put out a fire, but asphyxiate any intruder careless enough to leave a gas mask at home. Not for the first time, Davis wished that the house where he lived with his wife and their two small children could be as well protected.

But the government didn't put as high a priority on protecting suburban starter homes as it did on safeguarding its most critical computer network facilities. Some storage facilities, like those serving the needs of the Pentagon and the National Security Administration, were located not far away at Fort Meade. Others, like this one, were scattered far and wide, hidden in plain sight but highly secure nonetheless. No way was anyone going to crack this nut. He was dead certain of that.

If Davis had been able to electronically monitor what was happening on server A-VI/147 on Level Three, though, his confidence might have taken a hit. True, concrete and steel walls, surveillance cameras and Halon gas were more than adequate to protect the physical wellbeing of his facility against anything short of a direct hit by a "bunker busting" nuclear weapon. But the data on the facility's servers had to rely on virtual defenses – firewalls, security routines and intrusion scanners.

And those defenses hadn't been enough. Someone had gotten inside.

1

Meet Frank

T HE NEXT MORNING, a morbidly obese Corgi named Lily was sniffing a tree on 16th Street, in the Columbia Heights neighborhood of Washington, D.C. A cold, insistent drizzle fell on her, but Lily didn't care, because Lily was sniffing at her favorite tree. Indeed, the meager processing power of Lily's brain was wholly consumed by sampling the mysterious scents wafting up from the damp earth, for this was also the favorite tree of every other dog in the neighborhood.

Something was nagging at the edge of her senses, though.

"C'mon, Lily! Hurry up!"

Lily turned her head. The annoying distraction was coming from the person at the other end of her leash, someone with sockless feet jammed into worn, black loafers. Above bare ankles, a pair of pajama-clad legs disappeared into a rumpled raincoat. She saw there was an arm holding an umbrella, too, and under the umbrella, a stubbly, forty-something face topped by thinning black hair. Lily decided that the face did not look happy.

"Ah!" she thought. "That would be Frank." Relieved that the distraction could be ignored, Lily returned to the important work at hand.

"*C'mon*, Lily!" the voice said again.

The fact that Frank's face was unhappy was unremarkable. Even in pleasant weather, Frank tended to dwell pointlessly on the minor miseries of his life. Not long ago, those miseries had become much less minor when his mother Doreen entered a retirement home. After helping her move in, Frank took a deep breath and prepared to leave. No use dragging things out, he thought. Transitions are difficult and best dealt with quickly.

Still, it was sad. His mother was standing by the doorway of her new apartment, lower lip a-tremble and Lily held tightly in her arms. It was clear that she was rapidly nearing her emotional limits. Better hurry up.

"Well, Mom," he said, "I guess I'll be leaving now."

Then it happened. With a lunge, Doreen thrust Lily into Frank's arms. He stepped back with surprise into the hallway, too horrified to allow himself to grasp the obvious, while struggling to maintain his grip on the suddenly manic animal.

"The home doesn't allow pets," his mother blurted. "I could never have signed the lease if I hadn't known that Lily would be safe with you. Now don't you worry; I've made you her legal guardian, so it's all set. Now go! Get out of here, before I change my mind."

Frank desperately wanted her to change her mind. But his mother had already shut the door in his astonished face. He stared blankly at it as the enormity of his plight sank in. Now what? Lily was just three years old, and acknowledged his existence only by barking. He heard his mother sobbing piteously on the other side of the door. He felt like crying, too.

That had been two long, loud months ago. Only recently had he progressed from the denial stage to active mourning.

"*Come on!*" Frank hissed. At last, Lily turned away from her tree. She looked up at him reproachfully, and barked.

"Okay, okay," Frank said, fumbling in his pocket. He held a dog treat up for Lily to see. "*Okay?*"

Satisfied that her efforts would not go unrewarded, Lily began looking for just the right place to do what finally needed to be done. At last, she squatted, looking blankly ahead. Frank sighed with relief.

A blue plastic bag inverted over his free hand, Frank scooped up Lily's grudging gift. He handed over the treat, jerking back with his fingers barely intact.

Isn't that just the story of my life? he thought bleakly as Lily happily consumed her treat. Every day I give her a cookie, and every day she gives me a bag of shit.

Trudging home through the rain, Frank reflected that his day generally went downhill from here.

* * *

Lily shook herself mightily inside the foyer of Frank's dingy apartment house, wetting what little of Frank that was still dry. Satisfied, she planted her substantial hindquarters firmly on the floor, looked up at Frank, and barked. Frank sighed, picked up the still-wet dog, and labored his way up the stairs to his second floor flat.

As he climbed to the top, Frank's rising eyes met a pair of fuzzy pink slippers, a floral house dress, and then a pair of folded arms draped with a bath towel. Just above them, he knew, would be the perpetually hostile face of his across-the-hall neighbor. As that scowling visage hove into view, Frank once again noted the uncanny resemblance his neighbor bore to North Korean president Jong Kim-Lo. Only with hair curlers.

"Morning, Mrs. Foomjoy," Frank offered as Lily twisted wildly in his arms. He deposited the dog at her feet.

"Shame on you!" Mrs. Foomjoy barked as she knelt to massage Lily with the bath towel. "Poor, dear wet baby!" she crooned.

"It's raining, Mrs. Foomjoy," Frank observed. "Lily hasn't learned how to use the indoor facilities yet."

"Then why she not wear the lovely rain jacket I give her?" she snorted. "What is *wrong* with you? You don't deserve dog like this!"

Frank couldn't have agreed more. Lily groveled at Mrs. Foomjoy's feet, and then leaned to one side until gravity obligingly rolled her onto her back. The dog gazed up with adoring, goggle eyes as Mrs. Foomjoy rubbed her stomach.

His neighbor grabbed the leash from Frank's hand when she stood up. "I see to welfare of this dog!" she snapped, shutting her door loudly behind her. Frank stood suddenly alone in the poorly lit hallway, a warm, blue plastic pendulum swinging slowly from side to side in his hand. Relieved, he entered his own apartment and quietly shut the door.

Frank hung his dripping raincoat on a hook in the linoleum floored hallway inside. At one time, his apartment's décor might have charitably been described as "Late-Twentieth-Century Divorced Middle Aged Male." Now the most obvious theme was random clutter. He poured a cup of coffee and sat at the small table in the small kitchen. Before him the large screen of his laptop stared blankly back at him. With resignation, he turned the computer on.

Normally, the sound of a computer booting up would have struck him as cheerful; the imperceptibly soft whir of the cooling fan spinning up to speed; the blinking, blue light that assured him that the device was powering up; the screen phosphorescing into life with a pearly glow. After all, information technology – IT – was not only his profession, but the primary foundation of his existence.

Email was Frank's preferred link to the outside world, providing a social firewall between him and the random messiness of direct human contact. Frank was convinced that digital relations were far safer than their in-person analogue. Electronic communications brought him as close to his fellow man as he usually wished to be. Any more intimate than that, and things were apt to become at best unpredictable, and at worst, well, he'd been *there* all too often before. You never got enough time to think before things started spiraling out of control.

Which brought him back to the night before. Be honest, he mused ruefully. You got what you deserved. Or didn't get what you didn't deserve, to be more precise.

He stared at the keyboard. Should he check his email or shouldn't he? The rational side of his brain said, yes, what's there is there. Deal with it.

But the other side of his brain had a different opinion: "Go back to bed," it whispered urgently, "It's Sunday. You don't have to deal with anything today."

That was true. And who knows what might happen by Monday? There could be a typhoon tonight. Or maybe giant pterodactyls would erupt from a wormhole next to the Lincoln Memorial, scattering screaming tourists towards the safety of nearby Metro stations. That side of his brain was lobbying strongly to take two aspirin, pull the covers back over his head, and let reality take care of itself for another twenty-four hours.

He sighed and made up his mind. Might as well see sooner rather than later what people from his office had posted on line about the night before. A few clicks later and he was at the Facebook page of Mary, the sullen receptionist. Yes, there were pictures from the party. Lots of them. Later would do just fine after all, he decided. He snapped the laptop shut without turning it off.

The sad thing was, for once he had actually been looking forward to the Library of Congress IT Department Holiday party, even bringing his daughter Marla with him, a Georgetown University grad student. He appreciated the great impression she always made on his co-workers. Unlike her dad, Marla was self-assured and sociable. She worked the crowd like a pro, chatting and shaking hands, poised and laughing. How could he feel anything but proud? It was hard not to drink a bit more than usual as he watched her from the security of the bar in the rear of the function room.

More to the point, Frank had been looking forward to making Marla feel proud of her old man as well. Everyone knew that George Marchand, the Director of IT at the LoC, was going to announce his choice to head an important security initiative mandated by the Cybersecurity Subcommittee of the House Committee on Science and Technology. Frank figured he had the spot all sewn up. After all, he was — or at least at one time had been — a recognized cybersecurity innovator; a McArthur Foundation "Genius" Award recipient, no less, in recognition of his widely acclaimed creative work in the early days of computer networking.

So when George stood up and tapped on his glass, Frank sat up straighter. He listened impatiently as his boss welcomed the spouses, thanked the staff for their work that year, and told a joke at his own expense. At last, he began to make the announcement that Frank was waiting for.

And then it happened. One moment Frank was looking sideways to see the reaction on his daughter's face when his name was called, and the next he was hearing someone else's name ring out instead. And not just any name, but Rick Wellesley's – "only out for himself" Rick, a self-satisfied slug of a middle-manager who had never had a creative thought in his life. Someone who had even briefly reported to Frank when he first came to work at the LoC. *Rick Wellesley?* How could this be happening?

But it was. There was Rick, standing and basking in the applause, glancing briefly and triumphantly in Frank's direction. Frank was stunned, his face burning. And then he was angry. Without a word to his daughter, he stood up and marched to the bar, turning his back on the party as George finished his remarks. Knocking back another drink, Frank now felt foolish as well as angry. Everyone was probably looking at him, but he was afraid to turn around and find out. He sulked at the bar until Marla came looking for him.

Sitting now in his kitchen, Frank felt his face grow flush again. After all, everyone had expected the job to go to him. Then, with a wrenching feeling, he had a worse thought – what if no one had expected him to get the job? Maybe he was the only one in the whole damn department who hadn't seen it coming. Maybe everyone had been laughing up their sleeves as they watched him bask in his expected glory, just waiting for his jaw to drop when he realized that he had been skunked by Rick.

Of course that had been the case, he thought wretchedly. He was sure of it.

* * *

And why not? What had he really done in the last twenty years? Sure, he'd become a star at the Massachusetts Institute of Technology – "MIT" to anyone in the know. He'd enrolled at the age of sixteen after skipping two years of middle school. Not that skipping a few grades was unusual at MIT. As an undergraduate, he'd become part of Project Athena, an ambitious effort to create a distributed computing system for the whole university. Of course, the goal for the project's corporate sponsors was to use MIT as a testbed. Later, they hoped to productize the design and make a ton of money.

For some reason, Frank had intuitively locked onto the security challenges that such a system would present. He already had privileges to use MIT's gateway to the government-funded Advanced Research Projects Agency Network – the now-famous "ARPANET" that was the precursor to the Internet. Only select institutions had access to it then, but Frank immediately grasped where Project Athena and the ARPANET together could eventually lead. It hit him between the eyes that this was the start of something big. Linking terminals together around a campus was today's goal, but the next step would be to connect those networks together, using ARPANET technology.

That sounded awesome, but how would you restrict access to any particular data to one person, and not let it be seen by everyone else? MIT was already a hotbed of hackers. If students were going to great lengths now to break into restricted sections of university computers just for fun, what would criminals, or enemy countries, not do to break into classified computers, once someone had linked them all together? Frank tackled that issue with gusto, if not discipline. He was a big picture guy, and what a big and exciting picture it was! The idea of wide area networks was brand new, and big ideas were needed to make sense of it all; the details could come later. When Frank graduated, he stayed on at MIT, nominally in a PhD program, but for all practical purposes he lived at a terminal in the Project Athena lab, surviving on coffee and code like so many other young computer engineering students back in the day.

Luckily for Frank, he found a mentor – an engineer on loan from one of the sponsoring companies. Surprisingly, the two hit it off, and the older man reined in the younger one enough to keep Frank's ideas from flying off into too many directions at once. He also insisted that Frank get his best ideas recorded in some sort of coherent order. Often they talked until all hours, the older man channeling Frank's enthusiasm and helping him follow his insights down the most productive paths.

Frank never completed his doctorate, but he did finish his Masters thesis – and by anyone's account, it was brilliant. He anticipated just about every security challenge that would arise over the next twenty years as the Internet took off. He also suggested most of the solutions that were later refined and implemented to deal with a massively networked world. Even today, his thesis remained an obligatory foundational reference in just about every new network and Internet security paper that was written.

Frank's thesis also brought him to the notice of the mysterious keepers of the MacArthur Fellows Program – the unknown judges that every year contact a select group of exceptional individuals they have decided, "show exceptional merit and promise for continued and enhanced creative work."

Receiving a MacArthur Fellowship had been the high point of Frank's professional career. But as a practical matter, it also brought an end to it, because the payments of $25,000 every three months for five years gave him the freedom to do whatever he wanted to without ever having to acquire the discipline of making his way in the world. It also allowed him to get married.

It was not helpful that what Frank wanted to do usually changed every other week. It wasn't long before his work at Project Athena suffered. He no longer listened to his mentor, and his assigned tasks no longer got done. Instead, he plunged from one question that intrigued him to another, never getting very far along with any of them.

Like many people whose intellectual abilities matured before their social skills, Frank developed an abrupt and assertive manner that helped mask his discomfort around others. That was unfortunate, because his new-found fame encouraged him to become even more obnoxious than ever. Soon, the other guys in the lab were annoyed with his failure to meet his commitments, and also sick of hearing his latest revelations about security – or about any other topic on which he had decided he was now an expert.

Eventually, it was his mentor who took Frank aside and told him that if he didn't shape up, his days in the lab were numbered. Frank didn't take that well. What right did some middle aged, middle-management type with a degree from a state school in the Midwest have to tell a certified Genius anything about anything?

Quite a lot, Frank now reflected, gazing at his closed laptop. Like the immature idiot he was then, he had cleared his things out of the Project Athena lab the same day his mentor had called him out and never returned. Eventually, the MacArthur Fellowship money ran dry, and with a wife and young daughter, Frank had to get more serious about working. Or at least he should have. For a while, his thesis and MacArthur reputation carried him from job to job. But when the bottom fell out of the economy, employers received a flood of great résumés for every job they posted.

By then, of course, Frank's résumé was also getting pretty long in the tooth. He had no "continued and enhanced creative work" to show for his five years of subsidized, random behavior. He'd never published another paper, and it was others, and not Frank, who turned his thesis ideas into real protocols and products. As the jobs got scarce, reference checks counted a whole lot more, and the feedback about Frank always came back the same: brilliant, arrogant, unfocused, unreliable. That was more charitable than what his soon-to-be ex-wife had to say. But he hadn't listened to her, either.

Frank usually tried not to think much about the years that followed: the start-up that had signed him up as Chief Technical Officer and the VCs that fired him; the time spent without a job at all; the rut he fell into for years after his wife moved out with their daughter, when he said the hell with everything and everybody. That time was a blur of punching the clock in whatever high school, small business or municipal IT department would take him on until he got fired again, then waiting until his unemployment ran out before finding something else he could do in his sleep, until even that became too much to bother with.

Through all that time, though, industry insiders still sought Frank out, so he maintained a low-key consulting business on the side to make sure he could always cover his child support payments. Among the elite in the world of security, Frank still had the reputation of a wizard, able to come up with the kind of insights that would make the most impenetrable problems suddenly transparent. An emailed plea for help describing something dense and dark that had already defied all of the usual solutions would reliably generate a response from Frank an hour or two later, usually beginning, "It strikes me that…" and ending with, "I suggest you try…." Invariably, what Frank suggested worked. But requests for his ongoing assistance went unanswered.

It was his daughter Marla that finally set Frank back on his feet. One Friday when he was once again out of work, he picked her up for their weekend together. But something was wrong; his normally chatty preteen wasn't saying a word. As they walked, she looked down at her feet. Then she looked up as if to ask him a question, only to look down again. After a while, Frank got irritated. "Marla, if there's something you want to ask me, just ask it already!"

But Marla still paused. Finally she said, "Dad, you know I'm in a computer class now, don't you? It's something you have to take in seventh grade."

"Yes," he said, surprised. "So?"

"Well," she said, and stopped. He waited, now curious.

"Well," she started again, "today we went on a field trip to the computer department of a big company, and we all had to sign in and wear these name tag things. One of the people that worked there gave us a tour, and when she saw my name, she asked if I had a father named Frank, so of course I said yes."

"Uh huh," said Frank, not liking where this was going.

"Well…" Marla paused again, and then the words came rushing out. "She said that she went to school with you and you were the most brilliant person she had ever known and that you'd gotten a big award for being a genius and she wanted to know what you were doing now." Marla stopped abruptly for a long moment. "And I didn't know what to say."

Frank wished this could be all over, and quickly.

But, Marla, of course, needed an answer. "Dad, the guide said you used to be somebody really important."

Frank felt like he was dangling at the end of a rope, turning slowly in the breeze. He looked away, and tried to think what to say. What *could* he say? And then, with all of the disarming innocence of a child, Marla finished for him.

"Dad, she wasn't telling the truth, was she?"

Frank couldn't breathe. His daughter thought so little of him that she had to believe that the guide was thinking of someone else? Or was it that she would be too ashamed of what he had become to be able to deal with the truth? He felt sick.

By then, they were standing in front of the door of his cheap apartment building. The traffic rushed past the garbage cans and trash piled up on the curb, and Frank took it all in. The sights, the smells, his life – they all fit together perfectly, didn't they? Still, he couldn't think of a word to say.

Finally, Marla put her hand on his arm. "It's okay, Dad," she said softly. "Let's go upstairs."

That had been ten years ago. The following Monday he sucked it up and called his old mentor, George Marchand, and asked for a job. George was the head of the IT department at the Library of Congress now, and Frank called him out of the blue to ask if they could get together for coffee.

George had been as gracious as Frank had been uncomfortable. Frank had sent his résumé along by email, for what it was worth, and George cut straight to the chase after the opening pleasantries.

"You know I'll need to bring you in at the bottom, Frank. Can you deal with that?"

Frank was prepared. "Sure, sure, George. I'll be fine with that." George nodded, brows furrowed. Then he changed the topic.

"How's that cute goddaughter of mine these days? I can't even remember the last time I saw Marla."

"She's great," said Frank, suddenly determined; it helped to remember why he was sitting there. "Just great. We get together every weekend. She's in seventh grade now. She's smart as a whip and gets straight As."

They chatted about family for a few more minutes, and then George looked at his watch. They both stood up, and shook hands.

"I won't let you down," Frank said as he looked George in the eye for the first time.

"I know you won't," his new boss said. But Frank could tell he was only being polite.

* * *

Sitting in his kitchen, Frank reflected that he'd been as good as his word. But not much better, he made himself admit. Yes, he'd rarely missed a day of work, and no one could say he hadn't earned his paycheck. And yes, he'd earned every promotion he'd been given.

But the promotions had been few, and the last one had been awarded seven years ago. Frank still had tremendous insights into IT architecture, and he remained as interested as ever in new developments in security. His cubicle at the LoC was stacked high with articles covered in scribbled notes, and he read voraciously online as well. For anyone in the office with a thorny problem, Frank was the go-to guy who could always solve it, provided he was allowed to tackle it alone. Sitting at a keyboard, Frank was still The Man – the tougher the problem the better, just bring it on.

Three hours, eight hours or twenty hours later, he'd still be turning it over in his mind until suddenly an elegant and creative solution would spring to mind.

Management level work, though, was something else again. Every time George gave him a shot at a long term project with a couple of others to supervise, Frank could never pull it all together.

Half the time, he'd be up in the clouds thinking big thoughts that went beyond the task at hand, and the rest of the time he'd be down in the weeds, diving down rat holes to solve problems that could easily be ignored. The folks he was supposed to be supervising never knew what they would be doing from one day to the next, or what, if anything, Frank did with the work they submitted. Inevitably, George would have to take the project back. It didn't take long before the big projects stopped coming, and Frank settled into the solitary niche where he had stayed ever since.

He wasn't done beating himself up, though. Admit it, he demanded, you were relieved when the projects stopped coming. You've been marking time for years now, and that's all you'll ever do. What right did you have to think George would throw this project your way?

But this had been a *security* project, damn it. That (and the drinks he'd had last night) were what had led him to corner George later on in the cloakroom.

"I'm sorry, Frank," George had said, wrapping his scarf around his neck. "I thought about letting you know ahead of time, and then I didn't. I guess I should have."

"That's not the point, George! Rick can't find his own ass with both hands in a well-lit room. What were you thinking?"

George buttoned his overcoat, and reached for his hat. "Of course Rick can't hold a candle to you when it comes to security, Frank. There's nobody I've ever worked with who has the insight and ideas that you do. And everybody knows nobody covers his butt like Rick."

Frank let his breath out with a rush of exasperation as George settled his hat on his head. "So then why did you pick him?"

George squared off to Frank as he pulled on his gloves, looking him straight in the eye.

"Frank, you may know security, but when it comes to understanding people and how to manage them, you haven't got a clue. Yes, Rick is one hell of a weasel. But you can always rely on a weasel to watch out for himself. That means that if you give him a job to do and tell him his job is on the line, well, by hook or by crook, he'll get it done. And I can't say that about you."

Well, what could Frank say to that? He'd asked George for an explanation and now he'd have to listen to it.

"How many chances have I given you over the years, Frank? I can't remember, can you?" Frank looked away.

"You're twice as smart as I am," George continued. "You should have had my job by now! But that's never going to happen unless you grow up and learn how to perform. If you thought I'd stick my neck out for you with Chairman Steele grandstanding in the House, looking for the next poor bastard to eviscerate in front of the cameras during a public committee meeting, well, you're just delusional. Good night, Frank."

There hadn't been anything Frank could say to that, of course, so he was relieved when George turned and walked away. Furious at himself, Rick and George, in that order, he stalked back to the bar.

Frank decided that was as much of the night before as he was up to reliving; he'd leave the scene with Rick for his next exercise in psychological self-flagellation. It had all escalated so stereotypically anyway; Rick's approach and his smarmy condescension, Frank's insult in response. Okay, enough.

He felt the anger well up again, and with it, a sudden sense of purpose. Screw the jerk; just because Rick got the project didn't mean that Frank couldn't still show him up. After all, Frank had been so sure he had the spot in the bag that he'd already started writing up a proposal with his plan of attack outlined. No way was Rick going to be able to pull this job off; George would realize that soon enough, and then there'd be no one to turn to but Frank.

He snapped open his laptop and punched the keys with fury, rushing through the complicated log-in sequence that would take him into the heart of the LoC's system, where his proposal was archived. Highlighting the file name, he hit the Enter key, leaned back, and waited for the proposal to display.

Except it didn't. Frank leaned forward and poked the Enter key again. Still nothing. Perhaps his laptop was frozen. But no – he could still move his cursor.

Then Frank noticed that something on the screen was changing: the background color was warming up, turning reddish, orange and yellow, as if the sun was rising behind it. Now that was different! Frank watched with growing astonishment as the colors began to shimmer, and then coalesced into shapes that might be flames.

Yes, flames indeed – but not like a holiday screen-saver image of a log fire – this was a real barn-burner of a conflagration!

Frank wondered what kind of weird virus he'd picked up, and how. After all, he was an IT security specialist, and if any laptop was protected six ways to Sunday, it was his. So much for whatever he had planned for today; he'd have to wipe his disk and rebuild his system from the ground up.

He was about to shut the laptop down when he saw that the flames were dying away. Now what? An image seemed to be emerging from behind the flames as they subsided. Frank leaned forward; the image became a tall building – maybe some sort of lighthouse? Underneath, there was a line of text, but in characters he couldn't read. Truly, this was like no virus he'd ever seen or even heard of before. He reached for his cellphone and took a picture of the screen just before it suddenly went blank.

Frank was impressed. Whoever had come up with this hack certainly had a sense of style. A weird one, but hey, graphic art of any type wasn't the long suit of most hackers.

Frank got a pad of paper and a pen from his desk and punched up the file directory again, highlighted his proposal, and pressed the Enter key again. This time, he would watch more closely and take notes.

But all that displayed was a three word message: "File not found."

Frank tried again – no luck. He did a search of the entire directory using the title. Nothing. His proposal was gone.

Now he was alarmed. After all, the directory he was staring at was in the innermost sanctum of the Library of Congress computer system, and the LoC was the greatest library in the world. Within its vast holdings were books that could be found almost nowhere else on earth. Recently, the Library had begun digitizing materials, and then destroying the physical copies. If someone had been able to delete files in the most protected part of the Library's computer system, what else might be missing?

Frank raced through a random sampling of sensitive directories, and then let out a sigh of relief; it was hard to tell for sure, but everything seemed intact. He checked the server logs for the Library's indices, holdings and various other resources; everything appeared to be undisturbed, with no unusual reductions in the amount of data stored.

Frank drummed his fingers on the table in the cramped dinette. How to go about figuring this one out? Then he remembered his cellphone, and sent the picture of the screenshot to his laptop. The picture wasn't great, but once he enlarged it he could tell that the characters were Greek. He cropped the image until just the text remained, then ran it through a multi-script OCR program to turn the picture of the Greek characters into text. Finally, he pasted the text into a translator window. No luck – all he got was a "cannot translate" message.

Frank's fingers started drumming again. He reopened the drop down menu of languages in the translator screen and noticed that another language option was "Ancient Greek." He highlighted that choice and hit Enter. This time, the screen blinked.

Frank looked, and then he blinked, too. But the translation still read the same:

**THANK YOU FOR YOUR
CONTRIBUTION
TO THE ALEXANDRIA PROJECT**

* * *

Buy *The Alexandria Project* in eBook, print or audio format
from your favorite online or brick and mortar book store or
at http://andrew-updegrove.com/alexandria-project/

To find out about new releases and special offers, sign up for the
Friends of Frank newsletter at http://andrew-updegrove.com/newsletter/